I0542308

The Seventh Colour

WILL DAVIDSON

2ND EDITION

Published by Upavon Press, 2017

ISBN: 9780995765009

SECOND EDITION

The 'Vectis' font on the cover is used under license from Greater Albion Typefounders

N

THE REALM OF
ASKURIA

DESERT

GRAND
LANDING
HAYMOUTH

FAR
TOWN

PEACEWATER

RIVERTOP

TRYACHAN

CAR PERONEL

CAR VANDRA

BRAED TOR

FOR VAINGEL
(LIMBEL)

DRAGONSBACK
MOUNTAINS

ESKELLION

YESTLE

REVIEWS OF THE SEVENTH COLOUR

"Will Davidson writes with a controlled, descriptive style that draws the reader into the narrative through its very economy... intense statements of the strange world he sets before us sucking the reader into the plot... [c]oupled to very strong descriptions of each individual character... the reader soon becomes a co-conspirator in the direction and dissemination of this tale.

...a new restatement of the old, old story of political repression by a political class unable to envisage change as it admires its own reflection in the mirror... This is good writing, intelligent, amusing yet challenging on what is a very relevant subject. It is also an excellent tale which describes, excites and pulls the reader all the way through to the final denouement."

Nigel Robert Wilson

British Fantasy Society

"...the setting's cool, the story's cool. And the characters are amazing! By the end of the book, none of them are who we thought they were, and some of the twists and turns that Davidson pulls off are really cleverly done."

Flasheart2006

4* review on amazon.co.uk

"A compelling fantasy adventure packed full of surprising twists."

The Wishing Shelf Book Awards

Will Davidson "creates a rich setting full of mysterious plots and strong characters and keeps you enthralled to the end."

MisterMike

5* review on amazon.co.uk

"The story is told in multiple ways... One would think, from all these different story-telling approaches, that [it] would be a confused mess. But while it doesn't always cohere perfectly, the result is truly compelling. The Seventh Colour is essentially a heist story, with conspiracies and betrayals and unreliable narrators telling just enough to keep the reader guessing at the next revelation, at what's true and what's not."

Donald Crankshaw

Black Gate Magazine (online)

"OOH! This was really wonderful. A bit of an epic in fact. I see from the blurb it is inspired by Tolkien, amongst others. I can see that. Good characterisation and a strongly designed plot. Well done!"

Reader for the Wishing Shelf Book Awards

DEDICATION

To Emma. For everything.

PROLOGUE

Tryachan, 1,773 years ago

The corpse of the last dragon made an incongruous backdrop to the farewell ceremony.

Too massive to be moved, its skeletal remains lay on the cliff edge where they had been picked clean in the week following the battle. First the head and tail had been taken as trophies by the powerful Lord of Tryachan. His champion had, after all, brought the beast to ground. The feet too had been taken, though no-one knew by whom, during the first confused night of revelry. After that, the scales had been plucked by any who dared, as mementoes. Once the scales were gone, scavengers of various types had lost no time in devouring the flesh within.

But the great mass of the dragon's skeleton remained, even if it was now strewn with banners proclaiming a victory accomplished.

In the king's opinion, it would have been more fitting to afford the mighty creature a decent burial. But the king's opinion had not yet been sought on this, or any other, matter. Instead, freed for a short while from his formal robes of office, he sat with crossed legs on the muddy ground and simply considered what he could see of the macabre spectacle.

Around him on the hillside servants ran about, readying seating for the forthcoming entertainments. In theory they did so at his order, but in his short reign the king had already learnt the futility of trying to countermand their instructions. The only benefit that seemed to come from his status was that while activity took place all about him, he and the small circle of ground he occupied were left discreetly alone. The smooth mud made an ideal surface for drawing. With his dagger the king idly sketched out an image that he had spent most of the last week considering, as he sat through interminable meetings of the Interim Council.

Askuria. His Kingdom. From the desert coast in the north, to the cooler more fertile lands in the south. He had memorised the bays and headlands of the western coast and of course every turn of the new border with their neighbours to the east. He felt that he had examined every inch of the territory won in his father's name and now, presumably, occupied in his. As he had seen the council and their advisers doing, he marked on the major landmarks and resources. A tower to symbolise Castle Peronelle, his capital. An anchor for the trading port of Tryachan, the site of their most recent battle and forthcoming farewell celebrations. Eskillion, Yestle, Rivertop, Far Town: each of them had their own symbol and place on the map.

Nor was it only the centres of habitation that had been pored over. A great deal of time had been spent in discussions about resources and how they were to be exploited. Forests, mines, farmland - all had been divided up and responsibility had been agreed. In among these allocations had been discussions about such exotic concepts as labour relations, trader tariffs and revenue. All these had been wrapped up in something called the Markt, which was as close as the advisers ever seemed to come to a religion.

Most of these discussions had been incomprehensible, but the reactions of the council members had been even stranger to the king than the unknown words they had used. He scratched savagely at the mud with his dagger. These were men he had grown up respecting and fearing. Not one of them had less than half a century of years on him. Each of them usually bore himself with the seriousness and severity that befitted his position. Yet over the last week of meetings the king had seen his counsellors sitting as eager schoolchildren while their glamorous advisers moved among them dispensing instructions in their musical lilting tones. His own childish enthusiasm had been worn out much more quickly.

As his dagger retraced the outline of the Dragonsback Mountains, he remembered the excitement with which these particular lands had been considered. It was no surprise that this freshly won territory had taken a large part of the council's attention. But what had been the word that they and their advisers had kept mentioning? It was clearly a matter of some great interest, but only ever whispered or spelled out in his presence. He sketched poorly remembered markings - a mine in the northern mountains, a trail across the desert, a coastal port that he hadn't previously seen on any map...

"Bereland!"

He looked up, irritated. Only one person would use his given name in such a peremptory fashion.

"Bereland! Come here!"

Hastily the king used his sleeve to obscure the details of his picture. Then he pushed himself to his feet, his head barely emerging from the rows of seating that had been arranged around him, unnoticed in his preoccupation. There she was, at the bottom of the hill. Already pink spots were glowing on her cheeks and the king knew that the longer he delayed, the redder her face and the hotter her ire would become. He waved a hesitant hand to catch her attention.

"There you are Bereland! It's time you were dressed for this ridiculous ceremony. Come on!"

With a last scuff of one foot, the Dragonsback Mountains and their markings were forever obscured. Then the nine year-old king put away such grown-up preoccupations and ran downhill to his waiting servant, erstwhile nurse, and now surrogate family.

Three hours later, pressed back into his formal regalia, the child-king Bereland Berillion stood stiffly to attention as the departure ceremony drew interminably on. The clothing hung almost as heavily on him as the weight of his council's expectations. Every item of his attire had been fitted to the accompaniment of a droning recitation of the importance of this event.

With his undergarments had come the crown chamberlain. He was a man whose intricate knowledge of court protocol derived from years of experience in the service of both Bereland's father and, before him, his great uncle. With the ponderous severity of the aged and uncertain, he had found numerous different ways of emphasising to Bereland that he stood at a moment of profound significance for the future of the realm. With their foreign advisers returning to the west, a time when humankind would at last assert control over their own destiny.

Bereland's head had emerged from his tunic to discover the master herald, charged with the organisation of the day's festivities. It was apparent that he regarded his audience as a child first, and a king second. He had explained, again, that Bereland would play a crucial, yet seemingly entirely symbolic, role in the day's events. It would be for the young king to lead out the representatives of those races and kingdoms which had been brought together in the recently completed war on the Darkness. Each of them in turn would bid farewell to their departing advisers, with Bereland being the last of all to do so. It was emphasised to him on several occasions during this explanation that he would not be required to speak 'at any point' during the day. Once that duty had been discharged, the boarding of ships would be completed, and the departure would begin.

Even as he had left his robing chamber, making his way in the midst of a superfluous entourage back to the hillside selected for the ceremony, he had been beset, this time by the crown treasurer. Bereland had always viewed the man as greedy. It was a belief borne out by his considerable corpulence even after the deprivations of a war that had been fought since long before the new king's birth. His only concern was to make sure that if, as anticipated, the departing advisers were to present the young king with a gift, he should understand that it was not meant to be personal to him. It would instead be a gift to the Crown and should therefore be transferred into the crown treasurer's safekeeping as soon as might decorously be possible.

Now he stood impatiently, uncomfortably, in line. So far, everything had progressed entirely in accordance with his council's instructions. Just as anticipated, gifts did indeed seem to be being presented. Bereland watched as the small yet dignified party of representatives made their way closer along the line of assembled leaders and comrades who had gathered to bid them and their race farewell. At first the distance to the far end of the line had been too great to allow him to see much detail. Now the group was approaching his position, closest to the embarkation points on the shore. Being able to make out with greater clarity what was being bestowed provided him with a welcome distraction from his own preoccupations.

The advisers moved a position closer along the line. As always, however clearly Bereland thought that he could see them while he was looking in their direction, all that he was left with afterwards was a wash of impressions – beautiful symmetrical faces, pointed ears, brightly coloured clothes. He knew that there were seven of them in this departing delegation, and that they were tall, but details eluded him. It was easier to focus his attention elsewhere. The advisers had just started to speak to a tall man with yellow hair, long both on top of his head and about his face. His moustaches and beard hung down luxuriantly and were plaited and tied with elaborate coloured ribbons. From his briefings prior to the ceremony, Bereland thought that this leader might have provided cavalry during the later stages of the war. To him was given a golden comb, accompanied with some comments which, whatever they were, elicited a hearty laugh from the recipient and those around him.

The dwarf king, only slightly taller than Bereland himself but considerably more rotund, was next in the line. Bereland had met him once before, at his father's funeral, and had been touched by the old man's compassion as he had paid his respects to the grieving young king. Perhaps this made him particularly sensitive to the customary dismissiveness with which King Howel was now treated. The leader of the departing delegation, one of the advisers in whose company Bereland had spent much of the preceding week, wore a disdainful look that he made no effort to conceal. Nor did he make any effort to equalize the dramatic difference in height between him and the monarch to whom he was speaking. Indeed, as he held out the dwarf king's gift, a hammer made of some silvery metal that appeared to glow with internal energy, he did so in a way that required its recipient to stand on stretched toes in order to accept it. In this case, the laughter that followed was far less good-natured.

Bereland felt anxiety growing in his stomach. Only two more people remained in the line before it would be his turn. Focusing on the protocol that he had worked so hard to memorise, he did not even register the next presentation. Now the advisers stood next to him, exchanging laughing words with the man to Bereland's right. This was General Miroir, one of the great heroes of the War and regarded by many as likely to be a significant figure in the king's Council for many years to come. A large book, bound in a remarkably smooth animal skin, was handed across to him. Even in his youthful ignorance, Bereland noticed the significant glances that seemed to be exchanged between the general and the leader of the advisers. It also appeared that the farewells on this occasion were particularly heartfelt.

Now, at last, it was Bereland's turn. He felt heat rushing up into his cheeks as he imagined the attention of the collected audience turning upon him. The leader of the advisers took a step forward.

"So, child! We leave our realm in your capable hands!" The laughter underlying every word, normally so soothing, felt like mockery. Bereland felt his shoulders tightening, and the heat that had been spreading through him turned to cold embarrassment in his stomach. From the corner of his eye he could see the chamberlain tensing, and remembered his insistence that Bereland should simply stay silent.

The adviser seemed to smirk, his aura glowing brighter in his amusement.

"No words of farewell for us, little human child?"

Still, Bereland stood silent. Surely this would soon be over. The adviser turned to his companions.

"So silent! Such a proper little king!"

The mockery felt intolerable. He felt the words rising uncontrollably within him, something his nurse had said earlier in the day in her usual dismissive tone.

"I... I'm sure we'll manage to muddle along without you..."

He had not thought that he had spoken them aloud. Certainly, the words could not have carried far, but the lead adviser nevertheless seemed to stiffen. He turned back to Bereland, still smiling of course, but spreading his hands to reveal that they were empty of any gift.

With unmistakeable emphasis, the adviser spoke once more. "Keep *our* realms safe, Your Highness! Farewell!"

Bereland, preoccupied with the shame of his

thoughtless outburst, and at having failed his Council by not obtaining any gift, was unprepared for what followed. It was, in any case, entirely without precedent. The lead adviser stretched out his bare hand. Bereland watched in horrified fascination as his own hand rose up automatically to meet it, then to shake it. All at once, a wash of strange emotion, a sense of horrifying age and experience and cruel alien humour, ran through his thoughts. Visions poured into him, of the past and of the future tangled up together, overwhelming his mind.

Even as the historic handshake was broken, even as the advisers turned, waving their farewells to the crowd, the images and sensations coursed through him. His brain resounded with faint recollections of an ancient arrival, and with the sense of a plan that had been long in construction and which was far from completion. Heedless of the sounds around him, Bereland watched as if dreaming as the advisers' ships were boarded, the last farewell speeches were made, and moorings were cast off.

Even much later, as their sails dropped below the western horizon, Bereland stood alone on the cliff-top, wrapped in these troubling visions, and the echoing laughter of the departing elves.

From the unfinished draft Cyclopaedia:

Departure, The

...Within a year of the elves' journey into the west, all but one of their great strongholds had disappeared.

There appears to be no consensus beyond that about how quickly the process occurred. In fairness to the chroniclers of the time, it was a period of introversion, of every community returning to their own. A time for wounds to heal and damage to be repaired. Some adventurers had undoubtedly journeyed into the forests and the mountains, the remote places where the elves had hidden their homes. Whether they went in search of abandoned treasure or simply out of curiosity, history does not recall what, if anything, they found. The first organised expedition did not come for over a year, and eventually concluded that with one notable exception [see also **Great Tower, The**; **Car Peronel**] whatever traces of the elves' civilisation had been left from their time in the world had melted like dew after their departure.

Within ten years, popular culture had started to establish the world-view of the elves that has lingered across successive centuries. Whatever the reason, it was clear that humankind had disappointed their elven advisers. Our philosophies, our economic structures, all lacked the purity of thought and purpose that the elves espoused. If they were ever to be persuaded to return, humankind would have to demonstrate that they were worthy of their attention – and they would have to do so alone. Why else had the elves been so hasty to depart after the battles were done? Why else had they been so quick to leave the task of reconstruction, rapidly coming to be seen as by far the greater challenge, to humans alone?

By the end of that first decade, it had also become apparent that whatever magic had been in the world had faded equally rapidly following the Departure (now capitalised). The swift decay and disappearance of their buildings was symptomatic of that, certainly, but it was not exclusively elven realms that were affected. The dwarf king Howel was murdered in his bed by assassins, when the Hammer of Taran failed to warn him of approaching danger. Crops, rendered immune to pestilence for generations, started to wither and decay. Some of the effects went undetected, others were concealed. The Crown of Berillion sat on the heads of four more kings of the realm of Askuria before it was discovered that whatever wisdom it had once conferred upon its wearer, it now possessed no magical capabilities at all...

[Extract ends]

1

Rivertop, 2 weeks ago

If, as would sometimes happen, a gull were to fly inland from the coast at Tryachan in search of alternative food sources, it would find itself at the end of a day's flying close to the precinct of Rivertop. What it would see, illuminated by the rays of the setting sun, was a compact walled township, clustered tightly on the edge of a curved promontory, rising up out of the plains below. The river which gave the precinct its name emerged from a gorge which ran back from the escarpment deep into the highlands behind. Rivertop overlooked the point at which it broke free from its rocky confinement, and set off on its long meandering course through the lowland plains to the distant sea.

Behind the precinct, more grassy plains gave way rapidly to darker woodland which stretched almost to the distant mountains. The main road from the precinct ran away from that inhospitable land, though, bridging the gorge at its neck on a viaduct assembled from the same great grey stone blocks as the precinct's walls. From there it forked south, to the capital Car Peronel, and west, following the sweeping curves of the river.

Swooping closer, the gull would have passed along the route of the viaduct and over the type of shanty town that existed around all precincts, made up of tents and other impromptu structures that clung to the walls. Passing over those walls without impediment the bird would have found the buildings within, uniform in their whitewashed walls and black roof-tiles. As the gull moved along the curving streets, the curfew bell might have started to ring, and caused almost all activity to subside into stillness. Even so, snatches of music might still be heard in amongst the ringing bells, drifting up from the substantial opera house building located on one of the precinct's central squares.

Although every precinct enjoyed some sort of building at which music could be performed and enjoyed, very few had a dedicated opera house. Rivertop's was a source of considerable pride to the small precinct's citizenry, even though the building was slight in stature compared to either of the two such buildings in Car Peronel. It was immaterial, too, that the venue's owners were constantly struggling to book any performances deserving of the name opera, let alone the attendance of the well-known names (whether as performers or guests) whose mere presence drew in the capital's crowds with such regularity.

Instead, Rivertop's opera house hosted the occasional touring performance, local repertory work and, very rarely, some new composition by a composer whose pockets were sufficiently deep to offset the disadvantages of being unheard of, and thus inevitably lacking any endorsement from the Council of Style. Rivertop's populace were unconcerned – if they thought of it at all they probably regarded attendance at such events as part of their civic duty, setting an example of proper behaviour to those in less fortunate strata of society. But, truth to tell, the quality of the performance was of little relevance. The opera house was a venue at which society could meet itself, updating itself on all the latest evolutions in the complex ecosystem of the precinct's wealthy residents.

As with most aspects of precinct life, tradition had quickly taken root, and was slow to alter course. Producers, performers and guests each knew their part, and provided that each adhered to what was expected of them, nothing could be amiss. Difficulties only arose where someone sought to behave in a way which was unorthodox, or even 'novel'. Then society, or at least its more rarefied circles, was plunged into disarray.

The composer of *Thonthiel's Farewell*, seemingly ignorant of such considerations, had insisted on darkness in the auditorium, throughout the production. This curious, indeed unprecedented, stipulation had already guaranteed a negative critical reception from those whose opinions mattered. He had nevertheless insisted on it, and since he was also financing the production personally, the theatre had eventually given way. With profusely muttered apologies to those who had come to see and to be seen, staff had moved through the hall shortly before the performance had been due to start, extinguishing the candles in each box, and the lanterns set at intervals throughout the stalls.

Riv' Tomas Callan, heedless as always of society's whims, was perhaps one of the very few to appreciate the darkness. In the corner of his left eye, he could feel the cold heat of an incipient teardrop. The battle-scarring around the eye left it with a tendency to betray him with weeping at inopportune moments. Custom dictated that he should suppress this, but the darkness allowed him to surrender to his emotions, to the reaction being conjured by the performance before him. On the stage, men dressed as elves were enacting the last days before the Departure, but the mundane subject-matter was more than compensated for by the extraordinary ethereal music.

As another minor refrain swelled, feeling as if it was pushing directly up through Tomas's chest into his throat, he almost let out a physical sob. The tear, released, traced a slow path along the creased scar beside his nose. He resisted the impulse to raise a hand, to brush it away. Instead he savoured the raw ache conjured by the music, the gaping void and long-suppressed sorrow that it was articulating.

The debutant composer, only a few years older than Tomas himself, had done something remarkable with this piece. It was commonly thought to be impossible to find something new to say about the departure of the elves, the event which more than any other had preoccupied the culture of humankind for the best part of the last two millennia. To have found something not only new, but potent and dramatic, was almost unthinkable.

The tear took a long, slow detour around the edge of Tomas's mouth, expending itself in the process.

He wondered whether any of the other attendees

at that evening's performance were being similarly affected. Looking out of the box that he was sharing with his wife, Tomas gazed around the crowded auditorium, the minimal illumination from the stage creating the illusion of a shoal of pale faces swimming together in a darkened pool. Even without the darkness, emotional reactions would have been hard to read. The year's fashion dictated that everyone, regardless of their true feelings, should sit in silence, as if enraptured, throughout the performance. The applause at its conclusion was likely to be the best evidence of how affected the audience had been, but again this would probably be dictated more by the viewers' sense of propriety than by genuine emotion.

Even as this line of thought developed, Tomas felt himself drawn ever more deeply into the music's grasp. He wondered at his mind's ability to sustain conscious thought under the swell of emotions that threatened to submerge him. Somehow, the composer's work had been able to tap directly into a well of grief and loss that had been buried for many years. A second tear flowed more readily, tracing the same track as its predecessor, and consequently expending far less of itself to reach the same point. It flowed on.

On stage, the king of the elves was standing at the sea shore, dispensing gifts to his closest allies among the humans and the other earthly folk. The image was jarringly similar to one on the cover of Tomas's first school history book, lost from his memory since childhood until tonight. Like the simplistic image on that cover, the artifice before Tomas attracted him and connected with him in a way that dry history always failed to do. He felt curiously as if he were gazing out of the darkness of the present day through a brightly illuminated window into the past.

A hesitant succession of tear-drops was now progressing down Tomas's cheek, each one reaching a little further down towards his jawline before being caught and drying in his stubble. The sensation made Tomas wish that he had had time to return home to change and shave before the start of the performance, but as usual he had been working until the last possible moment.

The potent aria was reaching its conclusion. As the king of the elves knelt and extended his empty hand to the boy king, Bereland, Tomas heard in his memory the famous lines 'the empty hand of friendship/the greatest and the least of gifts'. The soaring music, triumphant in its despair, pulled Tomas forward on his seat. With her usual sensitivity to his moods, Idony placed a warm, gentle hand upon his arm. A slight sigh evaporated from his lips, briefly alleviating the growing pressure in his chest.

For a moment, Tomas's introspection lifted. However intense the effect of the music on him, it would be equally profound for his wife, who shared the deep sense of loss that lay submerged between them. Tomas glanced at her, but saw only a faint, encouraging smile. In that moment another teardrop, the seventh, broke through the last barrier, reaching the precipitous line of his jawbone. It hung there for an uncertain moment and then dropped without ceremony to the soft cushion of Tomas's sleeve.

The elf king retreated, his final gift dispensed, his face already turned to the west and his future home. A final instrumental fanfare was building, elaborately drawing together the themes from the preceding scenes into a single, strikingly coherent, whole. Tomas allowed his eyes to close briefly, as the music shivered its way up his arms and his back towards its climax. He felt himself completely immersed within it.

Until Idony's hand tightened on her husband's arm as unexpected light streamed into the box.

Tomas's eyes opened at once. Then he waited, immobile, just long enough for the young runner who had stepped unannounced into his box to realise his error and to retreat outside, drawing the curtain closed behind him. This also afforded Tomas the time he needed to compose himself. He donned his cloak, picking up his cane and the hat with his gloves tucked inside which sat on a shelf next to the curtained entrance. Then he turned to his wife, a quick hand gesture dismissing the slight moisture from his cheek, his eyes now filled with an apology. Idony, still smiling reassuringly, kissed him lightly and whispered her love into his ear.

Then Tomas was gone, the curtain barely disturbed by his passage. Half way down the stairs to the ground floor, a now anxious runner trailing behind him, the sound of the perfunctory applause from the auditorium barely reached his ears.

2

Car Peronel, today

[Extracts from the voluntary confession of [Subject T187356]. Interview 1. Collated from the files of the Justice Authority. Quaestor's words redacted throughout.]

To deal with the formalities, then, this is my voluntary confession. My full name is [Redacted: T187356]. I have elected to make my confession orally and with a full transcript and understand that by doing so I have waived the leniency which I would have earned by permitting the Justice Authority to assist me with my evidence. I understand that I must speak truly and completely on pain of sanctions to be determined by the coactors' courts.

I shall begin as requested with the first of the events that eventually brought me here. Shortly before the start of Fest, and so perhaps only two weeks or so ago now, although it feels a good deal longer, I rode over to Hartrick Hall to take part in the last hunt of the year. Lord Hartrick was the hunt master and I had been honoured with a personal invitation for the first time. I was determined to make a positive impression and recall that I had spent even longer than usual in consultation with my wardrobe, seeking to achieve a truly striking appearance.

I fancy that I attained my objective. Certainly there were few people that I encountered that day who did not comment on my apparel. Several of them stated that they had never been hunting with someone quite so sharply attired. Regrettably, fashion and fox-cats are a poor mix and, out of consideration for my tailor as much as for any other reason, I was obliged to retire early from the hunt before my best breeches became irretrievably sullied.

Nevertheless, the refreshments and diversions offered by Lord Hartrick were so charming and the company so conducive, that it was not until after twenty o'clock that I prepared reluctantly to depart for my homeward journey. In some ways, I was rather surprised that Hartrick did not invite me to stay overnight but, of course, if he had done so...

Anyway, that is not to the purpose.

I confirmed the return route with my host and, after a pause to allow him to make any offer of accommodation or further refreshment, which again he overlooked, I took my leave. It is not as if he did not have ample facilities to accommodate me... But then, perhaps he was acting on the instructions of others? That is a point which I had not previously considered. It would certainly explain the lapse...

I am sorry. At any event, the sun was touching the spires of the hall as I made my departure, casting long shadows ahead of me down the drive. The evening retained much of the day's warmth, and I was very comfortable as I sat astride my eight year old hunter, letting him take it at a steady pace as I reflected with satisfaction upon the successes of the day.

After leaving Hartrick's estate, the quickest route home took me across country for several miles. Much of the land is open farmland, and under the protection of the lord's forts, so I did not have any great qualms about travelling openly and alone. I had when younger been equipped with the usual amount of sword training and I flatter myself that I know how to wear a blade with conviction, and indeed to handle one if necessary, although I have rarely been obliged to do so.

Crossing the farmland in the morning I had been occupied with thoughts of the day's hunt, but I had more leisure to look about me on the return journey. I could not help but make comparisons between the farmsteads which I passed on my route, and the more meagre dwellings that represented my own home. Orphaned siblings have no choice in such matters of course, but there was an essential unfairness which struck me as I looked upon the thick walls and robust fortifications of the other farm buildings, and compared them with our own modest protection. The property we occupy, as you may know, has only the one fortified round tower adjoining the main farm buildings and we had for some time been increasingly conscious that the remainder of the property was extremely vulnerable.

It avails little now to berate my parents for a lack of foresight, indeed their deaths have made any such recrimination entirely otiose. Nevertheless, I have often wished that they had been able to acquire a properly fortified holding within the oversight of the lord's forts. Naturally, with two offspring and the law as it is, the precincts were forever beyond their grasp, but they might at least have attempted to secure something within the boundary road! Once past that road I knew that I would have to enter the forest for a short period and I did not relish the prospect of doing so in the gathering dusk.

Equally, however, I could not think of stopping and requesting a bed and shelter for the night before continuing my journey. It would have been unbecoming in me to show any anxiety about the coming darkness. There was also the consideration that my sister had been left alone in the farm all day, apart of course from the one or two farm-hands who worked our land, and was apt to become anxious if I had not returned by nightfall.

Heedless of the peril to myself, then, I continued on my way. I have often been told that I have a keen sense of direction, and it was no doubt as a consequence of the distracting thoughts of my sister's anxiety that I went somewhat astray on this occasion. In consequence, I encountered the boundary road about a half mile from the crossing point that I had been aiming for.

By that time the sun had sunk below the high pines that lined the main road on either side, and the way ahead of me was cast into gloom. I felt a chill of premonition, not fear of course, but enough to make me wary as I cantered along the road to the intersection. I am sure that it was because of this that when I first saw the mounted figures I did not call out to them quite as carelessly as I might have done, in daylight, on another occasion. It later seemed clear to me that it was that caution which had saved my life.

I do not know with certainty who I encountered on that evening. You will know, as well as any I dare say, that the roads are increasingly inhospitable places for the solitary traveller. I had no expectation of meeting anyone there, and the hour was getting late, such that any other respectable travellers would already have halted their journey. With all that has happened since, and indeed with the numerous re-tellings of the encounter which I have been obliged to provide on various occasions, it is difficult to remember precisely how I felt at the time.

I do, however, remember clearly the image that those men presented as I saw them ahead of me on the road. They were dressed entirely in black with no crest or other adornment on either themselves or their steeds. Even though we were still several hundred feet apart when I first hailed them, there was no mistaking the ferocity with which they suddenly turned and spurred their horses towards me. After that I had no cogent thought at all, other than the desire to flee.

I should say that I am no coward, but nor am I foolhardy. The number of my opponents made it inconceivable that I should seek to stand and fight. My only hope, as I saw it, was to reach the safety of the farm, and to hope that the place's modest defences were adequate to deter my pursuers. I rode straight back along the boundary road for nearly half a mile, with the sound of hoof beats loud in my ears. Frequent glances over my shoulder showed me that my pursuers were gaining ground. I believed that if I remained on the roadway much longer, I would be taken and, as I imagined, swiftly killed. With strength that derived purely from the fear of the moment I turned the horse and impelled him towards the darkness of the pines.

Of what happened next, I cannot say... No! No! I assure you, I am not attempting to withhold anything! Please, I beg you, not again! May I explain?

No sooner had we entered the dark canopy of the forest than something solid struck me across the temple. I do not know whether it was a weapon, thrown by my pursuers. More likely it was a branch of one of the trees. The result was horrific, blood seeped from the wound to stain my otherwise pristine collar and neck tie. The fabric was ruined beyond repair. But at the time I was unaware of this. I believe that I must have been dazed, at the very least. My recollection of the flight that followed is little better than a blur. All that I know, I do assure you, is that somehow in my headlong panic I left behind the hunters pursuing me and when I came to myself the sun had set, and I was quite alone in the woods about two miles south of the farm.

What became of them? I have not the faintest idea! Afterwards I assumed that they had lost sight of me in the trees and decided to try for some other victim.

I cannot account for it. To the best of my memory I encountered no-one else.

I swear it! I remember nothing more!

No! Please!

[Interview suspended]

3

Outside the theatre, a carriage stood on the cobbled square, waiting among the conveyances of those wealthy enough to have hired a vehicle and its associated guards for the entire evening. Nobody who actually owned a carriage would leave it in such an unprotected location, even within the precinct. Climbing aboard, Tomas barely waited for the runner to be seated next to him before striking the roof once with his cane to set the carriage into motion. Pausing for several moments to gather himself, as the carriage got under way, he finally turned an inquisitive glance to his companion. The young man flushed.

"Please permit me to apologise for disturbing..."

Tomas held up a hand.

"There is no need for an apology. Discretion and etiquette are important, as I am sure you know, but the substance of the work we do can excuse minor lapses in your conduct, provided that they are occasional."

A grateful gulp.

"Thank you, Sir. I believe that this is indeed a matter of some substance. The Arch-Investigator insisted that you, and only you, should be tasked with this enquiry. He said that it was essential that you should begin work immediately. We are not even to return to the armoury for tasking!"

It was plain to Tomas that the young runner had been greatly impressed by the nature of the instructions that he had received. He was, indeed, suitably impressed himself by the urgency of his summons. It suggested some matter of precinct security, some small part of the so-called "fight against fear" which never failed to give rise to new and interesting challenges for the investigators. If not that, then a murder seemed the most likely possibility – a fresh incident scene could quickly become contaminated and valuable clues lost as a result of delay.

A theft, perhaps, with investigators summoned to give "hot pursuit"? The carriage, although imposing, did not seem to Tomas to have been heavily armoured, and was only drawn by a pair of the day to day workhorses from the armoury's stables. As such there did not seem to be any expectation that he would need to leave the precinct, certainly not before dawn. The same calculation appeared to rule out the possibility of a kidnapping, a reflection which caused Tomas considerable relief.

"Do you have a briefing for me, or any papers?"

"Only this."

The runner handed him a small rectangle of paper. An urgent call. In one corner hung the Arch-Investigator's seal verifying the instructions contained on the slip as genuine – even if Tomas could not have recognised his direct superior's distinctive script. The slip was difficult to read as the carriage's constant motion shook the candle-lamp on its gimbals, but Tomas could see that it was nothing more than a name and an address.

"What is this? Are we meeting this person? Are they to give me further instructions?"

The runner hesitated for a crucial moment. Tomas felt his eagerness fall away.

"I have been instructed that this is truly a matter of considerable urgency, Sir. I... That is to say, it is a missing person, Sir."

Tomas was quite sure that none of the considerable surprise that he experienced at being allocated such a mundane task was visible from his face. At the same time, however, he permitted a certain amount of the tension that had been creeping into his shoulders, arms and hands to evaporate. A slight smile briefly turned up the corner of his mouth.

"A missing person? And this name... Riv' Rauor Tell. This is the person in question?"

The runner, who apparently had been fearing an outburst of some sort, also seemed to relax. "That is correct, Sir."

The name, or more specifically its prefix, told Tomas something. Whoever he was looking for was a citizen of Rivertop. The surname Tell was not one that Tomas was familiar with, however. Without a better knowledge of the lesser families that occupied the fringes of High Town, however, his understanding was not much progressed. He forced himself to relax all the way. It could have been worse, he supposed. He could have been left investigating the recent spate of graffiti that had been appearing around the precinct.

"Were you given any further instructions for me?"

"Not really, Sir. Only that I was to bring you to

that address as soon as possible, and that no-one else was to enter the building before you had completed your preliminary search. Even I am to wait outside, to prevent anyone else coming in after you. The Arch said that you would know what to look for, and that once you had finished looking, you should report only to him, first thing tomorrow. I'm sorry Sir, that is all he told me. That, and where to find you."

"Very well. I make no doubt that we shall be there within a few minutes, and then we shall see."

Tomas turned his face away, to look out of the carriage windows. He subdued his internal confusion and turned his mind to the question of their destination. The walled precinct of Rivertop covered barely two square miles and he had made it his business to ingrain a knowledge of its streets in his memory soon after transferring there from the army. Despite the uniformity of the buildings, all timbered white walls, regular rectangular windows and black slate tile roofs, it had not taken long to learn each street's subtle distinctive features. As such, a single glance was enough to tell him that they were on Exchange Street, close to the northern wall, moving parallel to it in the direction of the eastern corner fortress. At this point, furthest from the promontory and the winding street-ways down to the river port, the quarter was almost exclusively residential.

On the assumption that they were to remain within the precinct, this suggested that the person in question was likely to be someone of considerable wealth and influence. For these reasons, as much as the apparent mundanity of the task, Tomas seemed a strange choice for the Arch-Investigator to have made. He was not, he knew it, a flower of fashion. Some of his colleagues moved in fashionable sets. Some even sought to imitate the modes of the dandy elvish as far as the uniform permitted, although Tomas's occupation was not generally one which attracted extroverts. Any of those colleagues might have been more suited to a task which was likely to require any degree of interaction with the High Town. Tomas, whose blunt and straightforward manner had once been described as "refreshing" by a second order beau of the Council, was not accustomed to moving in those circles, a circumstance which to date had gratified all concerned.

Any further thoughts were curtailed by the arrival of the carriage at its destination. According to the subtle geographic hierarchy of the High Town the property was slightly too close to the wall to be of the first order. There were two floors above ground, which suggested a further two below along the usual lines, and in Tomas's mind this equated with a relatively small family, perhaps only two or three offspring, and a household staff of only three or four in total. The household budget was unlikely to run to the expense of a night porter, and Tomas wondered how they were to be admitted entry. Like many of its neighbours, the house was dark and shuttered in the late evening.

The carriage came to a halt, the horses' breath tracing gentle steam trails in the night air. Tomas turned to the runner.

"When we have dismounted, please wait at the roadside. If anyone enquires of your business show them your badge and tell them that I have instructed you not to answer any questions. If anyone seeks entry, take their details and ask them to wait in the carriage until I have concluded my business. There should be some suitable refreshments beside the driver, for you to offer them."

The runner nodded once, in assent.

Privately, Tomas considered that it was unlikely that anyone would approach either the property or the carriage. Even the more fashionable parties would be under way by such a stage in the evening, and anyone not engaged socially would have returned, within a half hour of the sunset, to the safety of their homes. The principal purpose of his superior's instructions, he reflected as he ascended the steps to the front door, was to keep the runner out of his way while he conducted his initial investigation, and Tomas was not ungrateful for that consideration.

Tomas's concerns about the prospects of gaining admission were dispelled before he had even had time to reach out to the bell pull that hung beside the door. A worried looking gentleman, of middle years, pulled the door open and ushered Tomas inside. The householder, for Tomas could not imagine that it could be anyone else, was dressed in what might only be described as a house-coat, but one with such opulent finishings and adornments that in other circumstances Tomas might have found it risible. The man's anxiety, evident from his features, spilt over into speech even as Tomas was in the act of producing his badge.

"So glad that you have come! Kerton! I mean, I am Kerton. Come in, come in! I've sent the servants to bed. Strange business. Didn't want any chat running around to the neighbours, ha! Sure you know what I mean. Didn't really know what to make of it myself. Not a big believer in the supernatural. Don't imagine you are either, ha! Should I... blast! Your man, is he coming in or just loitering outside?"

Tomas removed his cloak and started to hunt for

somewhere to leave it, without any intervention from Lord Kerton "He will remain outside, my lord. It is essential that I should not be disturbed in the early stages of this investigation."

"Quite right, quite right. Pity. Whole street will know you've been here. Can't be helped. Can't imagine what you're going to find, though. Not unless you are a magician, ha!"

"I beg your pardon, my lord?"

"Well, damme it all man, it's not every day that a member of the household vanishes from his room without a trace!"

This statement produced a slight twitch from the investigator's head, but then Tomas returned his attention to the folding of his cloak, placing it at last on the hall table with his hat and gloves. He almost left his cane with them, but yielding to a faint anxiety, at the last minute he kept it in his hand. Straightening and turning back to the excitable lord, he found him already at the foot of the stairs, leading up to the residential part of the property.

Looking up, Tomas could see that the rooms above were arranged off a roughly semi-circular landing, and he noted that the internal dimensions of the property would seem to preclude a second stairwell, even for servants.

As soon as he was satisfied that Tomas was following him, Lord Kerton began to climb, unleashing a further verbal torrent as he did so.

"O' course, I say he's one of the household, but scarcely flesh and blood, don't you know? Tutor. Educatin' young K minor. Son and heir, but a bit... delicate... if you take my meaning? Wanted to keep him close at hand. Tutor seemed like the best solution. Good chap, too, if you don't count the vanishing. Ha!"

By this point, they had reached the landing and

Lord Kerton's speech became punctuated by rapid-fire hand movements, describing a clockwise trajectory as he pointed out the highlights of the property to his visitor.

"My bedroom. Good lady wife fast asleep. Sleeps through anything, ha! My study. Boy's bedroom. Library."

The small, book-lined snug sitting at the top of the stairs and directly opposite the front door was the only room on the upper floor to have an open door. From what Tomas could see it barely seemed to deserve the lofty description given it by Lord Kerton, and Tomas drew appropriate conclusions about the remainder of the property. His host, and tour guide, had in the meantime turned right at the top of the stairs, making for a doorway set in the corner of the upper floor.

"Here we are. Those rooms" pointing further to his right, and completing the arc, "are guest quarters. Locked when not in use or being cleaned. This is Tell's room."

The door, like much of the rest of the upper floor, was entirely unremarkable. His host was about to lead the way inside when Tomas interjected.

"Pardon me, my lord. It would, I think, be much better if you were to let me take a preliminary look at the room myself. Then I will need to obtain your impressions and also take a note of any other information that may be important. Have you entered the room since the disappearance?"

"O' course I have man, had to look for the dammed fellow, didn't I? Couldn't be incurring the cost of an investigator when the man was fast asleep in bed, or passed out on the floor, could I? Didn't touch anything though, if that's your concern. Little enough to touch, man lives like a convict, ha!"

Without ceremony, Tomas stepped through the door into the tutor's bedroom, easing it silently shut behind him. The room was as bare as he had envisaged from Lord Kerton's description. Yet there was a subtle sense of a life interrupted, a feeling that at any moment the mysterious tutor could return. So strong was this sensation that Tomas looked, unashamedly, beneath the bed and in the wardrobe, to satisfy himself that he was alone, before commencing a more thorough enquiry. He also satisfied himself that there was no inter-connecting door leading to the guest quarters, thereby eliminating what had seemed to him one of the more likely explanations for the disappearance.

Thus far he had trodden lightly and touched as little as possible. Next, he returned to the doorway trying to recapture the sense he had obtained when first entering. The bed, though made up, was slightly rumpled and appeared to have an indentation running along it as if to suggest that someone had only recently been resting there. The wardrobe appeared to contain a reasonable quantity of clothes for a person of the tutor's station in life. Shoes and outer clothes were all where Tomas would have expected them to be.

The only other furniture in the room was a dressing table which appeared to double for a desk. A sheaf of parchment covered in a child's handwriting lay there, topped by a quill that was still loaded with ink, albeit dried. All of the normal accoutrements of a man's toilet, at least in Tomas's experience, were set out on and amongst stacks of books on a variety of subjects, at a first glance all being texts suitable to a young man's education.

Nothing appeared to be missing, nothing appeared to be disturbed. Looking more carefully,

Tomas noted that the light burning on the dressing table was nearly burnt out and, from the freshly opened pack of candles lying next to it, Tomas inferred that it may have been freshly lit that evening. Now that his mind was focused on flame and fire, his nose detected a sharp trace of paper smoke, at odds with the smell emanating from the beeswax candle. On his hands and knees again, Tomas discovered a small grate behind the dressing table, and in that grate a twist of ash which suggested that a small quantity of paper had been burned there very recently. An optimistic exploratory fingertip returned with a thin coating of fine ash, having crumbled this potential evidence into nothingness.

There was little more to see in the room. On a whim, Tomas lay on the bed, fitting himself as nearly as possible to the indentation. To his right was the wardrobe and beyond his right toe, the door to the room. To his left were the room's only windows, looking out across the darkened gardens of adjacent properties. A flicker of movement momentarily drew his gaze, but it was merely the local semaphore tower, signalling with lamps in the late evening gloom. Something about the window itself, however, caught and held Tomas's attention. One of the handles of the right hand frame was only half closed and he rose to push that window open and to peer out into the night beyond. The handle was loose and would not stay in the open position. It was thus possible that if someone had pushed it closed from the outside, it would have fallen as Tomas had found it.

A few moments' inspection served to satisfy him that such an explanation was highly improbable. There was no balcony outside, just a sheer drop to the ground below. It was difficult to judge the distance in the dark but Tomas thought it unlikely that the tutor had left by this exit. It would be a difficult fall for someone such as himself, who constantly trained in such physical activities. For an intellectual, a tutor, it was more or less inconceivable. In any event, a far more elegant and simple solution had presented itself to the Investigator's mind.

The hour was marked by a gentle chime of bells from the next room, drawing Tomas's attention. He returned to the doorway.

"I have completed my initial examination, my lord. There are no other doors into or out of the room, and the window is set too high, and with too little below it, for that to be a viable means of egress. It seems to me most likely that the man left your property by the main staircase and the front door, perhaps at a moment when your servants were otherwise distracted. Did the family dine at home this..."

But before he could elaborate on this theory any further, Lord Kerton cut him off, now in considerable agitation.

"But damme it all man, that is just what he cannot have done! Servants saw him enter the room after dinner, ha? Front door was locked, only key in my constant possession, ha?"

A further sudden thought overtook Tomas, causing him to halt where he stood. He lowered his voice, grasping his cane more firmly as he continued.

"Then, my lord, he is still within the house."

"No! No! Damme it man don't you think I've looked? Impossible anyway, ha! Haven't told you yet. K minor was sitting on the stairs reading his dammed book the whole time!"

4

[Extracts from the voluntary confession of [Subject T187356]. Interview 2. Collated from the files of the Justice Authority. Quaestor's words redacted throughout.]

It was late when I reached the farm, but a lamp shone in the ground floor of the fortified tower, where we maintain our kitchen. I knew that I would find Elyssa waiting there for me. In recent years she has become, I regret, as much a mother as a sister to me. I vex her greatly, I know it, but beneath the antagonism and the frustration I know that in her simple way she also loves me deeply.

Nearly unconscious, giving no thought at all to the spectacle that I presented, I came through from the stable, staggering slightly in the narrow stone flagged passageway, and burst into the kitchen. What an apparition I must have presented! I was still bleeding, as I subsequently discovered, from a wound to my right temple. My clothes, to the extent that they were not blood-stained, were marred with twigs, branches and even mud. I think at one stage I must have fallen from my horse and remounted, without even knowing it.

Elyssa, like any gentle soul who had been whiling away the day and night with fantasies of what might have become of her beloved brother, naturally screamed. My efforts to calm her were only partially successful, hampered by my own initial puzzlement about the source of her anxiety. It was many minutes before either of us were calm enough to have a rational conversation.

My sister recovered first. Leading me to the kitchen table she bade me sit and soaked any cloths that she could lay her hands on in order to staunch the flow of blood and cleanse my wounds. A generous glass of portwine, lightly warmed over the firepit, did much to aid my return to sanity. As soon as I was able to do so, I told Elyssa everything that I could recall, much as I have just related it to you.

I do not know whether you have in your records the details of our family circumstances? Our father and mother were killed around five years ago. An ork gang crossed paths with their carriage one night as they returned from the nearest precinct. There are few families living beyond the green who are not marred by similar tales. They left us the farmhouse, staffed, and a modest income. The farmhouse was secure but, being over ten miles from Eskillion it had little or no monetary value. A group of our parents' friends had supported us, as much as they could, but as far as we then knew they were none of them affluent. The most prominent among them, and the closest to us, was the southerner lawyer Merson Blare.

Consequently, once Elyssa had heard my tale and dealt with my injuries as well as she was able, her first thought was of "Uncle" Merson.

Merson lives over thirty miles away from us in Braed Tor. As such, there was no way in which we could have readily travelled to see him at that point. Certainly my fastest curricle and the match pair of racing greys that I had purchased to celebrate my majority could have made the journey within a day, but the conditions would have been too cramped for Elyssa. In any case, I was still suffering from the profound headache. Furthermore, I was reluctant to involve him. Blare and I do not have such a close relationship, a fact which owes much to his disapproval of what he termed the frivolous and dissolute way in which I have chosen to lead my life. I did not relish the prospect of another scolding from Uncle Merson. Moreover, I did not at that point perceive any danger that there would be repercussions from my encounter, beyond a prolonged period of physical discomfort for me, and the somewhat pressing need to visit my tailor for a new riding coat.

Unfortunately Elyssa, as she so often did, disregarded my views and compiled a short message to be signalled to our Uncle's office, informing him of the events. Our family code did not, understandably, quite contain the vocabulary to do true justice to the event that had occurred, but Elyssa was, I believe, able to imbue an appropriate sense of danger and to convey the fact that I had been injured. It did not, in truth, occur to me – and I am sure that it was not in Elyssa's mind – that this would prompt anything more than a polite expression of concern from our "uncle" together with the obligatory castigation on the next occasion when we met.

I was led to my bed, feeling quite the invalid and distinctly the worse for wear. Without undressing me Elyssa laid me under the covers, informed me tenderly that I was a fool who deserved everything I got, and urged me to fall asleep. I was still largely dressed in my day clothes and in any other circumstances the thought of the creasing and other harm that would befall them would have made sleep impossible until I had changed into my nightwear. Nevertheless I complied with Elyssa's injunction so readily that I do not recall that I even heard her return from the roof where she had gone to transmit our message, before night closed in.

It felt as if it were only a few moments later when I was awakened to find the significant presence of Uncle Merson, leaning his bearded face over my bed and examining my injuries. For a few moments I struggled to remember the circumstances which had led me to my present condition. When memory returned I must have let out a slight involuntary groan, for he, perceiving that I was conscious, stepped back to examine the sum total of the spectacle that I presented.

I, in turn, surveyed him. As ever, in my experience of the man until that point, he was dressed with unfashionable sobriety. For all that his collars were starched to perfection and his neck-cloth was adequately folded, his dull and sombre attire always put me in mind of a funeral. It was not an association that I relished, in the circumstances. In my precarious state of mind, I recall that I asked him whether matters were as bad as all that. Somewhat indelicately, he lost no time in informing me that I had made quite a mess of myself, albeit that my physical injuries were apparently slight.

This in turn spurred my own recollection of the fact that I was still clad in my clothes of the previous day, some of which were by now likely to be damaged beyond repair. I could perceive that there was much that he wished to discuss with me, but I impressed upon him the unlikelihood of his obtaining any useful intelligence until I had changed, made at least a peremptory toilet and consumed no less than two cups of coffee and a modest breakfast although, as it transpired, it was closer to dinner time on the following day.

Blare expressed a deal of impatience with these niceties, but being persuaded that I was not prepared to compromise, embarked on a brief tour of the farm with Elyssa while I made myself somewhat presentable. As a result it was nearly an hour later before he and I sat down in the farm's kitchen, myself considerably fortified by my sister's good, strong coffee, and I embarked for the second time on a narration of the previous night's events.

It is amusing to recollect that at the time I felt myself to be under an interrogation. I had no conception of quite what a true interrogation might entail...

[Pause – break for the prisoner's comfort]

I should clarify my last comment. I did not mean to suggest that I have in any way been mistreated or coerced into making this statement, which I am providing voluntarily.

I apologise, I have momentarily forgotten what I was saying.

Yes, I am grateful.

Uncle Merson's technique was abrupt and unsympathetic. Matters which my sister had been prepared to take at face value, he questioned in aggressive detail. I felt myself to be under criticism for some wrong-doing, although I knew not what it might be.

This was not an unfamiliar sensation when dealing with our uncle. I had indicated to you already, I believe, that he and I did not get on at all well together. In the past, out of consideration for Elyssa's feelings, and because I am by nature an amenable man, I had endeavoured to overcome these differences. On that occasion, however, I was in pain, I felt myself to have suffered a number of indignities, and I had no patience for an investigation into the detail of my journey times and the garb of my attackers. Frankly, Merson seemed to be unusually interested in what these footpads had been wearing, without showing the least interest in the far more serious matter of the effect that the adventure had had upon my own wardrobe.

A certain frustration began to manifest itself in my answers culminating, as I remember, in an outburst which I now look back on with some embarrassment. I will spare you the details but suffice it to say that questions were raised about Uncle Merson's lineage, upbringing and, well, habits.

As I spoke, I watched a curious transformation coming over him. It truly was the most remarkable thing. Even as the words were escaping my mouth I knew that I had gone too far, that I was provoking at the very least a stern chastisement. Instead my uncle's face softened, and he even started to smile. When I had concluded my peroration, he sat for a moment in silence, regarding me. Then, to my never-ending surprise, he apologised. Reaching across the table with his huge hands, he seized my wrists and looked deep into my eyes, telling me that he regretted the way that he had behaved, acknowledging that he was treating me like a common suspect – no insinuation intended I assure you! – and begging my forgiveness.

I was amazed. It was a side of the man that I had never previously encountered. Pressing my advantage, I asked him what he meant by descending on us in such a peremptory fashion and what precisely I was supposed to have done wrong. Calmly, reasonably and, above all, amicably, Uncle Merson explained that his behaviour was motivated solely out of concern for our well-being. He had heard tales, as had we all, of increased raids by ork gangs into the green lands around the precincts. Homes, previously considered to be safely within the green, had been attacked, looted and burnt. The inhabitants had been brutally murdered, or simply disappeared. He explained that he had, for some time, been considering our needs and best interests, and had been increasingly concerned about the vulnerability of our position.

It was true that we were, as I have said already, in an exposed location. Our farm, though of robust construction and possessed of a fortified tower, was very isolated. Apart from a couple of largely idle farmhands, there were only myself and my sister in the event of any attack. I have mentioned, I think, that it lacked any other more sophisticated defences. It was borne in on me by Uncle Merson's words that there was a good chance that, whether by following my tracks from the previous evening, or by chance in the future, there was the possibility of a marauder force stumbling across our homestead. If that happened, and particularly were I not there to lend my strength to the defence of the property, the consequences did not bear thinking of. I considered the fine wooden floors, the wall-hangings, my extensive wardrobe and library. All would fall victim to the flames. Elyssa too would be in considerable danger.

Upon those sobering reflections, it was my turn to make my apologies to our learned visitor. I acknowledged, without reservation, the propriety and good sense of his observations, and asked him with some urgency what thoughts he might have had in the direction of resolving this predicament.

He explained that in his view it was no longer to be tolerated that we should be living so far from the safety of the precincts. Somewhat caustically I observed that this was something that we were now painfully aware of, but that short of relocating our farmhouse to a more desirable location, it was difficult to see what was to be done about it. The thought of leaving our home had not, at that stage, even occurred to me. In part this was, to be sure, a question of sentimentality. Both Elyssa and I were very attached to the home in which our parents had lived since before our births until the time of their deaths. Moreover, it was a pragmatic reaction. We had, as I have explained, only limited resources. The property was of little value, for precisely the reasons that our uncle had so articulately identified. The prospect of renting it out was improbable, at least at a rent that would provide a sufficiently high income for us to be accommodated in any comfort nearer to even a second order precinct such as Eskillion. The idea of actually disposing of the property by sale was entirely unthinkable.

Fortunately Uncle Merson assured us that these remedies would not be necessary. In addition to keeping a watchful eye on his two charges he was, he disclosed, also the administrator of a fund of monies. This had been established by himself and a number of our parents' friends, to provide support in times of need. Such need had, in his estimation, now arisen and he confirmed that, in the short term at least, he had access to ready funds that would be more than ample to enable us to be accommodated in comfort and security. Longer term arrangements would be made, but his principal preoccupation was that we should be removed from our current position of exposure at the earliest opportunity.

At this juncture, Elyssa, who had until now remained as a largely silent spectator to our exchanges, interjected to enquire, as I had been about to do, what was meant by the earliest opportunity. I had half opened my mouth to explain that Uncle Merson undoubtedly meant some time within the next month, but he startled me by suggesting that we should depart at first light on the following day. This naturally provoked considerable protestations from both myself and my sister. It was however emphasised to us both that Blare's carriage was the only vehicle presently standing in the farm that would be capable of carrying us away for any prolonged absence. Certainly none of our own vehicles could have carried the significant quantity of luggage and accoutrements that we would require.

Merson's carriage, he assured us, would be leaving at the ninth hour on the following morning. If we were not aboard, then he would be, and we would have to make our own way to Braed Tor, carrying only what luggage we could securely attach to my open topped curricle. Once it had been established that he was in earnest, and that neither imprecations nor threats would alter his decision, Elyssa and I resigned ourselves to the urgent task of preparing ourselves for the journey.

[Interview suspended]

[Extracts from Report number 811 by Auditor [D] to the Committee on Internal Efficiency. Dated 3rd Nieumor XXVI Tor.]

"...As the writer has previously advised this committee, the effectiveness of a reconstruction of communications that have passed, after the event, is very frequently questionable. Commercial and domestic codes are now so prevalent that even contemporaneous interception of messages can result in a delay before those messages can be acted upon. Furthermore, it is increasingly common for multiple transmissions to be sent, by those seeking to conceal the nature of their correspondence, some or even the majority of which are sent purely with the intention of misleading investigators. I refer the committee to the recommendations contained in my report number 729 dealing with the acceptable delays at each hub-station that would come from ensuring that all messages are intercepted and documented before being transmitted onwards. Until such measures are implemented we put ourselves at a disadvantage in the fight against fear...

... Turning to the specifics of the matter presently under investigation, there is little enough to report, in light of the above general observations. Target [B099803] is known to have transmitted a series of half a dozen messages, late in the evening on 28th Finmae, XXV Tor. What prompted these transmissions is unknown. What the content of these transmissions were, is unknown. It is understood that Target [B099803] was already under surveillance as a result of a suspected connection with a spate of painted defacements of public buildings. In those circumstances the absence of a vigilator at his local semaphore station is an inexcusable oversight.

Recommendation: In addition to the general recommendations set out above, the local vigilator consul to be docked five pay points, only three of which may be allocated among his directly culpable subordinates..."

[Extract ends]

5

"You think it was play acting?"

"Absolutely!" Tomas laughed, shifting himself in the tepid bath water to look back over his shoulder at Idony. "I might have taken it for anxiety or even guilt if it had not been such an obvious affectation!"

Husband and wife were seated companionably within their large enamelled bath, an exceptional luxury in what was otherwise a sparsely furnished home. Idony paused in her task of massaging her husband's knotted shoulder muscles.

"Do you think that he could have had any involvement in the disappearance?"

"In my stomach I do not believe so. His lordship really did seem to be thoroughly perplexed by the situation and, affectation or no, the man was no actor. Speaking of which, I have not asked how you enjoyed the Opera?"

"I found it deeply moving as did you, I collect? Tomas, I do not believe that I have seen you so transfixed, not in a long year of theatre-going."

Tomas leant back into his wife's arms, although carefully so as not to put unwanted pressure on her more slender frame.

"I was moved, deeply moved" he confessed, "It was like nothing else I have ever seen. You know my views on most modern pieces. I went expecting absolutely nothing of that performance but, I cannot find the right words I fear! It amazed me." He paused, carefully skirting around the essence of his reaction, which would involve a subject that by common consent they rarely discussed. Feeling sure that Idony would intuitively have guessed this, he tried another way of expressing himself. "It was as if I had gone there expecting to find a field of grey, featureless, mud but instead discovered not just a green shoot breaking through, but a fully grown fruit tree, laden with ripe apples."

His wife laughed, as he had known she would. Tomas had no poetic pretensions. "What an image! And yet I would swear that there were not more than five or six others there who felt as we did. The majority I am sure deprecated it for its departure from traditional forms."

Nodding his head, Tomas leant forward to break the embrace, and prepared to exit the bath water.

"I was already half way down the steps with the earnest young runner, by the time the applause began. It certainly sounded slight."

"It was virtually non-existent. I was forced to moderate my own applause significantly so that I should not be summoned before the Council for a lapse of judgement, but even so I was by some way the most enthusiastic. But that runner! I hope that you did not chastise him too severely?"

Tomas gave his hand to his wife as she too stepped from the bath.

"No my dear, he well understood that he had made an error. He is a young man and will learn moderation. Moreover, he has turned out to be extremely useful to me. I had made up my mind that there was nothing further to be gleaned from inspecting the property and was descending the stairs, Lord Kerton still at my side, berating me for my failure to produce an instant answer to his conundrum. I admit it, I was at something of a loss, the only logical explanation being one which had, as it seemed to me, been rendered impossible no sooner than I had uttered it.

"As we reached the front door the runner, perceiving that Lord Kerton meant to press me to remain within the property until the case was resolved, stepped forward. Deferentially, but in a sufficiently loud voice that his lordship could hear every word, he informed me earnestly that the arch-investigator required a personal report on the development of this matter by no later than midnight, and that we were going to be hard pressed to make it back to the armoury in time. Lord Kerton's demeanour altered in an instant."

"I should think it did!" Idony smiled, handing her husband his night clothes, as he finished towelling himself dry.

"He could not thank me enough for my efforts, urged me to convey his gratitude to the arch for his thoroughness and looked forward to receiving my further report in due course. Within another minute we were inside the carriage and returning here."

Having dressed, the couple embarked on their nightly tour of the property, talking companionably together as they snuffed out the wall sconces and checked the window and door locks and bolts.

"He did not take you to the armoury then, despite his words in front of Lord Kerton?"

Tomas laughed.

"No, although I should perhaps be concerned at

the facility with which he practised the deceit! Once we were within the carriage, and in motion, he confided in me that the Arch-Investigator had left the Armoury some hours earlier, and had impressed on young man that I was to be permitted a good night's sleep before I reported before him."

"Sounds like prudent advice, ha!?" responded his wife, blowing out the last candle, and tugging on her husband's hand in the direction of the marital bed.

On the following morning, well rested in observance of his indirectly received instructions, Tomas boarded a public carriage and made his way across the precinct to the armoury. He was preoccupied by the puzzle presented to him on the previous evening, and paid little heed to his familiar surroundings. The monochromatic buildings and the more colourful pedestrians passing him by equally unnoticed. It was not until the dark walls of his place of employment were looming over the carriage that he was stirred from his reverie, and that was only thanks to an amiable carriage-man who had recognised Tomas as a familiar face. Asked jovially whether he was proposing to go round the loop again for another tour, Tomas coloured slightly, murmured his thanks, and dismounted directly in front of the forbidding black gates, set into the featureless, and window-less, building. To one side of the gates a clean up team were still scrubbing at the vivid dark blue or purple paint with which someone had daubed a rough circle shape enclosing a stylised number seven – the same mark that had been appearing across the precinct in recent months.

Presenting his card at the gate house, Tomas obtained his accustomed instant admittance. A message had been left that he would make his report to his superior, Riv' Victor Appelsin, at noon precisely. He immediately located a clerk and, perching on an unsteady chair beside the man's sparse desk, spent the remainder of the morning dictating and checking notes of the previous evening's investigations. He completed the exercise with no clearer idea as to the solution than he had had at the outset. With mid-day imminent, however, he gathered up the papers, tipped the clerk, and made his way onwards into the core of the building.

Members of the public, even if they succeeded in gaining admittance through the black gates, were only ever received in innocuous grey chambers close to the entrance, such as the room in which Tomas had spent his morning. Further exploration was strongly discouraged. Consequently they came away with an impression of bland, uniform and imposing architecture inside and out. Passing through a maze of identical unmarked corridors, however, Tomas emerged within the heart of the building, a large grassy square surrounded on all four sides by a covered colonnade, above which could be found the offices of the investigators and their associated departments. Every office, including Tomas's own when he could be troubled to use it, had windows which permitted views over this small island of greenery in the middle of the stone fortress, lending the place an open and relaxed air which was quite at odds with the public perception or imagination.

In the east wall, and therefore directly across from Tomas as he entered the square on that morning, were the wider windowed doors and balconies of the Arch-Investigator's office. There, on the first floor, Tomas could see his superior standing in the bright noon sunlight, one black gloved hand gripping the stonework of the balcony even as the other was raised in an informal salute. This Tomas returned, hastening across the square, thanking the runner for his services by way of dismissal. Within a minute, he had been admitted to that office, and seated across from his superior at the large and, uncharacteristically, cluttered desk.

"Good morning Tomas"

"Good morning Victor. Idony asked me to convey our thanks to you for the tickets to the Opera last night. We both of us had a remarkable evening, albeit that mine was somewhat curtailed."

"Please, do not trouble to mention it, Tomas. I was sorry not to be able to make use of them myself and I knew that the two of you were admirers of good theatre. I fear that perhaps an apology is in order, however, since I understand that the piece did not live up to expectations."

There was a trace of a laugh in Victor's eyes and Tomas, sensing his superior's true meaning, responded in kind.

"It is difficult to see how any right-thinking person could have enjoyed it, Victor. It had emotional depth, a detailed narrative and well rounded characterisation. And the music! If I had wanted to be moved like that I would have stayed at home with Idony!"

A brief laugh escaped from Victor. "You enjoyed it then? I was genuinely concerned that this morning was going to have to be all apologies."

While the words were still spoken with joviality, the humour rapidly ebbed away from the older man's eyes. Tomas leant forward.

"Victor, what is it?"

"I am sorry Tomas. I, well, I have involved you in something which it would have been far better for you to know nothing about. But you are the only investigator that I can really trust. To get results, I mean, but also to work to my agenda and not that of outsiders."

Tomas started to protest on his colleagues' behalf, but a firm hand gesture cut him short.

"You know me, Tomas. I have never been one to wish to be flattered, or to blind myself to the reality of a situation. If we were talking about the ordinary course of office politics, I would not doubt the loyalties of a good deal more of our colleagues. This is something far greater. It is also something a good deal more personal. I cannot entrust this to anyone else but... there is your wife to consider. For Idony's sake it is only fair that, before I go too far I give you the opportunity to decline this assignment."

Tomas sat back, gazing expressionlessly at the man whose every command he was contractually and morally obliged to obey. Beyond their professional relationship, Victor was like family to Tomas and Idony. He would be visiting them to broach a New Year's keg together in five days' time. Waiting for a few moments, Tomas weighed the proposal as he knew that Victor would wish him to do, but there was no chance of his conclusion altering.

"Out of the question, Victor. Tell me what I can do for you."

There was a faint suggestion of a sigh from the older man. Now that he came to examine Victor more closely, Tomas could perceive creases of tension on his forehead, in his eyes and in the set of his shoulders. There was a curious unreality in the contrast between this, and the view through the wide windows over Victor's shoulder, where Tomas could see bright sunlight on the grass. Younger personnel strolled about in relaxed mood, winding down towards the beginning of Fest. It seemed such a pleasant, ordinary day. In the persistent silence, Tomas felt a rare tremor of anxiety pass through him.

"Please, Victor! Tell me what you need me to do?"

Another sigh.

"I cannot tell you everything Tomas, even of what I know, and that is very little. There is a group of people. Probably quite small, no more than four or five at most. The government regards them as a threat. I should say, the government would regard them as a threat, for I have no way of knowing whether any in the government are even aware of them. I have kept them under close observation for some time. This is the personal reason I spoke of. I believe that these people were involved in the death of my wife. As you may know, that was the same incident that cost me my leg."

As he spoke, Victor's right hand instinctively stretched out to caress the joint on his right thigh where flesh was covered by leather strapping, connecting him to the wooden appendage which lay concealed and so often forgotten below his suit trousers. Tomas, who knew Victor better than most of his colleagues, was nevertheless startled to recall the injury. He was startled still more by Victor's unprecedented reference to it within the office.

"You have never told me how that came about."

Victor frowned, plainly wrestling with a deep concern. "I cannot, Tomas. I cannot speak of it even now, even to you. Suffice it to say that I have questions that I want to put to these people, to help me understand what happened to us. I want to do so personally, before they are tracked down by the 'proper authorities' and taken to the Tower for questioning. There is no satisfaction for me in that."

Unsure whether he understood what was being asked of him, Tomas asked "Who are they? How can I find them?"

"As to where they are, I wish that I knew. Two of them I had under relatively close observation. Indeed, they lived within this precinct. One was the tutor whose disappearance I sent you to investigate last night, Riv' Rauor Tell. The other was Riv' Lias Nefflor."

The second name struck a chord. His mind on a professional track, it took Tomas a few moments to make the connection.

"The composer? Why did you have tickets for something this man had composed after what he had done to you?"

Victor lowered his eyes. He paused for two deep breaths, giving Tomas further time to take in the surprising level of disarray in the office. Papers lay piled high on the desk, and one such pile had toppled leaving a number of documents scattered along the floor. Victor returned his gaze to meet his subordinate's eyes.

"It isn't so simple. If you had asked me that yesterday, I would have pretended to you that I did not know it was him. But time is short. The truth is that I was hoping you might catch sight of him, that I might have your opinion on the man, without the danger to me of a face to face confrontation. But of course you did not see him..."

"No, he did not make an appearance. The consensus was that he knew that the Council would deprecate his work. Indeed I understand it is likely that their critic will pen a death-notice. Is that what has you concerned? The fact that these two have disappeared on the same day? It could simply be coincidence, Victor. Disappearances are hardly an unusual occurrence in these times, even in the more rarefied air of the precincts."

"I wish I could believe that, Tomas. Part of me did not want to accept that I could have lost sight of them all after my years of painstaking work. So even while you were still at Lord Kerton's last night, I sent a semaphore message to one of my agents in Car Peronel, asking for an update on my target in that town. I received this response shortly before your arrival this morning."

He handed Tomas a thin ribbon of message paper, torn directly from the semaphore wheel. The message was concise: "Suspect vanished. Mode of escape, unknown. All her possessions taken for examination. Further report to follow." Victor took the slip back, crumpling it in his hand. "Now tell me about your investigations last night."

Tomas did so, describing his inability to reach any sensible conclusion on what had happened without any qualm of self-recrimination. "Mode of escape unknown" the message from Car Peronel had said, and if that was the case then there was no shame in his own ability to uncover the truth. Instead he set out what he had observed, and the few tentative conclusions that he had drawn, as fully as he could, hoping that Victor would be able to make something of them.

"That makes three, Tomas, three in the space of a single night. All without taking any of their belongings with them, all showing no sign of how they departed, or where they may have gone. I must find them. Something has driven them into hiding and I fear that it is the long shadow of the Tower. Before they are captured, and before there are any more victims, I must find them and talk to them. To understand what happened to us." There was a look of desperation on his face unlike anything Tomas had seen before. "I shouldn't say it, but I have no concern what becomes of them after that. I just have to know why my wife had to die, why I had to lose..." gesturing at his leg again "... so much."

Tomas felt himself surging to his feet, lunging forward, reaching out an impulsive hand to squeeze his superior's shoulder. The thought of another disrupted season of festivities barely even crossed his mind. He saw the arch-investigator before him, reduced to an anxious, pleading man. He thought of what it would feel like to lose Idony, worse even than the considerable pain of amputation. The swirl of feelings merged with and fuelled the burning loyalty that he already owed to his superior.

"Where do I begin?"

From the unfinished draft Cyclopaedia:

Fest (n. fest)

... In the first centuries after the Departure, discontent was rife. There was a tendency among parts of the populace to see the abandonment of humans by the elves as a judgement – a sign that the humans were unworthy (see also **Departure, The**). Some responded to that judgement by trying to improve themselves, following the example of the shining ones who had gone before. Others stored their resentment, waiting for anything that would ignite it.

A pattern began to emerge. In the hottest summer months, for an apparent variety of reasons, social unrest would flare up. Each individual incident had its reasons which undoubtedly seemed genuine and pressing to the protesters at the time. One year it was an increase in feudal impost contributions that provided the kindling. Another year, discontent from a shortage of food after a poor harvest. On other occasions, real or imagined misdeeds by those in authority set tempers aflame. Where prior generations would have accepted the situation, the new mood was not so subservient. Riots burnt through the cities. Marches, strikes and other protests spread from place to place, sometimes igniting other issues in their wake. Only the first cool rains after the heat of summer could bring an end to the disruption.

At last, wise heads recognised the pattern and responded to it. The merchant kings were most keen to see a resolution – it was the shops in their towns, the warehouses at their docks that were looted and set alight. Disruption meant loss of profit. Their response was typically mercantile. If the people wanted an outlet, why not commercialise it? Thus the holiday season of Fest emerged.

The first step was to alter the calendar, a process which was already being considered for a variety of other reasons (see **Calendar, New**). At that time, the year end came in the middle of winter, a cold and dark time when people were likely to be preserving their money for essentials such as food and heating. Moving it to mid-summer would be more lucrative, and provide an outlet for the pressure which started to build every year at that time. The year was re-divided into twelve equal length months, and the few surplus days were set aside for Fest. No shops would be open during the period of Fest. Only a handful of laws would be enforced, broadly being in relation to offences against the person (citation needed). All people were to be treated equally, whatever their social position or standing the rest of the year.

It was a great success. All of the emotional energy of the people, all of their resentments and anxieties and fears were purged in an annual festival of excess and chaos. It was equally successful commercially. From those who decided to celebrate the holiday season with lavish and debauched parties, to those who wanted to purchase additional security for their homes, to protect them from the rampages, the annual preparations for Fest gave everyone a reason to spend money.

And if the counter-point to this carnival of excess was perhaps a slightly greater emphasis on obedience to the law for the rest of the year, what matter? People might chafe under the cold shackles of their duty and obligation in the middle of winter, but they could always look forward to the heady freedom of Fest.

6

[Extracts from the voluntary confession of [Subject T187356]. Interview 3. Collated from the files of the Justice Authority. Quaestor's words redacted throughout.]

I was, I think, explaining how we came to be bundled out of our home in some haste by Uncle Merson.

I say! I hope that I have by now established my willingness to co-operate? I wonder whether I might be permitted the luxury of having my hands free?

I do give you my word of honour that I will not attempt any sort of escape.

I am much obliged to you.

Returning to the detail of the arrangements made on behalf of my sister and myself by our uncle, it was at a dashed uncivilised hour on the following morning that I was shaken awake and ordered to be down stairs and breakfasted within thirty minutes. Such a rapid toilet was inconceivable, particularly in anticipation of a long journey, and I fear that my sister and uncle were both extremely vexed with me by the time that I made an appearance. It was nevertheless my view that since it was I who had actually been in danger of losing my life less than two days earlier, I ought to be afforded a certain degree of compassion.

After breakfast Merson accompanied us to the carriage, handing my sister up into the sparse interior before strapping the last of our luggage down behind. I recollect that I spent a few more moments seeking to persuade the coachman that I should be permitted to ride along side of him, and perhaps even to take the ribbons for a stretch, but he was under strict instructions from his master, and I was ordered to accompany my sister inside for the duration of the journey.

Of the journey itself, I fear that my recollections will be of limited use to you. Elyssa had not travelled such a distance for some years, and was startled to discover that the roads did not appear to have undergone any renovation in the intervening period. To those more seasoned travellers like myself, the journey was neither unduly lengthy nor excessively uncomfortable, but Elyssa made for a shockingly poor travelling companion and I was rather cast into the role of nursemaid for the duration. The surroundings were mainly forest in any event, and entirely unremarkable.

Uncle Merson was left behind at the farm, with the task of packing up our remaining belongings and confining them to safe storage within the tower storage rooms or, in the case of certain items of apparel which I had specifically identified to him, ensuring that they followed on behind us so that I might be deprived of them for the minimal time necessary. As far as I know he left the premises in a secure condition although, as you will appreciate, I have not actually seen them since that departure.

You are correct, I am getting somewhat ahead of myself.

Our arrival at Braed Tor was inauspicious. It was raining and Elyssa felt very much the worse for her experiences along the highway. Nor were we conveyed to our uncle's home, the expectation of which had sustained us both throughout the journey. Instead, and no sooner were we through the precinct gates, we were deposited at some manner of coaching inn. As the driver, with Merson's purse, was making all arrangements for our accommodation, I was not in a position to gainsay him. In any event Elyssa was too fatigued from the journey to have any desire whatsoever to move from the sparse shelter that we had found.

How in all the shining stars should I know which coaching inn it was?

Oh very well. As best as I can recall, it was just inside the western gate on the right hand side of the road. A two storey building with an archway to the left hand side that led into the stable yard. In decoration it was unremarkable – whitewashed walls below and a timbered upper floor. Like everything else it had a sloping roof of black tile. The downstairs had a large front room with a bar, and a smaller parlour and the kitchens behind it. Upstairs was guest accommodation. The landlord was a short man with, I believe, red hair, whose wardrobe made no impression on me at all.

I hope that will suffice. I must confess the place did nothing to embed itself in my memory.

In credit to him, the driver was able to bespeak for us a small parlour with two connecting bedrooms, which with Fest approaching was nothing short of miraculous. We were of course informed that we would have to surrender the rooms by no later than noon on the following day, but that did not trouble me. Incorrectly, as it emerged, I assumed that by then Uncle Merson would have arrived and swept us up under his capable arm.

Elyssa and I dined simply, in our rooms, seemingly on whatever fare had been cooked but not ordered at the pass below. As I recall, most of our conversation centred on an attempt to identify the constituents of the stew which comprised the main course. We did of course also discuss the certainty, as we saw it, that on the following day we would find ourselves in the altogether more salubrious surroundings of Uncle Merson's town house. Not for him plain, white-washed walls and dusty curtains. It is indeed strange to think that we regarded ourselves at that moment as undergoing an unusual and onerous hardship.

As soon as the meal was finished, Elyssa retired, and I was left to review the events of the preceding day and to consider what the immediate future might hold. Unlike Elyssa, I had been somewhat struck by Merson's reference to a fund which might be used to establish us within close proximity to the walls of Braed Tor and I spent an instructive half hour at the bar in conversation with another of the house's guests, obtaining details of where the best cock-pits were to be found, and what other entertainments might be available to a young man of modest resources. Having never travelled as far afield as Car Peronel or Rivertop I had no frame of reference but it seemed to me that the range of diversions on offer would be more than ample for my requirements.

I was not, however, tempted to partake on that evening. I was tired, and grievously short of funds. I therefore pleaded fatigue after the long journey and retired to our rooms, but once there I found myself oddly restless, and unable to sleep. For a while I sat in the window with the second half of a flagon of wine from dinner, gazing down into the yard where carriages were now tidily arranged ready for the following morning, the horses safely stabled for the night. It being over an hour after dark there was no vehicle traffic of any sort passing through the gate, and only the very occasional pedestrian to be seen on the street.

After that, in desperation, I found myself browsing the limited library of books made available on a shelf in the drawing room. To my considerable surprise I found a copy of an old book of mage-tales tucked inconspicuously between more contemporary fare. It was a book which my parents had read to us as children and the cover, although austere by modern standards, instantly recalled me to those contented nursery days. By chance it fell open on one of my favourite tales, of the Rainbow Prize. Do you know it?

No, I rather thought not. It is a most amusing story, but...

I apologise. I was momentarily caught up in the memory, but you are right to correct me.

It was only that... no, you are right, it is unimportant.

My apologies again. After reading for a time I retired for the night. On the following morning Elyssa and I met at breakfast and concluded that we had neither of us slept as poorly as we had feared. Without instructions, we then waited, after having a house servant pack what luggage we had, and one of the stable lads carry it down to the yard. Noon came and went without any sign of Uncle Merson. The day was hot, and Elyssa and I retired to the lounge to consume cooling drinks and await our next instruction.

It was not until around fifteen, however, that a middle aged man, of considerably smaller build than Merson and with a hunched over, defeated look which made him appear all the smaller, entered the inn and enquired for us in the tap room. I watched as the landlord pointed us out, and then apparently in deference to the coinage passed to him in compensation for this minor task, saw fit to emerge behind the bar and conduct the gentleman over. His courtesy did not, however, extend to introductions and the hunched man was therefore left to speak for himself.

Seating himself at our table he explained that he was Merson Blare's factotum and had been instructed to attend to us and to convey us to alternative accommodation for the following night. When it became apparent that this was not to be accommodation within Merson's home, I lost no time in conveying my displeasure at the run-around we were being given. He explained, however, that Merson already had house-guests, who he was not in a position to disoblige. We were further assured that he was at his own expense providing us with suitable alternative accommodation throughout Fest and into the New Year.

Unable to argue with these considerations, Elyssa and I permitted ourselves to be led outside and into a waiting carriage. In that vehicle, once it had been loaded with all of our possessions, we were conveyed upwards and inwards towards the centre of the precinct, a development that I regarded as encouraging. Throughout the journey Merson's man of business, whose name was, I think, Skapgood, kept up a constant narrative about the history of the streets that we were passing through, and of the precinct as a whole. Despite first impressions, he was a forthright man, seemingly proud of his station but eager that we should have no cause to make anything other than a good report of him to his master. His size belied his strength, which was considerable. Indeed, when we arrived at the King's Shield hotel, we were hard pressed not to laugh aloud at the comical sight of this hunched figure, arms stretched out straight from his sides, as he carried all of our baggage to the reception area. Speaking for myself, my laughter was only quelled by the realisation that he was managing at once what had taken myself and Uncle Merson several trips to load onto the carriage at the start of our journey.

These new accommodations provided a marked improvement upon the coaching inn of our first night in Braed Tor. From the luxuriously appointed lobby to the sumptuously carpeted stairwells and the sensitively furnished rooms, the hotel did a great deal to restore our confidence in Merson, not to mention our personal composure. We bathed and had our wardrobes attended to by the domestic staff. It was, I confess, a level of luxury that we had neither of us experienced before and I certainly indulged myself to the full.

All the while that we were thus luxuriating, Skapgood waited patiently downstairs and when some hours later I descended the main staircase cleansed and in a freshly pressed shirt, I found him stood in the same position that I had left him in, no trace of impatience on his features. Once my sister had joined us he explained that we would be dining with Merson, together with some other friends of the family, and led us unresistingly out through the doors of the hotel and into a waiting carriage.

I wonder if I might test your patience a little and request a short respite? I have no way of knowing what time it is, as you know, but my stomach certainly believes it to be long past luncheon, and my throat is getting a little parched...

I am most excessively grateful to you...

[Interview suspended]

(From a critical notice, published in the Council Gazette on 30th Finmae, XXV Tor. Notice composed by Beau Respiri and entitled "Thonthiel's Farewell – Opera (a Death-Notice)")

"... But of far greater concern than these technical deficiencies, serious though they may be, was the apparent lack of any reticence on the part of the composer in putting this confection on to the public's plate. Indeed it is understood that considerable personal cost was incurred by Mr Nefflor in arranging for the staging of this, his debut work.

Any artist must be free to create, and to express himself – such freedom is an essential tenet of our society. With such freedom comes a responsibility, however. In return for a law which prohibits censorship, artists have a duty to self-censor, to prevent the pollution of the artistic dialogue with what may only be described as 'contaminants'. In the charmingly provincial Rivertop theatre two nights ago, I felt as though I needed to have a metaphorical handkerchief pressed to my nose for the duration of the performance. I am sure from the lack of any real reception at the conclusion of the piece that I was far from alone. Indeed. I even saw a man in the box opposite mine who was unable to tolerate the unduly saccharine and manipulative conclusion to the Second Act, and who rose to his feet and departed before the curtain fell. While unable to descend to such discourtesy I could certainly share the man's sentiments.

I am not, as shall be well known by my regular readership, an unjust man. Let it not be said that I would deny any erring artist the opportunity to redeem himself. But Mr Nefflor's redemption, if it comes, must not be permitted to come within the field of Opera. A theatre full of members of the public has lost three hours of their lives which they will never recover. For the sake of the emotional and mental well-being of any tempted to follow in their footsteps, I must not hesitate to state my views. Compassion for a young man's career must not stay me from declaring this effort, as I perceive it to be: flat.

Postscript: the writer understands that Lias Nefflor failed to attend the premiere of his work, and has not been seen or heard of since. While I would not be so uncharitable as to wish a life end on anyone so young, from a purely artistic point of view, such a conclusion to this misadventure could not be regretted."

7

Despite the imminence of Fest and the considerable sense of urgency imbued in Victor Appelsin's instructions to Tomas, arrangements for his departure took some time. Knowing that it was far from an ideal way to communicate, Tomas nevertheless took advantage of Victor's offer and availed himself of an official runner to convey to Idony that their fest plans were to be disrupted.

Two days of work then needed to be condensed into one, and there were very few of Tomas's colleagues who, with the holidays so imminent, were willing to shoulder an extra burden of work without time being spent in either blandishment or bullying them. Thus it was not until late in the afternoon that Tomas was able to collect his travelling accoutrements and weapons and leave the precinct, steeling himself both for the walk home through the crowded streets and for what was sure to be an emotional interview with his wife.

As he hurried back home on foot, in the height of the late afternoon crowds, he could feel tremors starting in his arms and across his chest, and the muscles in his shoulders and neck tightening uncontrollably. Every jolt from the crowds seemed further to shake loose dark and deeply repressed memories from the past. The anxiety which he had experienced on another race home, all those years earlier, muddled with fevered imaginings of Idony's reaction to the prospect of being abandoned until he could not tell which was which. He arrived hot and fearful, bracing himself for an evening of distress and well-earned recriminations.

Idony was not at the front door on his return. Tomas did not keep a permanent door staff, so he made his own admittance and went first to the parlour on the ground floor where he and Idony would usually spend their leisure time. There was no sign of her. Returning to the front hallway, though, he heard his wife's voice coming from upstairs.

"Tomas? Is that you? I am in our bed-chamber!"

He mounted the stairs, bypassing the guest chambers and the room which they seldom entered. He put his head around the door to their room and found Idony with his travelling case laid on the floor and various items of uniform and informal clothing strewn around on the bed. He hastened to her.

"I am so sorry my darling! I cannot imagine what you must think of me, abandoning you in this way."

She turned for an embrace, a sad smile on her face as she looked up at him.

"It cannot be helped, my love. I do not doubt that you would avoid it if you could."

"I would – I swear it! But Victor needs me to do this, and I cannot..."

She reached up a finger and pressed it to his lips.

"Peace, Tomas, all will be well. I have a good deal of reading to catch up with, and you would only have been a distraction during our forced incarceration." Her brown eyes twinkled with the golden light of laughter. "It will be quite a relief to be spared the necessity of providing for your constant diversion and amusement!"

Tomas let out a deep sigh, relief flooding through him. For several minutes they stood there in silence, savouring the feeling of the other's body in their arms, hungrily storing the memory to be called on in the days ahead.

So it was that the following morning, bathed, packed and breakfasted in readiness for his short trip, Tomas was at the coaching station in good time and was one of the first to climb aboard the stage coach bound for the capital city, Car Peronel.

It had been no more than a year since he had last travelled between the precincts. Even so, he had forgotten how great was the contrast between the sanctuary within their walls and the lawlessness of the lands beyond – particularly those beyond the so-called green lands, out of the precincts' spheres of influence. Tomas had been prepared for the throngs of unfortunates who lined the roads immediately outside Rivertop, although their numbers and abject poverty had been none the less discomfiting for that. But no sooner had the stones been passed which marked the boundary of the line of sight from the precinct's watch towers than an unsettling silence had descended over the landscape. Not one person was to be seen. Even the sound of birds and wildlife was intermittent and seemingly restrained.

Tomas felt a heightened sense of vulnerability, and from the reactions of his travelling companions he could tell that they all shared the same reaction. There was a large man to his right, seemingly some sort of merchant. From the moment that he had settled in the carriage, he had seemed to consider it his duty to regale the other passengers with the latest news from the farm-holds to the north. As they passed beyond the green, though, his narration of the many causes for the ever-rising price of grain had quietened and faltered. A young and obviously newly married couple seated across from Tomas drew yet closer together on the bench seat, despite the oppressive heat within the sealed carriage.

The further they journeyed from Rivertop, the more bleak the situation became. For large parts of the route the woodland had been cut back as much as half a mile from the roadway, so as to afford fewer hiding places for brigands. Within that dead land, no plant life higher than a hand span grew. Apart from the regularly spaced semaphore towers, locked and barred with no visible evidence of the garrisons within, the only breaks in the monotony had been supplied by the burnt out shells of carriages or, on one occasion, the skeleton of a horse.

Tomas thought with nostalgia about the towns and hamlets that had once been scattered along this road. While the precincts were still developing, long before Tomas's birth, the roads had reputedly been busy, friendly and above all interesting. The journey between two major towns might have taken several days, with regular stops at local hostelries or one of the occasional coaching inns. Tomas imagined sitting in the warm sunshine, enjoying a leisurely luncheon as he watched the post chaises and curricles racing by. Instead armoured carriages, those few that made the journey at all, raced along with no stops until they reached the safety of the next precinct.

Shortly after thirteen they passed a group of soldiers on clearing duty. It was no surprise to Tomas that the merchant should be the first to express his views. It was equally foreseeable that he should turn, elbow digging into Tomas's side as he did so, to speak directly to Tomas as the only uniformed traveller.

"It makes you sick to see them worked like slaves, doesn't it?"

Tomas was still struggling to think of a suitably politic reply when the man continued.

"I don't say that the work isn't necessary. But I remember when the Tower regarded it as convict-work. Gods preserve us, even the clampits could probably do it! But to see brave soldiers reduced to land clearance? It makes you sick!"

Tomas responded slightly more flippantly than he had intended.

"Knowing our brave soldiers, I should think that most of them are glad to have drawn a service which keeps them from the front."

The larger man seemed to consider this response carefully, as if searching for any implied criticism for speaking about the subject in the first place. He turned to the rest of the passengers.

"The investigator is pleased to jest. But that is precisely my point. These are men who should be at war, not cosseted away hundreds of miles behind their lines!"

The flat eyes in his round face peered intently at his fellow travellers, looking for any hint of encouragement. Whether out of deference to Tomas's officialdom, or out of general apathy, however, the others remained silent. Tomas knew that many would have shared the larger man's point of view. It had indeed been the custom to use convicts for the continual clearing work, but on several occasions the working parties had been set upon by orks, the guards killed and the prisoner workforce liberated. After the first sensationalists started to suggest that a conspiracy was at work, deliberately procuring the freeing of prisoners at the cost of the guards' lives, the practice was ended and ever since soldiers had been sent out in their place.

Tomas sat patiently, waiting for the next observation to come from his right. But perhaps sensing that he lacked any support for his views, the merchant closed the conversation with a phrase that Tomas was hearing with greater and greater regularity.

"Ah well, it's a problem for the Tower aright, and we've problems of our own".

To this trite observation, there were a few murmured assents. After that, the carriage subsided to silence. Tomas, a man used to taking responsibility and not abdicating it, felt an instinctive retort rising within him. He managed to subdue it, recognising that the rest of the party considered the matter to be concluded. Instead he turned his attention to the window and spent much of the remainder of the journey watching the scenery tumble past, and musing on the stark differences between the attitudes of his professional colleagues, and the minds of the citizenry at large.

As he neared Car Peronel, he turned his mind towards more immediate concerns. Car Peronel was jurisdictionally under the authority of the quaestors, a competitor organisation to his own investigators. There was supposedly an accord on matters of public interest, and Tomas could anticipate a certain amount of grudging assistance. Nevertheless he could not help but be apprehensive. With the beginning of Fest now less than a day away, he could ill-afford any delay in obtaining access to the lodgings of Victor's suspect in the capital, a woman called Forba Groenne.

His difficulties would be compounded by the fact that he would not be able to explain the urgency of his enquiries to the quaestors, without abandoning the secrecy that Victor insisted on. He gazed out of his window as his mind tried to formulate a compelling reason for urgency that would not betray Victor's confidence. As he looked out, Tomas started to see signs of habitation, suggesting that their carriage was at last within the green zone perimeter of the capital. If there was to be any chance of finding a clue to Mistress Groenne's whereabouts, Tomas decided that he would have to take a gamble. He would forsake the lady's home, which had in any case already been scrutinised by Victor's agent in the precinct and no doubt also by the quaestors. Instead he would make his way directly to the old cyclopaedia offices, to see whether any information could be found there.

The carriage slowed to a stop. They had reached the precinct's outer gates. Inbound traffic was inevitably heavy, and without fresh air being pushed into their carriage by forward movement, the interior rapidly became stiflingly hot. The large merchant to Tomas's right withdrew a handkerchief and pressed it to his brow repeatedly. The young couple opposite, who had been entangled with one another for the duration of the journey, now tried to achieve what separation the limited space within the carriage would allow. All of them knew better than to open any of the windows, let alone a door, with all manner of undeserving poor visibly in evidence on each side.

At last the carriage rolled forward into the

shelter of the gatehouse. Guards with long pikes were ready to dislodge any undesirables who might be reckless enough to try to secure access to the precinct by attaching themselves to the carriage's exterior. Without waiting for the others Tomas opened his door and stepped down, speaking to a quaestor runner and ensuring that his baggage would be removed and stored in nearby stables. He would return to retrieve it later, before availing himself of the hospitality of one of the quaestor barracks. While there were two or three people who Tomas knew well in Car Peronel, none of them were acquaintances that he would have felt able to impose upon at short notice, particularly during the Fest period. The quaestors might resent it, but they were obliged by their charter to give him accommodation and assistance.

Before that though, and before abandoning himself to a tedious isolation during the holiday period, Tomas was determined to glean what he could from the former working place of Forba Groenne. The carriage rolled on into the interior of the precinct, carrying the other passengers on to their accommodations. Tomas held a further short conversation with the runner who, for his part, certainly gave no sign of begrudging any assistance to his distant colleague. Moments later he held in his hand a map of the precinct with the location of the former cyclopaedia offices, and the stables where his luggage could be retrieved, carefully marked.

Tomas knew the capital well enough to be able to detect that the cyclopaedia had maintained an office in a surprisingly respectable part of the precinct. Three large plazas radiated off from the island on which the Tower was located, and the major ministries all occupied dramatic properties set on the edges of these plazas. Tomas could remember from previous visits how the substantial buildings were curved as if to ensure that as many windows as possible displayed the Tower centrally within their frames. The offices formerly occupied by the cyclopaedia project were only one street removed from the periphery of the north western plaza, and appeared to be located very close to the back entrance of the Council of Style's elegantly appointed premises.

Having arrived at the western gate, Tomas was able to walk more or less directly down a major thoroughfare towards the government district. The sun was nearing its highest point, and the Tower gleamed white before him as he made his way along the busy pavements. Everywhere there was noise, a marked contrast to the more muted Rivertop, and the almost complete silence of the countryside that his journey had brought him through. Music twisted out of doorways and windows, mingling with the calls of street vendors and the general chatter of conversations.

With the sun heavy on him, Tomas felt sweat dripping down his back, sticking his uniform shirt to his skin. In any other year he would be looking forward to a few days of loose fitting lightweight clothing, without formal starched collars or neckties. It occurred to him that he was going to look quite out of place in the quaestor barracks over the holiday, in his standard office lightweight fatigues. Around him already, even with Fest not yet begun, he could see fewer formally dressed citizens. No wonder the beaus were seldom to be seen in the time around Fest – they could scarcely move without seeing sights that would force them to reach for their smelling salts.

Tomas crossed the street, aiming for a shaded

patch of walkway which was, of course, all the busier for being sheltered from the sun's heat. As he did so, a flash of colour from an alleyway off the main thoroughfare caught his eye. He felt a strange prickling along his arms and across his shoulders. Daubed on the alley's wall was the same circled seven marking that had been appearing across Rivertop. Surely the same person could not be responsible for both? He shook himself, and returned his attention to more pressing matters.

The heat was intense despite whatever shade Tomas was able to find on his route. By the time he reached the shadow of the old cyclopaedia building, his arms and legs were also heavy with sweat. Without hesitation he mounted the steps to the building's main entrance and made his way gratefully into the coolness of the stone interior.

The entrance hall was impressive in its scale, but it had a neglected feel. Tapestries were hung on the walls and although well-maintained, there were loose threads on them and the bottom edges seemed soiled. Brackets and staining on the floor marked places where desks and counters had been removed and the room, which looked as if it had been designed to house around a dozen staff, had only a single occupant. At the far end of the hall, a simple desk was piled with papers, attended by a formally dressed clerk. As Tomas drew closer to him, he could see that the clerk was staring at him in what seemed to be a mixture of astonishment and disdain.

"Good heavens! What an admirable sense of duty!"

The tone was mannered and overly precise, emulating the sardonic humour of his superiors. Tomas stood patiently, failing to rise to the provocation, but it seemed that the clerk required no audience participation.

"The matter that brings you here must surely be one of great urgency!"

A further pause. The clerk must have been very junior, for he allowed a small expression of irritation to cross his face before suppressing it. He also tired of his sport far too quickly.

"To be compelled to board a common carriage is what I mean, my dear fellow, and then to proceed here without the luxury of bathing or laundry! Well, well. I had better not detain you further from your urgent business!"

Tomas seized the opportunity that the clerk had presented. He employed a tone of workmanlike civility, a stark contrast with the clerk's more delicate voice as it echoed around the stones.

"I am obliged to you. I need to speak to someone familiar with the cyclopedia project which was formerly undertaken from this building."

"Oh dear me!" The clerk pressed a starched white handkerchief to his brow before carefully examining it, presumably for any sign of discolouration. "I fear that your journey will have been in vain." He smiled archly at Tomas, as if seeking to include him in a conspiracy. "The project was something less than a success, don't you know? No-one here is likely to remember it at all, no matter how closely they might have been connected to it at the time!"

Tomas forced himself to smile encouragingly, and his own powers of dissembling were clearly far superior to the young clerk's who continued incautiously.

"Before my time, of course, but I hear the halls were veritable mountains of paper. Hundreds of clerks researching and transcribing, and all for what? Such a waste."

He sniffed and looked around him. "Can you imagine their hubris? Imagining that they should be the custodians of all human knowledge! The Council were right to deprecate it." The final comment recalled him to his proper purpose. "Which raises the question – what right thinking person would still have any interest in the project? It's been difficult enough keeping the cyclopaedians from breaking back in here and misappropriating papers. But I don't recognise you."

Tomas tried another smile, but the clerk was starting to look a little more reserved. Tomas decided that he would have to take a straightforward approach. "I'm an investigator from Rivertop. I'm looking for Forba Groenne – I believe she worked here on the project?"

"Groenne?" The clerk seemed to relax again. "She's been the worst offender! All of the others have abandoned this place now but still she keeps coming back..." he paused, looking thoughtful.

"Yes?"

"I wonder though. I collect that she may at last have resigned herself to the project's demise."

As in an interrogation, Tomas forced himself to be still, not to show too much interest. Carefully, casually, he responded "oh really? Why is that?"

The clerk would not last long in the Council unless he could learn to control his loquacity, but for the present, Tomas was grateful for it.

"It is only that I saw her this morning. I was near the southern gate and she was boarding a coach. I think it was the post to Braed Tor, and from the quantity of packing cases that she was having loaded aboard, I do not think that this was merely a Fest-trip. I think she was not planning to return."

Tomas raced back along the grand promenade with the Tower at his back, eyes cutting between the pedestrian traffic that filled the pavements in increasing numbers, and the shop-fronts to either side. At last he spotted a courier station and elbowed his way inside through the crowd of other citizens who had left it until the last possible moment before thinking of Fest messages they wished to send. Pushing his way to a desk he scribbled a brief note to Victor, updating him in the tersest terms, and indicating that he hoped to make Braed Tor before nightfall meant that it was unsafe to travel. He sealed it with both his professional and personal rings, as well as using the standard courier seal and thick wax candle supplied at the desk.

Despite his scepticism that it would assist in a prompt delivery, Tomas did what he could to encourage the courier by way of mild bribery and, when that failed, brow-beating. His negotiations completed, he had at least some confidence that the messenger would deliver the report unopened and in as much haste as was possible given the season. Tomas then left the courier service and made for the quaestors' stables by the south gate. His troubled mind was pre-occupied with the thoughts and concerns that he had not committed to paper. Victor was a loyal superior, and a good friend. But even if time had permitted, there were things that one did not say, thoughts which one did not commit even to triple-sealed correspondence.

In this preoccupied frame of mind he followed his direct course to the Braed Tor gate. Just as he was about to approach the quaestors' barracks, however, he was suddenly brought up short. A large, rough hand protruded from a black sleeve and splayed out an inch from Tomas's rapidly halted chest.

"Tomas? Tomas Callan!"

Tomas's hand automatically reached for the badge and papers carried in a pouch at his waist. Then he looked more closely at his interrogator. The ruddy features were thinner and seemed weary, but there was no mistaking the man's bulk, or his neat little black beard – even if that and his hair were now dusted with grey. Delight overtook the urgency which had been dominating his mind.

"Sure it is, Henrik!" He smiled, "Have I changed so much in the last two years that you no longer recognise me?"

Henrik gave a restrained laugh, but there something in his manner that Tomas did not recall from their past encounters. "Can't be too careful Tomas. Everyone is an enemy until it proves not so, or that's what they tell me."

"I'm sure the Tower wasn't talking about me, my old friend. How are you?"

"I'm well enough. I think it has been closer to five years since last I saw you and you are much as I remember. Always too busy thinking to look where you are going!"

Tomas shook his head. "Five years? Then your Gareth must be...?"

"Seven next birthday." Henrik had served with Tomas, had been in the field with him. He had been a good friend, but more importantly he had been an excellent source of morale. Even in the most difficult times, he had worn a constant smile. His generous sense of humour had always been able to find a way of lightening the danger and despair which they regularly encountered. Now, however, that usually open, good natured expression shut fast. As if recognising his friend's concern, but unable to address it directly, he leaned closer and took Tomas's arm. "Listen my friend, do you have a lodging secured for Fest?"

"I do not. I am here on an official investigation, but the trail leads on to Braed Tor."

"I... you are welcome to stay with us until after the madness, if that is not presumptuous of me?" Despite the reticent tone, Henrik's eyes urged Tomas to accept.

Old loyalty and current duty warred in his head as he hesitated. "It is very generous of you my friend, and another time I would gratefully accept the invitation, but I am afraid that I must make Braed Tor by nightfall."

A mixture of disappointment and relief moved across Henrik's bearded face. Speaking loudly Tomas continued "Now show me your livestock, because I know the sort of half-fed, run down creatures the quaestors stable here!" Then, as they turned to move into the stable-yard, he leant in to his friend's ear. "Is all well, Henrik? Can I help?"

His strong grip still on Tomas's arm, Henrik hurried through the stone archway and towards the wooden stabling that leant up against one of the stone walls of the interior of the quaestors' gatehouse. He stayed silent as he led Tomas to a horse which was tethered at some distance from the rest, eating in apparent docility from a nosebag. With hand gestures designed to convey the impression that he was giving Tomas a guided tour of the horse's anatomy, Henrik brought his head close to Tomas and murmured.

"Can I trust you Tomas, as a friend?"

"Of course. My word on it."

"I..." Another hesitation. Whatever it was, a slow blink of his eyes and a shake of his head told Tomas that Henrik was not yet ready to speak of it. "I am sorry Tomas. I have no business delaying you with my burdens."

Tomas placed an arm round the broader shoulders next to him. Even conscious of each passing moment, he could not leave a comrade in this state. Not without at least trying to attack the problem that was besetting him. Tomas realised that he was going to have to take the initiative.

"You have done me great services in our time, Henrik. I am not likely to forget the obligations that I owe you." For the moment he could not afford to care whether any onlookers might be attempting to discern the nature of their conversation. He turned to look up into his friend's hooded eyes, locking his gaze even as his mind raced to piece together the few clues that it had observed. "Tell me? What is the problem with your family?"

There was just a momentary widening of the pupils in surprise, and then suspicion narrowed his eyelids. For a moment Tomas thought that Henrik was going to break away from their conversation. Then a half chuckle escaped him, and he shook his head, the beard brushing against Tomas's right arm as it still rested on Henrik's shoulder. "So. Your insight is as good as ever. All right. We... we have a problem..."

After a furtive glance around, he continued, and on a topic that Tomas had not expected.

"You and Idony have no child, do you?"

Blood immediately pounded in Tomas's ears, and he struggled to maintain his composure. There was no way that Henrik could have known. No way that he could have imagined what pain this innocent question would cause his friend. Fighting to sound calm, Tomas tried to frame a measured response.

"No. You know how it can be with a career..."

Henrik, scarcely listening to the answer, still less

noting the whiteness in Tomas's cheeks, spoke across him, still carefully manoeuvring his way towards his objective. "Nevertheless, you will be familiar with the laws governing parenthood, within the precincts? It is the same in Rivertop, is it not?"

At last, Tomas saw where the conversation was heading. He stepped back to regard the man who at one time had been a brother in arms, and who even now, though employed by a competitor, was nevertheless a colleague and a friend. A man who now it seemed confronted a terrible choice and one which, if he chose unwisely, might spell the end of his professional career. A second child? He now understood why Henrik could not say aloud the trouble that he faced, even to such an old and trusted friend.

Even speaking as he had demonstrated considerable trust in their friendship. It also evidenced real desperation. Tomas, eager to show his solidarity, but desperate to avoid any indelicacy, hesitated before speaking. There was so much that he wished to say, but time was passing too fast. If he failed to reach Braed Tor before its gates closed for the night, the danger he would be in would overshadow even Henrik's predicament. Instead he simply clasped his friend's wrist in the old soldiers' sign of comradeship.

"I understand. I am so sorry, my friend."

Henrik locked eyes, unashamed of the tears that were welling there. "Yes, Tomas. In another time, we might have celebrated together. Sometimes I see what you and I fought for, and it..."

He turned his face away. His shoulders heaved and settled. When he looked back at Tomas a measure of the old spirit had returned.

"Do not despair for me yet! There are ways and

yet more ways to skin an ork. Now ride well, my friend, and give all our love and greetings to Idony when you see her."

"Farewell, Henrik. Good fortune in all your family's endeavours. If ever I can help in any way, send word and I will come."

With nothing more able to be said between them, Tomas turned and busied himself with the task of saddling his horse and mounting his travelling bags safely behind his seat. Henrik would be reluctant to draw any further attention to himself and Tomas correctly anticipated that he would take this opportunity to withdraw. Despite that expectation, when he swung himself up into the saddle his eyes could not help quickly traversing the deserted stable yard. He was alone, but the emotion he felt was locked deep inside and no sign of it leaked onto his face. Within a few more minutes, he was out of the gate and riding hard for Braed Tor.

[Extract from 'The Rainbow Prize' (a traditional mage tale)]

Long ago, before the Departure, there lived a man called Nail. Nail was not a very nice man – in fact I am sorry to say that he was a thief. He stole from rich hard-working merchants and the tax collectors who ensured the efficient operation of the realm, and he gave to the undeserving poor, those too indolent or mindless to work for themselves. By doing so he further trapped them in a cycle of poverty and ignorance.

One day, Nail heard of a treasure beyond anything he had ever before imagined. Far away from his home there lay an elvish citadel and within that citadel there lay a six-sided building with, at its centre, a weapon which could destroy the elves once and for all. Nail knew that it would be very well-guarded, but he was confident in his own deviousness and his abilities as a sneak-thief, and he decided that he must have this treasure for himself.

Greed motivated him, to be sure, but it was also an abiding and unreasoning hatred of the elves that drove him to do it. He dreamt of a world in which the elves, whose beauty and kindness were so alien to his own black heart, had been wiped completely from existence. So he set out on his quest and over the next year he did many terrible deeds in pursuit of his goal. An elf-lord was captured and forced to divulge the location of the citadel. A hero was betrayed, and his elf-cloak was stolen – thus Nail was enabled to travel invisibly while he was wearing it, the better to further his dark purposes...

8

[Extracts from the voluntary confession of [Subject T187356]. Interview 4. Collated from the files of the Justice Authority. Quaestor's words redacted throughout.]

That was delicious, I thank you.

We were, I collect, just leaving our hotel in the company of Mr Skapgood, in transit to dine with parents' old friend and my so-called uncle Merson Blare, and some other friends of the family.

Hampered somewhat by the necessarily curtailed wardrobe that I had been able to bring with us, I was obliged to dress in a rather less ornate style than I might have wished. For one as sensitive as I am to the gentle breezes of fashion I knew that I was nevertheless rather ahead of the vast majority of the citizens of Braed Tor. Since, moreover, it seemed important to uncle Merson that we should not draw attention to ourselves, I reluctantly reconciled myself to polished black top-boots, aethelskin breeches, a white shirt, and a deep red top coat. I wore, of necessity, my travelling wig, although I was at least able to re-powder it. In view of the limits of my wardrobe, it scarcely seemed worth attempting more than a dozen or so folds to my cravat.

Elyssa, with remarkable fortitude, wore the same dress which she had worn on the previous day to travel in. I am not sure that I could have borne it and I wondered at her resilience, but perhaps she had a better idea than I of the further trials that were yet to come.

Skapgood led us to our waiting carriage and with an astonishing informality, swung himself up into the carriage's interior once we were both settled. There he perched on a rear-facing seat, for the short duration of the journey.

No, I could not recall the route! I have the most lamentably poor sense of direction at the best of times, and with Skapgood's incessant conversation there was little enough opportunity to so much as glance out of the window.

I do recollect that the horses were facing to the right as we came out of the hotel, and that we seemed to continue in that direction for a little way. I would hazard, although I am no more than half certain of my accuracy, that we were in the carriage for a total of a little under one quarter of an hour. Certainly the sun was still just sinking behind the wall of the precinct when we arrived.

The building itself, however, I do recollect in detail. Even from the outside, and in the dusk, it was quite striking. There was a walled courtyard off the road-way where we dismounted from the carriage. As the sun was setting the gates were pushed closed hurriedly behind us, and bolted. Contrasting with the functionality of the gate fastenings, the decorative frontage of the building occupied the opposing side of the courtyard. A double staircase led up to the main doors set about head-height above the ground. Remarkably, this suggested to me, and so it proved, that the uppermost servants' quarters enjoyed some natural daylight!

The building was clad in a white stone which in the early evening light seemed to shine from within. Elyssa, I make no doubt, had the same thought that I did – if this was uncle Merson's home, it was quite remarkable that he could not find space within it to accommodate us. I was, I suppose, particularly conscious of the hardship that we would face in visiting over the following five days, with the revelries of Fest under way.

Skapgood led us up the front steps to the doors of the property, where Merson stood waiting to greet us. He wore, well, how can I explain this? Uncle Merson is an advocate by trade. They make, as you know, a fetish of dressing with ostentatious sobriety. I had not, I believe, ever known him to wear colour or to pay even the least regard to the requirements of fashion.

With all of those points borne in mind, you will appreciate that I was unprepared for the vision which greeted me as I ascended the staircase towards my host. His shoes were a sort of mirrored glass which reflected a rainbow of colour from the large bracketed torches situated on either side of the door. His breeches were a rich ocean blue, and perfectly complemented a shirt seemingly woven directly from a summer sky. His cravat was a single, pure white, multi-faceted cloud. I must confess that I stood in awe of the perfect folds, the neat precision of every line. I doubted my eyes! I must confess that I believed that I had made a mistake as to the identity of our host, and subjected uncle Merson to a scrutiny through my quizzing glass which I am slightly mortified to recall.

Any discomfiture which he felt, he kept concealed, welcoming Elyssa and me warmly and leading us into the entrance hall of his home. The interior of the house was equally impressive to the exterior. I was in particular most taken by the mirrored...

Oh, very well. You had given me to understand that you wanted a particular description of the property.

We were led down the polished stone-floored corridor to a large reception room at the rear of the house. It looked out over a surprisingly well-appointed garden, rather larger than I would have expected to see within the precinct. From sounds of laughter and animated discussion we already had a good idea of what to expect, and found our other two uncles seated in comfortable chairs, smoking and talking together.

Skapgood hurried past us to announce our arrival to the room. Uncle Rauor leapt to his feet and came towards us with enthusiasm. He clasped my hand in what I felt to be an unnecessarily tight grasp and gave no immediate sign of relinquishing it. With his other arm he reached out, enfolding Elyssa in a tight hug that caused us both a degree of uncomfortable proximity.

"How's my little bear cub?!" he bellowed. I am sorry, I cannot do the depth of his voice justice, at least not without risk of injury. He was always apt to call me that - "little bear cub" - an appellation which while fitting for a child was very much out of keeping with my present estate in life. It is Rauor's character, however, that you cannot begrudge him anything and I did not demur from the description. I contented myself instead with checking the lining of my jacket for damage inflicted by his energetic embrace.

That pressing task concluded, and peering past Rauor's bulk, I caught sight of uncle Lias, holding back, and seeming extremely discomfited He is, at the best of times, a timid man, and uncle Rauor's ebullience only serves to suppress him further. Even so, and despite my own considerable and not unnatural pre-occupations, I noted that he seemed to have a particularly pale aspect, and wondered whether he might be unwell. The true source of his imbalanced humours was not something that I would discover until later. Initially we were pressed to regale both uncles with the tale, once again, of how we had come to leave our home in such haste and to be with them.

It was around half way through our recitation of this tale that our aunt joined the party. We were thus obliged to commence again from the beginning and aunt Forba, ever the academic, posed a great many detailed questions about our journey and our experiences. As a result, the time had come to sit down to dinner before we had concluded our tale.

At dinner, attention eventually turned to news from the lives of our extended family. Uncle Rauor was working as a tutor in Rivertop and had obtained dispensation from his employer to travel for the duration of Fest and to visit family in Braed Tor. He entertained us at some length with a pen portrait of the family with whom he was employed, and in particular the master of the house who was possessed of a number of entertaining characteristics. Given his head, Rauor could keep a room occupied for hours with his anecdotes. As the meal continued, however, I became distracted from his tales and increasingly determined to get to the bottom of Lias' pallid temperament.

He had sat, throughout dinner, toying with his

food, pushing it about his plate like a fussy child. His pale complexion looked sweaty and he made noticeable attempts to avoid eye contact with his fellow diners – all of us well known to one another and company in which he was normally at his ease, as much as that were ever possible for him. I noticed at one point that reaching for a glass of wine his hand was shaking, and indeed there was a momentary danger that a few drops would have spilled onto my cuff, had I not snatched my hand away in time.

Eventually, Rauor paused to drink some wine, and there was a lull in the conversation. I turned to Lias and asked him in an undertone whether he was quite well. He looked at me, almost startled for a moment, and then began to explain what had befallen him.

Uncle Lias, you know, is a composer. While only in his fifth decade he had risen swiftly to prominence in his profession and had been accorded the honour of the airing in public of one of his own compositions – an opera set in the years immediately surrounding the Departure. From what he told me, the subject matter of the tale was traditional, orthodoxy itself. The music, however, was not. Amazingly, for someone accorded such a great honour so early in his life, Uncle Lias had squandered the opportunity presented to him, and put forward a piece comprised in large part of innovation, novelty and perhaps most shockingly to one of delicate sensibilities, a high emotional content.

I confess that sitting at the dinner table I started to feel a little unwell, merely in hearing the outrage described in Lias' abrupt, minimal style. How he was ever able to get the score past review by the Council, let alone persuade an orchestra to perform it, is only to be wondered at. As must inevitably have been foreseen by anyone with any pretensions to good taste, the piece had been poorly received in its inaugural performance, and uncle Lias understood that a so-called death notice was likely to follow. He had not waited to see the consequences of his deliberate provocation to convention, but had fled straight after the performance, seeking shelter with uncle Merson until the worst of the opprobrium had died away.

It... is a shock, I can tell you, to discover that someone close to you, someone for whom you have always had great respect, has taken such a perilous downward turn. It is, I suspect, not unnatural to feel tainted merely by association with such a person. Out of the filial affection I felt towards all of my extended family, and the consideration that we were both guests in Merson's house, I forbore from heaping any further criticism on him. I now well understood the deathly cast to his features, the forlorn disappointment which his whole body so eloquently conveyed. It may be, and I make no excuses for him, but it may very well be that he made a genuine error, that the natural excitement of the opportunity presented to him had led him to stray in unfortunate directions. I do not doubt that he now regrets what he did, but I fear that any such regret will be too late for the beaus.

During his explanation, the table had fallen silent. I could see from the eyes of the others sitting around me, though, that the shock and disappointment that I felt was not reflected there. Instead their reactions seemed curiously and excessively sympathetic to one who had caused his own downfall, and who really should have known better. Forba made an effort at lightening the mood with a description of her recent adventures following the closure of the cyclopaedia project (another ill-advised endeavour in my opinion) but it only served to reinforce the growing sense within me of a widening divide between us. Indeed it was very much to my relief that before long Merson announced that we must be returned to our hotel, and with the minimum of delay required by courtesy we made our way to the front door and out to our waiting carriage.

It was a difficult lesson for me to absorb, albeit one that you may say I should have learnt a good deal earlier. The realisation that dawned on me that evening must, I make no doubt, have informed some of my subsequent decisions. For as long as I could remember I had looked on that extended family as exemplars, if not of fashion, then at least of virtue and intellect. I could no longer do so. In light of what was to happen afterwards, it was intensely significant that I should have discovered that these guiding beacons in my life up until that time could be quite so tragically and completely misguided.

On the next day...

Yes, that would be welcome. I thank you.

Their full names? Why would you require those?

No, no difficulty at all. They are Rauor Tell and Lias Nefflor, both of Rivertop, and Forba Groenne of Car Peronel.

[Interview suspended]

9

In the end, Tomas's horse made the journey to Braed Tor in ample time, mainly by taking a minor risk and travelling across country in the latter stages of the journey. Rather than following the road which snaked around the landscape he instead followed the dry river bed which cut through it. This barren channel had once been the great river of Glanellen. An early experiment after the Departure in constructing dams and controlling the river's current, attempting to emulate some of the elves' great engineering projects, had been the main contributor to its demise. Now it flowed only with small streams, and then only in the rainy seasons. At this point in the year it was dead dry, and Tomas felt confident that before nightfall the time saved justified the modest danger.

As he at last entered its gates in the later afternoon, Tomas reflected that the loss of one of its two main waterways had done no harm to Braed Tor's status or affluence. It was not a precinct that he had visited before but he was aware of its reputation, as a trading centre above all else. Like all mercantile towns, it was reputed to have a rougher edge than some of its nearby neighbours. What it had, in abundance, was traders and all of the associated services that traders required. There were more livery stables than in any other city in Askuria, more warehouses, more bartering rooms and more hostelries for the passing travellers and transporters.

Consequently, Tomas was confident that even on the cusp of Fest he would be able to find lodgings for the night if he needed to. In fact it proved not to be necessary. The local investigators' headquarters had a number of rooms that they could make available for visiting colleagues from elsewhere, and Tomas was given a warm welcome when he presented himself at their gates. The headquarters were located close to the ruins at the centre of the town. A wizard's tower, or so legend had it, which had suffered some calamity prior to the Departure and had been left decrepit but surprisingly untouched ever since. As far as Tomas could tell, not even one stone had been recycled for use in the other nearby buildings. These stood in a splendour that was all the more dramatic when contrasted with the ruins that lay alongside them.

Tomas had no energy for exploring on that first evening. Instead, after a genial supper in the mess hall, he retired to his guest room to consider his strategy for the following morning, when he would begin in earnest his search for Forba Groenne.

The first day of Fest was always the most chaotic. Energy, pent up from throughout the preceding year, finally erupted through the streets of the precincts, filling them with a boiling lava flow of uncontrolled human-kind.

Early the following morning, Tomas made his

way warily down one of Braed Tor's main streets. Just as they had through the night, his thoughts returned again and again to Idony, at home alone in Rivertop, undoubtedly confined to their well-fortified house out of fear of making her way unaccompanied onto the streets. Within two or three blocks of the headquarters he was bruised from knee to shoulder, and only his size and strength had prevented him from sustaining more serious injury as he had attempted to make some progress across the town.

He wondered again at his wisdom in seeking to pursue his enquiries during this most challenging season. He could, he knew, have stayed with Henrik in Car Peronel. Despite their difficult circumstances he knew that Henrik's family would have made for convivial Fest-companions. Then, when the worst excesses had subsided, he would have been able to make a more measured journey to Braed Tor. He was not sure now what had prevented him from taking that course. Much of it he knew stemmed from the urgency with which Victor had despatched him on this investigation. But he was also determined that if he should be away from Idony, the time should be spent as productively as possible, even if that meant braving the worst excesses of Fest in order to do so.

His foot struck a couple grappling in the road way, whether in anger or in lust it was impossible to tell. In stepping aside he collided with a large, drunk man, and ducked under a surprisingly fast punch that would have rendered him unconscious if it had made contact. There was no way that he was going to be able to make progress by wandering the streets or, as seemed more likely, being swept along them by the currents of the remaining populace.

Up ahead, on one side of the street a wine

merchant had barricaded his shop and stacked a number of barrels full of cheap wine, spigots already inserted, on the pavement. This was customary behaviour from those who sought to satisfy the erupting crowds with offerings, in the hope that they would leave the remainder of their stock, not to mention their fixtures and fittings, intact. It served to draw the bulk of the crowd to one side and so Tomas was able to find a breathing space across the street, leaning against the heavy, water-soaked, wooden shutters bolted over another shop's frontage.

He had never really been able to enter fully into the spirit of Fest. As an investigator, it came very hard to him to set aside his sense of right and wrong, and disregard the behaviour of his fellow citizens. On any other day of the year a gathering of half this size, however well-ordered, would have been broken up and dispersed, the organisers and anyone else who obstructed the coactors being arrested and taken away. As a junior officer, Tomas had supervised such action, and had even felt the fury of the mob turned towards him on more than one occasion. He longed for a protective cordon now as he prepared himself to continue his progress down the street.

Another hour or two later in the day, and a good deal more bruised, Tomas found himself at last close to his target, the precinct's library. If the former cyclopaedian had any contacts in Braed Tor, he was guessing that they would be members of the academic community. If the library did not yield results, he would try the university and, after that, fight his way back to the headquarters to consider a new strategy.

The library stood in an isolated patch of ground, close to the precinct's eastern walls. The entire precinct lay on a slope, with the western side and its warehouses, tariff stations and trading rooms, lowest and closest to the river confluence. Thus, at close to its highest point, Tomas was now able to stand for a few moments looking out over the city that was arrayed below him, noting the first plumes of smoke starting to rise from a number of locations.

Again his thoughts, unsupervised, flashed back northwards to Rivertop. He closed his eyes and expelled air through his nose, trying to alleviate the building tension within him. Forcing himself to focus on the problem at hand, he turned his attention to the library building itself. As expected, it was carefully and comprehensively secured against marauders. The windows between each stone column were covered with reinforced oak shutters, and a sturdy metal gate stood in front of the heavy wooden doors. Also as expected, there were a number of academic types around, not participating in the festivities, but instead watching the crowds in nearby streets for any sign of a threat to their beloved institution.

Tomas approached the nearest of these and after providing identification, explained his purpose. The librarian, an elderly man in his seventies, seemed embarrassed by the approach, and still more so by his inability to be of any assistance.

"I do assure you, sir investigator, if I had any information at all, I would most gladly share it with you. I am not withholding anything, sir, but the name is not familiar to me."

"I beg you not to concern yourself" responded Tomas, "it would have been remarkable indeed if my first query had yielded any positive result."

"But I do wish to help you, truly I do" responded the older man. "Perhaps one of my colleagues might know something to assist your search."

He looked around him as if in a daze. "Did you say that it was a female cyclopaedian?"

Shaking his head at the novelty of the idea, the old man led the way across the courtyard in front of the library to a seating area, surrounded by several moderately high trees. Leaning against the trunk of the largest of them was a man of roughly Tomas's age, slim and with very dark features.

"This is Losar" said his guide. "He may be able to help you. Once again I do assure you that I am very sorry that I cannot, sir investigator"

At those final words, Losar stiffened and subjected Tomas to a detailed scrutiny as the older man walked away. "What is it you want?" he demanded abruptly.

Tomas sensed that a change of course would be necessary. He carefully hesitated and looked at the floor. "I am not making an official enquiry. I am ashamed to confess that I made some play of my position as investigator to secure your colleague's attention. The truth is that I have become separated from a family friend. We were to travel together from Car Peronel, but I was delayed in some administrative tasks with my colleagues at the quaestor armoury and so missed the time for the coach to depart. She, it appears, was obliged to leave without me."

The man snorted, but the explanation appeared to satisfy him. The tension which had entered his face and posture on the mention of Tomas's profession slowly started to recede. "Some friend! Leaving her to travel alone so that you could complete your paperwork? You ought to be ashamed."

Tomas carefully swallowed his natural reaction to such impertinence. Before he could speak Losar, who was plainly a man who felt that he owed it to his fellows to share his every opinion with them, continued.

"And as for seeking to make use of your, no doubt inferior, position of authority, to trick an old man into helping you! For shame, sir!"

Tomas clasped his hands together, consciously heightening the appearance of embarrassment. "I know it, sir. I must admit that my shame at losing touch with my dear wife's friend, and the thought of the consequences for me if she should not be found, were weighing very heavily on me. If you could but assist me, I would be extremely grateful."

At the mention of a wife, Losar appeared to relax further. A small laugh burst from his tight lips. "I see it now. Your wife's friend. And it is you who will be suffering the lash if her friend should come to any harm! I own that your conduct deserves much condemnation, but your plight deserves some sympathy, from one who can well understand it! Tell me about this friend?"

"Thank you sir, I am much obliged" responded Tomas. "She is a woman of middling years. I thought to investigate the library first because she is an academical, a former employee of the cyclopaedia in Car Peronel."

"I know of the project." For whatever reason, Tomas had once again put a foot wrong, and some of Losar's wariness had returned. Tomas hesitated, and Losar waved at him impatiently to continue.

"Her name is Forba Groenne. As the name suggests, she is of a Northerner family, and has the red hair common to that tribe. Other than that, I do not know how to describe her. She was not a very close friend. Of mine, that is."

As he spoke it became clearer and clearer that Losar knew something about this matter, even if it was equally apparent that the nature of the enquiry was unwelcome. But Tomas had no time to congratulate himself on the successful exercise of his deductive skills. Even as he finished speaking, there was the sound of splintering wood from a building just down the street. To Tomas's mind it suggested a heavy front door being broken down. Losar turned to glance around the square, as if weighing something in his mind. He did not turn back to Tomas before speaking, instead continuing to gaze downhill at the plumes of smoke now rising more steadily from many parts of the city.

"There is going to be trouble here before long. I remember years where Fest passed off with nothing more than a few bruises and many a sore head, but the last few years there has been a good deal of burning and looting. I and my colleagues are sworn to safeguard this place. I will not be able to leave the square until I am relieved at dusk."

There was a military cadence to his voice, reinforced by the terminology he used. Tomas, sensing an opening, prepared to offer his assistance, but again Losar continued speaking.

"I do not know your friend. But it is not a day for anyone to be separated from those who might offer them protection. You are right to think that she will be known within the academical community. If you will give me your direction, I will make some enquiries of my colleagues here, and send word to you at the end of my shift."

He turned back to face Tomas and there was a hard and cold look in his eye. "Now, I suggest that you return to your wife, and wait for me to send you word. There is nothing more that you can do wandering the precinct alone, and I make no doubt that your wife will value your protection, even if you do not value her company."

It was plain that the interview was concluded. Suppressing his scepticism, Tomas explained that he was staying at the armoury, and passed across a visiting card with his name and credentials on it. He thanked Losar for his anticipated assistance, but was waved away dismissively. Accepting the wisdom of the man's advice, however coldly it was delivered, Tomas turned and made his way across the square. For a moment he stood, noting the increasing numbers of smoke clouds rising across the width of the precinct, hearing with a professional ear the ugly note in the crowds' raucous shouting. Then, gathering himself, he descended back into the warren of streets, and the crowds of revellers.

The conversation with the confrontational Losar left Tomas feeling the gulf of the distance between himself and Idony. It was some small consolation to know that she was in the rather more civilised and restrained precinct of Rivertop. Even if he could not be there himself, Victor and others of his comrades would be close at hand and would think of her if the situation deteriorated. Returning to the Braed Tor armoury with these thoughts uppermost in his mind, he found himself unusually keen for company. Fortunately, a good many of the local law men seemed to share Tomas's sentiments about the anarchy of Fest, and had decided to reconcile themselves to a few days of enforced barracks leave. He sat with a couple of the men, playing at cards for a pleasant hour or so, and was even able to engage in a little sparring practice.

By early evening, however, he had retired to his room and decided that for want of any better diversion he would embark upon a letter to Idony, even though it was likely that he would end up delivering it in person. With a bottle of wine, and a plate of cold food to relieve him of the obligation of further company, he was therefore sat at a small writing table in the corner of the room when a delicate knock sounded on his door. Assuming that it was a servant come to refresh the lamps, or turn down the bedding, he uttered a peremptory "Come in!" and continued with his writing. A cough from the doorway caused him to look round. There, a nondescript man stood, his clothing concealed beneath an unfashionable grey travelling cloak, the hood of which he was in the process of lowering.

Tomas felt, instinctively, that he was an intruder. He was not dressed as one of the law men might dress when not on duty, and there was something about his manner that suggested that he was out of place. He had a ready, confident smile, however, and the manner of one who was accustomed to his charisma being sufficient introduction.

The full force of the man's charm was being turned on him, but Tomas pushed it forcibly aside as he rose to his feet. Nevertheless, his uncertainty about the man's identity meant that he was careful to moderate his tone. If he spoke abruptly, it was at least without heat. "What do you mean, bursting in to private guest quarters like this? Have you no manners?"

The voice in response was deep, and amused. "None whatsoever, or so my few friends frequently tell me. You are Tomas Callan?"

The man took a further step into the room, pushing the door closed behind him. As he did so, Tomas stiffened. The light material of his cloak had parted to reveal the hilt of a sword hanging in a scabbard at the man's waist, and there had been a flash of metal at boot level which suggested that further armaments might be concealed there. Other than the foil which he had used for sparring practice earlier, which lay out of arm's reach on the bed across the room, Tomas had no other weapons available to him. Indeed he had been obliged to hand in his own sword on entering the building. How then had this intruder managed to come, armed, to the very heart of the investigators' headquarters without being prevented?

"Come sir, it is not a difficult question. Are you Tomas Callan, or not?"

"You have the advantage of me sir."

"I am pleased that you recognise it," came the unexpected response. "You would be best advised to listen to me, and do exactly what I ask of you. Please sit down."

Tomas took a step towards the bed, and the hilt of his foil. There was a faint sound in the air, as of a moth flitting past his ear in the dusk light, and the man's sword was in his hand and waving negligently in Tomas's direction. "In the chair, if you please?"

Tomas's estimation of the danger posed by the intruder increased by a further significant measure. He had consumed several cups of wine, to be sure, but his reactions ought still to have been swift enough to see the man draw his sword. Keeping his hands out, and palms spread in a practised demonstration that he posed no threat to the other man, Tomas seated himself as he was bid.

"You are looking for Forba Groenne?"

"I am."

"But you are not, as you claimed to the man you spoke with earlier, a family friend of hers?"

Tomas considered his options. There seemed little prospect of being able to sustain the falsehood.

"No, I am not."

"Why have you come here looking for her, then?"

"That is an official matter. I cannot tell you."

The sword waved a little nearer to Tomas, lamp-light glinting along the length of its blade. The man gazed at Tomas, appraisingly, for a long moment.

"Will you tell her, if I take you to her?"

In the circumstances, there did not seem to be any other alternative available to him.

"Yes, I will."

A few minutes later, Tomas stood outside the headquarters on the far side of the street. He was watching the entrance intently. His unexpected visitor had told him that they would need to leave separately, and instructed Tomas that he would meet him shortly in this location. Tomas was curious to see the man's method for escaping without being intercepted. In part this was purely out of a sense of disbelief that it could be done, but his professional senses suggested that the most likely explanation involved the assistance of one of the officers who manned the gate. If that proved to be the case Tomas was going to be obliged to report the matter to the armoury intendant when he returned. A small internal smile acknowledged the presumption inherent in that thought. Perhaps he would not return at all.

Curiously, permitting Tomas to leave separately had enabled him to retrieve his sword and to borrow a short dagger from the Armoury supplies which was now tucked with its scabbard into his right boot. Since the stranger had no doubt anticipated that he would do so, this was perhaps intended to be a sign of trustworthiness. Equally, though, Tomas was alert to the possibility that he was now close to penetrating the circle of those who long before had cost Victor Appelsin his leg, and his wife's life. However trustworthy they might want to appear to him, he would need to be on his guard. The air was starting to cool and he took several deep yawning breaths, trying to expunge the lingering effects of the alcohol. If the man's speed and skill were indicative of those he was investigating, he would need to be at his very best.

Still crowds swirled around him, and Tomas had continually to shift position to keep the headquarters' entrance in sight. Finally, hemmed in on all sides by the press of people, he must have mis-stepped slightly and stumbled. He felt momentary alarm as he realised that in doing so he had stood on the foot of a passer-by who was rather closer than he had expected. During Fest, far lesser insults could result in a violent response. He turned hastily to apologise, and saw with ill-concealed surprise that it was the man from his room, the bemused half-smile still visible even in the now rapidly gathering gloom.

"Come on Callan, stop staring at me and let's move."

Without waiting for a response, he turned and started to push his way through the crowds. It proved to be quite a challenge for Tomas to keep pace with him, particularly while maintaining a watchful look-out to each side. At any other time of the year, the pedestrians who were still abroad in the early evening would be hurrying homewards, determined not to draw attention to themselves or to come into any conflict with those around them. They would also afford Tomas, in his uniform, scrupulous courtesy. This was an entirely contrary experience. There were those who wished to lavish affection on him, or aggression, and those to whom he was too insignificant to be avoided. Each collision and encounter had to be rapidly assessed and graded in the severity of the response that might be required. If those who had found him knew what his mission was, there was a chance that any one or more of these revellers around him could be tasked to assassinate him. It would be a quick death and inconspicuous. When his body was found it would be ascribed to Fest and even Victor would only be able to speculate that it had been anything else.

Matters were further complicated by the absence of any distinctive features in the man he was following. Again and again Tomas saw other men of his height, or hair colour, or build. Only the curious light grey cloak that he wore over his clothes gave any assistance, and the colour of that seemed to be fading even as the daylight did. This was where Tomas's unfamiliarity with the streets of Braed Tor counted against him. It rapidly became clear that his guide was setting a pace and choosing a route that would make it as difficult as possible for Tomas to keep track of his surroundings. The possibility that Tomas might be expected to return and retrace his steps gave him some comfort, but only a little. The precaution did not necessarily mean that he was expected to survive the appointment he was heading towards, only that those he was dealing with were extremely careful in their security.

Fortunately, it was not too long before they arrived at their destination. His guide had slowed his pace a little and Tomas was just about to catch up with him. Then, at an astonishing speed, a gate by his side opened and a pair of hands reached through, physically lifted him from the ground and pulled him through the gateway. The man that he had been following turned as if on cue and passed through the gate behind him, pushing it shut as he did so. The sound of the crowd immediately dropped and Tomas looked around to find himself in the torch-lit courtyard of an imposing residence. Walls bounded the plot on all sides as far as Tomas could see – the gate had been set into the wall which faced the road – but there was a distance of several carriage widths between those walls and the building itself.

Despite its obvious refinement and superficial decoration, the structure and layout created a more professional resonance in Tomas's mind. It felt like one of the fortified country houses that command staff had occupied when he had been in the forces. Doing what he could to take note of any potential exit points, in case he should have to leave in haste, he turned his attention to the man who had bodily lifted him from the street. This man was significantly shorter than his guide, but Tomas noted the musculature of his arms and shoulders. The careful way in which he ascended the main staircase at the front of the property while still keeping Tomas in peripheral sight suggested that the man was a fighter, probably a professional.

A none too gentle pressure to his shoulder from the man in the grey cloak, who had remained behind him, drove him up the steps and towards the main entrance. Inside, the ornate decoration continued as Tomas was led down several corridors to a large and well lit reception room which extended most of the width of the rear of the property. A red-headed woman, presumably Mistress Groenne, rose from a chair by the window and moved forward as if in welcome. The smile on her face appeared genuine, if somewhat tentative.

"Tomas Callan," she spoke inquisitively, with the strong accent of a Northerner tribe, "I 'ope you will come in, and meet with my friends?"

Looking around the room, Tomas saw that they

were far from alone. Closest to where he was standing, a slight man with red-rimmed eyes and an anxious appearance seemed unable to decide whether to rise from his chair or remain seated. Beyond him, a large table at the corner of the room held two youngsters who seemed to be playing a game of cards. However improbable it may be, the similarities in their appearances strongly suggested that they were brother and sister – perhaps even non-identical twins. The brother was dressed in the style of the dandy elvish and had a sour petulant expression on his face. Stood watching them play, with his back to the door, and seemingly without interest in the new arrival, was a heavy-set man of darker complexion.

Unlike the sense given by the exterior of the property, and his reception committee on arrival, this room and its inhabitants presented a positively domestic appearance. His two escorts were somewhat out of place with the rest of the company, thought Tomas turning to glance at them, and found that they had already absented themselves, closing the door silently behind them.

"May I ask, pray, who you are?"

In the time he had taken to glance back towards the door, Tomas found that the remaining occupants of the room had changed position. The light-haired young dandy had stood and was examining Tomas and his apparel through a quizzing glass, albeit at a safe distance. It was he who had just spoken, in a strained and artificially high voice. His sister remained at the table, and had turned her face away, although she appeared to be stealing glances at him through her lashes at regular intervals. Their older companion, now facing towards him to display an elaborate outfit set off by startlingly grey eyes, was advancing on

Tomas with a serious expression.

All semblance of a familial scene had evaporated. Recollections of training protocols flashed through Tomas's mind. There were signs that he and his fellow investigators were trained to look for, subliminal reactions which they had schooled themselves not to ignore or suppress. For all the apparent warmth and openness of his greeting, Tomas felt vulnerable. He glanced first at the woman who must surely be Forba Groenne, then at the slight, anxious man who was resuming his seat next to her. Each radiated the same indefinable menace beneath their benign exteriors.

Determined not to cede the initiative Tomas took two steps towards this last group, half-turning away from the elaborately dressed man as if to signify that he did not feel threatened by him, while still keeping him squarely in his peripheral vision. Tomas extended his hand and fixed an amiable smile to his face.

"Forba! Is it you? My wife will be so pleased that we have found you."

She was well-trained, and in skills which no scientist or cyclopaedian ever needed, but Tomas's own reactions were honed by fear. He detected the initial warming in her composure as she was greeted, even though it was quickly masked by a convincing appearance of confusion. Tomas sensed the others moving closer and took another step towards his quarry.

"Can it be that you do not remember me? Forba, I declare I am quite hurt!" He reached out and clasped her hand in his, preparing to pull her towards him if necessary in order to create some leverage. First, though, it would be necessary to throw her further off balance.

"Still – it must be quite some years, since I last

saw you. We were with our mutual friend Victor as I recall?"

Mentioning Victor's name prompted a definite reaction of surprise and Tomas tensed his hand to pull Groenne into a tighter grip. Before he could do so, however, there was a blur of movement to his left, a shout and then a sudden blow to the side of his head, which exploded bright after-images across his eyes before fading into blackness.

From the unfinished draft Cyclopaedia:

Gazetteer – Tryachan – Addendum

... It was from Tryachan, of course, that the several ill-fated voyages to pursue the elves were launched. Prior to the Departure, it had been impressed on those being left behind by the elves that they were not to be followed, and for two or three generations that edict had held any thought of pursuit in check. But progressive infrastructure failures brought home a growing realisation of the extent to which humankind had relied on the elves and their magic to sustain their way of life. Around 150 years after the Departure, a small fleet of vessels was assembled, captained by the traders and fishermen who worked their ways along the coast from season to season.

They set sail full of considerable optimism. When none of them returned, that optimism very quickly waned. As generations passed and fresh adventurers were born, further attempts were made, ending with a similarly inconclusive silence, and the apparent loss of valuable vessels and crew. Only one explorer, setting out some four hundred years after that first attempt, managed to travel into the West and to return news of his discoveries.

Erraziz Grancomo had inherited a thriving merchant's business while still young, and had made his own fortune before he was much older. Obsessed with the tales of the elves, and without the restraining influence of the Council of Style and Etiquette (which would not be formed for another three hundred years) he applied his wealth to the formation of the largest naval expedition ever assembled. Nearly fifty vessels, varying in size from large fishing boats to more substantial rowing galleys, anchored at Tryachan and set sail with a strong westerly wind behind them. From Grancomo's logs, the wind held for around three days before the flotilla was utterly becalmed. Nevertheless, utilising a network of ropes strung from vessel to vessel, Grancomo was, it seems, able to harness the power of the rowing galleys to keep the flotilla moving at a gentle pace.

The hardships endured by the crews of those vessels are difficult to imagine, and very little can be gleaned from the logs, beyond the almost daily record of bodies discarded to the depths. Several boats were abandoned, their crews and provisions as far as possible being re-allocated to those ships capable of proceeding under their own power. At last, what was probably two months later, a breeze returned, and the remaining vessels and their occupants were able to set sail and continue.

Land was ultimately sighted. To the explorers, the one possibility that had sustained them was the hope of finding the dwelling place of the elves, such that their hardships would not have been in vain. They were destined for disappointment. The occupants of the Western Landfall as it was known were very much like the participants in Grancomo's expedition. A little less sophisticated, perhaps, a little more naïve, but otherwise surprisingly similar. Their land lacked resources which Grancomo's homeland possessed in abundance, and they had little to offer which might have compensated for the long voyage. Most importantly, they knew nothing of the elves.

It was a matter of weeks, only, before the decision was taken to return home. Only three vessels successfully completed the journey. Grancomo died during the return voyage (of disappointment, according to popular local legend), and his body was delivered to the city elders at Tryachan for burial. The vessels were broken up for salvage.

No further attempts to journey into the West are recorded as having been made (checks needed!)."

10

[Extracts from the voluntary confession of [Subject T187356]. Interview 5. Collated from the files of the Justice Authority. Quaestor's words redacted throughout.]

On the following day, Fest now having begun, we made our rather more laborious way back to Merson's home. As one on whom the burden of fashion lies heavily, I was somewhat uneasy at the necessity of under-dressing for the second day in succession. It had been put to us that we should do so, in order not to draw too much attention while walking the streets. I confess that once we had left the safety of the hotel, however, I was so preoccupied with keeping a pomander pressed to my nose, and avoiding soiling my shoes or stockings with anything untoward, that I could not have told you whether more than about half a dozen individuals had even noticed my apparel.

After considerable difficulty and irritation, we reached Merson's home. The cook had obviously been busy prior to the holiday period and the table was heavy with refreshments. I was, though, somewhat surprised to note that the others, who were all of course already present, had not thought it appropriate to wait for us to arrive before addressing their own appetites. It brought to mind for me the regrettable conclusions which I had been forced to reach on the previous evening, in relation to the character of my parents' friends.

Lias Nefflor was still his miserable sniffling self. As I had made up my mind to do the previous day, I did my best to avoid engaging him in any sort of dialogue beyond the most perfunctory. As for the others, they were all in a festive mood, and the day quickly descended into the type of enforced revelry which I most abhor. In sensitivity to the presence of my sister and Aunt Forba there was to be no gambling, and instead we were obliged to play the most tedious table games that you can imagine – entirely dependent on chance and with all manner of frippery associated with them. I itched to think of the various gaming hells that, in other circumstances, I might have entered on the first day of Fest and not left until the celebrations were concluded.

I own that the entertainments were lighter on my pocket book as a consequence, but this was their only virtue, and if a man does not have the blunt to embark on such activities, the virtue of enforced thrift is but scant consolation.

That thought led me to take Merson aside and speak with him, man on man, about the subject of our allowance. At first he was loath to engage in such discussions, suggesting that I should come to his office after Fest was concluded, when he would have access to all of his papers and records. I wore him down though, and eventually he relented and allowed me a small purse of coin that would at least have seen to my night's entertainment.

But, of course, I was not to be permitted to leave. That is to say, it was not thought safe for either my sister or I to wander the streets of the precinct. Thus I was present for the first of the day's extraordinary intrusions, which occurred some time in the late afternoon. All of the servants, even the footmen, had been granted leave by Victor to return to their homes for the duration of the holiday. Thus, an uncouth hammering on the front door foreshadowed the arrival of an unsavoury individual who, before you press me for it, did not grant me the pleasure of a formal introduction. Instead he urgently drew Uncle Merson into a side room, there to conduct a very hurried conference. Whatever business they had to transact was concluded rapidly, the man leaving again within minutes.

I presumed him to be a client of my uncle's, but when I was civil enough to ask whether anything was the matter, I received a strong sense that secrets were being kept from me that went beyond the usual obligations of confidentiality.

The day continued much as if the interruption had not occurred. Indeed I had quite forgotten it, distracted as I was with my own thoughts. I was still hoping that I might contrive to persuade Uncle Merson to let me out into the precinct to locate a suitable venue for the evening's recreation. Yet after an early dinner, I found myself sat in the main drawing room, playing a version of Cheftain with my sister. As you may imagine, with only button wagers it was dull sport. I was eager to leave. Rauor, I noted, had been permitted to depart, and I therefore started to consider what I might do, if permitted the same liberty. First I would return to our hotel in order to be properly attired for the clubs and private houses that I planned to visit. Then, so that I might arrive there with my attire intact, I would need to ensure that I had a carriage at my disposal. I had made up my mind to tax Uncle Merson with these considerations, when the second interruption occurred.

Without the least fanfare or advance warning, a man was pushed in at the door, which was promptly shut behind him. He looked around him in something close to bewilderment. I appraised him instantly – it is a talent of mine, I confess. With his plain clothes, clean-shaven face and open demeanour, I guessed that he was either a merchant, a seaman, or an official in some capacity. It turned out that the last of these was entirely accurate – and that in fact he was...

But I am getting ahead of myself. The man stood a few feet inside the doorway to the room, scrutinising those of us already there. What he must have thought of Uncle Lias, sitting forlornly in the chair which he had not left for the large part of the day, I cannot imagine. The majority of his attention, however, centred on my aunt. Her red hair certainly does attract attention, and so I did not mark his particular focus at first, but he then took a few steps towards her, saying something about his wife being pleased that he had found her, and extending a friendly hand.

I fear that I did not have a very good view of what followed. To my surprise, it seemed to me that Aunt Forba, normally the very soul of propriety, shrank away from the new arrival and refused to match his greeting. I glanced away to look at my cards, but I can only assume that Forba's negative reaction discomposed our visitor. Whatever the reason, as he took his next step towards her, he appeared to lose his footing on the stone floor and tumbled sideways. Uncle Merson darted across the room to catch him, but the poor man had managed to render himself unconscious.

I am sorry. I collect that there was a humorous aspect to it at the time, but I suspect that it is a humour which loses much in the re-telling.

After a stunned moment of silence, I asked Forba to explain who this unknown man might be. Although she professed to be unable to enlighten us as to the man's identity, I noticed a glance exchanged with Merson which suggested otherwise. Once again, my suspicions were aroused that there was information that was being kept from me.

Since neither I nor Lias (albeit for very different reasons) were in any position to lend assistance, it fell to Uncle Merson to lift our visitor and place him on the table, sweeping aside the cards from our latest hand of Cheftain as he did so. I was surprised to note that my sister had been holding a remarkably good hand, and in that sense, if no other, the intrusion was a welcome one.

There are, I confess, certain skills which the feminine members of society are infinitely better equipped to perform. One of these is tending to the injured and wounded. I cannot count the number of times that my sister has ministered to me or my apparel when one or other of us has suffered harm. One of her few genuine accomplishments is her ability with needle and thread which has often enabled me to avert disaster and to avoid an unscheduled visit to my tailor. Now she turned her hand to the unknown visitor who lay on the table while she wetted cloths and pressed them to his brow.

It was, I believe, during this period of time and following an examination of his identity papers, that it emerged that the visitor was an investigator, and from Rivertop no less. As I told you, I had of course identified his position at the instant that he had entered the room. Rivertop, however, was Uncle Lias' former home, so I was somewhat surprised that the investigator's focus had been on Aunt Forba. I was also concerned, I confess, that the man had been rendered unconscious by a fall which, depending on his state of mind when he awoke, might well be regarded by him as suspicious. I reassured myself with the thought that I had been some way away from him, and seated, when the fall had occurred, such that no suspicion could possibly fall onto me. I drew additional comfort from the recollection that it was Fest and that as such the prospects of any penalty following from his injuries, even if he did not accept that they were accidental, were extremely remote.

Nevertheless, and not least as a consequence of the considerable regard in which I hold all members of the constabulary, I was extremely relieved when the investigator started to show imminent signs of returning to consciousness. As he came to, several of us were at pains to emphasise to him the accidental nature of his fall, and that we were in no way responsible for it. With considerable good grace he waved our comments aside and sat up on the table, looking about him with what I must describe as an air of bemusement.

We introduced ourselves, and he told us that his name was Riv' Callan. Since none of our party was about to explain that we had searched his pockets and perused his credentials while he was unconscious, I was intrigued to see whether he would admit to his profession and reasons for intruding on our assembly. He did not – which of course I do not seek to criticise him for in the least – but there remained an awkward uncertainty about his intentions.

His physical description? Why yes, of course. I think I have told you already that his clothing was plain. This was something of an understatement. Even were it not Fest his apparel would have been noteworthy for its under-stated quality. His attire was for the most part of a faded black hue, and he wore no flourishes, neck tie or cuffs. His wig was insufficiently powdered. His boots were of good, if serviceable quality, but they and his belt were the only items which appeared to have had any care or attention devoted to them. But for his references to being married, which I was therefore sceptical about, he struck me very much as one of those impoverished public servants that one meets regularly in travelling between the precincts, making a minimal subsistence on the fringes of good society.

Oh – as for his features they were unremarkable, but I did not have much opportunity to study them. I think that his hair was dark and, now that I think of it, also receding and swept straight back off his face. He was not excessively tall, but carried himself as one who understands his proper place in society. There was no question of his passing as a gentleman, of course, but equally he was the type with whom one could expect to have an entirely civilised conversation.

The same, regrettably, could not be said of the next intruders. I suspect at this point that my narrative will begin to overlap with your official reports, gathered from other sources. As such, it may be that there is not very much that I can add...

Indeed. Far be it for me to seek to instruct you in your profession.

Investigator Callan was starting to regain his composure and was experimenting with walking around unsupported. Aunt Forba and Uncle Merson were at the far end of the room in urgent conversation, close to where Uncle Lias still remained seated. My sister was tidying away the dirty linen and water bowl from her ministrations. Noting that there was little that I was likely to be able to do to assist any of them, I stepped out of the room to make an idle tour of the premises. To my surprise, I found Uncle Rauor, who had clearly returned unannounced at some point during the disruption, in the house's extensive kitchens in the upper basement.

Uncle Rauor is, as you may know, a man of quite considerable accomplishments. Why he should find it necessary to work as a private tutor, little better than a house servant, I have never understood. It seemed to me that his obsession with employment had clouded his conception of propriety – I can think of no other reason why he should have thought it necessary to take upon himself the task of preparing vegetables for the evening meal. It was true of course that the house was without any of its usual complement of staff, but the hardship of having to consume food that had been prepared in advance of the holiday, and left in store for us, was something that simply had to be borne for the duration of Fest.

I was in the process of remonstrating, unsuccessfully, with him, when movement in the house's courtyard attracted my attention through the high windows which admitted light into the sunken kitchen.

My first assumption was that revellers had broken through the outer gate. The new intruders wore varied attire, but there was a Festive theme, and most of them wore carnival masks. There was, however, something about their purposeful movements and the co-ordinated manner in which they dispersed around the building, that gave me a feeling of considerable anxiety. It brought to mind the feelings of instinctive anxiety that I had experienced on the road back from Hartrick Hall.

My conversation having halted in mid-flow, Uncle Rauor's attention was rapidly caught by the same intruders. As they continued to move through the grounds, I felt an increasing sense of menace. I do not scruple to confess that for a few moments I entertained terrible fears for my safety. Fortuitously, the masked figures paid no regard to the stairway down to the subterranean kitchen entrance, and this it seemed to me represented our best prospect of escape.

Rauor felt that we should discuss the matter before acting precipitately. I could not see what remained to be discussed. Whether the fresh intruders had any connection to my earlier attackers, I did not know. But I understood that I was in danger, and from that knowledge the only logical conclusion was that Uncle Rauor had an over-riding duty to escort me to safety. Sounds of a violent assault on the front door brought our debate to a rapid conclusion and we collected a few provisions before making our way out of the side entrance. A cautious exploration at ground level revealed that our assailants had failed to leave any guard on the exterior of the property. You may rest assured that we took advantage of the oversight, and very quickly were doing our best to immerse ourselves in the crowds that were still in evidence in the street outside.

How was I to know what had become of the others? There was no question of my returning to the property, it would have been the most profound folly. I had no doubt that the remaining family members would look after my sister, as indeed proved to be the case. It was the only sensible course for me to take.

No, no! I assure you! I really do not know any more. Please!

[Interview suspended]

[Copy of Urgent Call in Quaestor Feiger's own hand – dated 5th Nieumor XXVI Tor.]

Investigator Callan's reports for Fest brought to me – by dawn tomorrow.

Message to Quaestor's Office, Braed Tor: urgent review of procedures arising from raid on residence of [B099803] – suspect an inadequate external guard was mounted.

Without Fail.

[Ends]

11

He knew it was a dream, but Tomas still felt the nameless terror clawing at his insides. The cold air burning his lungs with every hasty breath, the shooting pains up his calves as he raced along pavements and across cobbles, the knowledge that all of his effort was in vain. All of this his mind drew directly from memory. But as always in this dream there was a contrast to the still of that early morning, when he had been summoned home unexpectedly from the middle of his shift. In the dream he found himself fighting his way through greater and greater numbers of people, as if during the celebration of Fest in full blood.

The panic tore deeply at him as it always did. This time he would be too late. The door of his house was visible over the heads of the crowds, but for every step he fought forwards he was carried several steps further away. This time, there would be no chance to say any last farewell.

Out of the surge of the crowd, a giant, dressed in black, his face masqued, seized Tomas's arm. Fearfully he clawed at the man's face, dislodging the concealment to reveal Victor's cold dispassionate eyes staring remorselessly into his own. The crowds began to fade as Victor's face drew nearer, swelling to fill Tomas's whole vision. At last, the face turned to one side, and spoke.

"Elyssa, I think he's waking up?"

Gradually, he blinked his eyes open. As he did so, the girl he had seen earlier sitting with what he thought was her brother, leant over him. There was a slight frown on her face. He felt his own face was slick with sweat induced by the urgent unreality of his feverish nightmare. Remembering his predicament, Tomas tried to force the thoughts of it aside, but it was all that he could do to retain his composure as he lay there, being scrutinised.

The girl, he noticed absently, was quite youthfully attractive. Her blonde hair hung about her face in waves as she leaned forward. There was an innocence to her pale blue eyes. This impression was reinforced when, seeing that he was conscious, she started slightly and blushed. She did not allow any sense of embarrassment to interrupt her inspection. Only once she had checked his wound did she straighten and confirm to the rest of the room that he had regained consciousness.

The dream-induced fear had not left him, and his present situation remained precarious. Even so, Tomas felt able to relax a little as he lay, gazing at the stuccoed ceiling, tentatively moving each limb in turn. Had the inhabitants of this property intended to hold him captive they could have tied or chained him up without resistance, but his arms and legs appeared to be free. Similarly, if they had intended him any serious harm, he might never have recovered at all. Despite this slight improvement in his apparent circumstances Tomas decided to remain still for the time being. With some experience of head wounds, he thought it best not to attempt to rise and risk causing a further black out.

Instead, he closed his eyes and concentrated on the voices around him.

"Honestly Al" this was his nurse, speaking (he guessed from her tone) to her brother, "not everything that happens is focused on you." Her voice was soft, and quite child-like in tone.

There was a low murmured response from her brother, masked by the sound of other conversations elsewhere in the room.

"I know you're special, Alyster! There is no danger of my being allowed to forget that, is there?" More murmuring "Well, if you refuse to help me, maybe you could go and lend Uncle Rauor some assistance in the kitchen?"

This last comment struck Tomas as strange, until he realised that the house servants had undoubtedly been allowed to leave for the holiday period. The name Rauor, of course, provided further confirmation if it were needed that Tomas had located the group that Victor Appelsin had sent him to find. What Victor would think, were he to see Tomas's present situation, was less easy to guess.

He opened his eyes again, in time to see the brother (Al, was it?) making his way out of the main doors to the room and closing them behind him. Letting his head roll to the side, Tomas could use one of several mirrors lining the walls to locate the larger, elaborately dressed man, in deep conversation with Forba Groenne. Behind them, in the dusk light, a small garden was visible through the room's high windows – careful planting working effectively to screen the walls that separated this plot from its neighbours.

For a number of minutes, Tomas lay in that position, watching the conversation. None of the other occupants of the room appeared to be in a hurry to rouse him, or subject him to questioning, and he was minded to take the opportunity to gather more information about those around him. He could not read their speech in the glass, but their occasional glances towards his end of the room suggested to him that he was the topic of conversation. He could hear the girl moving around to his other side, and prepared himself to turn and face that direction. As he did so, he caught a glimpse of movement in the garden outside.

At first, he simply assumed that this was a previously unnoticed guard, patrolling the grounds, and Tomas started to wonder how large the organisation was that he had encountered. This assumption was rapidly shown to be incorrect. It quickly became clear that a number of individuals were surging towards the rear of the property. In an incongruous echo of his dream, each was dressed completely in black and wearing carnival masks. These were removed from their faces as they drew closer. Tomas, with no real thought beyond his own self-preservation, called out and sat up too quickly, feeling his vision start to cloud from the edges as light patches danced in front of him.

In a coordinated movement the attackers split into pairs, one striking the centre of the large glass windows with a long pole before the other dived through the shattering panes. Sounds of breaking glass and tearing wood from elsewhere suggested that there was a concerted assault on the whole property under way. Tomas could do little more than keep the emerging situation under observation, and put all questions to one side until later. For the first few moments, it seemed to him clear that the attackers were the superior force. Their co-ordination and uniform appearance spoke of both military levels of training and many years of experience in action together. It took several more moments for Tomas to realise that, professional though they may be, the attackers were in every respect comprehensively outclassed by the occupiers of the property.

First to move were Forba Groenne and her companion. They did so with astonishing speed. The former cyclopaedian reached the doors at the moment that the first intruder succeeded in pushing his way through the fragments of the frame and entering the building. Seizing him with one outstretched hand, she turned with his movement, his body describing an arc through the air which lingered in Tomas's imperfect vision even as the sound of the collision between the man's head and the stone floor echoed in his ears. The grey-eyed man now moved into the attack, a sword in his hand which Tomas had not previously noticed. The solidity of his build seemed no obstacle to his ability to reach his opponents and inflict savage injuries with no more than a few minor twitches of his wrist. Tomas, an experienced fencer himself, recognised the level of skill and self-confidence that the man's careless demeanour was intended to mask. The onslaught had been rapidly halted, and the remaining attackers drew together, rather more wary of their enemies.

Those few moments, sat as a stationary observer, gave Tomas an opportunity to recall his sense of propriety. He had no idea who the intruders were, but he knew that his duty lay in getting the young lady to safety. He turned his head and found her backed against the wall, the width of the dining table between her and the violent activity taking place at the other end of the room. Seeing his glance, she started back around the table, but Tomas waved her back and, getting to his feet, backed himself around the table to join her.

"Is there another way out of this room?" he asked in a low voice.

"We'll be safe here. Promise."

There seemed some justification for the girl's confidence, from what Tomas had seen, but as he turned back to consider the situation at the other end of the room, a second wave of black clad invaders were making their way through the broken windows and doors. Anxiety tugged at Tomas, urging him to movement as Forba Groenne and her companion retreated across the room, the rapier's blade and her quick fists keeping their opponents at bay in what could only be a temporary impasse.

Like the intruders, however, Tomas had not remarked the remaining occupant of the room. The mournful slender man, who Tomas had arbitrarily decided might be Lias Nefflor, was still seated in the chair that he had seemingly occupied since before Tomas had been rendered unconscious. He had gone entirely unnoticed in the battle until that point. Now, rising with considerable agility, and after casting one brief glance to the garden to ascertain that no further waves of attackers were approaching, he moved.

Neither the distance, nor Tomas's recent concussion, nor even the increasing gloom as night fell outside, could adequately account for the blurring around the slender man's movements. His hands appeared to do no more than reach out, open handed, for opponent after opponent. Whoever he touched slumped to the ground in a manner which suggested utter finality. As soon as the intruders became aware of this attack from the flank, Forba

Groenne pressed her own advantage, her companion holding back but keeping his rapier ready. He swept his grey eyes around the room, only now glancing in the direction of Tomas and the young girl. Those eyes met Tomas's for a moment, taking in his stance of protectiveness, and his head inclined in a mild salute.

By the time each of them had returned their attention to the battle, it had concluded. A glance between the three combatants conveyed unspoken agreement, and all three turned and hurried down the room towards Tomas. The girl who he had been rather ineffectually protecting now pushed past him and hurried to her friends. The larger man, who in his manner and bearing seemed to Tomas to be the leader, was the first to speak.

"We need to leave at once. There will almost certainly be more coming to follow up on the initial attack. Do any of you have any belongings that you cannot bear to leave?"

The other two adults shook their heads. Tomas noticed that the formerly rather forlorn gentleman who had provided such an effective ambush in the preceding battle, was now looking far less melancholy. The girl seemed somewhat more reluctant, however, and the still unidentified leader came closer to her, taking her slender shoulders in his large hands.

"Elyssa, we cannot hope to outrun them if we burden ourselves with too much baggage. Even Alyster will have to leave his wardrobe behind!" His hypnotic grey eyes fixed onto hers "We need to leave. Now."

Elyssa, seemingly unaffected by the urgency in his voice, shook her head. When she spoke, her voice had a surprisingly warm tone, and the tired good humour of one who was accustomed to dealing with unreasonable demands.

"I know, Uncle, but I have already left my home and most of my belongings behind this week. I am sure that a short visit to the hotel will not delay us unduly. I do assure you that, unlike my brother, I am capable of readying myself quickly for travel." At this she, and indeed the others, all cast glances at Tomas. He wondered what their intentions were, having very little confidence that if they meant to kill him he would be able to prevail against their attack.

There was a moment's pause. Deferring to his apparent status as leader, the others all now glanced at the larger man as he considered his niece's request. Eventually, he seemed to relent. "You can go with Skapgood and Lias. Assuming, of course, that we can leave the premises unharmed!" The girl moved towards the thinner of the two men, confirming Tomas's original instinctive identification of him as Lias Nefflor. Before the two of them had left the room, the girl's uncle had turned away from her and approached Tomas. In an echo of the earlier tableau, shortly before Tomas had been struck unconscious, he again extended his hand in greeting.

"Investigator Callan – my profound apologies. It must be proving to be a somewhat perplexing day for you. My name is Merson Blare – will you give me your hand?"

This short speech was uttered with such warmth and good humour that Tomas, despite all of the circumstances in which he found himself, felt that it would be unreasonable not to take the proffered hand. His civility did not, however, cause him to lower his guard.

"Mr Blare, I cannot pretend to understand half of what has passed here. I have reason to believe that you have been an enemy to a very close friend of mine, and if you mean to be my enemy as well, I would prefer it if we could be straightforward about the matter."

Far from prompting fresh hostility, Tomas's response drew laughter from Merson Blare. He leant in close and spoke to Tomas softly, in a voice that would have been inaudible to Forba Groenne as she examined the broken doors and windows around the perimeter of the room.

"I think that you and I will deal very well together, Sir Investigator, if you will permit it. I would like nothing more than the opportunity to demonstrate my goodwill to you, and your "friend", who I take in fact to be your colleague and... superior? Victor Appelsin?" He made no comment on Tomas's poorly masked reaction of surprise, but continued "We have little time, however. I am forced to offer you a choice. If I am correct, you have already tracked us through three precincts and I am confident that you would be able to follow us further if we left you behind, albeit that you might be somewhat delayed in trying to explain the situation here. As such, I ask you whether you wish to accompany us willingly."

He raised a hand to stifle Tomas's sceptical response. "If you come with us, I and my companions will do our best to provide you with whatever information you require, on condition only that you in turn will give us a fair hearing, and reserve judgement until the conclusion of our tale. You have seen that we must leave without delay. I cannot permit any of my companions, all of whom I love like family, to take more than a few moments to prepare themselves for our departure. You would be treated the same. Worse than that, by accompanying us you would share the same risks that we have all willingly consented to, because those who are pursuing us would make no discrimination for your title or position."

He paused, looking at Tomas inquisitively, as if to see how this oration was being received. Tomas had endeavoured to keep his face as inexpressive as possible, but nevertheless the larger man clearly saw some sign of encouragement and continued.

"Will you come with us? I do not deny that there is a sentimental attraction to our travelling at full complement, but the choice must be yours. I must press you for an immediate answer."

Tomas shook his head, but more to clear his thinking than in negative response to the proposal. Of all the outcomes that he had envisaged since embarking on this investigation for Victor, the present situation was completely unanticipated. Ultimately, there seemed no better alternative than that offered by Merson Blare and his companions. Permitting himself a slight smile, and without reflecting on his uncharacteristic willingness to be swayed by the other man's charisma, Tomas stretched out his hand again.

"I will come with you and I will hear out your tale. I give you no other assurances about what my duties and loyalties might require of me."

Merson Blare inclined his head. "I ask nothing more", he responded. "Now we must leave."

At this point, Lias Nefflor returned with the young girl. They had with them the short fighter who Tomas had encountered outside the property. He explained to Merson Blare that Elyssa's brother, Alyster, and Rauor Tell had already disappeared from the compound. Far from expressing any concern for their companions, those that remained appeared to presume that they were making their way separately to a pre-arranged safe meeting place. The courtesy extended to Tomas did not include permitting him to know the details of this location, and he did not press the point. Without more than a perfunctory farewell, and an agreement to meet again prior to dawn, Lias Nefflor's group departed for the hotel.

For all the apparent urgency of their departure, Tomas and Mistress Groenne nevertheless found themselves stood for several minutes in awkward uncommunicative silence in the atrium of the property, waiting for their travelling companion to complete some urgent business elsewhere in the building. Tomas, his professional side beginning to reassert itself, found that he had far too many questions to be able to ask any of them, and it scarcely seemed the moment to embark on an interrogation in any case. Merson Blare returned carrying heavy saddle-bags, and a long box which looked very much like the case that Tomas kept his swords in when travelling, and which he was asked to carry.

Both of his travelling companions had put on pale cloaks over their clothes. Forgetting his experience earlier in the evening, Tomas thought at first that this would make them easier to locate in the throng outside of the compound, but no sooner had they emerged into the still busy streets, than he found himself apparently alone. After a moment of looking hurriedly about him, Tomas found that Forba Groenne was only one or two paces ahead of him, and had turned back to beckon him urgently on.

The journey to the edge of the precinct was extremely arduous. In addition to having to concentrate, merely to keep the others in sight, Tomas was also trying to carry Merson Blare's box without its being either damaged or stolen. This added demand on his concentration made it difficult to avoid the increasingly drunken and violent crowds. There were a number of changes of direction which appeared to Tomas to have no obvious purpose. He found himself at last forcing his way through a crowd which was determinedly travelling in the opposite direction, prompting a resurgence of the emotions that he had experienced in his unconscious dream. It took all of his professional discipline to keep pushing forward rather than surrendering to the emotion and the crowd. At last he found the throng starting to thin, and emerged from the back of it to find himself alone with the other two, in a dark and otherwise unoccupied street.

After that, they moved more quickly. He was impressed by the travelling cloaks of his companions, which seemed to have a strange trick of reflecting shadow. Despite their light tone they blended very quickly into the darker corners of the precinct through which they were now moving. At one point they passed the end of a long boulevard which led back uphill into the more heavily frequented parts of the precinct. In the distance, Tomas could see the buildings of the library, with what seemed to be flames and smoke around them. In the middle-ground, a large crowd of what might charitably be described as revellers, but which looked to Tomas more like rioters, filled the streets in every visible direction.

From his brief view of the city earlier in the day, and the sense that he was close to its lowest part, Tomas concluded that he was approaching the docks. In Braed Tor, these were unusually located within the precinct's walls. The Fest-madness had obviously not taken too deep a hold on the crowds. They were not prepared to do violence to the part of their precinct which was responsible for the majority of its income during the remainder of the year.

Returning his attention to those he was supposed to be keeping in view, Tomas found them further down the street, huddled together close to the high walls of what appeared to be a commercial facility. Neither of them was properly visible in their cloaks. Even so, as he approached he thought he saw Forba Groenne leap straight up the wall and land on the top of it without any obvious difficulty. Even allowing for the possibility that in the gloom he had missed her companion providing some form of assistance, Tomas was impressed by the athleticism involved. It was yet further evidence that this group had received levels of training and possessed physical skill entirely out of character with the public persona of the people that he had been pursuing.

Frustratingly, for a man accustomed to being able to act on suspicions at once, and to expect unquestioning co-operation in doing so, he knew that he would have to wait for an explanation of these matters. For the time being, escape from the precinct was their most pressing priority and if ever he was to have his curiosity satisfied, Tomas was willing to continue on the route now before him.

Equally, however, if Tomas was to have a conversation with these people as equals, it was going to be important that he should not display any inferiority to them. Indeed, he decided, it was time to demonstrate that physical accomplishment was not the sole preserve of this extraordinary group of individuals. Merson Blare was in the process of throwing the saddle bags he had been carrying up to the top of the wall, where a flash of bright red hair was the only sign of movement as they were safely caught. Accelerating to the wall Tomas noted that Merson Blare had turned towards him at the movement, crouched and extended his cupped hands for assistance. Disdaining them, Tomas ran straight at the wall. One part of his mind analysed the composition of the obstacle (large brick, loose mortar, a likely point at about half-height and slightly to his right) even as another part registered Merson Blare's open-mouthed look of surprise as he rose from his crouch and reached in Tomas's direction. Tomas tossed the heavy sword case straight into his outstretched arms.

Then he was at the wall. The trick was to convert horizontal movement into vertical acceleration as efficiently as possible. His right foot struck the ground forcefully, two paces from the wall. The toes of his left foot, in his supple leather boots, gained purchase a further three feet from the ground and Tomas's forward movement carried his upper body on towards the wall. His left hand struck once, driving a thin blade from the belt at his waist into the weak mortar he had identified, not too high so that there was still some rotational momentum that he could derive from this new pivot. His stronger right hand splayed upward and his fingers obtained a firm grip on the top of the wall, several feet away from where Forba Groenne still stood balanced.

At this point physical strength and momentum gave him the final boost he needed to reach the top of the wall. Admittedly, he did not land on his feet, but nor did he embarrass himself unduly by falling backwards to be caught by Merson Blare. A greater danger was caused as he stood to find that the sword box had been slung upwards after him, and instinctively leaned across to catch it. For several moments it seem that its momentum would cause him to topple over the wall into the dark courtyard beyond. Once steadied, he fought an inclination to rest awhile and forced himself into a balanced seated position. He turned in time to see Merson Blare's rather more effortless leap up, to be caught and secured by the red-haired woman's surprisingly strong grip.

Both of them were staring at him, an expression on their faces which was as unreadable as it was suddenly threatening. A moment of tension was quickly broken by a smile from Mistress Groenne, and the first words that she had spoken directly to Tomas since their initial meeting.

"I think you've been holding out on us, investigator?"

Belatedly, her companion also smiled. As he leapt sure-footedly down to the ground on the far side of the wall, his wry voice carried back upwards towards Tomas's ears, "Do you know, I am looking forward to that conversation of ours – more and more."

[Extract from 'The Rainbow Prize' (traditional mage tale)]

...Further deeds of treachery and cruelty followed until Nail was satisfied that he knew all that he could about his objective, the Rainbow Prize as the elves called it. At last he set out, and after several days of travelling arrived at the gates of the citadel. Shining white towers stood proudly above pure white walls, and everywhere there were elvish guards whose honesty and purity of purpose were entirely at odds with the black heart of our villain.

Using his stolen cloak to conceal himself, Nail entered undetected and congratulated himself on his cunning at having deceived the honest and friendly folk who occupied that shining city. Having done so, it did not take him long to find the building. Each of the six sides of the structure bore one of the six colours of the rainbow, and the hexagonal roof had six steps of tiles running around it, with red outermost and purple at the centre. It was smaller than he had imagined, but he knew that despite its small scale, many challenges lay within it before he could reach its heart.

Untroubled by any conscience, not even pausing to consider the enormity of what he hoped to achieve, Nail approached the simple and unguarded wooden door to the building. He opened it and went inside....

12

[Extracts from the voluntary confession of [Subject T187356]. Interview 6. Collated from the files of the Justice Authority. Quaestor's words redacted throughout.]

No, I did not anticipate that we would seek to escape from the precinct. My main concern as we left Uncle Merson's town house was that we should return to the hotel, bathe and change apparel. Then, if time permitted, we could make enquiries with a view to finding out which of our friends had survived and where they might have been.

It was not selfishness, I assure you. There was little prospect of my being of any assistance to my friends, one of whom I remind you was also my sister, after all, and every chance that I could have suffered a fatal injury in attempting to assist them. Moreover, the hotel was the only other location which Elyssa and I were aware of, and I therefore held out some hope that she at least, if she survived, would make her way there so that we might be reunited.

Unfortunately, the hotel was in a direction which involved making our way through several large crowds of uncivilised elements. Uncle Rauor did great service in forcing a way through for us both, but even so my jacket, breeches and boots were scuffed, soiled and damaged and I had been somewhat bruised, by the time we reached safety. I am sure that Uncle Rauor was also in some pain, and I invited him to come upstairs and refresh himself, something which he was initially reluctant to do. It emerged that he was anticipating that we would leave the precinct without delay, and some harsh words were exchanged, on both sides I regret to say, when it became clear that I did not agree with this view.

I am not a man to seek to deny it when I am in error. On that occasion, I own that I had not fully understood the seriousness of our situation. We had no way of knowing who the attackers at Uncle Merson's property had been, and as I lay in a hot bath run for me by the hotel staff, my reflections took an increasingly anxious turn. It was possible, as Rauor had suggested, that these attackers were not simple Fest-revellers on a rampage, but instead connected with the attacks previously made on me several days before. If that were so, and they had been able to track me to Uncle Merson's place, it was entirely possible that my address in Braed Tor was also known to them. Every minute that we remained at the hotel exposed me to greater and greater risk.

On reaching this stage in my reflections, I exited my bath and made my way, without any pause, straight into the adjoining room where Uncle Rauor was bathing. It is some measure of my anxiety that we were several minutes into the debate which followed before my undressed state fully registered in my mind. At that point, the conversation had become so heated that I did not like to withdraw. Nevertheless, I was deeply relieved when uncle Rauor finally assented to my proposal that we should leave the precinct without further delay, and I was able to return to my room to clothe myself.

Consequently, it was no more than half an hour later before both uncle Rauor and I were dressed and ready to make our departure. It was agreed that we should eschew the atrium to the hotel, and Rauor was fortunately able to persuade one of the footmen to permit us to use a side exit to the property. I was not privy to their conversation, but assumed that in the course of it Rauor had made arrangements for our luggage to be sent on. He carried a backpack and a second long canvas bag, which I subsequently learned was filled only with weapons, and none of the other essentials which we might have required for our journey.

In fairness to uncle Rauor, however, he did settle the account for my room and my sister's out of his own pocket which, to judge from his usual attire, was by no means as deep as that of uncle Merson. Then we departed, taking advantage of a momentary lull in the festivities outside of the hotel, and making for the nearest of the city gates.

I regret to say that even making allowance for the fact it was Fest, security was extremely lax. Indeed it struck me that the majority of the guards were probably to be found in the crowds which were by now converging on the centre of Braed Tor, intent on further acts of violent celebration. I, having no mind for commercial matters, hung back while uncle Rauor transacted with those guards who remained, and who proved to be perfectly amenable to his golden entreaties. Their generosity even extended to the loan of a horse, which naturally my uncle insisted that I should ride. Although it was by no means the sort of seat that I was accustomed to, it was bearable, and certainly provided an infinitely preferable mode of transport to walking, as my uncle was obliged to.

By this time, night had fallen.

I beg your pardon?

I am sorry to hear you express such scepticism. It is true, of course, that you must owe some loyalty to those fellows. But matters occurred exactly as I have described.

No, no, there is no need for such threats, and to be frank sir, I had thought us to be somewhat past such exchanges. I have provided you with all the evidence you could want against my parents' former friends, with no regard to the fact that I also implicate myself and my sister – albeit only by association. If this narrative strains your credulity, then there is a great deal in what is to come that will tax it further.

I do take offence, sir! Damme it, have I not been candid with you? Have I not ridden my recollections hard in your service? I did not expect amiability, in the present circumstances, but I think that a gentleman is entitled to expect courtesy!

Oh very well. It is begrudging and half-hearted, but I make no doubt that it is the best apology that I could expect.

I have entirely lost my train of thought, you know. Perhaps we could have a short hiatus, while I gather myself and seek to clarify my recollections?

I am grateful.

[Interview suspended]

[Interview resumed]

Indeed! I said as much to the warden. It is a very striking panorama, particularly on a clear day such as this. To look down from such a height is an unfamiliar experience as I am sure you must understand. The view from the higher floors must be even more impressive. I do not wonder at it that the lords and masters should have chosen to locate themselves here.

Quite so, but I was speaking to you of the more recent departure that I made from Braed Tor in company with Rauor Tell, if I remember aright? Passing through the gate without further incident, I mounted the beast that uncle Rauor had obtained for me, and we started down the Northern Road.

It was remarkable how quickly the lights of the precinct faded behind us. As a countryside dweller, I had thought that I would be more prepared than my companion for the darkness of the night. We were now in plains country, not forest, and I had never dreamed how the moon and starlight could illuminate the landscape. After a short ride from the gate we moved off the path to avoid a small encampment of those rather unsavoury types that one seems to see around all of the precincts. While most appeared to be asleep, we were under no misapprehensions as to the prize that our horse and other belongings would represent to these feral individuals.

Once clear of the infestation, we rejoined the road. I gathered from Rauor that we were heading for a pre-arranged meeting point. Any of the others who had managed to escape from uncle Merson's place would catch up with us there before dawn, and, so I was told, we would rest there during the day before travelling again at night to reach Car Peronel.

I was less than enamoured of this proposal. It was by no means certain that we had been the victims of anything more than opportunistic and well-organised burglars. Even if I granted the slightly fanciful possibility that we had been targeted specifically, it seemed to me likely that anyone else who was pursuing me, or indeed any of our group, might also be travelling along the same route. Furthermore, if we did have to leave Braed Tor, both Rauor and uncle Lias were more familiar with Rivertop. This would also have the merit, to my mind, of being a smaller and therefore less obvious destination. I did not appreciate, of course, that there were other considerations at play.

During this time we had left the cleared zone around the precinct and started to encounter occasional trees and bushes within arrow's reach of the road. After a period of debate Rauor ultimately accepted the force of my arguments. While he made it clear that any decision would ultimately lie with uncle Merson, who I gleaned was regarded by the others as a type of leader-figure, he said that he would certainly argue my point with vigour.

It was at around this point that I first had the sense of our being watched from near at hand. Uncle Rauor, perhaps fatigued after what had been a somewhat difficult day, rejected my concerns in terse terms. It gives me scant satisfaction to record that I was, however, almost certainly correct.

The meeting place? I could not locate it on a map, but I remember the route tolerably well. We left Braed Tor, as I mentioned, from the North Gate, and took the main Northern Road for a way. It was perhaps twenty minutes later, moving at a brisk walk, that we parted company with the main road and took a track that led uphill and east of north. It was at around this point that the cleared zone ended and plants began to reappear. The sun had set some time earlier and in the moonlight it was difficult to make out very much of our surroundings, although I was aware that the ground before us seemed to be rising and that rocks and boulders, as well as trees, were visible even in the gloom.

We continued on that route for perhaps another hour and a half. As the road rose higher, it became a path and then a track. We went single-file, with uncle Rauor leading my horse by the bridle. Rocks and boulders were piled to each side of the track and I had the feeling of being within a narrow valley or ravine. Of course in the dark I could have been mistaken.

At last we came to an open area of stony ground. It was surrounded by rocks but nevertheless uncomfortably exposed to the elements. We were in fact on one of the first foothills of the Central Spine, but it was only with dawn the following morning that this became apparent. Having tethered the horse, uncle Rauor started to establish a camp, signalling that he expected us to remain there for the night despite the uncomfortable conditions. That being so, I dismounted and waited for the others to arrive, with what I think in the circumstances must be regarded as commendable patience.

[Interview suspended]

[Extract from report of Quaestor Captain Boomel – dated 6th Nieumor XXVI Tor.]

In reference to the above urgent call, I hasten to report that the cyclopaedian, Forba Groenne is now in custody. Through diligence, my men were also able to apprehend her companion, who on enquiry has been revealed to be Merson Blare, also subject to a separate urgent call.

Both are delivered, under cover of this report. I am grateful to Quaestor Feiger for his consideration in favouring me with this assignment, and hasten to assure him of my continuing readiness to serve him in all matters.

[Extract ends]

13

For all that he might be able to compete with the
others in acts of athleticism and bravado, Tomas
found himself more and more in awe of his
travelling companions, as their escape from Braed
Tor proceeded. He regarded himself as healthy,
partaking regularly in the drills, forced marches
and routine daily exercise practised by his men. By
contrast Merson's stocky build and elaborate
clothing suggested a life-style of civilised leisure,
and Forba Groenne's dress, while without the
stiffening and under-layers of more formal attire,
still looked likely to hamper her movement.
Consequently, for all of the skill and dexterity
displayed by the others in the battle at Merson
Blare's house, he had remained confident that if it
were necessary for him to do so he could escape and
rely on his higher levels of stamina and endurance
to elude his captors.

It was now about an hour after they had started
their journey and Tomas was starting to find his
breathing laboured, and an unfamiliar burning
sensation in his leg muscles. The initial escape from

the precinct had not been too arduous. From the dock complex they had been able to find their way down to a tow-path which ran only a little above the level of the river, and was largely concealed from view by the docks and warehouses. At the river-gate, Merson Blare had jogged ahead and applied some force to the unguarded side gate which had barred the tow-path, holding it courteously to one side for the other two to pass through.

As soon as they had safely emerged beyond the precinct's walls, the pace had increased dramatically. Once again the outer cloaks they wore seemed to catch and reflect the shadows, making their movements hard to discern. For a time they continued to head westwards, following the tracks and paths that ran along the river-side. After a while and without warning, the other two veered to the north, following a path which led up the gently sloping side of the river valley and into the tree-line.

Tomas had kept pace tolerably well on the flat. As soon as he started up the relatively mild incline though, he found the going to be a good deal harder. By the time he reached the edge of the woods, he was several hundred feet behind the other two. He did not hesitate to enter the woods, despite the knowledge that he would be losing the moonlight which on open ground provided some minimal visibility. His over-riding concern was that he should not to lose contact with the others. He accelerated to a run, feeling the cold air bite in his chest, and wondering how long he could sustain such a pace.

Crossing the tree-line he found to his alarm that he was completely alone. He glanced left and right. Thick brush barred his way to either side of the path. The way ahead was dimly visible, and completely empty. He turned to glance at the deserted hill-side behind him.

Turning back, he found Merson Blare and Forba Groenne stood before him, a sword's reach away. Although expressionless in the minimal light, their voices when they spoke held tones of faintly mocking humour. Merson Blare spoke first.

"Did you think that we had abandoned you to the orks, investigator?"

Tomas, regaining his breath, and unable in any event to share in the apparent humour of the moment, simply shook his head.

"I think we've upset him Forba! Perhaps you had better speak to him for a while. I am not sure that our athletic investigator quite appreciates my sense of humour!"

Forba Groenne inclined her head. She spoke, low and with urgency, her accent strengthening and making her harder to comprehend.

"It is good that you can amuse yourself, Merson, although at my opinion no-one else is entertained! How certain are you that we are not about to have company?"

Merson's deep voice chuckled back at her in the darkness. "You have very little faith in my abilities, do you not? There is no living thing within half a mile of this position."

"Very good" she replied, "it may be that we can hazard a little light." Rather than reaching for matches or flint from her pack, however, she simply cupped her hands together. A glowing light, dim by domestic standards, but bright enough in the present gloom, blossomed between her palms.

Tomas started. Despite everything, a surge of childish excitement surged through him. Involuntarily he leaned forward, asking tentatively: "is it magic?"

No sooner had he spoken than the light dissolved into a number of small elements, each flittering up into the air and establishing a pattern in orbit around Forba Groenne's head. It appeared that she had acquired a halo, although the shape of the orbiting light changed constantly. Tomas was reminded of the enormous flocks of birds which would rise from the marshlands to the north of Rivertop, describing intricate geometric patterns in the air with their dark bodies.

Groenne, her face eerily illuminated from above, the rest of her in darkness, laughed gently.

"They're pixies." Even as she spoke she started to walk, Merson Blare having already set off ahead of them.

"Pixies?" asked Tomas, the word feeling ridiculous in his mouth. He shook himself and took a few hurried steps to catch her up, bringing himself within the range of the halo of light which was keeping effortless pace with Forba Groenne as if it was attached to her. "I thought that they had all died out?"

"So we all did, once. But there are a very many things believed gone from this world, which have only been mislaid, investigator."

Responding both to an innate discomfort with standing on formality in the circumstances, and also to the faintly mocking tone with which his title was used, Tomas spoke loudly enough for both of them to hear. "Please, do call me by my given name, which is Tomas."

"Merson", "Forba", came the unceremonious replies.

Groenne now continued to speak. "When we made our return from our great journey, the pixies came and found us. They were... well, how does one say it? They were drawn to us by what had happened while we were away. But I see that I must tell you the story entire, for you to understand it."

Unconsciously, their forward pace had been increasing. Tomas now found that he needed to keep his eyes turned to the ground, in order to be able to respond to obstacles which were illuminated by the pixie-light only moments before his feet encountered them. Nevertheless, he diverted as much of his attention as he could spare to the conversation. He focused on applying his skills as an interrogator: maintaining his scepticism; determined that he would reveal as little as possible of what he already knew; careful not to discourage them from continuing with their revelations. When he spoke it would be in open-ended questions, designed to prompt further detailed responses.

"I take it that your group have been comrades in arms for some time?"

His methods, though, were seemingly less opaque than he might have hoped. "Ever the Investigator!" Groenne chuckled, "It is true. We have had acquaintance all our adult lives, in some cases."

Perhaps a slightly more direct approach was required. He thought back to the room, where they had first met. "I also suspect that you are none of you actually related to the two youngsters with you, although you seem to be responsible for them."

"That is true enough. The two children have no mother or father any more. But we love that boy, and his sister, as if they were our own."

Tomas felt that some comment was expected of him. "That is very commendable I am sure. I take it that their parents' loss was in some way connected to the matters which you are all involved in?"

"We suspect so, though we cannot know it of a certainty," replied Groenne. "Whatever the truth of their passing, their deaths were a great loss to us all. They are also a part of the story which we must tell you, but they are not the start of that story."

Tomas marvelled at her ability to speak normally, almost casually, even as she once again started to increase her pace through the dark woodland. As if judging that they were now far enough into the woodland, and away from the river and the possibility of detection, Forba Groenne pressed her hands together again. Closer to her this time, Tomas thought that he detected her muttering something under her breath, but could not discern the words, or even the language. He did, however, see more clearly that the pixies (if that is what they were) did not simply materialise within her hands as he had previously thought. Instead they flew to her from all directions, each imperceptible flicker of light becoming apparent as they came closer together, and their glow flared.

Even as the tale continued, Tomas was conscious of a pang of disappointment. It seemed a shame for there to be a natural explanation when for a brief moment it had been as if magic had returned to the world.

"Before I can tell you how it was that we met with Alyster and Elyssa's parents, you need to hear something of the group of friends that Merson and I were part of. With the others who you saw at the house we were students together. My studies were of the ancient history, pre-Departure. Merson was studying the law, Lias was a musician. I do not bring to my mind what Rauor was studying."

"Politics" Merson Blare's voice floated backwards out of the darkness. Despite having moved ahead without any seeming regard for his companions he was clearly still attentive to the conversation that was taking place behind him.

As if she had not heard, Groenne continued. "Whatever it was, he had a lot of free time, and used to spend it scouring round the libraries of the University."

"University?" interjected Tomas.

"That is so. We were all of us students at Car Vandra. I met Rauor and we got talking about history and the state of the world, as students do. History was just as unpopular a subject then as now. It was quite pleasant to be able to speak to a like mind who had an interest in the topic, and we became very good friends. He introduced me to Merson and Pepina, Merson introduced us to the others that he shared a house with. There were six of us all together."

They came to a point where the path seemed to divide and re-divide as it threaded between the trees. Looking ahead, and with the light of the pixies visible peripherally, Tomas could not see which path Merson Blare had taken. Groenne though stepped forward sure-footedly and as they continued Tomas could make out the large man's shadowy form still receding in front of them.

"Lariad was the other house-mate to Merson and Lias. It might well be my romantic soul, but I believe that he and Pepina very quickly formed a deep attachment." A sound which might have been meant to convey disapproval echoed from in front of them. "It may have been a little while longer before all of us took notice of it. But we were all young, and in the grip of the excitement of discovering like-minded thinkers, some of us for the first time. Merson grew up among intellectuals, but Lias and I had both lived out our youth in environments where brain was looked down on, and strength prized above all."

"So the fact that some or others of us had found

romance took second place to the fellow feeling of being among people of our own minds. We went about scrutinising at the world around us, setting our brains to consideration of what was wrong with it, and how it might be set right."

Just as the pace and concentration required for his physical progress was now becoming comfortable again for Tomas, so the progress of the monologue he was hearing had started to adopt familiar lines. In his interrogation of radicals and dissenters, Tomas had often heard the justification that the world was ailing, that it needed to be cured. Curiously the medicine prescribed by these radicals often took the form of violence or acts of lewd public indecency. He braced himself to hear, and not to condemn, a description of student rampages, or acts of petty "political" sabotage. Instead the conversation took a different, although perhaps not wholly unexpected, turn.

"What is the biggest single ill that faces our world, to your mind?"

For all that attempts to engage him in a discussion of political theory were a frequent part of interrogations, Tomas still found himself momentarily nonplussed. In a formal interrogation, Tomas might have turned the discussion back onto his subject's beliefs, or simply refused to answer on the grounds that he was the one asking the questions. In this unprecedented conversation he sensed that neither response was likely to be met with much approval by his companions.

"I am not sure that I can really answer that question, Forba" he replied, forcing himself to use her given name casually. The less this seemed like formal questioning, the more he was likely to learn. "For myself, I admit that the government of our realm has its faults, but I think that it is a good deal

159

better than any of the alternatives which might be available."

Blare's laughter carried back to him. "Very good, investigator. You parroted the Tower's words back to us just like you really meant them. But it cannot have escaped your notice that this world is in very serious difficulty."

They did not seem to object to dissent. Tomas decided to test how far that applied.

"It is now when you tell me that we need a new government, new systems, a new start, is it not? That the violent overthrow of the established order is an essential cleansing process? That you cannot make emolattu without breaking an egg? I am sorry Merson, and I do not mean to deride your beliefs, but the world has been this way for a long time, and nothing you, or any of us, can do will make any difference to that."

Merson stopped in his tracks and turned to stare down at Tomas, his features curiously accentuated by the pixie-light. There was a ferocity in his eyes which slightly intimidated the shorter man, even though there was also a smile of what was clearly delight on his lips.

"Unwittingly, to be sure, you make my point for me, investigator. We will come to what we may do about the problems this world faces in time. For now, though, you have encapsulated those problems in a few eloquent words."

Before Tomas could ask what Merson Blare meant, he had turned back and resumed his rapid progress through the woods. The ground was starting to incline gently uphill again, and for a few moments Tomas concentrated on finding his footing, marvelling at how Blare managed to advance so swiftly even though he was out of the pixie-light. When he felt able to divert his attention from the path for long enough, he turned a quizzical glance to the woman who was now running slightly behind him.

She obliged his unspoken question by continuing. "Our discussions and deliberations took many forms. Some were restrained, like academic discourses. I found these to be tiresome. Equally Merson and Lariad found it hard when the more radical members of our group, like myself and Rauor Tell, fell to arguing more emotively. Over time, however, by not dismissing anyone's ideas without examining them, we came to some firm conclusions." Sensing the quiet rebuke in those words, Tomas remained silent to permit her to continue.

"From what we understood of the realm prior to the Departure, humankind had been progressing pretty well, in harmony (if that is the right word) with the other denizens of the world. The elves and the mages brought magic and what my people would call glamourie." Her halo gave a slight wobble. "The pixies too of course. The dwarves were skilled at technical matters. The orks and the humans were the hard workers – the lifters, the diggers, the assemblers. Then came the dark wars, of which you learnt in school and, when those were thought to be over, the Departure."

Tomas nodded. In the darkness he could suddenly see again the tableau at the staging of Lias Nefflor's opera, only a few days earlier. He could hear the soaring music of that final aria. He even felt again the same shivers over his skin.

"The mages and the dragons were all dead. The elves travelled out of the world, into the west. The pixies disappeared, becoming unseen but, as we now know, still very much present. The dwarves, already very much in decline before the Departure, survived in small pockets until at last they passed into extinction. But what became of the humans themselves?"

"We remained." Drawn in by her rhetorical style, honed he was sure from years of interaction with students, Tomas found himself answering involuntarily. He mentally cautioned himself to be more guarded.

"Yes, we remained. But we did not change. Though we took over the mines and the technologies left behind by the dwarves and the elves, we could not make use of them. Within a generation, most of the mines were in disrepair. We knew that the elvish citadels and the mages' towers had been sustained by magic. Having no magic we did not try to build tall towers and citadels. Despite the range of weapons that we had seen wielded by the other races, we remained content with the swords and axes, the bows and arrows, that our ancestors had been content with."

"We misthrived. Here we are, nearly two thousand years later, and nothing of substance has changed. We lingered behind when all the rest were gone, but we might as well have died out too for all the difference that we made to the world in our time here alone."

"I do not have your academic advantages, Mistress Groenne," objected Tomas, "but I do not entirely recognise the version of events that you are describing. A number of advances have been made: the precincts, the creation of the corporations, the quaestors and investigators for example. Even in the last few generations, semaphore has made a great difference to the speed of communication. You would concede, would you not, that we have not entirely wasted our time?"

This rhetorical flourish was marred somewhat as

Tomas finally missed his footing and tumbled face first to the path. He redeemed himself only somewhat, in his view, by turning his uncontrolled fall into something more elegant like a roll which brought him quickly back onto his feet. Immediately the other two stopped.

"Are you alright?" Tomas tried to brush their solicitations aside and resume their forward progress, but both remained still. Merson looked about him at the apparently featureless woodland.

"We are making good progress, Forba. I for one should be grateful for a few minutes' pause and there is, I believe, a small clearing not very far from here along the path. We can talk more while we rest."

Tomas was beginning to take for granted Merson Blare's unnatural ability to steer their way through the heavy woodland. Sure enough, after only one or two more minutes of walking, they came to a grass-covered clearing which was large enough for all of them to sit or, in Merson's case, lie down in some comfort.

As soon as they were settled, Forba Groenne responded to Tomas's question.

"The examples that you listed have a number of features in common. All of those features of our so-called civilisation reinforce our case for us. You must see that many of humankind's proudest 'achievements' are in fact nothing more than mimicry of the elves or dwarves who came before them? You should know, for example, that the precincts are inspired by the elven philosophy. Even their form is no more than a half-hearted attempt to remake the citadels of old. It is not any coincidence that the one building alone that remains intact from those times has become the seat of government since the Departure. The 'Great' Tower, as they say! In the time of the mages and the elves it was of little consequence.

"So too, the corporations have been made in slavish adherence to the elven theories of money matters." She paused, laughing quietly to herself. "I could continue at great length but you are not a student and I am not attempting to be your teacher. Perhaps for now it is enough for me to say to you that we thought on all of these matters at great length, over months and years. The conclusions that we have come to have been tested by all manner of ingenious arguments and have so far proven to be, how do you say? Indestructible. I am scientist enough to accept that we are in no way an impartial group. Our theories rest unproven, in the scientific sense. But I had and I have confidence in them. For the purposes of my narrative, the important thing for you to comprehend is that we all did."

Tomas shifted on the ground. Now that they had stopped moving, he felt the strain that his body had been under, and started a series of careful exercises to apply tension to first one set of muscles and then another, keeping himself in readiness for the further travelling that was no doubt still to come. Carefully removing any scepticism from his voice, he turned to face Merson's recumbent form, trying to bring him into the conversation.

"You shared those same beliefs?"

"I still do," the deep voice responded. "We are sure that our analysis is a correct one. Except in the most superficial of ways, civilisation and progress have come to a halt."

Tomas remembered a conversation that he and Idony had had several months ago. She had been commenting that the papers seemed to be full of nothing but fashion and gossip, that nothing of substance ever seemed to happen any more. He shook his head at the coincidence, but was taken to be disagreeing.

"It is not necessary for you to accept what we say, Tomas. We simply want you to understand how it was with us. How those beliefs inspired us to the steps that we took then, and which we are now taking."

He stilled his first instinctive response. This, of course, was the purpose of their conversation as far as he was concerned. He reminded himself, again, not to be drawn into debate. His overwhelming task was simply to listen to and record the information which they were willing to share with him, in the hope at some point of having an opportunity to make his way back to Victor Appelsin and submit his report.

By way of encouragement, he replied "I do not necessarily disagree with you so completely as you may think. I shook my head because you reminded me of a conversation with my wife in which some of the same observations had been made."

"Exactly so" responded Forba Groenne. "Many people are aware superficially of these problems. It is the same stagnation that fills our society which makes them think that there is nothing that may be done about it. They tell themselves that it is simply the nature of the world."

"But you were not so readily deterred?"

"Do not be so sure! There were those," here she glanced across at Merson Blare's recumbent form, "who felt that as our academic days came to an end, we should absorb the fruits of the discussions we had had, should carry them with us into our professional lives, but should not otherwise act upon them. Their view was, as I remember, that there was 'no point' in making trouble for ourselves."

Merson Blare's eyes were closed and his body was still. He spoke with a tone that was part bemused, but also part weary. "You cannot entirely say that I was wrong to think so, in all the circumstances, Forba."

"Of a certainty, Merson. You have been quite restrained in not reminding me more regularly that you foresaw much of our present difficulties. And it is good that you did, or we would not..."

Her voice became hesitant and trailed into silence. For the first time in the length of the conversation, Tomas had a clear sense of something being withheld, of some slip having been made that Groenne regretted. He stretched casually to conceal his awareness of the moment, even while wondering what the end of that sentence might have been.

"Once again though, I am getting my story somewhat out of order. At last, Merson and the others who felt that all was futile were over-ruled. To be more precise, we persuaded them that their beliefs (however honestly felt) were products of the problems of the time. A man must have faith in his friends, and confidence in their intellects, to let them overrule his instinctive reactions. I cannot be certain that I would have been able to be so disciplined if the situations had been reversed.

"But in the end the decision was made. For all we knew, we were the only ones in the whole realm to feel as we felt. But what was to be done? It was Rauor Tell, man of a thousand enthusiasms, full of all of the energy and inspiration that is generally absent from our age, who first suggested to us what we should do. I remember it very clearly. We were at Merson's apartment. Not the house you have seen – that came later, after his successful legal career. This was a very much more modest place in one of the outlying parts of Car Vandra. We were all there for one of our discussions. All except Rauor who was a late arrival as usual."

"I'll never forget the moment when he burst in upon us, ink soaking one of the sleeves of his shirt, his hair dishevelled but his eyes flashing bright. In the stillness made by his dramatic arrival, I have those words in mind as if he had spoken them only a moment ago."

She smiled and shook her head wistfully before speaking in what was clearly intended to be an impersonation of Rauor Tell's youthful enthusiasm: "I know what we need to do! I know how we're going to make everything well again! We have to go into the west... we have to find the elves!"

14

Car Vandra, 20 years ago

The reactions that greeted Rauor Tell's impetuous words were not, perhaps, all that he might have wished. With unusually quick wit for him, Lias Nefflor plucked out on his lyre the classical three chord progression which would often accompany moments of dramatic revelation in comic theatre. Nor was he alone in seeing humour in the situation, to judge from the deep laugh that escaped Merson Blare's reclining form. Lariad Etellion was the first to verbalise the group's reaction, sitting up in his chair, and in the process nearly dislodging his darling Pepina from her accustomed place on his lap.

"That's it! Your mind has finally lost touch with reality! I'm sorry Rauor, but we are going to have to commit you to an asylum!"

This drew further laughter, compounded by Rauor's faltering expression as it gradually occurred to him that his enthusiasm was not shared by his friends.

"Well, I have always known you to be an unsympathetic collection," he responded, stepping further into the room and letting the door close behind him, "but I thought at least some of you would be interested in the possibility!"

"What possibility?" Merson was quick to enquire, "I know that you are a history student, and cannot really be expected to know much about such things, but there have been a number of attempts to pursue the elves into the west. I think I am right in saying that none of them succeeded?"

Forba Groenne, seated closest to the door, reached up to give Rauor's arm a companionable pat, and found her hand smeared with fresh ink. Shaking her head, she leaned forward in her professorial mode.

"That is not quite correct, Merson, as I think you are very well aware. You are letting Grancomo's voyage slip from your mind, are you not?"

"It was hardly a success, Forba" responded Merson, "certainly not for Grancomo himself! And the dwellers of that western land had never even heard of the elves."

"Exactly!" interjected Rauor. The others, even Forba, looked at him in some bemusement. Lariad settled back in his chair.

"Perhaps you had better change your shirt, Rauor? None of mine would fit you, but I am sure that Merson will oblige, if you do not mind having the cloth cut rather shorter than your usual style." An eloquent hand gesture from Merson both invited Rauor to do as had been suggested, while simultaneously indicating a degree of disfavour towards Lariad. He continued, unmoved. "Then come and explain your latest ingenious notion to us all. For myself, I must say that I am quite in the mood for a mage-tale!"

After Rauor had left, Merson started up in his chair, plainly meaning to give Lariad a scolding. Lariad was there before him.

"You might give your sharp tongue a rest on this occasion, Merson. You are becoming a good deal too peremptory these days. You know what Rauor is like. Let him give voice to his enthusiasms and they are fleeting. Stifle them, and they can take root!"

Grudgingly, Merson assented, and when Rauor returned to the room, he was able to embark on his explanation without preface.

"Forba's reference to Grancomo is extremely apposite, for it was in Grancomo's journals that I found the solution, I believe. The popular misconception, repeated by Merson, is that the voyage was unsuccessful, and it is certainly true that the inhabitants of the western lands that Grancomo encountered were unaware of the elves or anything like them."

"Does that not conclude the matter?" asked Merson, "Even if you are going to suggest that there are yet more lands undiscovered and unexplored, we would have no way of knowing how to reach them. At all events, the histories all record that the elven vessels sailed due west until their sails disappeared below the horizon. If they had pursued their course, as Grancomo did, surely the westerners would have encountered them?"

"Not necessarily," responded Rauor with a smile, "I think that there is another way in which the accounts and the evidence can be reconciled" and he extracted a sheet of parchment from the sheaf which he had brought with him from the library.

"I was researching Grancomo's journals for a paper that I am writing, and for some reason I had retrieved one of the earlier volumes, from the outbound voyage, by mistake. I have never read those earlier volumes before. Even the 'interesting' sections of the journal, dealing with the western lands, and the return journey, are hardly ever referred to – the outbound journey is regarded as entirely uninteresting. But it would take some time for the correct journal to be retrieved from the central stack, so in the meantime I decided to read what I had."

"Much of the content was, as I had expected, entirely unremarkable. Details of the composition of the crew, a record of the nautical details and the ship's routine. In the seventh week of the voyage, however, there was one entry that quite captured my attention. This was towards the end of the period in which they had been becalmed. Water rations were low, and the surviving crew were all of them, it seems, supplementing their diet with such alcohol as was available. An annotation next to this entry suggests that it is believed to have been an hallucination. I will read it to you, and you can draw your own conclusions."

Despite themselves, the other members of the group found themselves intrigued. Rauor had started to draw them in with his dramatic and customarily charismatic delivery. Pepina Atto sat forward in her position on Lariad's lap, and even Merson was slightly less horizontal than he had been at the start of the narration. Rauor glanced around to check that he had carried his audience with him, and read the paragraphs that had so captured his attention:

"Day 48 – supplemental. A strange hallucination seized the crew at around four bells. Several crewmen swore that they could hear music. I myself was sure that I could hear a chiming sound. The sky appeared to lighten, to a brightness that many of us found unbearable. For the rest, accounts are so diverse and confused that I can only relate my own experience. I was pressed down flat to the deck, as if by a great weight, and at the same time I felt the vessel beneath me grow still. It was as if we had run aground, or been lifted up into the shining air. I do not know how long it was until the fever passed, and already the details of what we believe we saw and heard are fading from our minds. All of us though have a clear memory of a voice. It must have been someone among the crew but none of us know who. The voice was calling out one word over and over again: 'unworthy'."

There was a moment of silence. It was clear that all of them were considering the implications of what they had just heard. Equally, the look on several faces suggested that they remained unconvinced.

"I know that it is hardly conclusive," said Rauor, "but you can see, I think, what this might mean."

Forba was the first to respond, her mind and Rauor's as ever running along similar paths, her imagination captured by the possibilities. "You think that they found the elves after all? Not in the western lands, but in the middle of the sea?"

"Why not?" retorted Rauor, "They were by all accounts a magical race. Why should they need to make their next home on land in the way that we do? Why could they not make it at sea, or even in the air? They could well be out there, waiting for us to find them, waiting for us to prove ourselves worthy."

Lias Nefflor, generally the quietest and least confrontational of the group, leant forward.

"What precisely is your plan, Rauor? Are we to build a sailing ship and travel into the West? Even leaving aside the very great risk that we ourselves would be exposed to, even assuming that this journal entry means what you think it means, and even assuming we can find them, I really don't understand what it is you hope for in a meeting with the elves."

Forba smiled apologetically at Rauor "Do not take it amiss, my dear, but I must agree with Lias. Even leaving aside all of his very good points, there is nothing in the old histories that suggest that the elves might wish to return and help the humans, no matter how serious our predicament might become. It seems to me that by the very act of going searching for the elves, we almost certainly show them our own unworthiness."

It was clear that the others too were waiting to pour scorn on Rauor's idea. They had an agenda of other matters to consider, however, and so it was Merson, perhaps smarting from Lariad's earlier rebuke, who diplomatically brought the discussion to a close. "A fascinating idea, Rauor, and one that will repay further investigation I am sure. Perhaps this is something that you and Forba would like to undertake, exploring in particular what is known about the elves and their willingness to become involved in the affairs of humans. It is a field of which I must confess myself to be wholly in ignorance.

"Look into the histories, and when we have a clearer idea of what the objective of such an exercise might be, we can consider your suggestion again."

15

Dew was starting to form on the branches of the trees and on the shoulders of Tomas's cloak. They were moving at a more moderate pace now, and he was pleased to note that his two travelling companions were neither of them blessed with inexhaustible supplies of vitality. Even so, Forba Groenne was managing both to keep pace with him and to relate her narrative without apparent ill effect.

Putting his envy of their superior stamina to one side, Tomas listened as Forba related the many investigations that she and Rauor Tell had undertaken at Merson's suggestion. Tomas could discern considerable affection for her absent friend, but little of the concern which he would be feeling in the same circumstances, given the manner of their parting. He did not believe that any confidence she might have in her friend's abilities would be undeserved, but Rauor Tell was also protecting their young charge, the girl that Forba clearly regarded as her own daughter. In the same situation Tomas was sure that he would have betrayed considerably more anxiety.

He pulled his attention back to the narrative that had resumed beside him.

"... and for a time the research that Merson had tasked us with was frustrating, to be sure. But slowly I came to find the challenge of building a picture of the elves in the time before the Departure more and more engaging. That challenge was heightened by the fact that, as we rapidly discovered, very little of the information that you would expect to exist in relation to the elves could be located."

"How is that possible?" interjected Tomas, "I had understood that good records remained of the period."

"That is certainly what we are told, but..." Merson Blare suddenly turned and made a cutting gesture with his hand. For a brief moment Tomas believed that their conversation had strayed across some boundary and that he had been about to learn some deep secret for which he was not yet judged ready. Then he heard the sounds in the undergrowth.

Tomas's hand went instantly to his sword. How long had the subtle noises been continuing, unheard behind their own conversation? There was no time for self-recrimination now.

The other two moved fluidly into position. Their backs were turned on Tomas and he moved easily to cover the remaining sector. Eyes and ears on the alert for any sign of attack, he wondered how the three of them would manage to fight together, how their range of styles and disciplines might enmesh in confronting whatever opponents came from the darkness.

He could hear the noises more regularly now. The crackle of sticks on the ground. The occasional rustle of cloth on wood. It seemed to be quite a large group, circling them in a roughly clockwise pattern. They were perhaps only a sword's length away, but invisible outside of the weak circle of light cast by the pixies.

A hand, Blare's he thought, reached back and tapped a pattern on his sleeve. His brain received and processed the information automatically. It was not until later that Tomas recognised that the message had been in a tactical hand code peculiar to the investigators of Rivertop, and one that Merson Blare should not have known. In the moment, all Tomas was aware of was that he had been told, as clearly as speaking, that there were perhaps a dozen unknowns approaching from the northern and eastern quadrants.

If the attackers were dispossessed humans, or even the professionals who had attacked Blare's residence back in Braed Tor, the fact that their targets had stopped and closed ranks would make them pause, possibly even cause them to fall back and regroup. It was quickly clear that this was not happening. As such, the surprise to Tomas was somewhat lessened as the first of the creatures broke through the thick bushes and leaves and lurched out of the black to hesitate in the pixie-light.

Orks. The half-light emphasised their protruding jaws and flat sloping foreheads, stretched with hairless skin. These were the creatures of nightmares and horror tales. Rarely seen in the wild, Tomas had encountered several in his professional capacity, and knew them to be ferocious fighters, utterly lacking in the instincts to moderation or self-preservation that were ever-present in human combatants.

This made them dangerous, but Tomas and his

companions were well-trained and prepared. The pixie-light too gave them an advantage, taking the orks out of their preferred environment of pitch darkness. Even the half-light that hung over the group might have deterred another tribe, one that was not so hungry or so large. In contrast, this group betrayed no hesitation and Tomas concluded that they would fight until all three of the humans were dead, and that after that they would probably fight one another for the carcasses.

The ork nearest to him sprang forward. Shoulder to shoulder with the others, Tomas could not give ground. Nor could he risk lodging his sword in the ork's thick musculature, with a number of other potential enemies still in play. He had no time to plan. He punched out with his sword hand, striking the ork a hard blow directly on the bony plate of its forehead. The punch stunned it and caused it to stagger backwards. A half step forwards now, another change of angle to the blade, and he was able to bring it slicing down diagonally, cutting at first across the creature's face and then the hands that it had raised protectively. As the pain of this contact registered and the head lifted up and the hands were pulled instinctively away, the tip of his blade was able to conclude a back-stroke by dipping and slicing across the ork's throat.

He stepped back knowing, without wondering how, that Forba Groenne had also made a kill at around the same time. Merson Blare, by coincidence, was covering the south western direction and his sector appeared for the time being to be free of opponents. Another ork burst through the undergrowth to his left and Tomas took him on the sword point, letting his enemy's momentum do the work for him, withdrawing after the damage had been done but before his sword became irretrievable. A physical shove of the spasming body drove another of the creatures out of his path and straight into Forba's attack, her blades a blur in the limited light.

More appeared and more. There was no subtlety in the attack, but sheer volume of numbers threatened to overwhelm their position. Tomas cut and punched, stepped and recoiled. Some of the orks carried hand-made clubs that he was careful not to engage directly with his sword. The blade could become lodged and irretrievable for critical seconds in the hard wood that they were almost certainly constructed from.

Even as he managed to cut across the chest of an approaching ork, sending it spinning and writhing back into the darkness, Tomas felt a sudden pressure on his right ankle. He glanced down and could dimly perceive an ork's form pulling itself closer and closer to his leg, its mouth hanging open and its jaws extended, ready to sink into his flesh.

Desperately Tomas hacked downwards, fear causing him to swing the tip of his blade dangerously close to his own booted foot. A muted ork scream joined the other battle noises in the night air, before subsiding to a gurgle as Tomas's sword sliced into its throat. The arm that had gripped his leg clung on more tightly in the creature's death-throes, and Tomas hacked at this with his sword. Eventually, it was dislodged and he looked back up, panting, desperately scanning his surroundings for any sign of the next attack.

"Move! North!" Merson Blare's voice cut urgently through the night. Without pausing both he and Forba started to move in formation but Tomas, wrong-footed by the unexpected instruction, failed to move for several vital moments. The pixie-light rapidly evaporated, leaving him in darkness.

Self-control alone stopped him from calling after them. At last his feet were in motion and he threw himself after his fellow combatants. Behind him he could hear the sounds of more orks, pushing through the vegetation towards his position. None seemed close enough to pose an immediate threat and Tomas hoped that some might be distracted by the easier prey offered by their injured kin. He turned his attention ahead, where the tantalising pixie-lit forms of Merson Blare and Forba Groenne receded before him into the darkness.

Just before they vanished from sight he saw them halt and stand back to back. Straining to reach them, Tomas was only able to discern two blurred shadows moving in on them. One of the orks was rapidly despatched by Merson with a savage cut across its body that pushed it back several feet before it fell to the ground. The second caused Forba rather more difficulty, and Tomas was within a sword stroke of coming to her aid before a rapid left hand punch to the creature's chest stopped it in its tracks. It fell to the ground with one of Forba's sharp knives in its heart.

"It's a nest!" shouted Merson. "Too many for us to fight without injury, and we can't afford the delay."

Without waiting to see that Tomas had understood the implications of this news, the others moved on again. This time he was ready, and in any case the thought of what they had escaped spurred him on to keep pace with their urgent flight. Forba Groenne seemed to have complete confidence in the strange senses that Merson appeared to possess. Assuming that he was correct in what he had said it was imperative that they should make as rapid an escape as possible from the area and preferably across open ground.

Now Tomas heard Forba Groenne utter some louder imprecation, in a language that he did not recognise. The pixies multiplied in number, but those who had been with them from the outset were starting to flag, and their light was starting to dim. The troubling thought occurred that the light might not last for the duration of their escape.

A crash of branches behind him caused him to turn and lash out with his sword. He recoiled at the instinctive nature of the move, the way that it left his back and right hand side exposed to a counter-attack. By lucky chance, though, the tip of the blade made contact with the an ork's face, causing it to fall back, whimpering. That might hamper some of their pursuers, who would stop to kill and feed on their wounded brother, but Tomas had no way of knowing how many might be in pursuit, nor indeed how many might lie in wait to the sides or ahead of them. He was uncomfortably aware that he had to trust the guidance of a man who, fundamentally, he had no reason to trust.

It was impossible to know how long they had been running. Tomas had long passed the point at which he had thought all of his stamina would be exhausted. It was the continued movement of his companions, tired though they also were, and the thought of what would become of him if left alone, that spurred him onward. Afterwards they reckoned that it had been somewhere between two and three hours between their first encounter with an ork, and the point at which they emerged from the forest canopy into dim moon-light and open grassland. For some time they had been moving at little more than a gentle jog, but the prospect of safety encouraged them to increase their pace. They finally reached a small hillock, a good quarter of a mile from the forest border, and with what passed for a dominant position in the local landscape. As they started up its gently sloping sides, Merson Blare spoke for the first time since they had emerged from the darkness of the forest.

"We are going to be somewhat late for our meeting," he observed drily, "Tomas – how do you feel? No heroism please!"

"I could keep going a while longer at our recent pace," responded Tomas panting, "but if we stop moving I may not start again."

"I concur," interjected Forba, "I think that we are all of us close to our limits. But to keep moving is more important now than to rest. How far do you think we are off course, Merson?"

Despite the absence of obvious landmarks, Merson responded with conviction.

"We are not so far off as all that. We ought to have emerged from the northern end of the forest by this stage, but it will take us around an hour to get there from our current position. Equally though, we will move faster across the open country than we would have done under cover of the trees."

Appearing to take it for granted that they were therefore all agreed, he abruptly veered to the left, and set a course parallel with the edge of the forest on their left-hand side, but keeping it at all times at a safe distance.

Without the distraction of the perilous forest journey, Tomas became aware of the physical strain that the night had taken on his body. His feet and muscles ached and his bones felt chilled through. To distract himself, he returned to the conversation which they had abruptly abandoned hours earlier.

"You were telling me about your researches into the elves?"

Forba and Merson exchanged a glance which seemed amused in the half-light. Forba slowed a step so that she was walking beside Tomas, with Merson once again ranging ahead along the line of their route.

"Yes, that is correct. Rauor and I were tasked with finding out all that we could. I think that you expressed some surprise that we were unable to find very much information."

"Indeed. I was under the impression that we had very well preserved records dating back to those times in all of the main precinct libraries."

"That is true, after a fashion," replied Forba, her voice noticeably adopting again a more academic tone, "but what we found out is that the wealth of publicly available resources consist in reality of only one or two primary sources, repeated many many times. Most modern historians are writing commentary. Not commentary on the actual events of the time, not even on the contemporary accounts of those events, but instead on the writings of other historians. All of these, once we had conducted a fairly rigorous search, could be found to trace back either to the original official elven histories, copies of which were left with the Lord of Car Peronel and with the dwarf kings, or to the dwarves' own histories. Each of those original accounts, from what we could discover within the commentaries, were extremely selective in what they reported, and both sets of writers had their own prejudiced reasons for preparing those histories."

"So was your research fruitless then?"

"Not quite. I have told you what the position was with documents which the public could have sight of. What we also started to hear, when it was known in the academic community that we were researching in this field, was that other texts had been preserved. Some were accounts by humans, contemporaneous descriptions of the Departure and of the times leading up to it, which have never achieved wider publication."

"That seems improbable." Tomas's evident scepticism encouraged Merson to slow his pace and join the discussion.

"Most improbable, Tomas, as I said to Forba myself when she first reported these rumours to me. But without wishing to disrupt Forba's narrative flow, I can assure you that the texts were real. Forba saw direct evidence of them for herself, in the end, as we all did."

"And what did they say?"

"All in good time, investigator. There is another aspect to the story first, which is of particular relevance to you, I suspect."

Forba glanced sharply ahead of her at this cryptic comment, and then turned back to look at Tomas.

"Would I be correct to think that you came from Rivertop originally?" When Tomas nodded, she smiled grimly. "I had forgotten your reference to 'Victor' when we first met. Merson it seems has already made the connection."

She walked on a few more steps. "Indeed, he is quite correct. This next part will be of considerable interest to you." Tomas tried to maintain a neutral expression, but there seemed little purpose in doing so. Just as had been the case with Merson Blare's reaction at his house, however, it seemed clear that Forba thought none the less of Tomas for his connection with Victor Appelsin.

"Neither Rauor nor I had the contacts we needed to be able to see any of the documents held in private collections. Again and again we heard tales that a complete set of copies had been compiled by the Lords of Car Peronel in the first century after the Departure. This codex, as it was seemingly known, was said to be held within the Tower. Only the Lords' family members, or certain academics with suitable credentials, could get access"

"Short of marrying into the family, which held little appeal (although I confess there was a time when Rauor considered it!) the only real hope was to obtain the necessary credentials ourselves, or to recruit an assistant who possessed them."

Ahead of them Merson Blare stumbled slightly, and Forba made an anxious start towards him. He recovered his balance and continued without looking back to them. Tomas could feel his weariness threatening to overwhelm him and felt sure that the others did too. Like them, however, he pushed it aside and carried on.

"Rauor and I were at a, what is the word, a 'dead end'. Pursuing the necessary accreditations would take years of work and the careers that we had anticipated for ourselves would have had to be deferred or abandoned. Selfishly, we decided that the easier course was to find someone who would be willing to be our accomplice, someone who would be able to enter the archives without attracting suspicion."

"We considered a number of possibilities. There were not very many academics in Car Vandra with the right qualifications, and none of those that we knew of were likely to be even slightly sympathetic to what we had in mind. We asked careful questions, pursued countless avenues of inquiry which came to nothing. We started to look outside of the main academic community at Car Vandra, writing to librarians, researchers and historians at Rivertop, Car Peronel and many others. We even wrote to the library at Braed Tor. You have seen that library, which will help you to understand how desperate and wide-ranging our enquiries were."

"Were you not concerned about attracting attention?"

Forba nodded sharply, approvingly – the nod of a teacher, pleased with an apt pupil. "Merson had taught us well by this stage. We used as many different pretexts as we wrote letters, Rauor maintained a journal to keep track of them all, and the answers that we received. To each we asked nice gentle general questions to draw out anyone with a specific interest in the history of the elves, without saying anything that would give away our objective."

As they walked, Forba Groenne explained the painstaking process by which they had sifted through the numerous respondents to their initial enquiries. With occasional interjections from Merson Blare, she also described to Tomas the frustrations that she and Rauor experienced, and the extent to which they became ready to abandon the whole idea.

"To some extent," explained Merson, "that had been my purpose from the start. Rauor was, and is, a man of changeable moods and preoccupations. It was not inconceivable that this fascination with the elves, manifested in his desire to track them down, would be another such passing whim. It was in the nature of our collective to support one another in each individual's projects, without at the same time necessarily having any real belief in the objectives."

Forba resumed her narrative. "We surprised you, I think, with the seriousness with which we both approached the subject. I surprised myself too. For all that we had been ready to identify the sickness of lethargy that gripped our world, we were slow to take note of the same sin in ourselves.

It had been a long time since I had embarked on any project with such enthusiasm. In contrast to my usual approach, the regular set-backs we encountered only spurred me on, spurred us both on."

"Then just as even Rauor's wells of enthusiasm, and my own new found stamina, looked as if they would finally desert us, Maryam made contact."

Now it was Tomas's turn to stumble and nearly fall as he glanced sharply to the side. The coincidence was too great for it to be chance. He brought himself upright to find Forba and Merson watching him, their gazes sharp and penetrating in the moonlight. For a few critical moments they stood still, the three of them, staring at one another in the frozen darkness. Tomas was suddenly conscious of the distance that they were from civilisation. He felt the aching realisation that it was hours since he had last had any thought of Idony, and was nearly overwhelmed by the anxiety that he might never see her again.

But most of all, his thoughts were of Victor Appelsin. Victor, several years earlier, after Tomas's first major success, inviting his ascendant subordinate for dinner at his home. It had been the first occasion on which Tomas had been so honoured. He remembered the entrance hall, panelled with dark wood, candle-lit. Directly opposite the front door there hung a full length portrait of a woman, an arm extended as if in welcome. Struck by her beauty, and by the vivacity that the artist had captured, Tomas had stood transfixed by it.

"That's Maryam," Victor had murmured beside him, taking his elbow to draw him through into the reception room, "that's my wife."

Tomas stared in disbelief at Forba Groenne,

seeing now an unfamiliar expression on her face. His body, sensing danger, was sending spasms of energy through his limbs and yet he remained stationary. The pixies, seemingly relieved no longer to be in motion, had all sunk down to cluster on Forba's hair and shoulders, their light dimming further and outlining her in a barely visible shimmer.

It was Merson Blare who broke the silence, his regretful tones carrying out of the gloom.

"Yes, Tomas, it is true. We recruited Maryam Tedo, later known as Maryam Appelsin. We recruited her, we persuaded her, we used her to penetrate the private chambers of the Lords of Car Peronel, to obtain the Codex. Above all, in the end, we killed her."

16

From the unfinished draft Cyclopaedia:

Government – Council of Style

... Officially, it must be said, the Council of Style has only very limited powers. Recommendations can be made to certain agencies of government, recommendations which, within the governing statutes of the organisation at least, were intended to be non-binding.

It is indeed arguable that the early beaus never intended that they should assume any sort of power for themselves. Many of them were gentlemen of substance (women having never been permitted to participate in Council sessions, except in a menial capacity) and those that were not were often purveyors of fashionable items. This latter category saw the Council as an opportunity to further their commercial interests. The former category regarded it as a part of their obligation as gentlemen, to set an example that the rest of society would follow.

Blame then, perhaps, ought to fall on society as a

whole. Very quickly it became clear that the establishment of the Council had provided a focus for what was already becoming something of an obsession within social circles, namely matters of etiquette, form and appearance, at the expense of action, principle and (above all) substance. Within the first year of its creation, in the city of Car Peronel alone, twelve thousand separate 'style disputes' were referred to the Council for adjudication [insert table].

A significant percentage of these, to be sure, appear to have been gambling disputes, which were excluded from the various ordinary courts by reason of the inherent risk in the transaction. Even so, the figure is remarkable, not least when it is considered that within that precinct there were at the time only around nine hundred or so gentlemen of substance who might have been entitled to submit matters for Council determination.

Equally, however, it is true that as with all political structures that are perceived to exercise power, those who aspire to power were drawn to it. Before long the beaus were peopled largely by those determined to exercise (whether on their own behalf or on behalf of their paymasters, whoever they might be) stringent control over every aspect of creative and aesthetic activity.

Far from being an organisation dedicated to the furtherance of the arts and of culture the Council had, within no more than a generation, become an instrument for censorship and suppression. Moreover it was an instrument that was wielded in the shadows, and without attracting attention. It was present in the deprecating laugh, the raised eyebrow, the disparaging sneer. And it was surprisingly effective..."

[Extracts from the voluntary confession of [Subject T187356]. Interview 7. Collated from the files of the Justice Authority. Quaestor's words redacted throughout.]

I state that I, [T187356] have today seen my sister in Tower accommodation, and verified that she is well and has not been ill-treated. I am grateful for the courtesy.

I must say that I had not thought that you would work so efficiently. It has been only a day or two since I gave you their particulars.

I was, of course, relieved to see that they had all been located.

You are sure that they could not have recognised me under my hood?

I am obliged.

Yes, indeed, there is quite some distance still to be covered. I believe that when we spoke yesterday evening I was describing the nature of our journey from Braed Tor, the discomforts of a night spent in the wilderness?

Quite so. We had been waiting, by uncle Rauor's reckoning, a little over an hour after our arrival at the pre-arranged meeting point, before any of the others arrived. Much of the time was spent in trying to ensure my comfort, which ultimately could only be achieved by laying all of our blankets and cloaks together on the ground for me to lie upon. Uncle Rauor kindly agreed to take the first watch, and patrolled the perimeter, looking out for orks or our pursuing friends.

Even with the layers between my delicate frame and the rough ground, I was unable to sleep. I was most pre-occupied with the consequences of our flight, with the thought that what few belongings I had been able to carry with me were abandoned, perhaps irretrievably lost, in Braed Tor. There was a particularly fine jacket which I shuddered to imagine the hotelier pawing at and perhaps even attempting to fit to his extensive frame. You may well shake your head – it is difficult to believe, but no consideration had been given to the practicalities of our wardrobe and toilet in the event that this headlong rush in the wilderness did not simply result in our early deaths.

It is scarcely surprising that with such thoughts to preoccupy me, I was unable to gain much rest. Imagine, therefore, my delight when the first of our companions to arrive were my sister, with uncle Lias and Skapgood, bringing with them a small pony drawn cart, laden with my luggage and other accoutrements that I had thought lost forever. I gleaned that they had been able to acquire a creature to harness to the cart from a selection owned by the hotel, and that uncle Lias had pledged to return it to the rubbing post at the next precinct which we reached. This accounted for the good time that they had made, and I in turn lost no moments, while uncle Rauor verified the well-being of my sister and uncle, in checking the contents of the cart to satisfy myself that all was well.

Chivalry at this point would in any event have obliged me to vacate the somewhat uncomfortable bedding that had been assembled for me, and thereafter to offer it to my sister. She was manifestly exhausted by the short journey, and at once gratefully accepted my offer, wrapping herself in one of the blankets and very quickly lapsing into sleep. It can only have been such total fatigue which permitted her to sleep as she did without complaint, and I confess I envied her that facility.

Without hope of sleep, I took it upon myself to keep Lias and Rauor company as they undertook their respective patrols, and to my mind the night passed rather more quickly than it might otherwise have done without the pleasures of our idle conversation.

Nevertheless, the others were clearly becoming concerned by the prolonged absence of the last members of our group. This showed itself in a tendency to become irked at the most trivial of comments. I had no notion of what might have become of Merson and aunt Forba, and overheard at least one muttered conversation between Rauor and Lias which suggested that come first light they might be inclined to move on, with or without my absent aunt and uncle.

Where we were proposing to move on to was my most pressing concern. Thanks in no small part to my efforts at persuasion with uncle Rauor earlier in the evening, the scheme was to avoid Car Peronel. Lias and Skapgood both agreed that its prominent status and its convenient proximity to Braed Tor made it too predictable a destination. Thus the preference was to make for Rivertop. It now emerged, however, that from our current location this would be a journey which would take us several days, even on horseback. Naturally I had not appreciated this, but I found it remarkable that Rauor had not brought the point up in our earlier discussions. With the majority of our party on foot, it was inconceivable to me that we should attempt it.

It was while this debate was still unresolved, and at about the third hour before the moon set, that I found myself alone on the perimeter of our temporary camp with uncle Lias. Rauor was, I believe, attempting to sleep in advance of the day's exertions. It was the first proper discussion that Lias and I had had the opportunity to have since our conversation over dinner at uncle Merson's property. It proved to be a somewhat uncomfortable interview for us both.

I taxed him, naturally, with the question of what he could have been thinking of, to attract the negative attention of the Council so early in his career. I am by no means a manual labourer in the aesthetic arts, but I flatter myself that my appreciation is as acute as any man's. He had toiled for near on twenty years in order to ascend to the position of being permitted to compose an opera and to have it produced, albeit in a provincial setting. Why then simply squander the opportunity at the first occasion?

Symptomatically, Lias would not see the matter in that way. At first he strove to deny that his composition and approach had been in any way as controversial as it was now portrayed. When it was clear that I was not to be so easily persuaded, he accepted that there were elements which in retrospect might be regarded as regrettable, but contrition remained peculiarly lacking. Nevertheless, I fancy that I left him with a clearer understanding of my own views on the matter, and for his part he confirmed for me my initial view, that he was highly unlikely to be making any further contribution to the arts, except perhaps as a patron.

I could not but reflect, as the night moved closer to dawn, that uncle Lias' failings were not to be viewed in isolation. It was an unsettling thought, particularly for one whose every hope of advancement and expectation of income lay with uncle Merson and his friends, but their judgement was shown to be lacking in their handling of Lias' case. They might well say that they were simply showing support for their friend at a time of considerable mental anguish. For my part, a truer friend might have left him to feel the full force of the social disapproval that he had incurred, and not cushioned him from it. By doing so they might have brought him sooner to a realisation of the wrongness of his conduct.

I am ashamed to say that it was not long after this tiring encounter that my stamina, albeit as resilient as any man's, finally succumbed. I fell asleep for a short while, my back pressed against a vertical stone face which stood to one side of the clearing.

As a consequence, I was not awake when the remainder of our party finally joined us. Nor did I hear first hand of the details of their flight from Braed Tor nor the reasons for their delay. From what I could glean from later discussions, it seems that they encountered a relatively large band of orks, perhaps even a nest, and were obliged to fight a running battle in order to escape them. I must own that I viewed this narrative with some scepticism – I have never yet heard a tale of combat, particularly with orks, which does not assume far greater dimensions in the re-telling than it ever did in the actual undertaking of the combat.

Living on our farm, my sister and I have occasionally been required to fend off an ork raider, and she and I – unversed as we are in matters of combat – nevertheless managed to hold our own against it.

I awoke to find plans being made to remove to Car Peronel without further delay. My revised preferences had been vindicated even as I slept, an irony which I was well able to appreciate. The prospect of a forced march to Rivertop, in a journey spanning several days and exposing us to considerable inconvenience and, indeed, some danger, was clearly not to be borne.

The next problem then, as it seemed to me, was to arrange for some water to be heated so that the gentlemen at least might make a perfunctory toilet. To this interjection, which I made in as moderate a manner as I knew how, uncle Merson's response could only be described as cutting. I think that I was not alone in feeling that his subsequent tirade was somewhat ungenerous in view of the precarious situation in which he had placed me, and Elyssa. Without the handcart that she and uncle Lias had delivered, I would have been without even a clean shirt to change into. As it was, the range of collars and other standard essentials of my wardrobe was significantly limited.

If I found this a hardship, I cannot imagine how much more so it must have been for Merson and Lias, both of whom, I collect, were accustomed to living in some comfort and finery. For aunt Forba and for uncle Rauor, the present squalor was perhaps not so very different from their previous lives as academic or tutor. How they were all able to bear the circumstances without complaint, however, I shall never understand.

Nevertheless, our vagabond group made a peremptory breakfast and departed. In daylight, the landscape was actually quite striking. Being accustomed to the foreshortened horizons of the forests, it was truly remarkable to reach that first rise and to find the northern lands laid out before us. We had come rather closer to Car Peronel than I had realised, and the Tower was instantly identifiable in the near distance. More surprisingly, I could make out in the further distance as the landscape dissolved into a green and brown patchwork, two or three other patches of white. These, I realised, were several more distant precincts, gleaming in the early morning light.

After those moments of aesthetic pleasure, however, the mundane reality of the lengthy foot journey that we had before us quickly reasserted itself. Nor, once the march began in earnest, was there very much in the way of diverting conversation to recommend the journey. I think that for the first hour or so of travel I neither uttered nor heard more than a dozen words.

After that first hour we reached more level ground and the Tower, which until then had offered us a significant land-mark to aim towards, granted us only fleeting glances between the thickening woodland. After a time, debate began about the comparative advantages of maintaining our existing course, which seemed destined to take us through every briar patch, thicket and saturated gully that lay between our position and Car Peronel, or seeking out a more straightforward course. We knew, for example, that a little to our west there was a road which cut a relatively direct path through the woodland in the precinct's direction.

It was quickly clear that the differences in opinion under-pinning this discussion were borne out of our differing views of the attack on Merson's place in Braed Tor the previous day. Consequently the discussion turned gradually to a more general attempt to assess how much of a threat those attackers might still pose to us. It was, I think, at this point that I began to perceive that at least some of our number might be rather less ignorant of who those attackers had been, than perhaps I would have assumed.

I see that this suggestion causes you some amusement. I acknowledge that my sister and I have been extremely ignorant in our dealings with this group. The point remains, however, that up until the co-ordinated attack on Merson's home – an attack which could not simply be discounted as the work of bandits, in the way that the earlier attack on me might have been – Elyssa and I had been given no reason to suspect that our family friends, our "uncles" and "aunt", were anything other than they had told us.

Even though we were all enduring the same hardships on our difficult route to Car Peronel, the others spoke guardedly when I was close by. On another occasion, I might have made nothing of it. But I had told you, I think, about the blossoming concern about their probity and motives, which I had been cultivating since our meeting a few days earlier. It was perhaps as a result of this, or in default of any other distraction, that I found myself concentrating rather more than I would ordinarily have done upon the manner and the content of their dialogue.

No, I cannot recall the precise terms used in their conversations. At the time I did not appreciate that detailed knowledge of their discussions would be beneficial. Nor did I wish to provoke further disagreements by being too ostentatious in my eavesdropping. The sense of them was very much that my extended family were convinced that they knew the identity of the attackers, or those who had directed them to Merson's house. There was much debate about whether, and if so how, Elyssa and I might be left in a place of safety. I should not like to comment on their motivations for such a course, although no doubt they would have described them as altruistic.

Thinking of the attack which had been the genesis for the previous few days' peregrinations, I was far from satisfied that leaving my sister and me on our own was the best guarantee of our safety.

There was a superficial attraction, I admit, to uncle Merson's theory that the original attack on me had been meant to provoke a reaction from him and his fellows, in order to "flush them out". Having now done so, he reasoned, Elyssa and I had no further importance or relevance to the group and hence to their attackers. There was considerable rational force in this – for certainly neither Elyssa nor I represented a threat to anyone. Even so, I could not dissuade myself from the anxiety that I would remain in danger if I were to part company with the others.

There was also the not inconsiderable factor that most of our belongings and any expectation we had of recovering a tolerable situation in life for the future, was bound up in the fates of the people around us – the closest family we had. Any arrangement which saw Elyssa and me left in a place of safety would, I felt, be incomplete if it did not also provide the means for furnishing us with a secure and comfortable future. This consideration did not seem to enjoy the same prominence in their deliberations as it did in my, and I am sure Elyssa's, mind.

As for my sister, she struck me at this point as being somewhat preoccupied. It is unlikely that she was oppressed by the same weighty thoughts that I was endeavouring to shoulder – she has never really been the type to indulge her mind in philosophy, let alone strategic considerations. I flatter myself that she would always look to her older brother to address such matters of genuine concern.

As an example, an hour or more into our morning's journey, we had descended most of the way to the plain. With the advantage of a descent in daylight, we had been able to select a route which brought us to the end of a sheep trail which led through open hillside and coarse bracken in a downward curve to the foot of the hills and a small village (long since abandoned of course). As we were all picking our way along the track, keeping a watchful eye on the undergrowth even though it was broad daylight, Elyssa suddenly cried out and went running off the track. You may well imagine the consternation that she created with this moment of impulsive folly. And what prompted this behaviour, and such anxiety among her travelling companions? She had seen a butterfly!

Is it so? The time certainly rushes by, does it not? I am told that I have something of a gift for narration, although I have never felt any great vocation in that direction. I wonder if you would care to join me while I dine? It is only a light nuncheon, but passable, and there are two or three particular words that I would say to you concerning [redacted].

[Interview suspended]

*[Extract from report of Quaestor Lieutenant Yan –
dated 7th Nieumor XXVI Tor.]*

With their customary efficiency, my men have
undertaken a detailed and urgent search of the area
indicated by Quaestor Feiger's intelligence. The
point of departure from the Northern Road was
immediately identified by reference to our men's
exemplary local knowledge. It was impossible to
track specific individuals at this point, but it is clear
that the side road is well-used.

We have also been able to detect three or four
points at which further branching of the way leads
to routes which match the characteristics described
in the esteemed quaestor's intelligence, and our
men are tracking each of these in turn with all due
diligence. A further report will follow.

[Extract ends]

17

From where Tomas stood on the trail, the cave mouth was barely visible. Indeed, if he had not seen the others disappearing into the cliff face, he never would have detected the opening. As he stood in the morning sunlight, waiting patiently with the two young siblings, he reflected again on the strange tension in the others' behaviour towards him. On the one hand, he was at liberty, armed and seemingly in receipt of their frank confessions and confidences. On the other, they remained guarded towards him, and he felt himself to be constantly under scrutiny.

From the time that he had been shaken awake in the early dawn-light, he had been constantly accompanied, albeit discreetly, by one member or other of the party. Even at his most private ablutions one of the other men would find that nature had made its demands of him at precisely the same time. They would then stand conspicuously close at hand, keeping up a disconcerting stream of conversation. It had been done with civility, even with some humorous acknowledgement of the awkwardness of the situation, but none the less it had been impressed on Tomas that he was neither trusted, nor wholly free.

About an hour after they had broken camp, the terrain had changed. They had emerged from a narrow rocky pathway to find rolling grass-covered hillsides before them, sloping down to heavy woodland. Beyond, shining in the morning sunlight, lay the Tower, with Car Peronel nestled invisibly beneath it. Almost immediately Tomas and the youngsters had been told to take a break and to keep an eye on the wagon, while Merson Blare and the others had worked their way through the waist-high grasses, along the line of the cliff-face, and then disappeared from view. Symptomatically of the group's inconsistent behaviour towards Tomas, he had been allowed to see the location of the cave, well enough that he could find it again in future if he wished to, but not to see inside.

His shoulders ached. It was good to be able to focus on something so trivial, in the swirl of emotions running through him. It had been far too long since he had taken part in the training camps which as a reservist he was still notionally expected to participate in. He was out of condition, had forgotten what it was like to undertake forced marches, or to snatching a few hours' comfortless sleep on the hard ground. He reached his left hand up to his right shoulder and rotated the joint, feeling the gentle pop under the surface as some of his tension was released.

As he did so, he watched the two young people, sitting together on the tail of the cart, watching him covertly even as they gently bickered together. There was something jarring about seeing the two of them together, so similar, so obviously tied by that bond of sibling affection. The law being as it was, it was simply unprecedented within the precincts. It was a sad loss, for people to grow up without the possibility of that connection, the under-current of warmth that Tomas could see even as superficially Alyster directed another snide barb at his sister, and she in turn rolled her eyes and shook her head.

Inevitably, his thoughts turned back to his friend Henrik, cast into a dangerous predicament by his normal human desire for a larger family. Every precinct was subject to a similar law restricting families to a single child, and Tomas had been required to enforce that law on numerous occasions. He thought of the families that he had expelled from their homes and the precinct, with young babies screaming at the disruption. It had sickened him every time, but it was a law which was widely publicised and no exception was made for rank and station, until of course the highest echelons of society were reached.

He thought of his comrade in that situation and despite the warmth of the mid-summer morning his heart felt a chill run through it. He knew that he was being emotional – that tiredness and the strangeness of his surroundings were making him feel detached from his usual sense of professional duty. But he could not bring himself to contemplate leaving Henrik and his family to their fate – still less actually reporting them for their crime.

The girl, Elyssa, looked up and caught his eye. She smiled shyly and turned to whisper something in her brother's ear. He in turn stopped talking and also turned to look at Tomas, who found himself slightly uncomfortably subject to their concerted gaze. Neither of them seemed hostile, just intrigued, and Tomas decided that he would take advantage of their interest, and the absence of the older adults, to start up a conversation. It would be interesting to see how much these two were aware of what their extended family were involved in.

Even as he took a step towards the two youngsters, however, a cry came from the direction of the cliff. Tomas' head snapped around. Half in and half out of the cave entrance, Rauor Tell was waving back towards the cart. His face betrayed considerable anxiety, and unthinkingly, Tomas broke into a run, pausing only to shout back to the two on the cart to stay where they were.

The ground was uneven under the tall grasses. Rocks broke the surface here and there, and clumps of roots posed regular hazards. Tomas was sure-footed enough in the daylight to make his way to the cave mouth without falling. As he got closer he could see that Tell's clothes were caked with cave dust, and his hands were dirty and bloodied.

"What has happened?"

"A rock fall. Will you not help me to shift it?"

It seemed a strange way to ask for help, as if he almost expected that Tomas would refuse. Tomas' response was eloquent. He flung down his cloak, unbuckled his sword belt, and plunged into the cave system.

The light faded quickly. The familiar oppression which stole over Tomas whenever he was in a confined space started to make itself felt between his shoulder-blades. He forced himself past it and deeper into the cave, turning a corner up ahead beyond which he could see a light flickering. The roof, all jagged exposed rock, lowered and the sides of the tunnel became tighter. As he came round the corner, Rauor Tell close behind, he could see the rock fall, illuminated by the light of a stub of candle that was resting on an exposed rock shelf to one side of the passageway. Tomas stepped towards the pile of rocks.

"Careful!" Tell's voice was sharp and echoed mutedly in the dusty atmosphere. "One of them may be trapped underneath!"

But Tomas' training had taken over. He heard the warning and it was incorporated into the three dimensional puzzle which was forming within his mind. Without thinking, he took charge.

"All right. You stand to this side. Be ready to move if the fall starts to slip in our direction. I won't put any weight on the larger rocks, but I am going to need to start shifting some of these heavier blocks from higher up."

He didn't wait for a response. Every moment counted. Bracing one leg against the seemingly solid cave wall, he stretched out his arms getting a solid grip on a large rock close to the top of the pile. Moving it dislodged a few smaller stones and some dirt from around it, but did not precipitate a further slide. Carefully Tomas passed the rock over to Raour Tell's waiting hands, and he laid it down behind him before turning back to receive the next block.

Once the first few substantial boulders had been moved, he began to claw at the loose rubble and soil that had packed in around them. As he did so, a narrow gap started to appear close to the ceiling of the tunnel and Tomas found he could hear Merson's voice on the far side of the fall, talking calmly to the others. Pausing for a moment from his frantic activity, he called towards the opening.

"Merson? Is everyone alright in there?"

Through the rock, Merson Blare's voice came back muffled and indistinct. It sounded like he called "Karsten, is that you?" Tomas glanced back at Raour Tell, but he was in the process of hauling one of the larger boulders towards the exit.

"It's Callan! Tomas Callan! Is anyone hurt?"

There was silence for a moment. "No Tomas, thank you. We are all well. How big is the fall?"

"Not too bad – I think I have made an air hole already. Can you move away from the pile?"

"All right." Merson replied. Then his voice lowered as he gave instructions to his colleagues. "Is there any difficulty with my continuing to try to clear it from this side?"

Tomas took a step back. Clearing the hole at the top did not seem to have precipitated anything further. Even with what had fallen already, though, it was going to be a significant task to clear a large enough hole to evacuate the three trapped people.

"Thank you Merson. Please work from the top on your side. We will try to clear a large enough passage for the three of you to crawl out."

Knowledge that those trapped on the other side of the rockfall were depending on him spurred Tomas on to further exertions. Even when the gap seemed wide enough to him for the purposes of escape, Merson was still hard at work at the far end, and Tomas kept going, trying to ensure that they had consistent dimensions throughout. Within another half hour, a substantial hole had been cleared and Tomas, who had been saving his breath for working, paused to call through the gap.

"What do you think Merson? Is the hole large enough?"

The only parts of Merson Blare visible until that point had been his hands and forearms, working hard at the far end of the tunnel in a mirror image to Tomas' own. Now his face appeared, dimly visible in the darkness.

"I should say so investigator," he called along the

narrow gap "I'm going to send the others ahead of me."

First Forba Groenne came crawling along. She had removed her dress which was bundled in a ball which she pushed ahead of her, crawling along behind in her vest and petticoats. Never one to let gallantry interfere with practicality, Tomas reached both arms into the tunnel and first pulled Forba's dress to safety before returning to retrieve her with a hand under each armpit. To his surprise, she enfolded him in a warm embrace as soon as her feet touched ground, whispering "Thank you! Thank you!" before picking up her dress and taking Raour Tell's steadying hand. Tomas watched them heading for the exit and then turned back to the tunnel. Within another few minutes Lias Nefflor was also through, brushing himself down fastidiously if ridiculously given the amount of dust that Tomas' exertions had thrown up.

Lias turned back to the tunnel.

"All right Merson, you can send them through now!"

Tomas started. Were there more people in there? Peering into the tunnel, though, he saw the first of what proved to be several large crates being pushed through the opening. Merson's additional clearance work now made sense – the crates' dimensions only just fitted into the gap. They were also as heavy as they looked and Tomas was glad of Lias Nefflor's assistance in reaching the first one down. Clearly the man had muscle beneath his effete exterior, although Tomas was beginning to feel that this group could not surprise him any further with their physical prowess and training. Even in the height of the danger from the rockfall, each of them had responded calmly and efficiently.

As Lias and Raour Tell carted the first crate into

the open air, Tomas returned to the hole where a second crate was now being pushed through. As it reached his hands he placed a firm grip on each side and pulled it towards him, staggering slightly. Merson's voice echoed faintly.

"Hold on Callan, the others will be back shortly to assist you" but Tomas was eager to get some hint of what the crates might contain and he pulled it further towards him, lowering it as gently as he could to the ground. Melted leads seals decorated every join in the timber, excluding any possibility that he would be able to see inside. A scuffing sound from the hole alerted him that Merson was on his way through, and Tomas quickly tried tipping the crate on one of its long edges, rewarded at last by the faint sound of metal scraping on metal. It was a feeble clue, but coupled with the weight of the boxes reinforced in Tomas' mind his initial supposition that these crates were packed with weapons.

Quickly he returned the crate to rest and when Merson Blare's head emerged from the hole it was to find Tomas leaning against the rockfall, recovering his breath and stretching out his back. Tomas reached out his arms to support Merson's descent and as they both steadied themselves in the half-light Merson Blare reached out his right hand, clasping Tomas' forearm in a firm grip.

"Thank you investigator. More than you can know, I am grateful that you came to our aid."

Tomas felt a surge of affection for the man standing before him, which he quickly suppressed. He coughed in the dusty air and turned his attention to the crate, trying to conceal his confusion. Without a word the two men hefted the crate between them and made their way back into the daylight.

Half an hour later, the crates were stowed on the wagon, precious drinking water had been expended in rinsing the hair and faces of those who had been trapped underground, and the party was on its way once again. The blue sky, the sunlight, the sounds of nature, all conspired to create a sense of unreality in Tomas. Could it really be that only an hour before three of their number had been trapped underground, possibly in genuine danger?

Yet despite their superficially unchanged marching order, it was clear that Tomas' unthinking willingness to pitch in and help with the rescue had changed the way in which he was treated. On several occasions, Tomas noticed one of the adults staring at him appraisingly as they walked along. More overtly, the young man's sister had responded to her brother's latest complaints about his hunger and the state of the road by bringing from her supplies a cloth wrapped bundle, which she proceeded to distribute to them all, starting with Tomas. Expecting some dried meat, or other preserved product appropriate to such a journey, he had been slightly surprised to be handed a small package wrapped in what seemed to be leaves, and containing a small disc of lightweight, white coloured bread.

Tomas' relief, that someone in the party had at least had the foresight to bring provisions, was tempered with dissatisfaction at the size of the portions. Each of the others consumed their share with relish, however, and Tomas could not bear to disappoint the youngster so he took a bite, steeling himself to compliment the undoubtedly stale morsel.

The taste, though, was like nothing he had ever experienced. It stirred a deep feeling within him, as if warmth and comfort and security were tastes that he half-remembered from childhood. A small part of his rational brain protested that no food could be so good that it produced this reaction, but the rest of him was swept up in a sense of euphoria. Behind that initial elation Tomas found himself re-energised and for the next few minutes walked purposefully with the others, lost to his surroundings and to the extraordinary sensations coursing through him.

The path began to descend. As the group moved downwards, the Tower began to loom more and more significantly on the horizon. Even Tomas, law-abiding officer of the investigators though he might be, could seldom look upon the Tower without a shiver of anxiety. At that moment, though, he felt only peace, and a sense that nothing was to be feared. Tomas thought again of Henrik, determined to help his old comrade in whatever way he could, and newly certain that he would find an answer to the dilemma faced by his friend. To help him, though, he would have to meet with Henrik again. Even with the added optimism given him by his uplifting breakfast, Tomas recognised that the continual scrutiny he was under made the chance of such a meeting extremely remote.

For all that he may have surprised his travelling companions with his willingness to come to their aid, Tomas knew that more would be needed if he were to be entirely trusted. If he was to be free on the following day to meet unsupervised with Henrik, he would first have to win his new companions' trust. Their descent towards the plains continued, and the pace of their forced march settled into a comfortable rhythm. This was the opportunity that Tomas needed to be able to earn the trust of the others, and particularly of Merson

Blare.

Although Merson still remained an intimidating presence to Tomas, it was clear that the reverse did not hold true – the taller man's features were adorned with a warm and seemingly genuine smile as he caught sight of Tomas approaching him. Nor was he averse to picking up on Forba's tale from the night before. He started by acknowledging that they had not yet provided answers to many of Tomas' inevitable questions, arising from the revelations about Victor's wife.

"I am sorry Tomas," he began, slowing his pace slightly so that they could walk together at a comfortable speed, "I do not mean to be ever tantalising you. But just as it is important to you that you are able to understand the role we played in Maryam's death, so it is important for us to be able to relate the story to you in our own way. So much happened, which is relevant to why we have done what we did. So much of what happened then is relevant to why we are doing what we must now do."

Tomas nodded, and courteously indicated that Merson should proceed as he thought best.

"The first thing to say is that the plan by Forba and Rauor to involve Maryam in their investigations struck me as being subject to unnecessary risks. She was affianced to a promising officer in the investigators. We would be asking her to undertake activity which could not but be regarded as questionable, if not completely unlawful, by her intended and those who employed him. With no discourtesy meant to your profession... we had no desire to bring ourselves under official scrutiny if that could possibly be avoided.

"Forba and Rauor, though, persuaded me that

while there were risks, they could not be said to be unnecessary. Through this hunt for the codex, it had become clear to us that a significant body of knowledge about the elves was being withheld from the population at large, and that suggested to us that it was either very valuable, or very powerful. In either case, it was information that we, if we genuinely intended to take a step towards improving our world, and breaking its cycles of despondency, needed to obtain.

"At my insistence approaches were made extremely carefully. The initial response to Maryam's contact, as I think Forba was trying to describe to you last night, was carefully set out in the most anodyne of terms. We were not about to implicate ourselves through an outright expression of interest in something which, for all we knew, might pose dangers to us simply for having known about it. It was Maryam who, undeterred by the blandness of our reply, followed up with the suggestion of a meeting, and it was only after several such meetings that I gave Forba permission to discuss with Maryam the nature of our interest in the codex.

"I wonder if you can anticipate her reaction?"

Tomas opened his mouth to respond, and then paused. Not for the first time he was struck with admiration of Merson's rhetorical techniques. Already, he was caught up again in the tale and had been about to make an unguarded observation which, while innocuous in itself, would have paved the way to a freer and fuller dialogue. With such lack of restraint, as Tomas was very well aware, came danger, and ultimately self-incrimination. He took a deep breath.

"I never knew the lady of course. I can only imagine that she was less than pleased to be implicated in such a scheme."

Merson laughed. The reaction was natural and spontaneous but the source of the humour was not immediately apparent to Tomas.

"She scolded Forba for not coming to the point more quickly. She had, it transpired, been well aware of the subject of our interest for some time. For all our endeavours at subterfuge, she had deduced precisely what materials we were interested in. She had in fact already made use of her privileged position of access to write out copies of several key texts located within the Codex. These she delivered to Forba, recklessly, as I thought at the time, including with them a short hand-written note in which she openly used both of their names. Maryam later explained to me that it had been designed to cement the bond between herself and Forba, to demonstrate her own commitment to the enterprise."

Merson glanced at Tomas, as if gauging how much information he ought to share.

"That first document showed me that Rauor and Forba had been right to insist on pursuing their investigations. It was a report of an examination of a dead elf, one that the codexari (as the authors of the document called themselves) had found unconscious and killed, without any other elf's knowledge. The report itself was fascinating, revealing a number of features that I had never previously been aware of. For example, the elves are always portrayed as much taller than humans, are they not? Well, this report revealed that at the moment of death the elf's body seemed to shrink on itself. One of the surgeons who had undertaken the examination suggested that the body itself may not have changed, but that some elven magic may have been at work while it lived, creating a more imposing impression than was the reality.

"It was another annotation, however, that proved to be of the greatest significance. At the conclusion of the report was written in the strongest terms a reminder to all who read it, that they must be scrupulous never to allow themselves to come into close contact with an elf, or to share the information in the report with anyone who might have reason to encounter any of the elven-kind. The report reminded the reader that elf magic included the ability to know another's thoughts, and that the purpose of accumulating the collected information which they had on the elves would be defeated, were the possession of that knowledge by humans ever to be discovered."

Tomas looked sideways at the taller man, and found himself caught in his unsettlingly direct stare. "That description does not sound to me like the writings of an ally. Were there groups of humans in opposition to the elves, then?"

"It is more than that, Tomas. We did not simply cohabit these realms with the elves. They were an occupying force, and all humans, apart from the few who collaborated with the elves and implemented their will, were held in subjugation." He held up a hand, recognising Tomas's instinctive reaction of disbelief but hastening to forestall it. "I know that you will doubt this. I did, even with copies of the written evidence in my hand. Even after Forba had managed to see the original documents for herself, and to satisfy herself of their apparent age and authenticity, I still struggled with the idea. We have been taught a lie, but it has been taught so repeatedly, and so well, that none of us have ever thought to challenge it. And if the essence of our relationship with the elves is other than what we had believed, what else of our ancient history can we put our trust in?"

The question hung silently between them for a while as they continued to walk, gradually catching up again with the rest of the group. They were starting to have to take a more circuitous route toward their destination. Ahead of Tomas, the only others of the group still in sight were Forba and Elyssa, and Tomas found himself watching them for several minutes, walking hand in hand in apparent leisure. Despite his confusion, his exhaustion and the whirl of thoughts occupying his mind, he found himself feeling suddenly calmed. Indeed, he found himself imagining for a moment of vivid fantasy that he and Merson were walking behind Idony and some other friend of hers on an idyllic afternoon's recreation. The play of the sunlight over the trees in the woodland beside which they were walking, the sound of birdsong and the fresh scents of mid-summer in the air, all conspired to generate a feeling of peaceful satisfaction in Tomas's spirit.

The moment passed as the two women, on some unseen signal, disappeared without warning from the path, a flicker of movement within the woodland the only clue to their direction. Tomas tensed himself to increase speed, to close the gap before losing sight of them, but Merson placed a restraining hand upon him, drawing him into the shelter of the trees and gesturing him to crouch down out of sight.

"We will catch up to them soon enough, Tomas" Merson's faintly amused voice reassured him, "and when we do, I think that it is probably time for Forba to tell you how Maryam died."

[Extract from 'The Rainbow Prize' (traditional mage tale)]

...he found himself in a long corridor, with red walls, red curtains and red tiles on the floor. Rising from the centre of the floor at intervals were red columns, atop which were delicate ceramic busts of famous figures from elven history.

Nail's hatred of the elves increased every time he saw another such figure, the beauty and purity of their faces almost driving him out of his mind with rage. Yet he did not succumb to his base urge to strike these figures and destroy them, falling prey to the powerful protective magic which would have killed him on the spot if he had set off that trap.

How he resisted, we shall never know. It is likely that, however strong his anger, his greed was stronger, and that he was thus able to set aside this first temptation and pass safely to the door on the inside wall of the corridor.

Beyond it, he found himself in a similar looking corridor, but this one without any columns and coloured entirely in orange. Like the red corridor its ends bent inwards, and had he had the time to explore Nail would have found that each formed a complete hexagonal circuit. On the walls were hung floor length mirrors and it was to these that Nail was drawn, finding himself entranced by the sight of his own, orange-lit reflection.

There he might have stayed, captured forever in self-adoration, but somehow the arch-deceiver knew that he was himself deceived. He found the strength to lift the hood of his stolen elf cloak and render himself invisible, freeing himself from the mirror's power at once, and enabling him to continue on his malevolent quest...

18

(Car Peronel, 20 years ago)

Lariad Etellion lay on the roof tiles of a modest town house, not far from the periphery of Car Peronel, in a section as yet untroubled by the construction of the wall that was gradually enclosing the entire city. Careful to keep his head below the ridge-line, he turned and spoke conversationally to the woman lying beside him.

"You know, I trust, that Pepina will give me no peace for some time if I tear this jacket?"

Forba laughed quietly. One could always rely on Lariad to alleviate tension.

"If you fear that the jacket will come to some harm, you could remove it and let it rest here."

This was met with a reciprocal chuckle. "You don't really think that there is any danger, do you? For all his premonition of disaster, I notice that Rauor was not sufficiently troubled to make the journey with us this time!"

Forba stifled the urge to leap to Rauor's defence. She knew that Lariad had drawn certain conclusions about her relationship with Rauor, and even though they were incorrect, she did not want to lend any credence to his mischievous speculations. Instead she focused on the first part of the question.

"I have nothing more to base it on than I ever had! I know well that Maryam takes every precaution on these occasions, and I should be content with that. She has every right to be where she is, even to be making copies of the documents she is reading and writing out. It is only the superstitious part of me that thinks that if something is going to go wrong, it will have to be today, on this last visit. It may please you to laugh at me, but after such a close escape a month ago, I cannot help to fear that we are placing a great strain on our luck."

Lariad did indeed laugh, but he also reached out a hand to treat Forba's shoulder to an affectionate pat. "You are too dismissive of superstition. Pepina and I knew that we were fated to be together from the first time that we met. We've never doubted it, never questioned the chances that brought us together. I agree with your anxieties, but for much more practical reasons – you cannot repeat the same trick too many times. The audience becomes bored, they start wondering how it was done, and then why it was done. We should have stopped a month ago."

"If you thought so, you should have said it!"

"By the same measure, should you not have spoken of your concerns, Forba? I did not speak for the same reason that you did not. You know Merson – we could not have dissuaded him even if all of the rest of us had agreed. The most I could do was volunteer to come along when Rauor said that he thought that Maryam would benefit from some additional protection."

Forba sighed. "We are not going to be of much assistance to her from this position. When is that ork's son guard going to move?"

On the other side of the ridge line, the roof sloped back down but, unusually for the architecture of Car Peronel, beyond that it butted directly up against another building, with a flat roof and a raised half height wall around it. From this roof-top, they would have had an excellent view of the entrance to the Tower, and have been able to provide some cover and assistance in the unlikely event that Maryam needed to make a dramatic escape. Unfortunately, however, the strategy depended on their being in occupation of the roof, which in turn required there no longer to be a guard there. Yet there the guard remained, leaning against the northerly wall, where his gaze would have to shift around only a few degrees to be looking directly at the ridge of tiles which currently concealed Forba and Lariad.

This misfortune was adding to the sense of anxiety that had been lying in Forba's stomach for the past few weeks. Maryam had provided excellent, and voluminous, intelligence from a good portion of the documents of the codex, stored within the Tower. Making regular, but never too frequent, visits to the room in which the records were stored, she had been able to add substantially to the knowledge which Forba and her friends possessed about the elves. Indeed their existing knowledge had not so much been supplemented as supplanted. So much of what they thought they knew had turned out to be a lie.

But for all the questions and doubts that the information provided by Maryam had provoked, her self-assurance and confidence had persuaded the group to be confident that no harm could befall her. It was this complacency which had been badly shaken a month earlier. Maryam had been on a very rare visit to Car Vandra and had been staying at a coaching house on the outskirts of the city. On her second night there, several of the group had joined her for dinner, but she had left the party early complaining of a headache and retired to her rooms.

Several minutes later there had been a sound of breaking glass and the others had run upstairs to find Maryam alone and very shaken. Her dress had been torn and her arms were scratched. She stood staring at a broken window which bore traces of blood and a scrap of black leather on the sharp edges of the remaining glass. An intruder had apparently been in her room, searching her belongings for something, and had put up something of a struggle when she had sought to accost him. While the inn-keeper was content to assume that it was a simple burglary, and to express his thankfulness that Maryam had not come to any harm, Forba and some of the others had been rather more sceptical. According to Maryam, certain items of jewellery, and even a purse of money, had been cast aside, and the intruder's attention had been focused on a wallet which contained, as it happened, purely innocuous correspondence.

Forba had communicated her concerns to the rest of the group, but Merson and Lias in particular had neither of them been persuaded. Ultimately Maryam had returned to Car Peronel with no additional arrangements having been made for her security. Undoubtedly, part of their unconcern stemmed from the length of time that Maryam had been operating on their behalf undetected. It had also been agreed that for the time being only a very few further documents would be needed to complete their preliminary understanding.

After the next delivery proceeded without any difficulty, Forba, who had already been half persuaded by Merson that she had over-reacted to what was perhaps nothing more than a simple burglar, endeavoured to convince herself that all would be well for the final delivery. Somehow, she could not do so. It was shortly after she had confessed her difficulty in eliminating the last traces of anxiety about Maryam's well-being, that Rauor had taken up the argument. In the end he had persuaded Merson that one or two of the group should make the journey to Car Peronel to mark the final delivery. If nothing else, he argued, it would be a good way to demonstrate to Maryam that they took her well-being seriously.

Forba had immediately put herself forward, with a grateful smile in Rauor's direction, but to her considerable surprise Rauor himself did not volunteer. Instead it was left for Lariad to half-heartedly put himself forward, expressing the view (to feigned outrage from Pepina) that she would never forgive him if he turned down the chance to purchase some gifts for her in the capital city.

Since their arrival in the capital, she and Lariad had done their best to fit with the image of a couple of friends at liberty in a new city, making various luxury purchases, dining well, and even attending a play. At the theatre they had made their pre-arranged meeting with Maryam and reassured her that, as far as they could tell, all was well.

Today, they had spent their time more carefully, walking the plaza outside the southern gate to the Tower, taking note of angles and sight-lines. Having identified two or three likely buildings, they had made their way to each in turn, and selected the flat-roofed square house for a variety of reasons. None of these had included the presence of a guard on the roof.

Time was now starting to become pressing. "Is he still there?" Forba murmured. Lariad, who had managed to smuggle his quiver and arrows past the guards on entering the city, and who now wore them strung tight against his back, crawled up to the ridge-line once more. Forba watched as he inched his head up above the tiles and then stiffened, seemingly in shock. After far too long he lowered his head and gestured urgently for Forba to join him. A sickening certainty growing inside her, she made her own way up carefully to see what had provoked his horrified reaction.

As her eyes took in the situation on the far side of the roof, she felt her stomach drop away from her, as if she had suddenly slid from her position and was tumbling down to the street below. Lariad's knuckles were white on the tiles next to her. The flat roof which they had selected for its strategic overview of the Tower's southern plaza was now occupied by a detachment of half a dozen guards. All were lightly armoured, armed with bows and short swords, and from their demeanour and their positions of concealment, they appeared to be very much in earnest.

Ducking his head down, Lariad whispered urgently in Forba's ear. "You need to go and get a coach and some horses, and wait with them at the Western Gate. I'll keep watch here. I doubt that these men have anything to do with Maryam, but if they do I will do my best to get her to you." He stilled any attempt at further conversation with a gesture of his hand. "What can you do from here? Whatever their target, these guards are serious, and

I am sure there will be a number more in other locations. Now get going."

Forba nodded once, and was about to move when she was stilled by a sound from the far side of the roof, the sound of a loose tile shifting underfoot. Silently, Lariad, the humorous light gone out of his eyes, reached behind him and extracted his bow, notching an arrow to it even as he kept his eyes nervously on the ridge-line. Without knowing how long it might be before someone appeared, he prudently drew the bowstring back to the half way point, preserving his strength but ready to apply full tension at a moment's notice.

If there was any further noise from the far side of the roof, it could not make itself heard over the uninterrupted background sounds of the city. Forba was cutting her gaze from the ridge-line to Lariad's anxious, sweat-beaded face. Consequently she missed the flicker of movement that provided him with his only clue, and saw instead the arrow drawn back and then released unhesitatingly. Turning in a futile attempt to follow its path, she found a man's head framed against the blue afternoon sky, the feathers of one of Lariad's arrows protruding from his throat.

Her moment of distraction was the only opportunity that Lariad needed. He kicked out, breaking Forba's grip and leaving her to slide down the roof-side towards a perilous drop. "Go!" he called after her. "Make sure you save her!". Then he leapt to his feet and had disappeared over the ridge-line. As Forba's uncontrolled slide continued, the clatter of tiles marked Lariad's parallel descent on the far side of the roof.

Scrabbling around with both hands, Forba was just able to slow her descent as she approached the roof edge, albeit at the cost of a wrenching sensation in her left wrist which she knew was likely to be a serious injury. A moment's madness almost saw her re-climb the roof to go to Lariad's assistance, but she knew that she could not help him. Instead she needed to escape and, if possible, bring Maryam with her. She hunted along the edge of the roof, finding the marked tile which showed where there was a convenient window-ledge below, and swung off the roof even as the faint sounds of battle began to carry to her ears.

Several minutes later, bruised and scared, she was on the plaza, resisting the urge to look back to the flat-roofed building behind her, terrified of doing anything that might betray her to the archers who she imagined even now sighting their arrows at her back. Her left wrist was really throbbing now. Ahead of her, a second detachment of guards appeared to be undertaking some drill practice on the plaza. Closer inspection showed them to be in full armour and looking remarkably alert and senior to be drilling in public. Forba consciously slowed her pace and her breathing, as much as she could, and let the flex of her muscles confirm that her short knives were still where they belonged, strapped in place on her forearms. She wished that she had had more time to practice using them, but they were a comforting presence nonetheless.

Remembering how she and Lariad had behaved the day before, she slowed still further, gazing up at the Tower in simulated awe. She even paused and spun slowly as if trying to find her bearings, looking without being too obtrusive for any other groups of guards that might pose a danger. The drilling group were close at hand now, and Forba was careful to maintain a sensible distance from them, observing proper deference as she circled their location and continued onwards, even more slowly now, to the southern gate.

She was perhaps a hundred paces away from the gate when she looked up, and locked eyes with Maryam as she came down the steps and onto the plaza.

Maryam's eyes widened instantly, taking in Forba's unexpected presence, and the knot of soldiers behind her. A look of betrayal flickered across her face and Forba started forward, wanting to reassure her that she would be kept safe. Maryam took a step backward, and that was all that the guards behind Forba required. There was the sound of swords being drawn, a quietly muttered order. Forba crossed her hands, palm to forearm, glanced one last time at Maryam who was now rooted to the ground in fear, and then turned, drawing her two daggers even as she did so.

The guards, soft from city centre duty, seemed to be stunned motionless by the sudden appearance of an armed woman between them and their intended target. Their officer pointed his sword, and opened his mouth to give an order. A slight flicker in the air was the only warning that Forba had, and the man fell, an arrow protruding from his back. Forba noted with something approaching amusement that Lariad had used one of the guards' own black flighted arrows for the shot, a little detail of mischief that would undoubtedly contribute to the confusion among the men that Forba was facing.

She took a step forward. The men, though mature, were uncertain without their leader and took a step back. A second guard fell, and then a third, to arrows from the rear. Panicked, they reacted by moving away from the greater threat, but unfortunately this path brought them back towards Forba. She sought to emulate a style of weaving hand motions which she had seen demonstrated but never troubled to practice, hoping to further discourage them. Instead, she nearly ended the fight ignominiously early when one of the blades dipped a little too close to the artery in her swollen left wrist.

Three guards were left. Their drawn swords had far greater reach than Forba's knives. She was also conscious that if this developed into a stand-off she would soon be very seriously outnumbered. She started to move backwards, towards the position in which she had last seen Maryam. The guards kept pace with her. Another arrow fell short, taking a man through the thigh and causing him to cry out in a way that drew even more attention to the fight. This was the moment, Forba knew, to capitalise on the inattention of the remaining two guards. She should strike before further forces arrived. She had not been able to help a glance towards Lariad, however, who would undoubtedly have regarded the last shot as a disappointing miss, and in that glance she saw flashes of what could only have been sword blades, on top of the distinctive flat-topped building which marked his location.

Time had run out. All that remained, as far as Forba could see, was to safe-guard Maryam, who she had drawn into this and therefore felt personally responsible for. In a moment of clarity, she wondered whether Merson would regard the information which Maryam had obtained as worth the price that she and Lariad were going to pay for it, knowing ultimately that whatever calculation he might make, she could not leave endangered the woman who she had encouraged to risk so much.

Creating confusion was the key now. She turned to a group of three men in labourers' clothes who stood close together nearby watching the developing fight. "It is no use!" she called, watching surprise and alarm flash upon their faces, "we shall never make it inside! The three of you must flee while you can!" The results were gratifyingly instantaneous. The men glanced at one another, turned and ran. In the subsequent confusion and inattention on the guards' part, Forba took three steps forward, intending at the very least to injure one of the two men and to leave the other one to speculate to his superiors that, whatever their original purpose on that day, they had stumbled upon some other, wholly unconnected, conspiracy.

The guards shifted their weight forward to meet the charge. Forba felt her focus narrowing. The sounds of the plaza, the bright sunlight overhead, faded away to invisibility. It was as if she stood in a tunnel, with the two swordsmen ahead of her obstructing the light. She took another step forward.

At first, she thought that the guards were backing away from her. There was a moment of stillness, a startled look on each of their faces. Then each in turn toppled forward, a further black flighted arrow protruding from their backs. Forba thought she heard the echo of an anguished cry coming from the rooftop far ahead of her, but her common sense did not desert her. Without even a backward glance at Maryam, she turned and fled the plaza, following the direction taken by the three labourers that she had previously set running.

That evening, a gala performance was taking place at the Pinnacle Theatre, part of the elite cultural district which clustered close under the shadow of the Tower. Far from the front entrance, where carriages queued in a painfully slow procession to deposit their occupants in front of enraptured crowds, a cloaked figure handed a roll of money to the stage doorman, and made her own entrance without an audience.

Inside, she hung the cloak on a peg conveniently close to the door and, dressed beneath in the uniform of the serving staff who waited on the wealthier patrons, made her way to the kitchens deep in the theatre's basement. There, she was able to circulate undetected, running imaginary errands, and reinforcing her knowledge of the most rapid avenues of escape, if that should be necessary.

Shortly before the first interval, she located a serving tray and some drinks and made her way to one of the smaller boxes on the lower tier. As she heard the applause begin she stood outside the box, glancing in both directions in a vain attempt to locate any sign of a potential trap. Reaching out for the door handle, she caught sight of her shaking hand and tried to steady it. The applause was starting to taper away. Steeling herself, whether for shock or disappointment, she pressed down the handle and entered the box.

Inside, Maryam started and turned anxiously. Her tension was plainly not alleviated by seeing Forba standing there. She was struggling to speak, but Forba's eyes were drawn to the other occupant, an unprecedented second occupant. The man continued to look out at the audience through his theatre glasses, scrupulously ignoring the intruder.

Maryam stood, a pink flush on her throat and cheeks, taking a step towards Forba and mouthing inarticulately. Forba, who had spent a lonely hour earlier in the evening sobbing uncontrollably, was now able to keep her emotions in check. No sign of her suppressed anguish at Lariad's loss, or her present fear, showed upon her face.

"I'm sorry to have intruded Madam. I've brought your drinks order?"

Forba waited for the response that would tell her that Maryam had been compromised, that she should leave. In front of her the younger woman took two deep, gulping breaths.

"Y... yes, thank you" she responded, "do you know where I might obtain a spare programme? This one is a little creased."

Several thoughts chased each other through Forba's mind. Taken at face value, the coded message meant that she was not under surveillance, and that she still had the papers that she had copied out earlier that afternoon, ready to make the delivery. Forba found that remarkable, perhaps even implausible. She thought back to her own hurried first minutes on returning to her hotel room, as she had systematically destroyed any materials that might identify her beyond the false travelling documents under which she still hoped to leave Car Peronel. Could Maryam really have been so much less affected by the afternoon's events?

The other explanation was rather more sinister, that Maryam had betrayed them and that delivery of the papers was intended to secure her freedom, but at the expense of Forba and her companions. While Forba did not want to believe it, she knew that such betrayals were possible, and it would certainly account for the presence of the unfamiliar man sharing Maryam's box.

Forba knew that, whatever the circumstances, she had to respond.

"I am sorry Madam, I do not believe that I do. It does not look to be very creased?" Translation: are you in danger? Have you been coerced into this meeting?

"What a pity – I had hoped to keep it as a souvenir." No – there is no danger.

Forba could not help but let her eyes flicker

again to the man, who held himself with a certain tension in his bearing that suggested that he was, at any event, not without some knowledge of the danger which might shortly be upon them. Maryam, noticing the glance, stepped forward and took the tray, placing it on a small trestle table at the rear of the box and, at her closest approach to Forba murmured, "He's my husband. He knows everything. You can trust him."

19

Tomas, not a specialist interrogator, was nevertheless well known amongst his colleagues for his skill at extracting confessions without excessive force, and for his restrained demeanour, even when hearing the most shocking confessions.

"What?!"

All of his famed composure had deserted him at that moment. He stared disbelievingly at Forba, unable to credit what she had just told him. The young girl, Elyssa, was still walking between them. Now she looked mutely back and forth, seemingly unable to understand what the heightened emotion stemmed from. Noting her distress, Tomas smiled reassuringly at her, and continued as calmly as he could manage.

"I apologise for my outburst. But you must accept that this history of yours strains credibility. I had difficulty enough believing that Maryam might have been involved in this matter behind Victor's back! But I cannot believe that he was complicit in it. We are both aware of the occupation which he was practising, even in those days, and which he still practices now."

He brushed aside the response that Forba was starting to formulate.

"You cannot seriously be suggesting that an investigator, a colleague in all likelihood of the guards who had been assaulted and killed earlier in the day, outside the Tower, was aware of what had happened and his wife's part in it, and he had made no objection!"

Forba stopped walking and turned to face him. The sunlight, filtered through the light canopy of leaves above them, cast dappled patterns of shade over her features. Ahead of them the rest of the group were pressing on through the woods, seemingly untroubled by the outbursts behind them. Anxiety showed in Forba's face, but when she spoke her voice was firm and her tone was surprisingly unapologetic.

"I am saying nothing of the sort, as you would know if you had been listening to the words I used. Tomas, I comprehend that this has been something of a shock for you. Knowing, as we have done for some time, that it must have been Maryam's husband who sent you to find us, Merson and I have wrestled with how best to introduce this subject. It is why we have explained so much of the background to that meeting – so that you might understand how someone might come to believe so strongly in what we were investigating that they would put their own life in danger."

"I do understand that. I never knew Maryam but I can readily believe that the serious matters which you have been talking about would have captured the attention of an academic in her position. I still struggle myself with the enormity of the revelations you have made to me, and I only know a fraction of what you and Maryam must have discovered.

But..."

"Tomas, understanding Maryam's motivations is not easy. I will never fully know what made her commit herself so readily to our cause. In Victor's case, however, it was all a good deal more straightforward. He loved his wife. Loved her enough that the duties he owed to the Tower, or his colleagues, were nothing compared to that."

Shyly, Elyssa slid a hand into Tomas's and tugged at it, urging him to continue along the path after the others. Grudgingly he did so, and was rewarded by an innocent radiant smile which once again seemed to lift a weight from him and gave him a chance to calm his thoughts.

Forba evidently took the loosening of his shoulder muscles, and his willingness to start moving again, as a sign that he was also willing to persist with the conversation. She shouldered her pack, and resumed her steady pace on Elyssa's far side.

"I spoke to him, you know? Not that evening. There was no time and for all Maryam's words I had no reason to believe that he could be trusted. But I was soon to be given all the evidence I could have wanted on that score.

"I simply thanked Maryam for the papers, and assured her that we would resume contact after a discreet period of time had passed. In the meantime, I urged her to maintain a low profile, but to continue to behave as if everything was normal. Then I left, just as the next Act was beginning, returning to the kitchens and finding a moment unobserved to slip away from my role as waitress, retrieve my cloak, and leave the building.

"But something still kept me from leaving the area. Even after so many years of dwelling on that night I cannot tell whether it was my superstitions, or whether it is just that I was not ready to return to my hotel and be alone again with my thoughts of Lariad's loss. Whatever the reason, I made my way into another building a street or two away. Its roof seemed likely to offer a good observation point for the front of the theatre. At the time, I think that I had persuaded myself that I just wanted to see that Maryam made it home safely. In the end, there was little I could do to secure that."

She paused, and Tomas glanced at her over the top of Elyssa's head. Forba was staring straight ahead, and Tomas imagined that she was reliving the evening as she described it. Her profile had a bleak expression and Tomas suspected that his own features were set in similarly grim lines. For the time being he had suspended judgement on the issue of Victor's alleged involvement, and indeed his own views on the propriety of the actions that Maryam and the others had taken. Instead he found himself impatient, while far from eager, to hear the fate which had ultimately befallen Victor's wife all those years ago.

Forba remained in her waking dream for another few moments, and the three of them continued in silence. Tomas subconsciously gave the hand that he was holding a reassuring squeeze, as if it was Elyssa and not Forba who was battling with her painful recollections. A break in the tree canopy showed Tomas the Tower looming ahead of them. He wondered how Forba felt to be coming back here after so recently fleeing to Braed Tor. That in turn prompted him to wonder why she had chosen to come to work here at all, after the traumatic events of her youth.

Forba too, looked up at the Tower and sighed.

"That evening, as I switched my attention between the entrance of the theatre and the moonlit shadow of the Tower looming up out of the darkness behind it, I had a lot of time with my thoughts. I dwelt again on the concern that had been troubling me for a while. What good were any of us really doing? It struck me that we had put Maryam in very considerable danger, and that nothing had changed with Lariad's death. Now, it seemed, there would be even more desire for us to keep going, so that Lariad would not have died in vain. I feared that reaction, even as I could feel it within me. Lariad had not, I was sure, given up his life with any thought of a higher cause. He had put himself in danger to protect Maryam, just as I had. He had also been trying to protect me.

"I wondered how those in the Tower, the families of the guards that we had killed and injured earlier that day, would view what Lariad and I had done. We would be thought by them – by the majority of the citizens of Car Peronel – to be a dangerous element, little better than criminals. You may think the same. Who, indeed, was to say that we were not? By the laws of the land that is precisely what we were, and for all our belief that our course was set for the betterment of human-kind, we might very easily have been wrong."

She glanced across at Tomas, tears on her cheeks. Ahead of them, the others had stopped and taken cover yet again, prompted no doubt by some sound or movement on the path ahead. Elyssa darted forward to join the larger group and Tomas and Forba left the track and entered the shelter of the undergrowth. No sounds, beyond the background natural noises of the woods, betrayed the group's presence, or indicated what threat might have caused them to hide. Peering ahead Tomas saw Merson in conversation with Lias Nefflor. The composer stood abruptly, pulling the hood of his travelling cloak over his head and seeming to merge with the trees, moving forward as if to scout out their path. Forba continued to speak as if there had been no interruption, murmuring quietly in the stillness of the woodland air.

"I came as close as I have ever come to loving the Tower that night. Seeing things suddenly through the eyes of those who we had set ourselves against, I saw the futility of what we were trying to achieve. Nothing we had learned of the elves by that time gave us any great confidence that they would think us anything other than pitiful and worthless. Why would we try to bring that attitude back into the world? Was not the order, the mundanity of everyday life, preferable to the chaos which had plagued the past? I sat there, unable to move from my self-appointed vigil, but in my mind practising for the discussion that I would have with Merson, as I explained to him that we had made a terrible mistake.

"And then Maryam and her husband came out of the theatre."

Forba seemed to shrink into herself. Her voice became fainter and Tomas had to strain to make out her words. Ahead of them, the woods remained silent and still.

"She was extremely beautiful, you know?"

Tomas nodded absently, his mind cast back once again to that funereal picture hanging in Victor's entrance hall.

"I saw her coming down the steps with her husband. In my memory she was radiant in the torch-light, a bright point in the darkness. They boarded their carriage, and the driver flicked his reins, setting them in motion. As they reached the corner where my look out point was located, they started to gather speed. Foolishly, perhaps instinctively, I leant out from my cover to look straight down on the roof of the carriage as they took the corner."

Another pause. Another deep breath.

"You must remember to yourself that in the darkness I had only fragments of images and that I have spent a long time thinking on what may have happened. I pledge you no oath that events unfolded exactly in the way I am describing. As I looked over the edge, I had an impression of a sudden flash of light. From what I saw afterwards, I believe that a man, standing on the corner, had unmasked a dark lantern directly into the face of the outside horse of the oncoming pair. In doing so he took a terrible risk, of course, but as was fairly likely the horse shied away from the light and into the path of its inside neighbour. Both panicked and the inside horse fell. Something else may have been involved in that, because afterwards it seemed that one of that horse's hamstrings had been sliced clean through. The carriage capsized.

"Even before the sound of the crash had faded, and long before anyone was able to react, a man bearing a lantern approached the driver, sprawled on the road. I think it was the same man from the corner. Another man climbed up on the carriage, which lay on its side with wheels spinning. He opened the passenger door and dropped down into the interior. He was back in a moment, in which time the lantern-man had knocked the driver unconscious and knelt to do something to his head. I... even now I cannot believe that I did nothing, but I assure you that it was over in moments. People were streaming down the hill from the theatre, and the two men had barely made their escape into the next street before the carriage was surrounded by anxious helpers. By that time it was far, far too late."

Responding to an unnoticed signal, or simply eager to bring the conversation to a close, Forba suddenly motioned to Tomas to get to his feet and gestured to him to move forwards to join the rest of the group. "Maryam was dead. We heard it was the impact that killed her, but of course we cannot be sure. Victor had a head injury and looked dead to me when they pulled him from the carriage, but he was lucky. He only lost a leg. As for the driver..."

They were nearing the rest of the group, and Tomas saw Merson's face, peering anxiously at them both from the undergrowth, a hand gesturing them to get themselves into concealment. Forba finished her sentence as they settled themselves into their new position.

"...they cut out his tongue."

From the unfinished draft Cyclopaedia:

Precinct (n. pri-sinkt)

Although the precincts are, in historical terms, a very recent innovation, it would be remiss in the extreme for them not to be included within this landmark collection of knowledge, so significant is the part that they have come to play in the life of Askuria.

A precinct is a walled city administered by a corporation operating under royal charter, and with leave to raise taxes, set internal by-laws and administer the infrastructure of the city. Consistently with elvish orthodoxy (see The Markt, Corporations and Economic Purity), the corporation itself is a private body, contracted by the Crown for the sole purpose of administering the precinct, albeit that successful corporations have begun (at time of writing) to tender for the charters to run other, less successful precincts.

The tax revenue levied from the citizens of each precinct is applied by a corporation exclusively within the confines of its precinct. The successful corporations are those which are able, as far as possible, to administer the precinct entirely from within their tax revenue, so that the greatest possible part of the charter fee paid from the Royal Treasury may be taken as profit. A necessary by-product of this has been that as a general rule service provisions for which the precinct corporations sub-contract, have necessarily also had to become self-funding.

As predicted by the prevailing economic theory, this has led (even in the short time for which precincts have been in operation) to a uniformity of approach. Very little research is permitted to be undertaken into these matters, but from the investigations of this body, it is clear that in real terms the cost of living within the precincts has increased. Commensurate with that, there has been a rise in the perceived status of those living within them.

This in turn has created a tension. Existing occupants have paid increasing amounts of money for the services which they enjoy, through direct taxation but also through the added costs levied by the corporation's sub-contractors in the fields of tax-collection, law enforcement, education and sanitation, among others. Having done so, they are reluctant to see those services over-stretched. On the other, there are those who live "beyond the green" (that is, outside of the areas covered by the precinct authorities) whose sole means of support is directly from the Royal Treasury, or whatever they can contract for themselves. In the case of this latter group, there has been large scale emigration, from the towns and villages, and from the countryside, by those seeking the prosperity and perceived status that derives from occupancy of the precincts.

To date, this tension has been resolved in favour of those with the largest resources. The walls of the precincts have got higher, and more well-defended. Those unable to get leave (by demonstrating possession of some useful skill, or through some other qualification such as wealth) are trapped beyond the walls, unable to improve their circumstances by being denied access to the quality of services enjoyed by their brethren within the precincts. This is described, euphemistically, as their "freedom of choice".

Life within the precincts does not come without its price, however. In addition to the monetary cost, there is also the inescapable fact that the erection of barriers to the movement of workers, goods and services is entirely contrary to the economic orthodoxy of the elves which is professed to motivate the precinct-dwellers. Nor is border control the only regulation to which those within the precincts are obliged to subscribe, as a price for the quality of life which they wish to enjoy. Thus, consistently across every precinct in Askuria, there is a trend (examined in more detail in Appendix CXIV) towards stringent population control..."

20

(Extracts from the voluntary confession of [Subject T187356]. Interview 8. Collated from the files of the Justice Authority. Quaestor's words redacted throughout.)

... My dear fellow! That is precisely what she said!

(Laughter)

That was most convivial. It has been some time since I have had the pleasure of a civilised dining companion.

Yes, I suppose that one must. I had told you, I think, all that you needed to hear of our footsore journey to Car Peronel. No, that is not quite correct. Shortly before we reached the precinct we had a somewhat unexpected encounter. We were being led by Lias Nefflor and Merson across the woodland lying to the south of the precinct, and less than an hour's brisk walk from the gates. You may tell me that this is no longer regarded as safe land, but by my reckoning we were well within the green at that point.

I was therefore both alarmed and dismayed when, forging on through the woodland as we were, we stumbled upon a marauding band of orks. This was in broad daylight mark you, if it could ever truly be said to be light under the canopies of the trees. They were a small group, of about a dozen or so, and I fancy that Merson and Rauor Tell, both uncommonly good sword-fighters or so I understand, gave a decent account of themselves in the end. You will well imagine that I took no part in the combat. I possess not the least martial skill, and would undoubtedly have proved an obstruction to my rather more athletic uncles.

At any event, unexpected as they were, the orks did cause us a significant delay, and it was not until late in the afternoon that we found ourselves before the gates of the precinct.

What say? Yes, allow me a moment to tax my brains. I have no great flair for geography, but I believe I recollect one of the others stating that it was the western gate. That would certainly explain my recollection that the sun was casting our shadows before us as we approached.

No, we were not challenged, quite the reverse. I confess that I assumed that uncle Merson enjoyed some special status with the guards, since he had no sooner begun speaking with them than the gates were swung open and we were being ushered inside with smiles and all compliments. Now that I come to think of it, it is certainly possible that he did pass some small package or purse to the captain, but I was not close at hand and I hasten to say that I would not wish to implicate any man on what is little more than mere supposition on my part.

Once we were within the precinct, aunt Forba assumed command of our group, leading us through the thronged streets running in a circle around the inside of the city wall. I do not know what the roadway might be called, but we turned right from the gate if that is any assistance?

I was forgetting that you know the location of the property in any event.

I noted, as we passed it, a guard post close by the southern gate. You will know the one – its walls connect directly to the outer wall of the precinct and it has a large courtyard and stabling within its confines. In contrast to the western gate, here the guards were vigilant and subjected us to a close scrutiny as we passed. I am sure that our dishevelled apparel attracted attention and I commented to the others that it would be important to ensure that we were all able to make a proper toilet before we next went out amongst the populace.

At the same time, I wonder whether some part of my mind was already considering how best I ought to deal with the situation that I had found myself in, and was drawing my attention to that guard post. It certainly made more of an impression on me than most of the other buildings we passed, and indeed than the accommodation, for want of a better word, that aunt Forba then proceeded to obtain for us.

To be charitable to her, the house was far from small. It was, indeed, far from anything, being close up against the outer wall, and inconveniently distant from the main thoroughfares of the precinct. Each of us had our own room, but with only the most basic of amenities. We had to fetch our own water for washing, although Rauor was kind enough to do so for me when I requested it. I cannot speak for the others, but I found the selection of clothes hung in the closet of my room to be wholly inadequate and some of it several seasons out of fashion. From what I saw of the others' apparel when we met for dinner, I suspect that we all had to grapple with the same difficulties.

It being Fest, and without any person having had the foresight to ensure that some servants were retained, we were all required to assist with the preparation of dinner. Despite my protestations, that included me, and I found myself with uncle Lias, cleaning and slicing vegetables. After our shared watch the previous night, we had not had any further opportunity to speak during our journey. Indeed, he had throughout the day separated himself from the rest of us. Mistakenly, as it transpired, I thought that we might while away the time spent in our chore, by discussing again his situation, and what future he might look forward in light of the consequences of his most execrable decision. I had had a number of thoughts as to how he might seek partially to redeem himself, were he to wish to involve himself further in the cultural sphere, and it might have been expected that one in his position would be slow to reject any advice or assistance, honestly proffered.

To the contrary, however, uncle Lias lost no time in making clear to me – in unnecessarily vulgar terms, that my assistance and advice were not required. The remainder of our time was spent in silence and I must confess that some of his more colourful observations wounded me deeply. I am not, as you may imagine, accustomed to hearing such language, certainly not directed towards myself. Even though I had the consolation of being the innocent party in the exchange, this did little to soften the injury. Consequently, I was somewhat shaken, and it was no doubt apparent to the others through my demeanour at dinner that something was the matter. Nevertheless, and unaccountably, not one of them took the time to enquire after my mental or emotional well-being, whether at table or privately afterwards.

I had much to reflect on and retired early for the night, spending many hours rehearsing the varied invective to which I had been victim, but also the wider predicament in which we had found ourselves. Gradually, as I deliberated on these matters, it became clear to me that both were aspects of a wider endemic problem. There was little doubt from what I had seen that far from being the types of people to whom our parents should have entrusted us following their deaths, our uncles and aunt were embroiled in matters which were apt to expose me, and my sister, to considerable danger. Whatever their part in matters, innocent or otherwise, it was clear to me that continued association with them would be extremely prejudicial to my future prospects.

Where else was I to turn, however? With no other family that I knew of, and without any of the means of sustaining an independent lifestyle within the precincts, absent the goodwill and support of those from whom I was resolved to distance myself, I was at a loss.

It was as I lay there, anxious and perplexed, that I glanced out of my window into the moonlit night. By chance, rising up above the roofs of the buildings around us, shining strong and dependable beneath the stars, I could make out the upper portions of the Tower. I hesitate to suggest any sort of spiritual component to my decision, but I confess that I felt a sudden lifting in my heart, as at last I perceived that the solution to my problems lay before me.

I wonder if might have a little more wine? I confess that the emotion of the moment is still quite fresh with me.

I am obliged to you.

After that I fell into a largely untroubled sleep, and it was late the following morning before I awoke. Naturally, I understood that any plan to avail myself of the assistance of authority was not without its difficulties. I was quite sceptical that I would be afforded the opportunity to do so, but after a light breakfast it proved to be surprisingly easy to contrive a reason to leave the house. Once I had been able to do that, it took very little time to find my way back to the guard house that I had taken note of on the previous day. It was then, I think, the third day of Fest, and the festivities were still in full flood. At one or two points on my short walk to the guard house I felt the temptation simply to take the coins in my pocket, and make my way to some gaming hell, losing my concerns in drink and games of chance. I did not do so, however, and once at the guard house and confident of not being observed, I presented myself at their reception area, demanding to speak at once to the most senior officer on station.

Yes, it took a little while. All proper procedures were followed. Once it had been established that I was not a reveller drunkenly attempting to enter the premises as part of a Fest-prank, I was admitted. I must, at this point, give proper praise to the quaestor captain who I was introduced to, Captain Boomel. Not for him any declining standards reflective of the holiday season. His uniform was neatly pressed, and his cravat well folded. I was much taken, in light of the constraints placed on him by the exigencies of the uniform code, with the small ways in which he had been able to reflect current fashionable requirements.

My own appearance at that stage was of course

some way from being in the pink of modernity. At once I had hastened to assure him that this owed more to a temporary impoverishment of circumstances, rather than any general lack of fine feeling or disregard for the strictures of style. Once this matter had been satisfactorily resolved, we quickly found that we were of one mind on many subjects, and dealt very well together.

Captain Boomel was indeed most sympathetic to my tale. Without the requirements of full confession which I am now under, I was able to deliver the salient points to him with considerable efficiency. He in turn, showed his insight by commenting first upon the considerable hardship which I, personally, must have laboured under. Thereafter we turned to the question of what may be done. For his part, his main concern was that I should be able to furnish some evidence of wrong-doing. In one sense, I had seen such evidence with my own eyes. All of those with whom I had travelled, apart of course from my sister, had been party to coercion of the guards of at least two precincts. They all carried concealed weapons and, as I now know, had at the time of the battle at uncle Merson's place in Braed Tor, been committing treason by seeking to resist apprehension.

In light of the circumstantial nature of that information, the captain averred himself to be interested to securing some further evidence. He sent for certain files which it appeared were already being maintained in relation to certain of my family, that is to say, my parents' friends. It was during the course of our review of these files that I appreciated, for the first time, quite how close I had come to being enmeshed with a group who were, by any standards, beyond the pale of civilised society. I had known, of course, of Lias Nefflor's conduct –

and as you know, I had deprecated it from the first. I had however, been unaware of the extent of Forba's involvement in the cyclopaedia project. I was quite shocked by the manner in which the editors of that work had perverted its true purpose, making it a vehicle for the most obscene sort of radical propaganda.

Many of these matters are already known to you, of course. Of all that I heard on that day, the greatest shock to me was to discover that uncle Merson was himself implicated in the same sort of radicalism. I had begun to think more highly of him, both in light of the manner in which he had come to my aid, and after seeing his obvious sartorial sense and the elegance of the establishment he maintained at Braed Tor. The unflattering picture painted of him by Captain Boomel, however, was of a man active in campaigning for so-called popular rights, something which even my naïve and provincial mind knew to be the preserve of the indolent, the corrupt or the morally base. His entire career appeared to have been predicated on the protection of such individuals from the appropriate supervision and control of the realm. The betrayal which I experienced at that point brought home to me that whatever I might be able to reveal of their secrets, I would be doing society a considerable service.

Luncheon was served and our discussions continued. The meal was one of the best that I had partaken of for some time, and all the more delicious coming after several days of intense deprivation. By the time we had finished eating,and were sat sampling a matured portwine from the armoury's cellars, an understanding existed. I would return to my supposed family, and through varied displays of loyalty and affection, acquire further information about their offences to date, as well as any further plans they might have for the future. Even then, shocked as I was by the extent of their collective depravity, I little imagined quite how far their plans might reach, or quite how low they had allowed their moral standards to decline. But it is best that I do not speak of my later discoveries now, for the reasons that I explained to you while we were dining.

Indeed. And on that very subject, were you minded to continue this interview now? My evening is bespoken with a concert under the supervision of Captain Boomel, and albeit that I must attend under some secrecy, and manacled, I would nevertheless welcome the opportunity to make myself as presentable as possible.

I am grateful to you. Let us resume tomorrow morning then, as you suggest.

[Interview suspended]

[Handwritten note from Captain Boomel to Quaestor Feiger – dated Fest XXV Tor.]

"My lord Quaestor,
The most curious coincidence. T187356 has just made an approach. There is more to this than we had supposed, assuming that he is to be trusted.

I will cultivate the source and report further at the end of this blasted Fest-time.

All courtesy and respect,
[Signed] Capt. Boomel"

[Extract ends]

21

Tomas was awoken by intense cramp in his left calf. Quietly, in order not to wake Idony, he rolled to the side of the bed pressing his mouth shut to forestall the outburst that was swelling in him. After a minute of agony, the cramp started to subside, and at last he was able to sit up and to reach for the carafe of water that usually stood at his bedside. Even as his eyes registered its absence, an aching body reminded him of his adventures over the previous two days. Grudgingly his mind accepted that he was in a strange bed, and far away from his wife and home.

Standing one-footed he lifted the cramped leg and massaged his calf, leaning on the window-sill of the room with his other hand. Doing so, he was able to look out at the busy streets of Car Peronel beyond. The house had its back to the outer wall of the precinct, an unobtrusive location which was perfectly suited to their requirements. Tomas was once again struck by the apparent extent of the resources available to this group who, as far as he could tell, were only half a dozen or so in strength.

He had not been party to the arrangements that Forba had made to procure the key to this house, but it seemed to him that it had been standing empty, waiting for their arrival. As he had seen the previous morning, even in the midst of the countryside, they had access to concealed stores of weaponry and other material. He suspected that they might also have some slightly more esoteric equipment.

For all its humble status in the geographical hierarchy of the precinct, the house commanded very useful lines of sight in all directions. The bay windows gave a clear view of the curving road that ran left and right around the inner circumference of the wall. There was also a major thoroughfare directly in Tomas's line of sight, which ran slightly downhill towards the island complex at the far end of the precinct, housing the government buildings and, of course, the Tower. In each direction, the streets were packed with the massed populace. This far into Fest, some of the more remote precincts would have subsided into stupor, the initial excesses of alcohol and violence having extracted a heavy price. The citizens of Car Peronel had rather more stamina, however, and even with the sun still rising in the sky the energy of the crowds was perceptible from his distant vantage point.

Tomas put his foot tentatively to the floor. The cramp had subsided, but he was cautious about placing any further strain on the muscles for another few minutes. He stood patiently, conscious that the rest of the household were probably already awake, but preferring tardiness to any evidence of physical inadequacy. The thought prompted a faint smile, dimly reflected in the window's glass. He had not been so preoccupied with his physical capabilities, or with a desire to show himself an equal to those around him, since his days of military service. He admitted, within the confines of his private thoughts, that his present company made him feel both old and inadequate, even though in truth his age was not so very different from theirs.

It was impossible to think of his time in the military without thinking of Henrik and the others. Henrik, of course, in particular had not been far from his thoughts over the preceding days. Tomas was troubled by the despair that he had sensed in his former comrade-in-arms when they had met on the eve of Fest. Even with all his other preoccupations, he was determined that now that they had safely managed to enter the capital, he would seize the opportunity to speak again with Henrik at more leisure. Together, he was sure, they would find a solution to his friend's difficult dilemma.

As he dressed and prepared to make his way downstairs to join the rest of the company, his thoughts turned to his own problems. He felt that he was constantly in danger of losing sight of his purpose in associating with this group. Whatever his intentions, every conversation seemed to end up further eroding the distance he was trying to preserve from them. It was inevitable perhaps, that their shared experiences of danger had made them closer. Between the ork attacks during the previous night and shortly before their arrival at Car Peronel, and the incident in the cave, it had been an intense couple of days.

He wondered whether the door had been locked. Testing it now, he found that it was open, although of course that was not to say that it had remained so all night. Nevertheless, it meant that once he had finished dressing he was free to explore the interior of the house. With only a qualm of guilty feelings, which he quickly suppressed, he set out to do so.

From below, perhaps even from one of the subterranean levels, the echoing sound of voices, raised in some spirits, rose up to his ears. The wood panelling within the central stairwell muffled the sound so that individual words were inaudible, but Tomas did not detect any anger or animosity in the voices of the speakers. He looked around him. Confirming his impressions of the previous night, he saw that the floor was made up exclusively of sleeping chambers. As far as he could recall, he, Lias Nefflor and the two younger members of the group had each had a room on this floor. On the next floor down had been the larger sleeping chambers which Merson, Forba and Rauor Tell had occupied.

Peering down the central stair-case, noting the dust in the air which streams of sunlight picked out at each level, he could see the tiled entry hall. From memory this opened onto a number of formal reception rooms. They had dined in one of these on the preceding evening, on food collectively prepared in the kitchens and service areas located underground.

All in all, it was a standard design of town-house, instantly familiar to Tomas from numerous similar properties which he had visited in the course of his employment in Rivertop. He put his hand on the banister to begin his descent, when suddenly he felt a faint shiver on the back of his neck, a signal from his intuition that there was something of interest that he had not yet considered. Pausing, he looked again around the landing, at the various open doors and the strewn bedding and clothing visible within. At first, he dismissed without reflection any thought of intruding on the privacy of his hosts. But as he stood there, unable to move, he collected himself and recalled his purpose and duty. This was an opportunity, and perhaps only a fleeting one, to discover something more about their plans and purposes, so that he could make his report to Victor.

Thoughts of Victor opened yet another layer of complexities. Even as he turned and stepped back up onto the landing, Tomas acknowledged to himself that he was deeply conflicted as to Victor's place within the stories that he had been told. On the previous day the narrative had been interrupted at the point of Maryam's death by an encounter with what turned out to be a small group of orks. In daylight, the skills of Tomas's travelling companions made the contest very one sided, although he had given a good account of himself. Nevertheless the time for discussion had passed and the approach to Car Peronel had preoccupied all of their attention. It was only after dinner that Merson had resumed the tale. He had explained that, following Maryam's death, all of the group had been careful not to cross Victor's path, and readied themselves for the possibility that he would initiate an investigation into their involvement. Forba had been particularly anxious that she would be implicated in any such inquiry.

Eventually, however, news had reached them that a diary had been discovered which appeared to demonstrate that Maryam had been pursuing her enquiries alone, for her own interest, and without the least thought of sharing the information with others. Victor had demonstrably known this to be untrue, after the meeting with Forba at the theatre, and yet had not contradicted it. From this, Merson and the others had concluded that Victor was determined to keep any wider implications a secret.

Forba had encountered him again, several years later, when she was attending an official function at the Tower on behalf of the Lord of Agriculture. He had recognised her at once, and had not been discourteous, but it had been plain that he had no intention of acknowledging any prior connection. With nothing but their guilt to be satisfied by pursuing the matter, the group had resolved to risk no further contact with him.

Preoccupied with these thoughts, Tomas found that his feet were leading him along the landing, and towards the nearest of the open doors. This was Lias Nefflor's room, and Tomas's experienced eyes noted that the bed, though rumpled as if to suggest occupancy, had not in fact been slept in the previous night. Instead a chair, placed so that its occupant could stare out of the window at the streets leading up to the Tower, had around it various scattered pieces of detritus that suggested that Nefflor has spent the night in sleepless contemplation.

There was little else to be seen in the room. Tomas wondered what his reaction might have been, days earlier, if he had known that he would so soon afterwards be standing in the bedroom of the composer whose music had moved him so profoundly. From the colour and vibrancy of the man's compositions, he would never have anticipated such a dull, small and uninteresting chamber, although it did seem to suit the man himself. On the previous evening, Tomas had finally had the chance to tell Nefflor how much he and his wife had been moved by the performance of Thonthiel's Farewell that they had attended. The composer had smiled weakly, thanked him, and retreated once more into silence.

Tomas left the room, and continued his exploration around the landing. He determined that he would not linger in any of the other rooms for longer than it took to get an initial impression of their contents. After that, unless his intuition guided him towards anything out of place or remarkable, he would make his way downstairs and join the company.

The first of the two rooms was that belonging to Alyster. It seemed entirely unremarkable. Alyster himself, however, was another matter and Tomas remained unsure how to read the younger man's character. Last night at dinner he had, in contrast to his behaviour earlier in the day, given the appearance of being at ease and comfortable in the group. He had told jokes which, although laboured, received a warm response from the others. There had been a sense of some obstacle overcome, some burden lifted, which had lightened the young man's face and removed for a while the perpetual scowl which until then Tomas had taken to be a permanent feature.

Then, without warning, this mood had passed. Tomas had taken a little wine by this point and, having until then been content to observe the to and fro of conversation along the table, had leaned forward to venture some opinion or other on the quality of the food which they had been enjoying. None of the others appeared to have regarded this as remarkable, but Alyster had looked startled, and immediately dropped his head and subsided in his chair. Apart from the occasional sullen glance, Tomas observed no further contribution from the young man to the evening's discourse.

The absence of any reaction from the others indicated that these rapid changes of mood were far from unprecedented. Still Tomas had the sense that the withdrawn and brooding appearance were a performance that was being staged for his personal benefit, even though he could not imagine what the purpose of such behaviour might be.

The final room was Elyssa's, and Tomas merely darted his head inside, doubly concerned not to commit any impropriety where this young lady was concerned. To his amazement, however, his gaze was met by those hooded blue eyes, gazing serenely out of that pale and placid face. Elyssa was sitting, entirely motionless, in a chair set in the middle of the room, close to the foot of her bed. Tomas could not now withdraw without seeming to implicate himself further, and from the simple smile which brightened Elyssa's face he could tell that he was not an unwelcome intruder. Nevertheless, he scrupulously stood with one hand on the door, while he tried to formulate some explanation for his presence there.

In her quiet, gentle voice, Elyssa took the initiative.

"Did Al send you to get me? Is it breakfast time?"

Tomas swallowed and forced a smile. "I was just going down myself. Are you coming?"

Elyssa stood, unabashed by the fact that she was clad only in her nightwear. Tomas averted his gaze. For some inexplicable reason he felt a hot flush of embarrassment on his cheeks, in a way that he had not experienced for many years. "I'll.. I'll tell them you will be down shortly, shall I?"

Making a confused retreat, Tomas's discomfort was not decreased by the musical peal of laughter that followed him teasingly down the stairs.

As Tomas had anticipated, the next two floors were devoid of occupants, but his appetite for investigation had been sated for the time being. He continued straight down to the main servants hall below ground, where the others were breakfasting. Still struggling to maintain his composure, Tomas relayed the message that Elyssa was not yet dressed and may be joining them later.

In a further reversal of his previous manner, Alyster thanked him warmly, and apologised on behalf of the group that they had not waited for him before starting breakfast. Tomas in turn apologised for rising so late, and in this cordial fashion was soon seated amongst them all, consuming a plate of eggs and bacon, cooked simply in the country style, but none the less delicious for that.

He soon discovered that a consensus had been reached that, now that they were within the walls of Car Peronel, there was little to be gained by urgent travels elsewhere. Fest continued, and the group had been remarkably lucky so far, their battles with the orks notwithstanding, not to encounter more sustained threats during their journey. While each of them had lives to which they wished to return, all seemed reconciled to the fact that this was going to be considerably easier to achieve once Fest was past.

Tomas had the sense, too, that for all the disruption and uncertainty of the previous two days, and his own unexpected intrusion into the group, Merson at least was not dissatisfied with their current situation. At one point, as he returned with water from the basement well, so that the breakfast things might be washed, he heard Rauor Tell exclaim,

"It doesn't exactly make things easier!"

Slowing his pace, so as not to interrupt their discussion, Tomas heard Merson's calm response:

"Nor does it make them more difficult. We are on course my friend. Our paintwork project has caught on as we hoped, and the markers are getting attention in the right places. As for our own strategy, we may have had to improvise a little, but for all that we are still on our schedule."

A chair scraped in the room ahead and Tomas jerked guiltily. He took two quiet steps backwards and then made more noisy progress back into the servants' hall, to find each of the speakers engaged in other matters, with no sign of the curtailed conversation which had just taken place.

In light of the new-found complacency amongst his hosts, Tomas felt that it might be timely to make the request which he had been formulating in his mind since he had awoken that morning. Returning to his seat, he turned to Forba who was sitting at the head of the table.

"Do I gather that we are to remain in Car Peronel for the time being?"

It was Merson who answered, however, pulling out a chair and interposing himself between Forba and Tomas.

"We are indeed," he said, placing a smiling emphasis on the first word. "You will appreciate, I am sure, that in the present circumstances I would be reluctant for us to part company. There is much for us still to tell you, and quite apart from that, the journey to Rivertop would not be without its difficulties. Some of our number will be returning there as soon as Fest is ended, and I am sure that they would be very happy to give you safe conduct back to your home."

Tomas resisted the urge to express gratitude for this indication that he might be returned safely to Rivertop. For all the trust that had been engendered between them, he knew that he had no real reason to take Merson at his word. In any event, he had more immediate concerns.

"I had another reason for asking, in fact. An old comrade-in-arms of mine lives in Car Peronel. I met him very briefly on my way through here prior to Fest. He is troubled by some personal matters and I had hoped that, if we were to remain in the precinct today, I might take the opportunity to find him out."

"I can see no objection to that," Merson responded, "one of the others will be very happy to accompany you."

Tomas hesitated. He had made up his mind that conducting himself straightforwardly was the only way to retain whatever trust he had earned from the group. Even so, there was a chance that his motivations would be mis-read.

"There is a problem, however. My friend is employed by the quaestors. I may have to seek him out at the guard house, and in any event I did not want to conceal that he is in that sense a professional colleague, albeit employed by our competitors."

To his surprise, Merson laughed.

"You may go where you wish Tomas, I would not seek to restrain you! Indeed, for all that I would prefer otherwise, if you feel that you must make a report, I will not prevent you, whatever terms it may be in. You see, I choose very carefully those in whom I place my trust. Almost all of them are in this room."

There was a general ripple of good-natured laughter. Tomas found himself instinctively joining in, but this only added to the confused turmoil within him. As the laughter subsided, Merson continued.

"I would like to send Alyster with you, however." He raised a hand to forestall Tomas's objections. "Not into the guard house itself, I assure you. But he would like to see something of the precinct, and I do not wish more of us than necessary to be away from the house. Let him know when you have tired of his company, and he will be capable of finding his own way home, have no concern about that."

And in a peremptory manner which suggested that to his mind it was already agreed, he moved on to new matters.

"At what hour do you wish to make your visit?"

Tomas mentally conceded defeat, for the present at least. "Not until after the lunch hour," he replied, "if the guard post runs on standard lines then the busiest time is the hour after noon. I would rather visit my friend a little later if that is convenient." Perhaps, he hoped, Alyster would have forgotten his ambition to explore the precinct by then.

"Very well," responded Merson. "I imagine that you would like to resume our conversation from the other day. Unfortunately there are some matters that I feel I must discuss with young Alyster. Full grown he may be, but I still have a great deal to instruct him on, if he is to make a name for himself in the world."

No sooner had the opportunity of escape presented itself, however, than it was withdrawn.

"Our discussions will not take anything more than an hour or two to complete," he continued, "so perhaps in the meantime Rauor can illuminate any areas in which you feel that our explanations to date have been lacking."

"Gladly," replied Rauor Tell, jumping to his feet. "The pooliard room receives a good deal of indirect sunlight at this hour of the day – perhaps you would like to play a frame or two while we talk?"

With a resigned sense that there was not a moment of his day that had not been choreographed in advance, Tomas smiled his agreement to this proposal, and stood.

It was strange to Tomas, to be talking at last to the man whose disappearance had set him in motion, several days before. Raour Tell had been a constant presence since the group had met up in the wilds outside Braed Tor, but Tomas had not yet had an opportunity to speak with him alone, and without prospect of interruption.

Strangely, now that he had the chance, there was only one question forcing itself into his mind. With none of his usual subtlety, without even any preliminary conversation, he asked it.

"How did you leave Lord Kerton's place, without being noticed?"

Rauor glanced up from filling the major rack with its truncated diamond of many coloured balls, and smiled.

"You don't waste any time - I appreciate that! Merson can keep his rhetorical flourishes, I prefer to speak simply."

He paused to press the diamond into place, but it was plain that he was intending to continue. Tomas filled the triangular minor rack with its three whites, and positioned it accordingly near to the opposite end of the table.

"If you have met my lord Kerton, you will know that I could not ask him for assistance. When I received the message, I knew that I had to get to Braed Tor as soon as I could. I really had not intended to attract any attention in the process," he glanced up at Tomas and there was a strange half-smile on his face which quickly disappeared, "but as I went to the door of my room, I heard Kerton and his brat, arguing in the stairway, and I could not face the confrontation. I left by the window instead!"

Rauor plainly found the recounting of the tale entertaining, but Tomas's puzzlement deepened with every word. Clearly some of his confusion showed on his face as Rauor leaned across to pass him a cue. He smiled and came around the table, patting Tomas on the arm as he did so. "I am sorry, I am obviously not doing a good job of clarifying this. Perhaps I should deal with one matter at a time!"

Tomas laughed – Rauor's good humour was certainly infectious. "I thank you!" He located the black and placed it behind the fence of whites in a traditional starting alignment. "You will have to make allowances for this simple investigator. We prefer to receive our information in linear fashion." Rauor waited for him to take his first shot, and for the brightly coloured balls displaced by a well-deflected central white to come to a rest, before he continued to speak.

"Very well. To explain something more of our circumstances: Merson, Forba and the rest of us remain in regular communication concerning our two young wards. Whatever our other commitments and obligations, we have each of us stood ready when required to come to their assistance. It has been so ever since the deaths of their parents."

"Forba and I have both taken a special interest in the pair, indeed it was the two of us who moved out to the farmhouse immediately after their parents died, in order to educate and protect Alyster, and Elyssa of course, as they grew up. That is not to say that Lias and Merson are not equally fond of them both, but Merson's work would not have permitted that he left Braed Tor for such a prolonged period, and Lias is not really temperamentally suited to the work of tutor or governess!"

Tomas smiled involuntarily at the image conjured by this last comment. In his distraction, an attempted deflection shot off the central firm cushion rebounded poorly and resulted in a penalty. Rauor barely paused as he lined up his first shot, sinking his target without any noticeable effort.

"There was also, of course, an element of concern for their safety. I do not know how much you know of their situation before last week?" He was lining up a long shot and glanced at Tomas from his position leaning over the table. He seemed to read the response in his face before Tomas could frame it, "No? Well, they were located in a farmhouse, deep in the countryside, thirty or forty miles to the east of Braed Tor." His next shot required a difficult screw back, and Rauor attempted it gamely, but unsuccessfully. Tomas, perversely feeling that he was not contributing a fair share to the conversation, stepped back up to the table.

"That certainly sounds remote. Did they have very much difficulty with orks?"

"Hardly!" Tomas looked up from his shot, and Rauor, appearing to recognise that he needed to provide some further explanation, hastened to continue. "I mean to say that Forba and I were very quickly able to establish in the minds of the orks that the farmhouse and its immediate surroundings were dangerous territory for them to stray into. We were greatly assisted by the fact that the land in question lies just within the marshallcy of Lord Hartrick. Even though he took no special interest in the two children, he has always been diligent in sending out patrols and maintaining border posts. Ork attacks and other banditry have been correspondingly rare in the lands that lie under his baton. It did not deter their recent attackers, however."

For a few minutes he sketched out the details of an encounter that Alyster had had with a group of unknown attackers in the week prior to Fest, and Merson's decision to move the "children" to safety within the precincts. "We all understood that there might be a time when the two of them were endangered, when we might need to put their safety ahead of any priorities in our own lives. Merson's message told me that the time had arrived, and the urgency of it made me feel that I had not a moment to lose."

Raour turned his face from Tomas – crouching down to examine the table before taking another shot. "I am certainly sorry that in the haste of my departure I gave Lord Kerton any anxiety, let alone that I have caused you the considerable disruption of investigating my disappearance! But my only thought was of the children and their safety, I do assure you."

Rauor clearly still viewed the two youngsters as his responsibility, and that led Tomas's thoughts in a different direction. After playing an unsuccessful shot of his own, he rested his cue, straightened and asked "Who were their parents? It seems plain that it was not Pepina and Lariad as I had originally supposed."

Rauor sank the last of his colours and with a ricochet potted his target white as well. Placing his cue carefully on the table, he gestured towards a couple of armchairs which were bathed in indirect sunlight. "There are several aspects to that question, and there are matters which it would be better for Merson to explain to you. But I will tell you what I can, if it will assist you to understand."

They seated themselves comfortably, and Tomas

declined a proffered drink.

"Forba has told you, I think, about what became of Lariad?"

Tomas nodded.

"She blames herself for it, even though we all of us shared in the guilt of his death. Pepina, though, felt it the most acutely of all. Grief and remorse are powerful emotions, and Pepina was never quite the same after that. We were still all living in Car Vandra at that stage. After Lariad's death, and indeed Maryam Appelsin's, we all needed some time to come to terms with what had happened. I think it took us too long to realise that Pepina was drifting away from us."

"One day, she simply disappeared, and we never saw her again."

22

Car Vandra, 20 years ago

"In the name of all the gods, where is she?"

Merson's eyes were staring round the room. Rauor had seldom seen him in such a rage. Yet the cause of the present outburst was not without precedent. Pepina Atto was missing again. More and more in the weeks following Lariad's death, she had distanced herself from the other members of the group. At first only Forba had remarked on it, carrying her own share of survivor guilt and thus more sensitive to the reactions of others to the dramatic events in Car Peronel. She had confided her concerns to Rauor, and he in turn had become more watchful.

Soon though, it had been clear that Pepina's changed attitude was not confined to any one member of the group. It had become clearer from the moment that Merson had over-ruled any prospect of revenge being taken against the officialdom of Car Peronel. She gave up on them. Each of them had their grief, and none begrudged

Pepina the right to grieve more profoundly and more intensely than the rest. As such her absence from the house, from the meetings in which they tried to devise a strategy for what they should do, went unremarked for longer than it should have done.

With the benefit of hindsight, Rauor saw that he ought to have spoken with Pepina, tried to understand the need that drove her to want vengeance, even at the risk of everything they had been working towards. Even Lias would have been a better prospect as a counsellor than Merson, but it was Merson, increasingly their leader by default, who had gone to see her. It was Merson, with his idealogical certainties, his lack of empathy, who had now driven her away.

They were meeting at Forba's place for once. A last meeting, convened at Merson's request, to decide on the direction of their group and whether Pepina would play any part in it. She had assured Merson, through Lias, that she would be there, but she was late and Merson was convinced she would not come at all.

"We do not know where she is, Merson, which is to say that none of us have discovered new information since the last time you asked." Only Rauor could speak like this to Merson, their long familiarity softening the harshness of the words. Even so, the man was making him feel nervous with his constant angry motion. "Sit down please, you are going to ruin Forba's rug with your pacing."

Merson gave no sign of having heard. Forba and Lias were engaged in quiet, urgent, conversation on the other side of the room. Suddenly Forba's voice carried more loudly "well, for heavens' sake you have to tell him, Lias!"

Both Merson and Rauor turned their heads at

this interjection. Merson was first to speak.

"Tell me, Lias? Tell me what?"

"I don't know where she is," Lias was stammering, blushing hotly, as he did in any confrontation, "but I talked to her yesterday. She was talking about showing you, showing us all, what could be done. Showing us what courage could do."

Merson stalked closer. Rauor resisted the urge to rise from his chair and restrain him, conscious that it would present an impression of them both converging on Lias, who continued as hesitantly as before. "I thought she was talking about plans. About coming to the meeting with a new strategy or something like that. Now I am less sure."

Merson stood staring at Lias for a few moments. Then his head sank and he drew in and expelled two deep breaths. He surprised Rauor by lowering himself into a chair before speaking, and when he spoke it was with a weary tone, the anger seeming to ebb out of him.

"I have had the same sense myself, and like you I fear that I have greatly underestimated the intensity of Pepina's sentiment in this matter. I am sorry Lias, all of you. If I am angry, I am angry with myself. I am very much afraid that we will not see Pepina again."

A silence spread over the room. This tone of resignation was one that the others were unaccustomed to hearing from Merson. All of them sat quietly for several minutes, each preoccupied with the same thoughts. Finally, Forba rose and walked to the windows, pulling the wooden cover aside to allow the last of the daylight into the room. "We can all of us find reasons to recriminate with ourselves. I have been as much to blame as any..."

She trailed off, and Rauor glanced round at her,

surprised by her hesitancy. He saw that she stood with her face to the window, and that her body was tight with tension. He sprang to his feet and made his way quickly to her side.

"What is it Forba?"

The question was redundant as soon as it was spoken. Across the town, dark black clouds boiled from the military district. It seemed that a dozen or more fires had taken hold within the barracks and armoury compounds, and there was no way of knowing what other damage might have been caused.

The four of them stood at the windows long into the evening. There was no question in any of their minds that this was Pepina's work – the coincidence was too great for it to be otherwise. Rapidly they made their plans. Knowing how slowly investigations would move, there was no urgent need to depart, although each personally resolved to pack their most valuable possessions and make ready to travel at short notice, if they detected any sign of closer scrutiny from the authorities. Equally, they knew that they could not rely on Pepina's involvement in these attacks remaining undetected, and that ultimately all of them would need to leave Car Vandra. They discussed their strategies, agreeing on plausible cover stories that would justify their departure from the city in the near future, preferably obscuring their trails in the process.

Finally, when all of these arrangements had been rehearsed and agreed, Merson prevailed upon them for a few more minutes. Sitting them down, he summarised the importance of the research that Rauor and Forba had undertaken and the contribution made by the lamented Maryam Appelsin. He explained his own conclusions, based on that work, and outlined what would need to be done next if those conclusions were accepted by the group.

They stood, and piled hands in silent agreement. The arrangements they were now to put in place meant that it would be several months before they saw one another again. Each of them would carry Merson's final words with them during that intervening period.

"We alone, perhaps, of all those living today, know something approaching the truth of the history of our world, and of the part that the elves played in it. We know something of their power, and that without it, our world is likely to remain stunted and undeveloped. We need that power, but we also understand the dangers – to us and to the world, if we invite that power back in unconditionally."

"We have lost Lariad and, I fear, we must assume that we have lost Pepina. You know how they need to be replaced. It is the only way in which we can have any hope of the ultimate victory that we need to achieve."

Car Peronel, 19 years ago

Rauor could never cross the open square at the foot of the Tower without feeling an uncomfortable tickle of remorse and anxiety. He knew well enough the location at which Lariad had died, from the plans of the city that Forba had used to brief the others after her return to Car Vandra the previous year. He could not bring himself to look directly at it, fearing even now that any inappropriate display of interest in the location might attract attention to him.

The sense was more intense on this particular

occasion as he made his way to a planned meeting with his former companions. It would be the first time that all four of them had met since the night of the Car Vandra fire. Forba's new found role as researcher on the staff of the Lord of Agriculture had also brought her to Car Peronel. They had met a few times, without intending to, but as far as possible they had tried to keep separate from one another. Rauor had been busy in any event, establishing a new life of his own, and a new circle of friends who placed considerable demands on his time. He had met with Merson once, in a short meeting contrived to look entirely accidental, and kept studiously brief for the benefit of any scrutiny that they might be under. He had not seen Lias at all.

It was not only the prospect of their imminent reunion which caused Rauor to be anxious. The meeting would also be an opportunity for the others to meet the two newest recruits to their cause. These were the candidates who, without their knowledge, had been selected by Rauor and proposed by him to Merson in their last meeting.

On the far side of the square, Rauor could see a colonnaded building from which spilled a collection of tables and chairs, filled with citizens taking advantage of the afternoon sun. To his surprise, Artesso and Shallia were both there already, the former stretched out languidly to his full length, even as his wife sat stiffly and properly upright. Rauor raised a hand in greeting and received a limp flap of one loosely held glove in return. Shallia did not make any acknowledgement of his presence. He felt a moment's regret that he had not had a chance to meet with the others, before they took this irrevocable step. Of course, as Merson had rightly decreed, this approach meant that there was far less chance of any of them betraying themselves, as they might have done if they had first had some time to speak freely to each other.

As Rauor came nearer, Artesso rose and gestured to a vacant chair at their table.

"My dear Tell, how pleasant the day is! My wife was just remarking on it to me when we espied you."

Slipping with practised ease into the conversational forms, Rauor first bowed to Shallia, and then turned to her husband. "It was well observed. I had not hoped for such fine weather." Pausing to seat himself, he continued the well-trodden steps of their conversational dances. "Are you both well?"

"Shallia is well, I thank you. For myself, I must confess to something of the headache. It is, I regret, a symptom of the fine weather, but a burden that I am willing to bear for the sake of my beloved's constitution." In a mocking aside which had no prospect of being inaudible to his wife, Artesso continued "She will have it you know that 'fresh air' is the only thing for her, and it seems a harmless enough fantasy. I confess I do not have the heart to deny her. At least it is a recreation which the lords and masters do not yet seek to regulate!"

Rauor relaxed – as he had hoped, the conversation was moving onto ideal ground for the meeting that was shortly to occur. Artesso was constantly complaining of an excess of intervention into his way of life from the authorities. Most recently he had been aggrieved at the suggestion that gaming hells ought to be subject to some form of inspection to verify that no unfair advantage was being taken of those under the age of sixteen who might somehow contrive to attend them.

A cynic might have suggested that regulation in

this area was likely to have a disproportionate effect on Artesso's fortunes. He was adept at relieving such youngsters of their allowances, in the interests (let it be understood) of "teaching the young pups a lesson". For Artesso though, opposition to regulation was a matter of principle, and Rauor could not deny that his new friend would probably have taken just as robust a line against regulation which did not have any such direct impact on him.

Keen to keep the conversation on this course, he responded in kind. "You have it a'right. I was at the races only last week, and there was some young lamb there, who had lost his locks in an ill-advised wager. He was protesting the haircut, and threatening to write to the King, as if he had not had perfectly free choice to be there and to make the bet! Gads, he was seventeen if he was a day, and yet there are those who would willingly set down rules to protect him from himself."

A short barking laugh issued from Artesso. "Drunk as well, I collect? If a man needs his hand held to that extent, he should have the sense not to spend his time or his money at the track or the table!"

A faint half-smile briefly touched Shallia's lips, in response to her husband's witticism. As she regained her composure, Rauor started backwards and stood up as if in shock.

"Gods alive! I beg your pardon madam. Can it be Merson Blare?"

Artesso betrayed the correct level of polite disinterest in his friend's outburst, but Rauor noted that he withdrew his quizzing glass and subjected the new arrival to detailed scrutiny. Rauor also looked his old friend up and down, pleased with what he saw. Merson's newly established law practice in Braed Tor was obviously rewarding him well – he was dressed in the pink of fashion and made an elegant spectacle as he stood in bemusement at Rauor's sudden appearance from the crowd.

Scarcely glancing at Rauor's two companions, Merson stepped forward and extended a gloved hand.

"I declare, Rauor Tell! It has been too long my dear fellow. How do you fare?"

"Well enough, Merson, and I have no need to ask how you do! Always the height of fashion."

He paused, and then as if remembering his manners, said in a perfunctory way "May I introduce my good friends Artesso and Shallia Trale?"

Merson audibly clicked his heels, and bowed over Shallia's proffered hand. "Enchanted, madam" he murmured, and then "and I am very pleased to make your acquaintance too, Trale. I see that young Rauor has started to move in more civilised circles at last, although it appears to have had lamentably little impact on his wardrobe."

Artesso tensed at the comment, which between strangers would have been regarded as rather too far beyond the line. Rauor, noticing, forced a laugh and shot Merson a warning look.

"Merson is a fellow of strange humours," he said, seeking to reassure his companions, "but he and I are the oldest of friends, and I have quite fallen into his way of our slighting one another at the least opportunity! Do not take it seriously – we will cut and cut at one another all day, but will never draw blood!"

Artesso's lips twitched in a somewhat sceptical watery smile, but his shoulders relaxed and he leant back again in his seat. Rauor, fearing that they might lose their prey at such an early stage in the conversation, decided to deploy their most attractive lure.

Turning to Artesso he said casually "Merson is a lawyer, don't you know! He specialises in schemes for the mitigation of tax."

Merson's eyebrows arched slightly, but he picked up his cue.

"Yes, the burden of tax can be a considerable one for most gentlemen, don't you find?"

"How very true" responded Artesso eagerly, all reticence forgotten, "I myself am taxed at nearly every turn. There seems to be little that I buy, sell or own that does not cause me a cost. Even dying will result in a payment to the realm!"

"It really is too, too bad" agreed Merson, languidly. "Yet there are ways in which such costs can be reduced, even sometimes avoided, with the right advice."

"You interest me a good deal. I assume that such schemes are expensive though?"

"Not at all. Taking my own example, I am only ever paid a percentage of the tax that has been saved. I find that I am very well remunerated for my services, and my clients are certainly satisfied."

Artesso leaned a little closer, and lowered his voice. "The authorities. They do not trouble you?"

Merson gave a deep chuckle. "I have defended several of my schemes in the courts. Judges are wealthy men too you know. To their mind, it is the duty of every right-thinking gentleman only to pay what the law requires. Exploiting the loopholes that exist is a civic obligation" he hesitated and then continued casually, "and of course it is entirely consistent with the elvish orthodoxy."

Artesso raised his quizzing glass once more and subjected Merson to a deeper scrutiny.

"You speak true. I positively shudder to think

what the elves would make of the world that we have constructed, supposedly in their image."

Merson too leaned slightly forward. Rauor, conscious that the two men were now communicating as much through their manner as their words, carefully stayed out of the conversation. He could not help but notice, however, that at the mention of the elves, Shallia had shown an interest in the conversation for the first time. While still preserving an air of decorous indifference, her features were turned to scrutinise Merson as he continued speaking.

"It is disgraceful. Do you know that I and some friends of mine are engaged on a project to analyse the laws and economic principles of the realm? What we have found both saddens and disgusts us. Everywhere superficial observance is paid to the elvish orthodoxy, but the reality in almost every case is sadly wanting."

As if warming to his theme, he continued "Take the recent revisions to the precincts' charters, for example. No one could deprecate the placing of essential services into the control of the private sector – it is the only way in which competition can guarantee the best prices for those services. But the execution of the scheme is so half-hearted. Again and again we hear concerns about what is to become of those unable to pay! The elves used to have a saying for that. The Markt will provide! Any necessary attrition in numbers will inevitably be of those least deserving of a place in the society we are building."

Merson expressed his views with conviction. Rauor, with the advantage of not being observed, carefully watched the faces of Artesso and Shallia, anxious to detect any sign of opposition to Merson's ostensible philosophy. There was none. Indeed, both of them could be seen to be nodding their agreement.

Remarkably it was Shallia who spoke next. There was an unmistakeable eagerness to her voice. "If the elves should return, chance be, how would they judge us on our respect for their principles?"

Merson turned a charming smile towards her.

"The return of the elves is not so remote a possibility as you may think." Then he hesitated, looking past them to a poor unfortunate at a nearby table who had taken that moment to glance in his direction. Turning his attention back to his audience, Merson went on. "This is rather too public a forum for this discussion. I do not normally rush to judgement about people that I have just met, but if you truly are interested in this subject...?"

Shallia nodded, perhaps a little too eagerly. Artesso laid a restraining hand on her arm, but nevertheless showed with a courteous incline of his head that he too wished Merson to continue.

"... well, I and my friends are meeting a little later today for a more detailed discussion about these very matters. You would both be more than welcome to join us." This proposal having been met with approval, Merson was mid-way through writing out the details of his address in town when he paused, and looked across at Rauor. As if in afterthought, with a cold dismissiveness which suggested that it would matter little to him either way, he added: "You are, of course, welcome to come as well."

23

"So these were Alyster's and Elyssa's parents?"

Rauor grinned at him from his semi-reclined position in his armchair. "Are they not what you were expecting, Investigator?"

"They are quite the reverse. The way you have depicted the father is certainly reminiscent of Alyster, but..." Tomas pushed himself to his feet, moving haphazardly around the room as his mind tried to assimilate the story that Rauor had laid out for him. "I do not understand how these people could be your comrades, your collaborators?"

Down the corridor they heard the sound of Merson's voice, in conversation with Alyster but coming nearer. Rauor jumped up from his seat and moved closer to where Tomas was standing.

"I don't want to keep you from your appointment, and I am sure that the lad will be equally keen to escape from these confines for a while. We shall resume this discussion later. Just remember what we knew of the elves by then. They were mind readers, and they would only accept the 'worthy'. We had to make sure, if we were going to find them, that we had some of the 'worthy' to introduce to them! That is why they were chosen, why I chose them."

Tomas had been left with little choice as to his companion, but made a good job of appearing to be content with the arrangement. Indeed as they readied themselves for departure, and with Rauor's story still prominent in his mind, he persuaded himself that it would be a valuable opportunity. He had not had many chances to speak privately with either of the younger members of the party since their interrupted discussion the previous morning, and after the brief interview that he had had with Alyster's sister, he suspected that the brother might be the more forthcoming of the pair.

In that, however, he was to be disappointed. Even as they passed through the entryway to the house, and saw the thronged masses of Car Peronel's citizenry embarking on a third day of revelries, Alyster fumbled urgently in his pockets for a handkerchief. He pressed it studiously to his nose, as if to ward off unpalatable odours. Conversation seemed likely to be impossible for as long as Alyster persisted with this affectation. After several unsuccessful attempts to engage the young man's attention, Tomas decided that he would try to rid himself of his company at the first opportunity.

With that in mind he took a more direct route to the guard house than he might otherwise have done. On arrival he bid farewell to the young dandy, leaving Alyster staring somewhat nonplussed into the sea of humankind which threatened to submerge him. With only a slight pang of guilt, Tomas presented his credentials at the gate. Within moments he had been admitted to the relative calm of the training quadrangle which took up nearly half of the interior space of this modest guard's outpost, and thoughts of Alyster rapidly faded.

Tomas was led by a young cadet across to the officers' building where he was assured that Henrik could be found. The cadet had taken a little coaxing to abandon his comfortable situation by the gate, from which he appeared to have been doing little more than watching the passing revellers. He continued to cast resentful glances at Tomas as he led him across the training ground.

As Tomas walked, he looked around with interest at the quaestor's guard post. It was by no means directly comparable with the armoury in Rivertop. While Rivertop was rather smaller than Car Peronel, the armoury was the central administrative and training hub for the entire precinct. This collection of buildings was a mere outpost of the Tower, and in a sense it was all the more impressive for that. The buildings, encompassed by an exterior wall which abutted directly onto the main fortifications of the precinct at the rear, were arranged around two expansive courtyards, and Tomas' path across the front yard was frequently obstructed by an impressive array of training devices and racks of practice weaponry.

On all sides of the yard, simple brick partitions extended inwards from the surrounding wall, dividing the edges of the space into small workshops and rest areas. In one, a table and chairs had been set out, and a group of guardsmen were sat comfortably, playing what looked to Tomas like a very low stakes variant of Royal House. Piles of loose chain links lay in front of each player, presumably borrowed from the smith's forge two alcoves further along, from which a desultory percussion of hammer on metal echoed around the confined space.

A food preparation area, a surgeon's post, a uniform store – all the necessary ingredients of a basic guard post appeared to be present. To the rear of the yard, and directly opposite the entrance through which Tomas had first been admitted, large double gates stood closed across a wide entryway. This would comfortably have accommodated a highway coach and its team, with room to spare. Ducking through a small wooden door set in the larger gate Tomas found himself in a second courtyard, identical in size to the first. Where the front yard had been covered with sand, however, the rear yard was laid with grass and Tomas saw that rather more substantial structures had been built along its walls. This included stabling for the post's allocation of horses, and even storage for two medium sized armoured carriages.

The more substantial construction at the ground floor meant that here it had been possible to erect an upper storey around the side and rear walls. At this upper level, if the standard layout was adopted, the officers would have separate rooms in which to work while on duty, or receive guests. The cadet led him to a staircase, saluted and indicated that Henrik's office was the second on the left when he reached the top of the stairs. Without lingering, the boy turned and sped away, back to his post by the front gate and his vicarious enjoyment of the celebrations going on in the street outside.

Tomas was half way up the steps when he suddenly paused, his hand coming to rest hesitantly on the rail. He had made his plans to come back here, and the more elaborate and half-formed plans to help Henrik, in the confidence that his old friend would welcome his interference, that he would be grateful for the help that Tomas proposed to offer.

Only now, when it was really too late to do anything else, was Tomas accosted by anxiety, a fear that his decision to return would be unwelcome. In Henrik's shoes, he knew, he might even regard it as meddling.

He shook himself, grasped the rail more firmly, and continued. In the circumstances, with all that he had done and been told over the past two days, Tomas was bemused to find that this meeting with his old friend was what had made him most anxious. Reaching the top of the staircase he turned left, barely noticing the impressive sight of the Tower looming off to one side over the guard-post's walls, and unhesitatingly approached Henrik's office. The door was open, and he leant inside, knocking the door with his knuckles as he did so, and blinking to adjust his sight to the gloom within.

"Tomas!"

Henrik's reaction was instantaneous and genuine. Leaping up from the desk where moments before he had been slumped, head in hands, he hurried to the door. First he seized Tomas's right hand and shook it warmly. Then forsaking all military decorum, he threw his arms about the other man and embraced him.

When, after a few moments, they separated Henrik stepped back to look in puzzlement at his friend. "What are you still doing in Car Peronel? I thought you had gone to Braed Tor for Fest?"

"It is a long and complicated story, I assure you." Tomas had known that this question would come, as surely as he had known that he did not know how he would answer it. He could not lie to Henrik, but the truth would take considerable thought, and a great deal of time.

"I will not be here in Car Peronel for long. I think that I will be returning to Rivertop as soon as Fest ends. Nor is very much of my time free to dispose of as I wish. But," he paused, watching Henrik's reactions carefully, "I have had your predicament on my mind a great deal of the past few days. I think that there might be a way in which I can help."

He watched the emotions march across Henrik's face as they talked, and as Tomas outlined his plan. Hope appeared briefly, rapidly followed by scepticism. It was a scepticism that Tomas could not help but share. The world that both men inhabited had taught them never to hope, and always to fear the worst. Tomas had a sense, though, that as they talked Henrik's instinctive doubt had come to be mingled with a sense of calm. Whether the plan would succeed or not, Henrik now knew that there was another person in the world who understood the pain that he and his wife were suffering, and who was determined to help.

Still, Henrik was right to express scepticism that Tomas's half-formed plan might be converted into something workable. What he was proposing was, without question, entirely illegal. If ever it were to be discovered, it would mean the end of both of their careers, and the sanctions could potentially be even more serious. Tomas was also very aware that he had started to devise his plan without any reference to Idony, even though his wife would play a central part in it. All of those doubts had to be overcome. Instinct told him that Idony would support him with all her heart, and for Henrik and his wife, the risk of discovery grew with every passing day.

In the end, Henrik leaned across his desk and clasped Tomas's hands in his own.

"We have done all we can, Tomas. I must do some paperwork now if I am not to attract attention. Bodila and I will owe you our lives if this plan of yours can be made to work. First, though, I must speak to her. The solution you propose is not without its risks for any of us."

"You must do so, of course." Tomas stood to leave, but anxiety about the consequences of any delay prompted him to continue "is there any chance that you will reach a decision before the end of Fest? I will be travelling back to Rivertop on the first day that coaches are running, and if we are to put our plan into action, I will need to find a way to communicate with Idony before then."

Henrik frowned, clearly imagining the conversation that he was shortly to have with his wife. Tomas felt moved to apologise, but his friend waved it aside. "You are quite right, Tomas. We have let too much time elapse already, and nature is not patient. I am afraid that we have both of us been guilty of ignoring a problem that is only going to grow greater." He sighed then clasped Tomas's hand even as he showed him to the door.

"Come to our house tomorrow. You have the address now. If you come for dinner, we will have made our decision."

24

(Extracts from the voluntary confession of [Subject T187356]. Interview 9. Collated from the files of the Justice Authority. Quaestor's words redacted throughout.)

It was very pleasant! An unfamiliar experience, certainly, to have attended in such circumstances, but it is a very impressive theatre.

I did, and trust that you did too?

By all means.

[Pause while prisoner reviews the written confession prepared to date in redacted form]

I have not read every word, but it seems to be accurate, yes. Where do you wish me to sign?

Very well. That brings us then to the more difficult part of my narrative. As you know, following my initial meeting with the excellent Captain Boomel, now Major Boomel as I am given to understand, I was not afforded any further opportunity to leave the property until Fest was concluded. At that point, some of our party, whose details I have already provided you, returned to Rivertop. Those that remained had as their most urgent priority the location of a property that might be rented for me to occupy, with my sister of course.

It was the evening of the first of Nieumor. Elyssa, worn out with the day of investigating suitable properties, had already retired for the night. I too was exhausted. Not one of the properties we had seen had matched my exacting standards. After an early supper, I had bade my aunt and uncle a good night and gone up to my room.

It was a hot night, and I felt decidedly uncomfortable. I soon discovered that, although one or two of Forba's servants had returned to work during the day, they were either insufficiently numerous or inadequately trained. In temperatures as high as those we have been experiencing, you would not think that something so critical as a jug of water by one's bedside was capable of being overlooked!

Having discovered the oversight, I saw that there was no other solution than for me to descend the three flights of stairs necessary to take me to the property's internal well, and draw water for myself. After the hardships of the preceding days, the manual labour that was required seemed trivial, but I found that the meniality of the task deprived me of all my energy. As a consequence I probably descended the stairs more slowly and more quietly than I would normally have done.

Reaching the ground floor of the property, I had been about to descend further, when I overheard voices in the drawing room. Forba and Merson were engaged in some private conference.

I hasten to assure you that I am far from the type who will usually be found listening at key-holes! Nevertheless, my discussions with Boomel, and what he had been able to tell me of these people's activities, had impressed on me the importance of knowing what else might be their plans.

I really do think that it is important to note that I did this not out of any personal inquisitiveness, a trait which I abhor, but in service to the needs of the realm.

I am much obliged to you.

It is certainly fortuitous that I did. As I have already alluded to in our private discussions [redacted].

All thought of the water was driven from my head. In only the first few minutes I heard them refer to [redacted] and Lord [redacted] and a meeting which they had been planning with several of the [redacted]...

(The remainder of this transcript is to be found in sealed record T187356-VS-001. Not to be accessed without the written authority of Quaestor Feiger personally, and one other of the Approved List annexed to this file.)

25

It was curious. Tomas had just committed himself to a course of action which he knew to be criminal. He was feeling greater and greater kinship with the subjects of his investigation. He was being buffeted by the monstrous drunken angry crowds of Car Peronel in Fest. There was very little in his situation to account for the sudden lightness that he felt within him as he left the guard post and started to make his way back across the precinct.

Yet for the first time since his night at the opera house with Idony, he did indeed feel at ease with the world. Perhaps it was the further insight that Rauor had given him in their discussions that morning. Maybe it was that he had unconsciously started to accept the truth of their remarkable claim to have contacted the elves, a claim that the emotional part of him desperately wanted to believe.

Whatever the reason, he found himself smiling as he ricocheted down the street like one of the balls on Rauor's pooliard table. There was something intensely liberating about the experience of being carried forward at the whim of the crowd, responsible only for the small bubble of space which he occupied at any given moment.

And then he saw her.

Clampits, they were called, like the small and foul smelling sea creatures that clung to the rocks on the sea-shore. It was a derogatory term for those who existed on the periphery of any precinct's society. Properly, they should never be able to gain admittance to the interior of the city, but just as in Rivertop, their presence was a daily inevitability. Like most other investigators, Tomas had developed an instinct for picking them out.

Once identified they were required immediately to be expelled. Rivertop's municipal code provided for the relaxation of this rule during Fest, but Tomas was well aware that this was unusual. Most precincts, and certainly the capital, would never entertain their presence. This girl had tried to disguise what she was with a brightly coloured Fest-scarf, probably stolen earlier in the day. Beneath the scarf, however, her clothes were drab and ragged, and Tomas knew that it would only be a matter of time before she was detected.

She was dancing through the crowds with apparently haphazard abandon, but Tomas was experienced enough at seeing such things that he quickly recognised her true purpose. Every carefree step, every twirl, even every carefully choreographed stumble, brought her close to a pocket, or a purse. A dipper then, and a very accomplished one despite her youth.

Rather than darting forward to seize her, however, he found himself moving slowly in parallel. He was captivated by her performance, the effortless fluidity of it. In another life she could perhaps have been a dancer, even a ballerina. The thought occurred to him that perhaps she had been. After all, not all clampits had been born in impoverished circumstances.

The crowd ahead of them was thickening and slowing. There was an obstruction in the road. As the people before her started to bunch and slow, the girl saw her opportunity and extended her arms in a long fluent movement, the end point of which was the bulging pocket of an obese reveller directly in front of her. As she turned, she happened to glance in Tomas's direction and their eyes locked for a fatal moment. He saw the shock run through her, saw her movement lose some of its fluency, saw her hand miss its target and strike the man full on the back.

In a moment the mood of the crowd changed. Whoever the man was that the thief had inadvertently struck, he plainly had a number of friends around him. Before the girl could move, a group of men had formed a loose circle around her, one reaching forward to pluck her scarf away.

"Lookee here – she's a gods-dammed clampit!" came the cry.

Insults quickly followed as snarls replaced smiles on the revellers' faces. Acting without thinking Tomas lunged forward, broke the circle, and stood with the girl. He pulled his cloak to one side in an oft-practised gesture. Only when it did not seem to be having the desired intimidatory effect did he remember that he was wearing attire that he had borrowed from the house that morning. His uniform, which admittedly had been starting to acquire a very stale odour, was now hung up and airing in a wardrobe in his room. That was not going to assist him with his current situation, which was suddenly looking very precarious indeed.

"Who the hells is this?" the overweight man

demanded of his friends. He had a synthetically high-pitched voice, in accordance with fashion, and as Alyster had done earlier in the day he was holding a perfumed handkerchief up to his nose. A tall bald man stepped forward. It was not clear whether he was one of the man's friends, or just an interested bystander, but when he spoke it was clear that he had no sympathy for Tomas or the girl.

"One or both, it's all the same. Shouldn't be here, should they? Should be thrown out."

"Thrown out?" came a shout from the crowd, "where've you been? 'Tis the death penalty for clampits nowadays and none too soon."

Tomas tried to project a calm appearance, but he could feel sweat forming down his spine. This was why he normally stayed indoors until Fest was over. He stepped between the tall man and the girl, although, with a crowd all around them, the gesture was largely symbolic.

"I am an investigator, out of Rivertop. I will deal with the proper processing of this girl. You can all disperse."

This was met with laughter, but no movement.

"An investigator is he? Where's his uniform?"

The bald man spoke up again. "Even if you are an investigator, which I doubt, you've no authority here! We all pay our dues to the quaestors and they'd know better than to interfere with this."

"With what?" Tomas was speaking fast now, feeling a hot flush coming over him. "Rough justice – is that it?"

"Quick justice" came the answer. "The law calls for your deaths, even in Fest. And there's none here to stop us."

There was a growing murmuring through the crowd. The phrase "string them up" seemed to echo through their voices. This was it. Tomas had no choice. He was not about to let himself be hung up from a gibbet to satisfy the crowd's blood-lust, and while he might just be able to escape without having to injure any of the crowd too severely, it would mean leaving the girl to their mercies. Law or no, he would not be able to live with himself if he did that.

Decision made, there was no purpose to further delay. Rather faster than the watching crowd could follow, Tomas's sword sliced through the air and, with only a little more resistance, across the bald man's forehead. Blood flowed freely, obscuring his eyes, and he stumbled backwards, no further threat. The rest of the crowd took several steps away from the flashing blade, making life considerably easier for Tomas as they gave him room to press his advantage.

Before anybody else could draw a weapon, Tomas had spun a complete circle, his sword extended at a high level so as not to threaten the girl behind him. More backward steps were taken, and Tomas identified two or three likely gaps that had started to open in the mob. To his surprise, the obese man at the centre of the original collision was the first to respond. Drawing a short sword, he rushed forward. He had no style or finesse, but he posed a threat and Tomas had no time to neutralise him without injury. His sword flicked out once, twice. The first strike took the man across his knuckles and his sword fell to the ground. The second caught his upper arm and a thin line of blood started under the fabric of his sleeve, across the line of the muscle.

The man's recessed eyes darkened. He shouted, in a far less effete voice than he had been adopting previously, "You have no idea who you are crossing!" and then to his friends in the crowd

"What are you waiting for? Deal with him!"

Even as these instructions were being given, however, Tomas was in motion. He whirled and seizing the girl's grimy hand, pulling her in the direction of the thinnest part of the crowd. As he had expected, the few remaining people in their path rapidly made way and they were out in open space before the girl regained her feet. As soon as she had done so she demonstrated the most important skill of any successful pickpocket, and accelerated away, leaving Tomas doing his best to keep pace with her. Behind him there were shouts of outrage from the crowd, and very shortly after that, the noise of determined pursuit.

After ten minutes, Tomas was still running and rapidly coming to feel that his earlier act of chivalry had not been worth the trouble that it had earned him. The girl, not once voicing any gratitude, had within minutes taken to the alleys. This was a route which Tomas, with his inferior knowledge of the precinct, was reluctant to follow. One small solace was that it had divided their pursuers, but from the sound of the shouts that were being directed towards him, Tomas was aware that there were still a significant number of people following him. Nor did they seem to be inclined to afford him any quarter if they were to get their hands on him.

Fear lent him extra speed, but his reserves were rapidly approaching exhaustion and still they kept coming. With his superior physical fitness Tomas was starting to extend a lead over his pursuers, but not quickly enough to give him confidence that he would be able to lose them if he kept to the precinct's wide avenues and open plazas. Perhaps the alleys would be preferable, although Tomas knew that he would in all likelihood choose one that brought him back out closer to his pursuers, or in a dead end.

Even so, that might be his only hope of escape. Just as he had come to that conclusion, however, he turned a corner onto the inner circle road which ran around the whole precinct, and found another solution before him. There, on the far side of the avenue, its tall tower stretching up into the sky with its various flags and batons in constant motion, stood a semaphore post. Tomas breathed a sigh of relief and hurried forward. Hammering on the door he shouted the code which would secure him admittance.

Instantly, there came the sound of bolts being withdrawn, and the door was pulled aside. He ducked in as quickly as he could, pushing the door closed with his body even as he pressed his eye to the spy hole to look back in the direction of his pursuers. Fortune was on his side. The door had been pushed closed for only a few moments when the first of the pursuers rounded the corner. Tomas felt a certain wry amusement as they stumbled to a halt, looking around them in bewilderment. He stood there watching for a minute, until he was satisfied that they had no suspicion of where he could have gone. First one or two, and then more of them started to dissipate, and with relief Tomas finally slumped and turned to face the semaphore operators who he had so unceremoniously barged in on. There were two of them, young and looking very apprehensively at him as he stood there with his bloodied sword still drawn. Hastily Tomas wiped the blade and sheathed it.

"I am terribly sorry to intrude! I am afraid that I was in some momentary danger, but that now appears to have passed."

The two young men gazed mutely at him, their

brows furrowed in comically identical expressions of puzzlement. It was clear that Tomas could not expect much in the way of conversation from them. Nevertheless, now that he was here, there was perhaps one other way in which they could assist him.

He smiled encouragingly at the two operators, stepping towards them open-handed to show them that they were not in any danger. "While I am here, I wonder if I could prevail upon you to send a short message for me?"

Half an hour later, Tomas had emerged back onto the circle road, having first satisfied himself through the spy hole that there were no potential enemies still lingering around. He called his thanks one last time to the two mute operators, pulling the door firmly closed behind him. The semaphore tower had served as an excellent hiding place and it had given him an unlooked-for opportunity to communicate with Idony and to give her advance notice of his return.

The message he had sent "Returning 1 Nieumor. Please air guest room 3" was entirely innocuous, but to Idony it would be replete with hidden meaning. It was the room which at one stage had served as their nursery, and Tomas was surprised that he could think of it quite easily without pain. All of the events of the past few days, and in particular the decision that he was hoping that Henrik and his wife would make, somehow cushioned him from the emotion that previously had always threaten to overwhelm him. He could only hope that in seeking to give Idony some forewarning of the news that he expected to be bringing home with him, he would not cause her too much pain.

Looking about him he could see that the afternoon was significantly advanced. Gathering his bearings, Tomas realised that he had a fair way to go to return to the house, and he set off immediately in what he hoped was the right direction. Fortunately, with a couple of wrong turnings aside, Tomas found that his broad sense of the geography of Car Peronel sufficed to help him find his way back to the vicinity of Forba's property. It helped that he knew that the house was located in an area that was about as far away from the Tower's island as it was possible to be, staying within the precinct's walls.

Soon he would be back at the house, several hours after the time that he had hoped to return. He would have to trust that Merson and the others would accept his explanation when he provided it, an explanation that would certainly be lent some veracity by the traces of blood on his sword blade.

He reached the wall of the precinct a little further anti-clockwise than he had intended, and chose a street at random to turn right. There, before him, was Henrik's guard-house. Relief washed over him. Finally he had a recognisable landmark which would guide him the rest of the way home. That relief was almost immediately overtaken by curiosity and suspicion, however. Emerging from the very gate house that Tomas himself had come out of several hours before, was young Alyster Trale. In contrast to his earlier demeanour, he now wore a satisfied smile on his face, and he started walking quickly and without any affectation back in the direction of the house.

Baffled, Tomas started after him. He could not think of any good reason why Alyster would have been at the guard house, certainly not for the time that it had taken Tomas to have his own adventures. It was just possible, he supposed, that Alyster had returned looking for him, after he had failed to return to the others within a reasonable time, but it hardly seemed likely. Furthermore, Tomas could not imagine what answer Alyster might have obtained to such an enquiry that would cause him to emerge smiling and at ease.

Afterwards, he could not be sure what caused it. Although his back was turned to Tomas, Alyster suddenly stiffened and halted in his steps. He spun round without giving Tomas any opportunity to conceal himself. No sooner had his eyes met with Tomas's, than his face resumed its accustomed scowl. There was also another emotion there which, although the distance between them was relatively great, Tomas read as fear. He raised a hand as if in greeting, but Alyster turned on his heel and, displaying a turn of speed of which Tomas had not suspected him capable, ran off in the direction of the house.

Even without the exertions he had already undergone that day, Tomas was not sure that he could catch the younger man. As such, he chose not to try. Instead he simply strolled at a steady pace, giving every impression to the world at large that he was a man totally at peace. Internally, however, he found himself gripped by considerable anxiety.

That anxiety was not in the least alleviated when he reached the house. Opening the front door he found an impromptu conference convened at the foot of the main stairs. Alyster stood with his back to the door but whirled to look over his shoulder as Tomas came in. Forba stood with him, stretching out a hand, although whether to reassure or restrain him it was not clear. Merson was stood facing them, but he was the last to raise his head and make eye contact with Tomas. Nevertheless, it was he who first stepped forward to speak.

"All right, Alyster. I will deal with this."

Alyster began to protest, but was silenced with a glance.

"Forba, take him upstairs. I will come and speak to you both, once Tomas and I have had a few words."

He stood gravely, pinching his forefinger and thumb under his chin as Forba led the young man up the staircase. Tomas, realising that the door was still standing ajar behind him, half turned to close it. Then he looked back towards Merson, consciously trying to relax his posture even as he wondered what Alyster had been saying and quite what jeopardy he was in.

To his considerable surprise, once Alyster had disappeared up the stairs Merson's stern expression dissolved into something rather like a grin. He rapidly closed the gap to Tomas and clapped him on the arm.

"You are nothing but trouble to me, investigator! But I can see that the time has come for us to be wholly frank with one another, at last."

He stepped back, and looked at Tomas appraisingly. "You have not had an entirely straightforward day, I think. If you would prefer to bathe first, we could speak later, but I would really prefer to say at least a few things to you without delay."

Tomas could not understand what might be the cause of this joviality, but his impatience with yet more mystery was such that concerns as to personal hygiene had to take second place.

"Let us speak now, Merson. The sooner I can understand quite what this is all about, the happier I shall be."

Merson led the way into an empty room. It

would probably have been the house's library, but although every wall was lined with shelves, they were all empty. Seeing Tomas looking around him as they seated themselves at a table in the room's centre, Merson took his cue from that.

"This house belongs to Forba, did you know that?"

"I think that I had assumed it, based on her apparent familiarity with the place. But when I came to look for her before, the address I had for her was a good deal less impressive."

"Indeed. Nor would this property be disclosed by any search of the Land Corporation's records. She owns it under a different name – in fact her true name."

"Her true name?"

"Yes. The names that you know all of us by are names that have been selected for the particular operation that we are involved in, and after that is completed we shall have no further use for them."

Once again, Tomas felt a rising sense of frustration. Rather than clarifying the mystery of Alyster's presence at the guard post, Merson appeared to be introducing yet another layer of confusion. As if sensing this irritation, Merson raised a hand to forestall further comment.

"There is a relevance to what I am telling you, Tomas. A pattern is being created, a pattern that has taken us some twenty years to devise and engineer. Rauor, Forba, Lias and I all have our parts to play. So too does Alyster. His part is rather less significant, perhaps, but I trust him to play it properly."

Tomas again began to interrupt, but Merson simply continued speaking.

"In all of our plans, in all of the years of careful strategy that have led us to this point, however, not one of us foresaw your involvement. How could we? It is the purest coincidence that after all of this time Victor Appelsin would still be keeping a watching eye on our group. We never anticipated that the patterns we are creating, which are having precisely the effect that we intended of attracting the attention of certain others, would also cause him and then you be to be drawn into our web.

"So, the time has come to speak frankly. We need to know where you, and indeed Victor, stand in relation to our group. Does he intend to incriminate us and, in doing so, himself? Or is he secretly sympathetic to our cause, as Forba and I sensed all of those years ago?"

Impatiently, Tomas shifted in his chair. "Merson, it seems to me that if we are talking about questions of trust, there is someone rather closer to home who you should be examining."

"Do you mean Alyster?"

"Precisely. Did he tell you what he was doing, where he was coming from, when I spotted him this afternoon?"

"He was coming from the guard post. He says that he was worried about you and had gone (at some personal risk I might add) to find out what had become of you. Do you have any reason to doubt it?"

Tomas flexed his shoulders. Sitting still after his afternoon's exertions was starting to cause his back to stiffen. He struggled to find a way to frame his response.

"Merson, you know Alyster a good deal better than I do. There was just something about his manner and bearing. He did not look concerned when I saw him, he looked positively relieved."

"Tomas, what I think you are suggesting is entirely inconceivable. Alyster would be betraying himself by betraying us. I fancy that even if he were willing to take that chance, the ties of familial loyalty that bind us all would keep him from such a course."

"I am sorry Merson, I really do not want to impugn the young man's motives. But I cannot help but doubt his explanations."

Merson smiled, and locked Tomas' gaze with his deep grey eyes. "This perhaps brings us to the most central question of all, Tomas. Even granted that you are accustomed to giving credence to your intuition in matters of this type, why does the possibility of Alyster's betrayal trouble you so much?"

The question was entirely unexpected, and yet as soon as he heard it Tomas knew that it was a question that he should have been asking himself. Rather than replying instinctively he forced himself to sit quietly for a moment. He had understood on a subconscious level that the reason that Merson and the others were telling him their tale in such detail, was that it was an elaborate courtship. He had even recognised that to some extent the strategy had been successful. But for all that he felt considerable sympathy for their views, and for them individually, he could not overcome his professional reactions.

Uncertain how Merson would react to anything other than unambivalent approval of his cause, Tomas drew a deep breath.

"I know what you are asking me. There are many who would say that I am already in dereliction of my duty for not reporting you and your group to the local quaestor captain. My ultimate loyalty though is to Victor. All that I have done has been done at his instruction, and he expects me to report. We have fought together, back to back. I am sure that you, Forba and the others have saved my life on occasion. For that, and for your frankness and openness, I feel that I owe you something."

Merson's eyes continued to bore into him. Tomas found himself curiously short of breath. He felt an unbearable pressure to tell the truth and he wondered whether this came from within him, or from outside. The scar next to his left eye was starting to sting, and in a moment the eye would start to water. But he could not look away.

Summoning all of his discipline, he squared his shoulders and tried to return Merson's gaze with equivalent force.

"I cannot be party to any act of violence against the realm. I know that that is probably not what you want me to say, but I have duties and responsibilities that I believe in. After Fest, I shall make my report to Victor, and no-one else, because that is what he wishes. What happens after that will also be up to him."

At once, the pressure lifted. Merson seemed to recede from him even as he stayed sitting, apparently relaxed, across the table. An encouraging smile prompted Tomas to continue. Relief made him laugh aloud.

"I had been afraid that you were trying to recruit me to your cause."

Merson also laughed.

"Perhaps we have, Tomas. Only time will tell. But giving us an open-minded hearing is all I have ever asked for, and I value it more than you can know."

26

Tryachan, 19 years ago

The memory struck Merson forcibly. When he had been a child he and his family had travelled to the coast, staying with family friends for several weeks. The children of the family had introduced Merson to the pleasures of beach games, and he and they had particularly enjoyed building elaborate structures out of the sand. Even the most carefully constructed fortress, however, had only survived for as long as it took for the tide to come in. Morning after morning, Merson would come hopefully down to the beach only to be confronted with the half eroded ruins of his construction. Sometimes the side nearest to him, and furthest from the sea, would be more or less intact. But always the side facing the water would be broken down and destroyed.

Now he found himself gazing at the same pattern, on a far grander scale, in the ruined port city of Tryachan.

He and Forba were riding on the first of three

wagons laden with supplies. Theirs contained food and other perishable provisions. Behind them, Rauor was steering an equally large wagon carrying the fresh water barrels. Artesso and Shallia were bringing up the rear, with a wagon which held the trunks comprising the group's wardrobes and other personal effects.

Approaching from the landward side, it was not immediately obvious that the city was ruined. The walls, though unmanned, were still largely intact. It was only in occasional glimpses through the broken down gates that they were approaching, that the devastation beyond could be seen.

As befitted a place which no longer had a fresh water supply, the entire city had a dried out appearance. Making their way through the gates they immediately noticed signs of wind erosion on the buildings. The streets were strewn with detritus, a combination of flotsam from the sea that had been washed or blown ashore and remnants of whatever possessions the inhabitants of Tryachan had not felt able to take with them.

As they descended through the town towards the waterfront, the erosion became worse and worse. Entire houses had collapsed. More substantial structures had large fissures through their walls and interiors that were significantly weather damaged. Merson started to become anxious that the facilities that he was hoping to find might not still be functional.

Forba echoed his anxiety.

"My gods! They have not left the place in a very useful state!"

"I fear not. Nevertheless, we must hope that the dock area has been constructed rather more robustly."

Forba jerked her head backwards. "While you

are hoping, you should hope that we will not have have to stay overnight! There's some with us who I do not think would relish the idea of sleeping among the ruins!"

"That depends on Lias. If all runs to schedule, we should be seeing his sail very shortly."

Their fears proved to be groundless. If the town itself seemed to have been half demolished by the elements, the harbour had been built far more durably. Not only were the stone quaysides still regular and intact, but there were even winches in their covers whose mechanisms looked as if they would endure for decades more. Unfortunately there were no ropes, but Merson had anticipated this need and several stout cables were unpacked from their wagon and threaded into two winches at the main dock, ready for loading work to begin.

Before that could happen, however, they needed a vessel, and nearly an hour elapsed before Artesso suddenly cried out "Look there! A sail!"

It was just possible that some other close shore fishing boat had made it this far south from Grand Landing or Peacewater, and so Merson counselled them to wait. As the vessel drew nearer and nearer, however, he saw that it was a rather more substantial craft, and as it approached the harbour Merson could even make out Lias standing at the helm.

Lias had a wholly different demeanour when at sea. He radiated confidence, in a way that was seldom if ever apparent while he was on land. Suddenly, Merson stiffened. Hauling on the ship's wheel, bringing the vessel closer and closer to the shore, Lias had suddenly barked a command. Unseen hands had let go sails, and the mainsail had swiftly dropped, followed soon after by the foresail. Even as Lias expertly used the last of the ship's momentum to bring it gliding carefully up to the quayside, Merson was urgently scanning the decks.

Forba was the first to spot the crew member. Her hand gripped Merson's arm.

"Was not he meant to be coming alone?"

"Those were certainly my instructions" replied Merson angrily. They could ill afford any disruption to their carefully laid plans at this stage. He had made it clear beyond question to Lias that if he did not think that he could handle the vessel himself, he must take one of the others with him, rather than risking any accident, or any outsider's involvement. Yet unmistakeably, now making his way to the foredeck where he started work in setting out fenders between the boat and the dockside, was the squat muscular figure of a stranger.

Lias, once the vessel was moored and they had all gone aboard, was wholly unrepentant. Standing on deck seemed to give him a stubbornness that he normally lacked, and he faced down Merson without difficulty.

"You gave me absolute discretion in the choice of the vessel, Merson. Indeed, in relation to all things maritime. This is a bigger ship than I had planned on obtaining, but when I saw it and the price at which it was offered, I would have been crazy to overlook it. A coast-trader, off with his fancy lady for a week's holiday, is going to come back to find that he has an irate wife, and no livelihood.

"Skapgood here was crew on the vessel. You have no idea what it is like up at Haymouth. Fewer and fewer ships are setting sail, and with every sea captain that no longer calls in to port, there are half a dozen businesses that find it that much harder to keep going. I do not exaggerate when I say that I have saved the man's life by bringing him with us."

Merson, albeit grudgingly, was soon forced to acknowledge that this Skapgood certainly seemed to know his way around the vessel. For all of his diminutive size he had considerable strength and he frequently seemed to be in two or three places around the deck at once, hurrying to and fro. Merson had wholly underestimated the amount of strength that the winches would require, and their voyage might not have set sail at all without Skapgood to lift the heavy water barrels and see them lowered and stowed within the ship's hold.

So it was that in a matter of hours, and long before the setting sun cooled the sea and caused the evening sailors' breeze to start to be heard among the rigging, the ship was ready to sail. Setting loose their horses, without at that stage any real thought of how they might make the journey back if it came to that, the inexperienced crew embarked.

Lias was still in his element. He moved among them, allocating roles, providing rudimentary instruction as he went. Skapgood followed in his trail with more practical assistance.

The sails were set. First one gentle gust, and then a stronger breeze blew off the land and filled the canvas. Merson, stood at the prow of the vessel, cast off first and then watched as his friends did so in turn. For a wonder, all seemed to proceed smoothly, and within what seemed no more than a few minutes, the ship's prow was looking tentatively out of the harbour-mouth.

Without any obvious task to perform, Merson wandered back along the deck towards the raised area where Lias stood steering.

"I meant to ask you, Lias. What is this vessel called?"

"She's the Lucilla."

"I wondered if we might rename her?"

Lias smiled indulgently. It was a strange experience, and Merson vowed that after this adventure he would try to keep Lias on land where he was more manageable.

"It is an ill-favoured name, I agree. Did you have something in mind?"

"I thought perhaps, the Empty Hand?"

Lias, schooled like all the rest in his ancient history, smiled again, but with genuine humour this time.

"Yes, very apt. It is good time that we should return the favour, for sure! The Empty Hand it shall be."

Behind them, the breeze stiffened into a good trader's wind, as if in appreciation.

The wind had stayed strong for the first month of the voyage. Eventually, though, just as had been experienced by Grancomo's expedition before them, they had found themselves becalmed. Another virtue of Lias's choices made itself apparent at this stage. Slung to the back of the Empty Hand had been a small rowing dinghy, and this was capable, with a couple of strong rowers, of towing the entire vessel onwards along the correct bearing. Skapgood took far more than his fair share of spells at the oars, but all of the gentlemen also took their turn. After a further couple of weeks they were all impatient and frustrated by the limited range of ship's rations, but the weather had stayed fair, and they were all of them feeling healthier than they ever had.

By this stage, Skapgood had become a firm part of the group. He could never quite overcome his sense of social inferiority to the others, however much some of them tried to persuade him that it was not at all justified. Even so, there is only so long that one can share a table at meals and share sleeping quarters, without the boundaries of formality and distance falling away.

Artesso made one attempt to explain their philosophies to Skapgood. He seemed to feel it important that the life-long sailor should understand what hope the elves offered to someone of his position, as much as to someone of Artesso's more elevated status. Skapgood listened to him politely for a few minutes and then clapped him on the shoulder.

"You're a clever man, Mister Trale, there's no denying it. You say that there's some purpose to chasing after mage-tales, and I'm happy to take you at your word. But you'll never persuade me that the Markt, or whatever it is you call it, has any relevance to me. I'm a simple sailor and will be until I die. I'm content with that."

Neither the snub, nor the over-familiarity, were taken well by Artesso. He retired to the captain's cabin for a more refined discussion with Lias, and after that made a point of never being alone in Skapgood's company. The rest of them took Skapgood at his word, and abandoned any thought of attempting to convert him to their cause. In Merson's case, as was no doubt true of some of the others, this also had the advantage that they did not have to discuss philosophy in the presence of Artesso or Shallia, and run the risk of either of them detecting some want of orthodoxy in their thinking.

Rauor's selection of the couple had been all too successful from this point of view. Each rigidly adhered, as far as they could, to all of the prescriptions of elven law and philosophy. What is more, they were fervent believers that only if all citizens of the realm did so would their current predicaments be ended. Any comment from one of the others hinting at a stance that favoured regulation of any type, for example, would be instantly seized on. On several occasions, only quick thinking and Merson's legally trained mind were able to rationalise the positions that one or other of them had unthinkingly voiced.

After the best part of a year of trepidation around such discussions, now compounded by six or more weeks of close proximity to the pair, Merson expected to be heartily relieved when this phase of their project was over. He only hoped that all of their efforts would be justly rewarded. Only if the elves would accept Artesso and Shallia as worthy, and moreover offer them some practical help towards restoring magic and power to the world, would Merson feel able to start to plan for the next stage of their scheme. This was naturally something that they had kept scrupulously from both Artesso and Shallia, for fear of the alleged telepathic ability of the Elven. Even within their own minds they had schooled themselves not to think ahead to what might come afterwards.

The days passed. Merson started to become afraid that they had missed their bearings. If any of the others shared his anxieties they, like him, kept it to themselves. Then, late one evening just over seven weeks into the voyage, as they all took their rest on deck after another uneventful day, it began.

Afterwards, Merson hastily scribbled down some impressions, mindful of the comments in Grancomo's log that the memory of the event had faded quickly. In fact, though, some parts of the experience were etched forever into his memory.

The silence was the first sign that something had changed. Despite the calm, all of them had become accustomed to the creakings of the ship's timbers, the occasional lap of a small wave against the hull, the little noises that even a becalmed ship at sea will make. So as a bubble of complete silence fell over them, they all looked anxiously at one another.

"I think it's starting" said Merson, but no sound came from his mouth. He could see the others' mouths moving, but like them he could hear nothing. Then, just as recorded in Grancomo's log, he felt himself pushed to the deck by an immense weight. Strangely, it felt as though the entire vessel was being hoisted upwards into the air. Light shone down onto him out of the darkening sky, and despite straining for several moments to see past the glare, he had to close his eyes against it.

Suddenly, he felt himself being lifted and turned. A buzzing sound filled the air. Through it, Merson could hear a musical and yet somehow threatening voice, repeating over and over "Unworthy", "Unworthy".

Despair filled his heart. Filled with the light and the strange sound in his ears, he felt a longing to be lifted, to be thought worthy. Desperately his mind sought ways to prove his value, anything to let him come closer to the musical voice. All too soon, however, he felt himself falling back down onto the deck, back under the same pressure that had weighted them down at the start.

Without seeming to diminish, he had the sense of the light's focus turning from him. His mind was once more his own. At once he strained to hear any sign that their plan might have succeeded. Still the voice repeated, seemingly endlessly, "Unworthy", "Unworthy".

Somehow, they had failed. Normal weight returned. The light faded and the buzzing sound disappeared. At the last moment, before he opened his eyes, he thought that he might have heard a faint echo of some other words. "Welcome, elf friends". Scarcely daring to hope, he sat up and looked around him. There was Rauor, already rising unsteadily to his feet. Forba lay prone as if unconscious, although her chest was rising and falling healthily. Skapgood and Lias too, could both be seen, struggling upright and looking about them in bewilderment.

But of Artesso and Shallia, there was not a single trace.

27

At last, Tomas was going home. With Fest over for another year, the carriage routes were reopened and Tomas was aboard one of the first post-chaises to be making the run from Car Peronel to Rivertop. It felt good to be back in his investigator's uniform. Certainly it had commanded a satisfying level of deference from the coachman when he had come to board in the main square earlier in the morning. Looking across the carriage, he caught Rauor Tell's eye and smiled. Both Rauor and Lias were travelling back with him, returning to the lives which they had so peremptorily abandoned prior to the holiday. Tomas suspected that, for Rauor, re-ingratiating himself with Lord Kerton would be a particular challenge, even with his reserves of charm.

All of them had said what they wished to say to one another in the preceding days, remaining in the house for all but essential journeys outside until Fest was over. With Tomas's clarification of his position to Merson, any remaining mistrust and tension in the house seemed to have evaporated.

Curiously, although Tomas was spending most of his time writing up a detailed report on their activities, they seemed more content now to speak freely to him, rather than in puzzling riddles.

They had provided him with more details of the scheme involving Artesso and Shallia Trale, and at last he felt that he understood why two such unpromising individuals had been recruited to their cause. Merson had also told him the story of their voyage, of their encounter with the elves deep in the becalmed sea, and of the success of their scheme. After that, it seemed that they felt that there was nothing more to be said. Tomas could only assume that the group either had an entirely unwarranted confidence that Tomas would keep Victor from betraying or pursuing them, or that whatever their project was, it could not be upset even by his making a full report.

The remainder of the time had been spent in more casual conversations, and Tomas had grown to know and like each of the others a good deal. Only simple Elyssa and surly Alyster kept their distance, but Tomas had too many other concerns to let their reticence trouble him unduly.

His only journey out of the house had been to attend the pre-arranged dinner with Henrik and his wife, Bodila. As soon as he saw her, Tomas knew that the scheme that he and Henrik had discussed would have to be implemented without further delay. Although he was looking at her with prior knowledge of her condition, it seemed plain to him that she was with child, and that it would not be long at all before that was apparent to even a casual and uninformed observer.

Their interview had been long and, despite the excellence of the dinner, a trying and emotional discussion. In the end, of course, as they all knew, there really was no other option. At least, no other option which any of the three of them would regard as palatable.

Once the decision had been made, Tomas left them to make the practical arrangements, and to say their farewells for what was left of Fest. Now, glancing to his left, he saw Bodila's impassive profile as she sat next to him. It was plain that she had been crying, but it was equally plain from the determined set of her jaw that she did not propose to do so in public.

Cautiously, Tomas had only explained to the others that Henrik's wife needed to travel to Rivertop to visit a relative, and that he would be accompanying her as a brother-officer of her husband. Lias had accepted this without any obvious reaction, but Rauor had looked sceptical. Now, as they were steadily jolted on their way across the countryside, Tomas saw Rauor glance first at him and then at Bodila. Rauor's eyes momentarily flickered down to her stomach. With an amused smile he returned his gaze to Tomas and tapped his lips gently with a single finger. Time would tell whether the promise implicit in that gesture could be relied upon.

At the coaching station within Rivertop, Lias parted from them without a word. His own relatively modest luggage was entrusted to a runner and he set off through the town, an apprehensive set to his shoulders. Tomas watched as the mail bag was taken down and also rushed away, bearing his sealed report for Victor's consideration.

Rauor though, lingered. While Bodila was supervising the loading of her luggage into a handcart, he drew Tomas to one side, shaking him by the hand.

"It has been a pleasure to make your

acquaintance, investigator. I hope that we may meet again in easier circumstances, but I fear that it is not to be."

Tomas mumbled some appropriately sincere response, but Rauor, it seemed, had more to say.

"None of the others would ask you this. I had almost made up my mind not to. But you are keeping secrets of your own I see, and I can assure you that we will keep yours, whatever may happen. Don't bother to deny it, it is not to the point. As I say, we will not betray your secret and that is not conditional on what I am about to say."

He pulled Tomas closer to him and spoke urgently, directly into his ear.

"I think we can trust you and Victor Appelsin to do the right thing, but Merson is a great believer in freedom to choose. Still, if you did want to choose to help us, whatever your motives, there is one thing that you both could do."

Tomas turned to look at him, impassively, unwilling to commit himself by asking what it was, even as he did not pull away.

"I know that you have written a report, but I also suspect that it is for Appelsin's consumption only. When you come to circulate the information more widely, why not have it that you parted company with us at Braed Tor? You could have made your own way to Car Peronel, Fest notwithstanding, and there is no need for it to be known that we were there."

He stepped back, looking anxiously at Tomas and releasing his hand. "I hope I have not offended you. It was not my intention. Can we at least part amicably?"

He extended his empty hand and Tomas, still trying to absorb this final demand being made on his loyalty, watched as if at one remove as his own hand extended and seized Rauor's in a firm grip.

The tutor turned, and in his confident manner called out to Bodila, "Farewell, my dear. I wish you a pleasant and productive stay in our fair precinct!" Then, with a final mischievous grin to Tomas, he turned and left, following in the direction of his friend. Tomas's own duties were for the moment clear, even if he could not yet see the shape of the conversation that he was soon to have with Victor. He turned back to Bodila, confirming that her arrangements with her luggage were complete, and extended his arm courteously to her.

The walk home was a slow one, and not only because of the heavy load of luggage that was following along behind them. Tomas spent most of the time looking anxiously around him in case he should encounter any of his colleagues, or the numerous other people who knew him, any of whom might wonder why he was escorting a strange woman who was not his wife. If they saw her luggage, let alone what else she was carrying, any number of questions might be raised, and rumours begun which Tomas could ill-afford.

For all that apprehension, however, it was the reaction of his wife that most concerned him. Soon, they were on the street where Tomas's house stood, and before he knew it, he stood at the bottom of the steps that led up to his front door. Leaving Bodila, at her insistence, to negotiate an appropriate fee with the luggage lad, Tomas took the steps two at a time towards a door that was already swinging open before him.

Idony had plainly been stood at a downstairs window, awaiting his arrival. Now she stood in the doorway, a confused and slightly hurt look in her eyes. This, Tomas knew he must immediately address, but all of the carefully rehearsed lines that he had spent so long considering fled from his mind. Instead he hurried forward and clasped his wife's hands in his own, looking deeply into her troubled eyes.

"My darling, can you trust me? This lady is the wife of a dear friend and she is in considerable trouble. She has come to us for help."

The rest could wait. The few words had contained all the straight-forwardness that a carefully rehearsed speech would have lacked, and it was the quality that Idony most respected in her husband. Brushing him aside she came down the steps without further hesitation.

"My dear friend," she called, in a voice carefully pitched so that it did not seem calculated to draw attention, but which would be heard by any whose attention had already been attracted by the scene. "My husband is an oaf to leave you standing there. Pray do tell the luggage lad to bring your bags inside and we can go in and catch up. It really has been far too long!"

Whatever reception Bodila had been expecting, it plainly was not this. Relief at the warmth of the welcome seemed to overwhelm her and she sagged where she stood. Again, Idony's reactions were equal to the task.

"Tomas, quickly!" He hurried down the steps to her side. "I think she's going to faint. Let us get her inside and out of the heat." Then in an undertone that only Tomas was meant to hear, but which to his relief was laced with a great deal of good humour, she continued: "and then, dearest, you have a considerable amount of explaining to do."

That evening, Tomas revelled in the simple pleasure of their companionable night-time routine. Bodila was settled in the main guest room, her belongings unpacked and a pleasant, if somewhat quiet, dinner having been eaten.

Now they were moving through the house, dousing candles and checking the bolts and shutters.

"There has been so much to discuss, this evening, and I have quite forgotten to ask how you spent your Fest."

Idony turned to him, putting a hand on her husband's chest as she leaned close. "I own that it was very dull in parts, but several friends came to pay their regards. Victor joined me for luncheon on the first day, and escorted me for a brief walk in the park the day before yesterday."

"That was good of him. He said he might try to."

"Yes, I think that he felt guilty for sending you off as he did. He spent most of the time we were together apologising for it."

Tomas hesitated. "It was good that he did, I think. I have a great deal to discuss with him tomorrow, but... yes, he will be glad that he sent me. It might have been the only chance we had to find out some information that will be very important to him."

They stood silent for a moment, the house in darkness around them, the lights burning in their bedroom illuminating the way ahead. In the end, Idony broke from the embrace and started for the door to their chamber.

Only once they were inside, and the door was closed, did she continue.

"I confess, Tomas, that your message left me very perplexed. I couldn't work out why you would ask me to give the old nursery an airing. I certainly never imagined the incredible news that you were bringing me."

"I know, my dearest. I know. I wish I could have

found a way to give you better warning, but..."

"Hush, sweetheart. It's alright."

Even as she said it, Idony's eyes started to fill with tears. All the repressed emotion of the day, and of the lonely week before that, surged up in Tomas and he found that he was weeping too, both of them clinging to each other as they had so many times against a tide of feelings that threatened to submerge them. Somehow, though, there was a cleansing quality to these tears. He felt his heart lightening as they flowed from him.

Perhaps Idony too had found something positive in the outpouring of emotion. Incredibly, within only a few minutes, he felt her shifting against him and heard a faint laugh drift up from where her head was buried in his chest.

She stepped back, and gazed up at him in the candle-light. Dishevelled and tear stained, she had never looked more beautiful.

"I am glad you came home safe to me. It's all I prayed for while you were gone. But now... now you've found a way to answer all our prayers."

Tomas, head full of all that could still go wrong, opened his mouth to try to limit her expectations. Idony smiled and shook her head, pressing herself back into his embrace.

"I know, Tomas, I know. Nothing is certain until it happens. After... what happened... I never thought that I could hope again. But somehow, I can believe in this."

She leant back, her smiling teary eyes glistening in the candle's gleam.

"I think at long last we're going to have a child of our own again."

After all of the disruption of the preceding days, it should have been comforting the next morning for Tomas to resume his usual routine. Yet from the moment he awoke the next morning he felt a growing apprehension growing in him. He was terse and uncommunicative over breakfast, and Idony, recognising that the only remedy would be for him to confront his fear, bade him farewell, assuring him that she and Bodila would be much happier getting to know one another without his interference.

The journey to the armoury in the bright summer sunlight passed all too quickly. He knocked and entered Victor's office and found his superior stood with his back to the door, gazing out over the green practice sward. The report, detailing every step that his investigation had taken, sat in a neat pile in the centre of his desk. Tomas stepped hesitantly into the room and Victor turned, his face unreadable against the bright sunlight which framed him. Then he said, "I think I might go for a ride, Tomas. Do you wish to accompany me?"

Briskly, and without conversation, they made their way to the stables. Victor called over one of the grooms, disdaining Tomas's offer of assistance in mounting. Serge Goodmartin, another investigator, came over, with a curious look on his face.

"Are we riding out? I did not receive any instructions."

Victor waited as he settled himself into his saddle. Then he turned a polite face to Tomas's colleague. "I am pressed for time today, Serge, and thought that Tomas might debrief me on his investigations over Fest while I take my constitutional. Nothing for you to be concerned about."

"Of course, Arch. I was very busy myself over Fest. Perhaps I might update you on those activities later, over a coffee?"

Victor smiled blandly, "I would welcome that, Serge. Speak to my assistant and have him fix the meeting, would you?"

Serge, ego appropriately massaged, bade them farewell and they made for the northern gate, passing not very far from Lord Kerton's house. Tomas spent a fleeting moment wondering whether Rauor had returned there, and if so what his reception had been.

Once out of the precinct, Victor called across to Tomas, "Let's give them their heads! Keep within the green!" For several minutes they rode as hard as the horses wished to go. They went directly north at first but before long they reached the edge of the woodland, which marked the limit of surveillance from the towers of the precinct. There they turned anti-clockwise, following the line of the boundary at a little over two arrow shots' remove from the tree line.

After a few more moments, Victor slowed his horse to a gentle canter, and signalled Tomas to come near him. Tomas smiled hesitantly, and was rewarded by a warm smile in return. Any lingering concerns that Tomas might have had evaporated with Victor's first words.

"This is about as discreet as we can be, Tomas. I have read your report and own that you have been more successful than I ever expected. I fear that you must have some further questions you would like to put to me, but I am certainly grateful for the opportunity to discuss matters with you before you circulated your information more widely."

"Not at all Victor," he started, feeling a faint echo of his discussions in the wilderness with Merson and Forba, "I simply need to know what you would have me do."

Victor shook his head with a regretful grimace. "Loyal Tomas. I really have caused you no end of trouble this time."

"I fear that the trouble is as much my making as yours. I started this thinking that you wanted revenge. I understood that. What I have heard though, makes me wonder whether that was ever your intention."

"It is as you say. I confess, I set you to investigate precisely because it would be so readily comprehensible. I though if I told you that I wanted to renew my contact with them, that you might not understand my motives. I am not sure that even now I quite understand them."

This was not at all the conversation that Tomas had been rehearsing fearfully in his head since waking. All of his carefully planned circumspection fell away.

"Is it true, what they told me? Did you know what Maryam was doing?"

Victor's head sank, but his voice still carried across the gap between them. "I knew it. Gods help me, I even encouraged her! We had no secrets from one another. Her role as researcher for the Tower on all manner of logistical matters ensured that she had access to more or less everything. Everything she saw filled her with horror. She hated what our world had become, and she taught me to hate it too.

"Our reactions were different. She wanted to break it all down and start again. I wanted to work from within. I think it was only once I had lost her that I realised that that can too easily turn into a coward's excuse to do nothing."

Despite the emotion that Tomas was sure must be churning within him, Victor spoke casually. It was as if he were speaking of someone else, of one of their cases.

"They killed her, you see. Killed her, and left me for dead. No secret is more important than a human life. And these were not secrets that mattered to anyone any more. I saw half of what she passed on to Groenne and the others. They were ancient history. But someone had decided that they had to be secret, and decided that the gravest penalty should be visited on those who broke the silence."

Victor's horse slowed to a trot and Tomas circled once before coming up alongside him again. There was a dark shadowy patch of woodland ahead that had been the scene of several small raiding attempts in recent weeks. Tomas took the unilateral decision to avoid any possibility of danger and turned his horse's head away. Victor followed suit, without question.

"So I decided that I would cover their tracks for them. I forged diary entries for Maryam which suggested that she had only been accumulating documents for her own purposes, and that she had burnt these before going out to the theatre that evening. Like a loyal officer I handed it in, and received a commendation for my loyalty. I waited a discreet period of time and then requested a transfer here."

"Why Rivertop?"

"There was no reason. It had always struck me as being a slow and quiet place. It isn't of course, but it has a quality which is entirely lacking in the capital nowadays. It still has compassion. I came here, and I tried to put everything that had happened out of my mind.

"But, somehow, a fascination with the people that Maryam had been involved with started to steal over me. I knew where to start: Car Vandra. Maryam had taken several trips there in order to meet with them. There was a series of fires, a co-ordinated attack, which I suspected them of being part of. Your explanation of that incident relieves me, because I had never had the impression that the group that Maryam dealt with would be willing to resort to indiscriminate violence. A number of innocents died in those fires.

"At the time, though, all I had were generalised suspicions. I could not find anything to connect any suspects to the attacks. I had almost given up searching when I found what I was looking for rather closer to home."

Victor described his shock at encountering Forba, although of course he did not then know her name, at an event in Car Peronel. Her distinctive red hair and accent had not been altered by the intervening years, but he had seen a difference in her. She had seemed to glow with an inner light. He shook his head at the idea that she and her companions had actually met the elves.

As Victor talked Tomas's mind returned to the main question which he had failed to resolve in his report, and which he was still grappling with. If, as their story suggested, Forba's group had been given something to assist them with their project to bring human-kind back out of its lethargy, where was it? What was it? True, their encounter with the elves would explain the peculiar properties of the travelling cloaks they all wore, and Forba had said that the pixies had been drawn to them on their return. But surely there was something more substantial than that. When Merson had spoken of it, he had made it sound as if the project had succeeded beyond their expectations.

Victor meanwhile was focusing on more practical concerns. "Their story is incredible, it is true, but knowing the details of it leave me no closer to knowing what we should do now."

Tomas laughed. "I had hoped that you would give me instructions, make some sense of all of this for me."

This drew a sigh from his superior. "I wish that I could do so, Tomas, truly I do. There is just so much that we still do not know. And I am afraid that what we do know makes our duty very clear..."

[Extract from letter from Quaestor Feiger to Arch-Investigator Appelsin – dated 4th Nieumor XXVI Tor.]

Dear Appelsin,

It has not been customary for our two organisations to show in practice that collegiate mentality which we both profess in public. Indeed I have been sceptical about the extent to which any such co-operation is really achievable between two competitors such as we are.

Nevertheless, it is to be recognised that we both serve the realm, in addition to our respective share-holders, and it is therefore incumbent on me to acknowledge and thank you for the prompt and comprehensive manner in which your subordinate, Investigator Callan, has provided his reports to me on the events that took place in Braed Tor, over the Fest period just past. I also own that I am impressed that your instincts had led towards the same targets that my quaestors have been investigating, supplementing the wealth of information which we had already gathered.

There are certain matters, indirectly arising out of that investigation, which may have implications generally for law enforcement as practised by your organisation, mine, and our smaller competitors. We are now at the point where it is important that intelligence be shared between us, and for that purpose, the possibility of appointing appropriate liaison personnel has been mooted. These will operate under my control and supervision, and it is I, in due course, who will formally submit a report to the lords and masters. Nevertheless some credit for the discoveries I have made will naturally reflect on those who are seen to have co-operated with, and in small measure assisted, the investigation.

You will no doubt be contacted through more formal channels in due course, but in the meantime I wished to bring these matters to your attention so that you might have an opportunity to consider whether you might bring yourself to part with such a valuable adjutant, in order to provide an appropriate representative on behalf of Rivertop's enforcement services.

[Extract ends]

28

Tomas felt a jolt of fear run through him, as the carriage door jumped under the force of an impact from outside. The two quaestor guards that rode with him made a great show of their implacability, but Tomas still noticed that they cast a brief glance at one another as the carriage rocked on its wheels.

Thick drapes hung across the carriage windows keeping out fumes and indeed protecting from the danger of broken glass, but they could do nothing to obstruct the smell which emanated from the horde of clampits. They were clustered around the vehicle, pressing, hammering, calling out in guttural voices. Tomas heard a scream, one who had perhaps come too close to the valuable horses and received an arrow from the gate guards for his lack of caution.

Grindingly slowly, the carriage made its way onwards. In the darkness, Tomas felt a building sense of anxiety, far greater than the low-level trepidation which he had felt ever since receiving the summons that had brought him back to Car Peronel. In truth, there had been a gradually building sense of inevitability to this return, ever since he and Victor had submitted their report.

For several days there had been no response. Then Tomas and his colleagues started to hear rumours that the quaestors had secured an important victory, one which (albeit discretely) they were determined to mine for all the political capital they could. Within another day the rumours had solidified into fact, fuelling Tomas's worst fears. The quaestors had secured the cooperation of an informer who knew the details of a significant conspiracy aimed at destabilising the realm. Tomas, without any more information, wished that he could reserve judgement until he had details. But the coincidence of timing seemed to be too great.

If Merson and his friends had been betrayed, it did not seem too difficult to identify the likely culprit. But if Alyster had betrayed them, there were certain omissions in Tomas's report that would surely be identified. Yet for several days no formal response to the report was forthcoming.

In the meantime, rumours continued to circulate within the law enforcement community. One of Tomas's colleagues, previously appointed as staff liaison to the Tower, returned to Rivertop at short notice, his tenure curtailed. He gave Tomas a wide berth, but stories which had plainly originated from him started to circulate in the mess hall. The quaestors had had a series of serious reverses prior to their recent success. A number of their elite special solutions teams had been lost in actions in Braed Tor and also outside the green, in the wild lands around Hartrick Hall. In the latter action Victor heard something about an intelligence-led raid on a farm house which had ended in an unexplained fire, taking the lives of all those who had made the assault.

The carriage groaned its way through the gateway as Tomas thought back over those anxious days. All of the information which had made its way to him was lacking in details and he could not have expressed any special interest in the matter without risking self-incrimination. Then, a week after his return to Rivertop, he had been called for a meeting with Victor. An express request had been made for Tomas's services. It was couched in the terms of a reward for his efforts in pursuing and identifying the members of Merson's group, but the effect of it was that he was summoned to the Tower to take up liaison duties without delay. Specifically, he was to attend on the final stages of the debriefing of the quaestors' secretive informer.

His thoughts skated over the difficult farewell from Idony. Instead he remembered reporting to the Armoury the previous night, the strange contrast between the congratulations and envy of his colleagues, and his own carefully suppressed sense of dread. He glanced across at his travelling companions, as the carriage cleared the gateway into the precinct and continued on up the main avenue towards the island complex where the Tower awaited him. They had been with him since he awakened that morning, courteous, but curiously remote for what were ostensibly his guides in the new protocols and environments that he would be encountering.

He leant forward.

"Do you know – I have never previously been invited within the Tower?"

The two men opposite him exchanged bland, disinterested, looks. It was the senior of the two who responded, his voice tinged with faint irony.

"Everyone should go inside, at least once in their lives."

"Tomas Callan, I am so pleased to make your acquaintance!"

An hour had passed – the time taken up with the issuing of Tomas's pass for the main levels of the Tower, and arrangements for his personal belongings to be taken to the lodgings he had been allocated elsewhere in the complex. Now he stood in a small ante-chamber on the fifth or sixth floor, greeted by a man in light-weight but carefully pressed pantaloons and a cut-away topcoat which revealed an ample belly, scarcely contained within a pin-striped waistcoat.

"You have the advantage of me sir" Tomas replied carefully. In the Tower of all places, the importance of the proper forms could not be over-stated.

"My dear fellow, of course, how remiss of me! I am Cap' Ensor Brattix. Quaestor Feiger sends his apologies, but as you may imagine he is busy finalising arrangements for the presentation later."

"The presentation?"

Brattix looked nonplussed. "Come sir, you are funning with me, are you not? You must know that all of the high town is a-flutter with expectation for Feiger's presentation of his famous prisoner, the culmination of his masterful interrogation!"

"Indeed," replied Tomas carefully, "I am eager to witness it myself. I had simply not appreciated that it was to be conducted in the manner of a public presentation."

"Oh no no, investigator," Brattix's hands fluttered at the buttons of his waistcoat, "not public, my goodness me. Just a carefully selected audience of four or five hundred, all the very best sort."

He dropped his voice to a whisper. "There will be things spoken of, don't you know, which must not be heard by untrusted ears."

Tomas leaned closer conspiratorially. "Is that so? You sound to be extremely well-informed. Is there anything you can tell me of the nature of the planned revelations?"

"Dear fellow, you must not ask! Feiger is a demon for secrecy and I know that he intends the occasion to have some drama – I would not deprive him of the satisfaction.

"But do not look too downcast my dear fellow – he has left special instructions for your diversion until the main event begins. We have a very special surprise prepared for you. Come this way!"

Tomas's heart was beating an excited rhythm on the inside of his uniform shirt, and his sword belt (stripped of its weapon at the entrance to the Tower) felt tight across his stomach. It took all of his self-discipline to arrange his features into a disinterested facade as he was led deeper into the Tower's interior.

In these inner corridors, no natural daylight penetrated. Secured lanterns cast a nauseating orange light through grimy glass panes, and illuminated bare stone floors and an occasional martial tapestry. As they reached the centre of the floor, Tomas saw for the first time the famous double spiral staircase which ran in a pair of uninterrupted flights from the basements all of the way up to the uppermost grand council chamber. Brattix carefully locked the door behind him as they entered the circular central chamber which encircled the staircase. Looking around the walls, Tomas could see several other recessed doors, all of them closed and presumably also locked.

"We shall use the transport cars later" explained Brattix, pointing to the rope and pulley system which hung down between the spiralling staircase.

"It is powered by some of the Tower's prisoners, don't you know?"

"So I had heard. Most ingenious."

"But for now we are only ascending a couple of floors. So it will be quicker to walk."

As they stepped onto the staircase, one of the transport cars dropped past Tomas at dramatic speed. He could not help but flinch, but Brattix took it in his stride, leading on up the curve of stairs. They passed two landings, each unmarked. At the third, Tomas, looking carefully, saw the elf number nine pressed into the stone step, like the crest in butter from a butter mould. Despite the number of feet which must have brushed its surface over the centuries, it did not seem to have eroded at all.

At the ninth level, the doors were certainly locked, and indeed the door through which Brattix and Tomas passed was guarded by two alert quaestors, armed with swords that were practical, rather than ceremonial. Beyond, there was a stillness. Tomas glanced about him, alert for any sudden attack, uncertain what he might do to repulse it. But there were just empty corridors in each direction.

"Follow me, investigator, straight ahead."

On one side of the corridor up ahead, a low wall provided a partial barrier to a large opening. As they drew level with it, Tomas realised that the opening extended downwards to the level below, and at once he knew what he had been brought to see. Drawing close to the wall and peering down, he found himself looking into the containment area, where a number of barred cells opened onto a central guard area, where three more armed quaestors stood at the alert.

Tomas felt a lurch in his stomach as he recognised the inhabitants of the cells, even though he had half-expected it. Merson was there, and Forba, and Raour. Lias Nefflor too could be heard, although not seen, intoning a mournful prisoner's lament in an off-key tone which, to Tomas's ear, was designed to be deliberately irritating. Of Alyster and his sister there was no sign.

"So, investigator?" Brattix whispered eagerly into his ear. "How is it to see them again? You must be very proud of the part you played in their apprehension. I own that I have never known Feiger to express so much praise for a mere... that is to say, for an investigator."

"Thank you. It is strange, certainly, to find them here. A testament to the efficiency of your forces."

"Indeed. They are an unusual group, is that not so? So varied in age, and in background. We could not find anything in their pasts to connect them or to suggest what led them to form this conspiracy."

Tomas looked around sharply, a frown creasing his forehead, but Brattix's thoughts had already taken him in another direction. "I must show you the girl. Of all of them, perhaps the strangest. Come on investigator, this way."

The corridor passed through a wall that stretched up from the floor below. On the far side, more cells, and another guard post. Here, though, the guards seemed more relaxed. Indeed as Tomas glanced down at them he could see that one had unbuckled his chest-plate and that all three were sat playing a card game.

He turned a look of enquiry to Brattix.

"It is well. These guards are strictly speaking off duty, but they are taking their break in this area in order to supervise her. They do not need to be terribly alert, after all. She has slept since her arrival."

Peering down, Tomas could see Elyssa on a low

wooden pallet bed inside the cell closest to the guards' table. Her blonde hair hung in disorder around her face, and a tranquil innocence radiated from her. He could not help but smile. She might just as easily have been asleep at home, without a care in the world, rather than imprisoned in the most secure fortress in the kingdom.

Tomas's smile faded.

"Why is she a prisoner here? She had no part in their plotting as far as I could tell."

Brattix shrugged. "The Tower knows. She is an associate of theirs after all, and it is not a time to take any chances." He glanced about him uncomfortably.

"I am sorry, investigator. Would that we had more time. But we must make haste to gain our seats in the chamber."

Without another word, Tomas was hurried from the room.

The audience chamber was a room unlike any that Tomas had been in before. Completely circular, it occupied the entire cross-section of the Tower. Narrow windows climbed from floor to ceiling at every side of the room, spilling sunlight into the chamber. No doubt the view from them would have been incredible, if any of the attendees had been so inept as to walk over and take a look. Tomas, recognising that he was in an arena where the Council of Style held close sway, made sure to observe and carefully emulate the behaviour of those around him. They all ostentatiously disdained any possibility of a glimpse of the view, so he followed suit.

Like the majority of the dignitaries invited to this event, Tomas had been required to ascend in the prisoner-powered elevator well ahead of the commencement. Only the lords and masters would arrive closer to the scheduled start time. As a result, he was left to wander the room, indulging in superficial conversation with his social betters, while anxiously awaiting a hand on his shoulder. His freedom to mingle with a substantial number of the most influential people in the realm strongly suggested that he was not under any suspicion, but every moment spent in this place represented considerable danger for him, for Idony and the family they soon hoped to have, for Bodila and Henrik, and for Victor.

There was no mistaking the purpose of the event. Everywhere, the banners of the Quaestor Corporation were hung, making the none too subtle point that it was they who were responsible for the earth-shattering revelations that were promised before the so-called presentation was concluded. Tomas noted with interest that among the dignitaries who now stood talking and helping themselves to refreshments, there were a number who wore extremely apprehensive expressions. Tomas made a mental note to investigate further those who he recognised, assuming of course that they would all be permitted to leave after the day's revelations.

A gong sounded, and the attendees started to seat themselves. Curved banks of seating, divided into three sections and following the curvature of the room, filled much of the floor space. The lords and masters were accustomed to having a section each to themselves, comprising around a dozen chairs and associated storage and desk-tops for their staff of advisers and note takers. Ordinarily, they would also be separated into three voting blocks, reflective of the three political estates which ostensibly represented the entire range of popular opinion. On this occasion, however, the staff were all excluded, and party political differences were put aside, in order that they should be consolidated into a single sector. The lords and masters consequently found themselves in rather closer proximity to one another than they were accustomed to, or found comfortable.

The remaining functionaries and high officials occupied the other two sectors. Whatever their background or their level of perceived elevation, however, none of them could entirely stop their eyes from being drawn to the hooded and cloaked figure who, after they were seated, was man-handled into the centre of the room.

There, a large gilded seat, like the base section of a throne without the backboard, was fixed in the very centre of the stage. The hooded man was seated on it, his cloak removed and his wrists chained on each side to rings set in the floor at some distance from the seat. This caused his arms to be pulled out to the sides away from his body. His clothing was the simple orange uniform that all prisoners of the realm were required to wear, in order to mark them out. The black hood was tucked into the collar of his shirt.

He was completely motionless.

The gong sounded again, somewhere close at hand, but invisible to Tomas from his seat. Around him there was a hushed flurry of activity as the rest of the crowd of onlookers settled themselves. Without leaving any time for conversation to set in, a quaestor inquisitor strode into the room, flanked by a series of staff members who fussed around the chains, set up a water jug and cup for the quaestor, and arrayed paper and a selection of quills for the formal record that would undoubtedly have to be made of the event.

Tomas peered as closely at the inquisitor as propriety would permit. So this was quaestor Feiger. As he stood there in his formal robes of office at the centre of the room he seemed determined to take sole credit for the conspiracy that he had uncovered. After all of Tomas's imaginings, he seemed a slight man in person, borrowing the authority of a very ornate outfit. The Quaestor Corporation had a very different aesthetic sensibility to the investigators, but at the moment it was the former that was in favour with the Council.

The quaestor raised a large staff and hammered it into a dark stone in the centre of the floor which bore the marks of many such ceremonial strikings. Silence fell.

[Extract from 'The Rainbow Prize' (traditional mage tale)]

...The next corridor, yellow in hue, was filled with a coloured smoke which matched the walls and saturated Nail's mind with terrifying imaginings. The horrors conjured up within the smoke tested his stubborn resolve almost to its breaking point. Any sane man would have given in to fear at this point, but Nail's implacable hatred of the elves was a madness which enabled him to withstand what others could not.

So it continued, as he advanced. Each challenge he confronted forced him to overcome yet another of his most base instincts. In the green corridor, he was forced to struggle with nausea more extreme than on the roughest sea voyage. In the blue corridor, he was almost overwhelmed by a crushing sadness which left him sitting, sobbing for days on the corridor floor before he was eventually, obstinately, able to pull himself onwards.

That brought him to the last corridor, purple in hue, the sixth and final colour. This was peopled by nymphs made of smoke and imagination, who teased and tantalised him in ways which you, my young listener, ought not even to be able to imagine.

It suffices to say that somehow, at last, he overcame them all, and burst through to the centre of the maze, and the prize which awaited him...

29

(Original note of the final confession of [Subject T187356]. Public Interview. Attendee list is appended to this document. Not to be distributed without redaction.)

Q. Feiger: Welcome my Lords and Masters, gentlemen. You have all received the briefing which explains how we came to be here, and the information which the quaestors, with the limited external assistance of other agencies, have been able to develop leading up to this point.

Q. Feiger: In a moment, I will introduce you to our guest here, although perhaps he is known to some of you already? Before starting, however, I wish to explain in a little detail how we were able to secure his remarkable confession, and the level of co-operation which we have been able to achieve [prepared statement to be annexed].

Q. Feiger: ...and so now, the time has come, to introduce you to our key witness. You will note that additional quaestor guards are taking up positions around the room. For the witness's own safety, he is going to deliver his most dramatic accusations now, in public, and for the first time. Those of you who are shortly to be implicated will in all likelihood know who you are already, and I urge you to surrender yourselves into custody now, so that you might receive some minimal clemency from the courts at your trials for treason.

[Pause. Silence]

Q. Feiger: Not a single person? How disappointing. Yet how predictable. Very well, without any further delay, may I present to you, Alyster Trale!

T187356: I say Feiger, I didn't think you were going to use my full name?

[Laughter]

Q. Feiger: It will be struck from the record. Strike it from the record! And these comments as well!

[Note: redact last line, anonymise T throughout]

Q. Feiger: Very well. Mr Trale, will you now please disclose to the assembled lords and masters, and those others who are also present, the matters that you and I have discussed.

T187356: Certainly my dear Feiger.

T187356: I should not wish to take too much of the credit for the discovery of this conspiracy. Nevertheless, it is almost entirely as a result of my own perspicacity that we find ourselves assembled her today. I and I alone have possession of information which has grave implications for the realm, and for the Lords and Masters who govern it.

T187356: I have outlined to my dear friend Captain, I am sorry, now Major Boomel, most of the detail that you have heard rehearsed before you today by the noble quaestor inquisitor. Equally, however, there were matters which I felt intuitively to be too sensitive for his ears. Having earned the trust of the worthy Feiger, I outlined for him the barest essentials of what I had discovered. He at once saw that my precautions had been correct. The conspiracy which my discoveries point to is so wide-ranging that I could not take the chance to imparting my knowledge to any other single person. The danger to my life that such a course of action would entail would be utterly intolerable.

Q. Feiger: Very well. You have explained, yet again, the considerations that have led you here. Now that we are here, perhaps you would start by vouchsafing to us the names of the conspirators that you have discovered?

T187356: I certainly intend to. I must confess, however, that while I am entirely of your mind as to the necessity of these restraints in principle, their presence is somewhat distracting to me. Is there any chance that they might be...

Q. Feiger: Certainly not! Whatever trust you may have earned with your confession only extends so far.

T187356: I am pained to hear you say so. After all, you have previously been content to let me attend the opera in public with Major Boomel. I had simply hoped that...

[Q. Feiger strikes the prisoner]

Q. Feiger: Be silent! You are in danger of confusing the issue. I must ask you please not to waste this distinguished audience's time with irrelevancies, but simply to disclose the names that you came here to disclose.

T187356: Quite so. You are right to remind me, although I cannot say that your methods entirely command my support. I am, you know, quite capable of being reminded of my purpose without it being necessary for you to descend to physical violence.

T187356: Now then.

T187356: I am sorry, I have quite lost any sense of what my next words were to be. Is it possible that I might have a small drink of water, simply to give me a chance to gather my thoughts.

[inaudible – Q. Feiger whispers directly into prisoner's ear]

T187356: Very well. I see that this is not an occasion for civility. I cannot see what may be so objectionable in a request for some basic refreshment but... No! No! I will do as you request.

T187356: I will name the conspirators.

Q. Feiger: Very good. Coactors! Stand by to arrest any man named! The rest of you, guard the doors and do not let any person in or out until this process is complete! Now, if you would be so kind?

T187356: Yes, of course. I explained to you the circumstances in which I overheard the conversation between my aunt and uncle did I not? I recollect that you had agreed to make it a matter of public record that I was acting at the specific request of the quaestors doing so.

Q. Feiger: Indeed. Pray continue.

T187356: I hesitate to say this. You will not think it discourteous I hope? You must see that I am in a somewhat difficult position. My closest family friends are implicated in a conspiracy and I have no immediate prospects or means of support. All that I have to my credit is my reputation, and I must, therefore, preserve it at all costs. I must do so, indeed, even at the risk of straining your not inconsiderable patience.

Q. Feiger: Please come to the point. There are a considerable number of important people here to witness your confession. I must ask you please to satisfy their curiosity without further delay.

T187356: I see. You perceive, I hope, the

difficulty that you place me in? On the one hand, you are all I am sure most eager for the information which I have come here to disclose. It would be a considerable discourtesy to keep you in anticipation for a moment longer than necessary. But at the same time I fear that I must, until my own status in the aftermath of this interrogation is confirmed. Your refusal to provide me with the comfort I require does not encourage me to think that the immunity that I had been promised is truly likely to be forthcoming...

Q. Feiger: Of course it is! We are the Tower, you arrogant child! If we make a promise to you, that promise will be kept without question. Assuming, of course, that you adhere to your part of the bargain. Now tell us the names!

T187356: I see that I have vexed you and I am sorry for it. Perhaps a compromise is in order. If you will show your trust in me by releasing my wrists from these uncomfortable restraints, I will take you at your word as to my well-being and situation once this procedure is complete.

T187356: Inquisitor? I am trying to be reasonable. Please will you extend me this one small courtesy?

Q. Feiger: You think I do not know your purpose? You have no intention of making a confession today, do you?

T187356: My dear sir, that is a preposterous assertion. You have all come here today to hear evidence of a conspiracy, and I am prepared to provide it. First, however, I simply ask that you would loosen these chains a little. I must say, Feiger, that I really am quite taken aback by your intransigence on this point. I had become quite accustomed to your solicitude to my comfort!

Q. Feiger: There will be no further concessions

to your "comfort". You need to remember your place, witness!

T187356: I could scarcely forget my place. I am chained to it.

[Further laughter]

Q. Feiger: You have been brought here to testify. So, testify!

T187356: Oh very well. Now then, what was I saying?

[Q. Feiger strikes the prisoner again]

Q. Feiger: The names, damme you, the names!

T187356: [inaudible]

T187356: I think you dislodged one of my teeth. I cannot think that this is the model of decorum which the lords and masters are accustomed to witnessing. For my part I do apologise to them most sincerely that they have been obliged to experience it.

T187356: Very well, Feiger, I will give you the names.

T187356: The conspiracy comprised the following individuals: Merson Blare of Braed Tor. Rauor Tell of Rivertop. Forba Groenne of Car Peronel, who may well be known to a number of you. Lias Nefflor, a failed composer, also of Rivertop. And lastly, though it very greatly pains me to say it, my own parents: Artesso Trale and Shallia Trale originally of Car Peronel but thereafter of a farm in the forests close to the marshallcy of Lord Hartrick. Ah, yes, there he is. Good morning my Lord!

Q. Feiger: Those names were already known to us! They are all already either dead or in custody. What about the others?

T187356: Yes, you are right. I do collect that I spoke to you of at least one other. There ought to be seven really, after all. You know what a fetish the elves made of the number seven. There was that story, was there not? Do you remember? Oh no, that's right, you had never read it – what a pity!

Q. Feiger: Is that so?

T187356: Indeed. The story was one that was taught to me from a young age, together with a number of other instructive mage-tales. Had you but known it, you might have understood more clearly the purpose of our conversations, you might even have realised why I chose to put myself so conveniently in your power in the first place.

Q. Feiger: [laughing] So you begin to show your hand at last, Mister Trale. Even now you think to taunt me with my apparent ignorance. But your arrogance has undone you. The fact is that I am well aware of what you are attempting to do. I have always known your purpose, but I have had my own reasons for permitting the charade to continue for as long as it has.

Q. Feiger: Mister Trale believes that he has carefully manoeuvred all of us into the position that we are in today. Little did he realise quite how transparent his schemes have been to the combined intelligence forces of the Quaestor Corporation! Indeed we know rather more about Mister Trale than anyone else alive, save for those others of the conspiracy that he named, and who are in custody below us.

T187356: Now see here, old fellow...

Q. Feiger: Be silent! You have had your entertainment at my expense and I have been willing to indulge it for as long as there was a chance that more of your co-conspirators would be revealed. Now it is my turn to speak. You see, we at the Quaestor Corporation have known about Mister Trale and his fellow conspirators for some considerable time. We have been watching them, ever since we learnt of a small journey that they made, into the west.

Q. Feiger: You will all struggle to believe this, but it is true, and I hope that we shall see some evidence of the truth of it before long. Six of them travelled into the west, and seven returned. How is that possible, you ask? With the help of the elves!

[General uproar, lasting several minutes]

Q. Feiger. You are all entitled to be sceptical, I was at first. But then this young man contacted one of my officers. No cause, no provocation. But it just so happened that through our network of informers, he and his fellow conspirators, the persons that he has named already, had already come to our attention. I alone realised that the timing was a little too convenient. That their careful provocations, their painted symbols throughout the precincts, were a little too deliberately ostentatious. That it was all part of an elaborate scheme, to bring us all together, to bring Mister Trale into our midst.

Q. Feiger: To what end? Maybe Mister Trale would like to explain that himself.

T187356: [mumbles]

Q. Feiger: What did you say?

T187356: It's not possible. How can you know all this?

Q. Feiger: We have sources, many and varied. But of course you were so confident, weren't you? So sure that the lackbrain quaestors would not see through your elaborate scheme! So you started dropping little riddles and puzzles into your oh so carefully tedious monologues. Teasing me with your references to the seventh colour, and the Rainbow Prize. And of course in your arrogance, you were quite content to believe me to be as ignorant as I pretended.

Q. Feiger: Many of you will know the tale of the

Rainbow Prize. As Mister Trale says, it is a common enough mage-tale. A villain, an enemy of the realm, had caused disruption to the elves' plans to bring the dark wars to an end. He had to be stopped. So they started to spread rumours, of a special maze comprising six obstacles, and at the centre of it a wondrous treasure which would be the death of the elves if it fell into the wrong hands. Have I remembered it correctly thus far?

T187356: You know that you have.

Q. Feiger: Six traps. The villain learnt all he could about these. They were set up sequentially using elven colour magic. He broke into the building which housed the maze and somehow managed to make his way past all six of the obstacles. He was after all very resourceful – it is why the elves feared him.

Q. Feiger: To his surprise, however, at the centre of the maze there was no treasure. Instead there was a seventh trap, the deadliest, and by the time that he realised he had been tricked, it had already snapped shut around him. He was never seen again.

T187356: Very good, you know your mage-tales. What of it?

Q. Feiger: The tale brings us directly to this man here, this apparently helpless prisoner. He is the seventh member of the group of six that he has always been so careful to implicate, the seventh trap, waiting to snap shut on us when we had killed the others or placed them safely into captivity. When we had become complacent and when we least expected any attack. What better place and time to do it than with all of the assembled lords and masters here, with important men from every corner of the realm gathered in one room?

Q. Feiger: And how did he propose to accomplish this feat? How was this reversal to be achieved? Mister Trale, you see, is not like the other six members of the group. Unfettered, I have no idea what limits there might be on his powers. It is why I had him bound you see, bound in iron. It is why he has been so eager to be released.

Q. Feiger: Six went into the west, and seven came back, as I said. They went to ask the elves for help, and that is precisely what they received. Help incarnate, I might call it.

Q. Feiger: Because just seven (seven!) months after their return, Shallia Trale gave birth to a child. A very special child. A child who looks to all intents and purposes like an ordinary human, but who is possessed of extraordinary powers. A child who grew up to be a man, confident enough in his abilities that he was prepared to give himself, and his friends, into our custody. Leading us on, teasing us, waiting for this moment when his powers would be revealed, and he would strike!

[Pause. Q. Feiger subjects prisoner to a further beating]

Q. Feiger: Well? What are you waiting for? Strike! My men are among the best in the realm. You might manage to kill some of them, but in the end you will be incapacitated. Then when the elves come to us, as they no doubt will, they will come on our terms. We shall hold their precious gift, and they will do precisely what we want if they are ever to secure his survival.

T187356: There are those, you know, who would kill me now, rather than see that happen.

Q. Feiger: I can certainly believe it. But where are they, these noble friends of yours? Are they truly willing to sacrifice your life in the service of their principles?

T187356: They are close at hand, believe me. But sacrificing me would achieve nothing for them, just as holding me will achieve nothing for you.

Q. Feiger: What do you mean?

T187356: I mean that there are still one or two matters that you have not fully discerned, even with all of the resources of the quaestors at your disposal. If you had truly understood the tale of the Rainbow Prize, you might have realised by now.

Q. Feiger: We have had enough of your...

T187356: Not quite. This is something that you would do well to listen to.

T187356: Elven colour magic had always been understood to work on the six colours of the spectrum. The so-called villain in that story had schooled himself to overcome each of the six branches of that magic. What he did not realise, what nobody knew, was that the elves had gone to dramatic lengths to create the trap for him. They created a seventh colour, indigo, and a new magic to accompany it. They made it up, simply to serve their purposes, and their creation was what lured him unsuspecting into his trap.

T187356: I may be the seventh colour, quaestor. But I am not the prize. I am not even the trap. I am just another part of a puzzle designed to keep you always looking in the wrong direction, until now, until that trap is sprung. You see, it is true that you know a great deal, quaestor: about my family; about their voyage to the elves; and about the gift that was given to them. A great deal. But...

30

*(19 years ago, several hundred nautical miles west
of Tryachan and one mile up)*

Artesso and Shallia blinked and looked about them.
Curiously, none of the others were near at hand but
from what Artesso had been able to discern, there
had been some sort of assessment process, and only
he and his wife had been found worthy. This was
not entirely surprising to him.

They stood in a room that seemed to be
comprised entirely of mirrors and light. Distances
were difficult to judge. Their reflections were
unclear and remote in the mirrors but they
nevertheless felt completely enclosed. Artesso drew
Shallia close to him and she looked up at him
apprehensively.

"Where are the elves, Artesso? I thought we
would meet the elves?"

"So we shall my love," he soothed her, "in their
own good time."

"What is this place?"

"I do not know. Perhaps it is the elvish sky-citadel that Blare and the others predicted?"

No sooner had the words been spoken, than Artesso heard an abrupt yet musical voice at his shoulder.

"It is a construct, elf-friend! We have no need of such physical spaces, but we wished to give you something that your human brain could assimilate! We have created it for you, but cannot sustain your frail bodies here for long!"

The elf's every word rang with bright enthusiasm. He moved past Artesso and turned to face them both. Artesso felt himself short of breath and turned excitedly to his wife. This was the fulfilment of all of their dreams. Shallia, though, had her eyes fixed on the creature before them.

The elf was *beautiful*.

"Thank you elf-friend! It pleases us to please you!"

It struck Artesso that it was inconsiderate of his wife to distract the elf with such superficial matters, particularly when time was short. He stepped forward, feeling that it was incumbent on him to take the lead in their negotiations.

"We bring greetings to you, from the realm of Askuria." Almost immediately, his carefully rehearsed speech was interrupted.

"We know, elf-friend! We know your purpose. If you had not been judged worthy, or if we could not help you, you would not be here with us now!"

Encouraged by these words, Artesso abandoned his script and forged ahead.

"And will you help us? Will you help us bring the realm back to orthodoxy?"

"Dear elf-friend! We already have!"

"How so? What assistance are you able to give us?"

"It is given! The most precious of gifts!"

There was a mocking musical laughter behind the words. Artesso tried to remind himself that the elves were superior beings, and that they were probably unaccustomed to dealing with humans after all their time away. He bowed and tugged Shallia's hand to encourage her to curtsy.

"We are most profoundly grateful to you, oh wise elf. But please can you give us some idea of the nature of your gift?"

"The gift? Can you not feel it? It grows within her!"

Artesso cast a puzzled look at his wife, who had suddenly given a sharp intake of breath. Suddenly apprehensive, he turned back to the elf.

"What is happening? What grows within her?"

Musical laughter echoed around him. "A child. She will have a child. And the child shall be the gift."

"A child?" Events were developing far too rapidly. This was not what Artesso had anticipated. "What will he be like? Will he be human?"

More laughter attended this question. Artesso sensed that more elves were nearby, perhaps all around them, although they could not be seen. For that matter, the elf's words, while seeming to emanate from the individual standing before them, could easily have been coalescing straight out of the air.

"Of course! We give you a human child, but one with all of the terrible majesty and power of the elves!"

"And what will become of him?"

Still the laughter rolled round and round him. The elf's delight was palpable, but Artesso felt himself utterly disorientated. He glanced at his wife who stood with an uncharacteristically thoughtful expression on her face, her right hand gently rubbing at her stomach.

"One day" the elf's voice continued, growing slightly fainter now, "the child will be the key that unlocks the barriers between your world and ours! Then we shall return! Only another generation, and human-kind's lonely waiting will be at an end!"

None of this had been anticipated in their discussions with Merson, Lias and the others. Artesso for the first time in his life felt himself wholly inadequate to the task that lay before him. There was so much more that he needed to understand, but even as he tried to formulate more questions, the mirrors started turning to mist around him, and the light began to fade.

Anxiously he reached out and seized his wife's hand. The elf seemed to be disappearing into the mist. Desperately, he called after it.

"Is there anything else we should know? What is he to be called?"

A faint laughing echo carried back through the deepening fog. "He! He? We said nothing about it being a male child, elf-friend! You should call her 'hope'!

"In our language, 'Elyssa'!"

31

Elyssa opened her eyes.

The cell was the same combination of aged stone and reinforced metal bars that it had been when she had laid down to sleep. It was a low priority holding cell, based on an assessment that she did not pose the same danger as the others. She inspected it curiously. Although Alyster and her friends were elsewhere within the structure, she knew with a thought that they were precisely where they were supposed to be.

It was time.

The same three guards who had been teasing her before she fell asleep were sitting around a table a dozen or so feet from the bars. They were playing a game involving cards which they appeared to believe was a game of chance – to Elyssa it seemed rather more straightforward. One of them nudged his neighbour.

"She's awake at last. Come on!"

Moving considerably more slowly than the thoughts that impelled them, the three guards lumbered to stand in a loose semi-circle, now only one or two feet from the cell. This was an improvement, but still not quite good enough. When she was certain she had their full attention, Elyssa sat cross-legged on the cold stone, maintaining eye contact with them, and began to sing.

It was a simple tune, a childhood tune, and utterly inoffensive, although the guards' reactions suggested that they thought otherwise. Insults, most of them of a lewd variety, were shouted through the bars at her. A sense of impatience grew within them, finally articulated by the leader, who by happy coincidence also carried the keys.

"Enough of this! I say we teach her a lesson. Come on."

Elyssa smiled as she sang. To the eyes of the prejudiced it was the smile of a simpleton who could not appreciate the danger that she was in. In truth, it was the smile of someone who was in no danger at all.

She was still smiling as the key turned in the lock. Still smiling as the lead guard stepped inside the cell and reached for her arm, anticipating an unresisting compliance which would make what he had in mind all the easier.

She was still smiling a second or so later, as the same guard hit the far wall of the cell, upside down, his neck cleanly snapped by the force of the impact.

Now there were two. One was the clever one, the one who always used long words when he insulted her. With a push of his arm he sent his companion ahead of him. Elyssa unfolded her body from the ground and bounced upwards. There had been too much stillness recently, too much restraint. Wheeling over the slower man's head, she caught the clever man with a sharp kick to the chest. He slumped to the ground.

The third man backed away. Elyssa had seen inside his mind and knew what he had planned for her, but she was not vengeful. As quick as breathing she stepped backwards, slamming the prison gate behind her. In a while he would realise that the keys were locked in the cell with him, but she did not think that he would be able to raise the alarm soon enough to cause trouble.

She paused, waiting to finish the song before she proceeded. Such things are important.

There was a glow surrounding her now, emanating from her. Contained within the song had been a trigger that caused her powers to manifest more fully than she had previously experienced, and strange new energies were racing through her. They would have killed a pure-born human. Elyssa, though, was barely distracted from her analysis of the rooms around her. As the power solidified in her, so the heavy stones of her surroundings seemed to melt and disappear. A glance upward would show her Alyster sitting hooded and in chains, waiting patiently for his interrogation to begin. Their new friend Tomas, who had played his unwitting part to perfection, was nearby. Closer at hand, in the high security cells at the end of the corridor, were Aunt Forba and the others.

Obedient to Uncle Merson's plan, just as it had first been outlined to them years before, Elyssa moved down the corridor to rescue her protectors.

At the entry point to the secure cells, the guards were considerably more alert. Even so, they could perhaps have been forgiven for their initial reaction when a young girl wandered round the corner of the corridor, smiled absent-mindedly at them, and then walked away again. Only two guards were dispatched to follow her, with instructions to find out why in the hells she was being allowed to wander free.

Several minutes passed before the guard captain realised they had not returned. He rang a handbell to summon nearby forces. Half of these he instructed to come with him to investigate, the others were left to guard the high risk prisoners, who were each isolated in their separate complex of rooms and cages. The prisoners, hearing the bell and understanding its significance, had all risen from their resting positions and were stood inside their respective cells, gazing out impassively at their gaolers.

One of the guards, facing the large dark-complexioned man with the grey eyes, found himself drawn nearer and nearer to his cell. The thought occurred to him that this man was not really a prisoner at all, and that it was time that he was released.

Meanwhile, the thin, sad-faced prisoner had edged closer to his bars. "I shouldn't tell you this," he intoned in a disappointed voice, "but I don't really know who else to trust." The guard looked at him quizzically.

"The thing is you see," continued Lias in muted tones, "I've buried quite a lot of treasure outside the precinct and, well, I don't have anyone else to leave it to."

This certainly captured the guard's attention. He leaned closer to hear the details of these wondrous riches.

Forba, as always, had a more direct approach. As her hands clapped loudly together the guard, startled, peered closer at her. To his amazement a green glowing cloud seemed to be coalescing around her bright red hair. A moment later he was collapsing under an onslaught of a million tiny stings. The cloud of pixies adroitly lifted his key chain and carried it back to Forba's outstretched hand before dispersing.

Once she had unlocked her cell Forba made her way to the central guard room, finding Merson and Lias already there. The sounds of combat echoing down the corridor suggested that Elyssa was still on her way to reunite with them. That only left...

"Help!"

"That's Rauor! What has the foolish one done now?"

Forba hurried in the direction of the shout, leaving Merson and Lias to go and see what assistance, if any, their young charge might require.

When Forba neared Rauor's cell she couldn't help but laugh. Rauor had somehow induced his guard to approach the bars, but he had mistimed his lunge and the guard had plainly seen him coming. Now Rauor was pulled up against the bars, his arms stretched through and wrapped about with rope which the guard was desperately holding onto, and awaiting assistance.

Forba made short work of him, but the look in her eye as she unlocked Rauor's cell suggested that he would be reminded of his inadequacies for some considerable time to come.

When they rejoined the others in the central administrative area, Elyssa was with them. impulsively Forba reached across and gave her a hug, causing her to beam with delight.

"How goes it with you?"

"Oh, you know Auntie. I'm alright."

Merson took charge. Rather than wasting time in reiterating what they all knew to be their next objective, he simply looked for the doorway to the central staircase that would take them upwards, towards the library archive. He led the way, calling to the others to follow.

Rapidly they ascended through the Tower's levels. Behind them, alarms were sounding as the incapacitated bodies of the guards were discovered. The stairwell itself, however, was only minimally guarded, suggesting that as planned the bulk of their forces had been drawn upwards to guard against the perceived threat that Alyster posed. While they ran, Elyssa provided them with a running commentary on the events upstairs, something which the others found extremely disconcerting.

Just as they reached the library level, she cried out in anger. "That horrid man just hit Al!"

"We had better hurry" said Merson. "Elyssa, Lias and I will be ready to carry on heading upwards, if Alyster seems to be running out of time. You two," pointing to Rauor and Forba, "find that codex as quickly as you can."

Fortunately, from her discussions with Maryam, Forba had a shrewd idea where the codex would be kept. Sure enough, despite the intervening twenty years, it was still hidden securely away, locked in its protective casket. Several large and heavy chains secured it in place, but Rauor made short work of these, simply crushing the links in his hands.

"Now, why was it not possible for you to have done that to the cell bars?"

"You know me, Forba, always looking for an easier way. Why rescue yourself if you can have an attractive redhead come and save you."

"Your mouth!" Rauor noticed to his satisfaction that Forba's complexion was notably pinker than it had been a few moments earlier as she quickly opened the chest and verified that its contents were intact. Then, they were back with the others.

"On and up" cried Merson, "You all know your roles, so move!"

32

"... But you do not yet know everything."

Tomas's heart leapt. Suddenly in a moment of inspiration, he understood. It was only his prejudice, the same prejudice which the quaestors seemed to have fallen prey to, that had blinded him until now.

Even as the realisation dawned, an enormous explosion blossomed from the corner of the room where the heavy oak doors to the stairwell had been standing. Now, all that remained of those centuries old barriers were a multitude of tiny wood fragments which drifted like confetti over the assembled audience.

Elyssa strode into the room, with Merson protectively at her side. Rauor, Lias and Forba were flanking them. Tomas fought down a childish urge to wave. Joy was bubbling up in him. He had watched the confrontation between Alyster and the quaestor inquisitor with something like despair, his realisation that Alyster had not betrayed him being overtaken by a dawning recognition that all of them had become pieces in a game which the quaestors seemed to have been controlling from the outset.

Now though, everything was reversed. Merson's group made their way to the centre of the room where quaestor Feiger still stood over Alyster. They took up positions in a rough circle around their companion, facing outwards into the room. Elyssa made her way to the centre of the circle and stood staring up at the inquisitor, a look of barely controlled fury on her face. Even suspecting what she might be capable of, Tomas could not help but feel that it was an incredibly unevenly matched contest.

The inquisitor obviously thought so too.

"So little elf daughter! This was the great plan! You could have escaped, you could have been far away, but instead you have walked up here and right into my power! Why did you not simply leave this one to rot?"

"He's my brother," replied Elyssa softly. Then, faster than an eye could follow, she hit him hard, once, in the stomach. Quaestor Feiger dropped to his knees and then to the floor with a finality that suggested that he would play no further part in the day's events.

"Hello Al!" cried Elyssa gaily.

"Hello sister." Alyster seemed to have a number of loose teeth, and the side of his face was already beginning to swell. Looking at him, Tomas felt that Elyssa had probably been quite merciful in her treatment of his interrogator.

That forbearance did not seem likely to win her any credit with the guards. Even as the assembled lords, masters and other gentlemen sat rooted to their chairs in astonishment, the well-trained quaestor guards surged forward, seeking to envelop the intruders in a protective cordon.

"Stop!" Elyssa did not speak loudly, but even

Tomas, quite some way back in the auditorium, felt the force of her command. The guards had no chance at all. Each of them froze rigidly into position, only their eyes and faces betraying that they did not do so entirely of their own free will.

Silence hung over the hall.

It was broken by a solitary slow hand clap. An innocuous man, seated half way back among the gentlemen and minor dignitaries, rose to his feet, continuing his faintly mocking applause as he did so. Just about able to turn his head, Tomas could make out a man who was smartly, but not elaborately clothed. His grey suit was neatly tailored, but in any other circumstances Tomas's eye might have glanced right off him. How was it that he was able to move, when the rest of the room remained so rigidly immobile?

"My dear... Eliza, is it?"

"Elyssa." She stepped forward to face him, even as Rauor knelt at Alyster's side and somehow caused the chains to fracture and fall away.

"Elyssa. My apologies. And my profound congratulations. You have played your hand exquisitely and, while some of us might wish that it could have been accomplished with rather less melodrama, I must say that I for one welcome the possibility of some fresh thinking in the upper echelons. It is not for me, a mere servant, to express any views on the subject, but..."

"Well, then don't!" Elyssa's sharp retort caused the man to pause in mid-stride. His smile faltered and faded.

"Perhaps one of the, ahem, adults might prefer to conduct this negotiation? There are after all certain forms to be observed."

Tomas awaited another angry retort, but there was silence. Merson stepped forward. In his bearing and manner the grey-suited man seemed to recognise someone with whom he could do business and he started towards him. Merson raised a hand.

"She instructed you to stop."

"My dear fellow!"

"I am nobody's dear fellow, least of all yours, Beau...?"

"I am Beau Exelon. Your perception does you great credit. Your strategy has also been masterly, bringing almost every person of significance in the realm under your control, at least for the time being. You must realise, however, even if your impetuous young lady does not, that if you intend to seize control you are going to need supporters.

"I, and the Council of which I am head, are entirely politically neutral you understand? We prefer order to chaos, to be sure, and if we have any small effect on the mores and morality of the realm, then we are grateful for our chance to serve. Let us therefore serve you! Any new government that is elected into office needs guidance, at least until they have grown in confidence. We, and our colleagues in the bureaucratic corporations, will I am sure have no difficulty in adapting to a new regime. Indeed I would expect that we could even make some useful recommendations about..."

"Enough!" Again, the beau, unaccustomed to be being interrupted, looked somewhat startled. Merson raised his voice, turning to address the entirety of the assembled throng. "We had two purposes in coming here today. Just two, and neither of them was the violent seizure of power.

"We are none of us administrators, and we none of us have any skill in political matters." Here Tomas saw Forba shoot a mocking grin towards Rauor "Moreover, we have always recognised that power that is taken by magic must be sustained by magic, and power that is taken by force can only be preserved by more force. Our wish is to heal the realm, not to rupture it. Certainly never again to see it subjugated."

The beau had recovered some of his bearing and, since he seemed to have appointed himself the designated representative of the assembled authorities, took it upon himself to interject at this stage.

"These are all laudable sentiments. But if you have come simply to fill our ears with trite intentions, might you not have found another, less dramatic way to convey your message?"

"We might," answered Merson, "if that had been our only purpose. One reason for coming here was to liberate certain information which we shall need for the future. We have now done that." Tomas noticed for the first time that Forba was carrying a large casket intricately bound in complicated metalwork. "The other was to deliver a message and a warning."

"And have you now done so?"

"Not quite. Our message is this: beware the elves. We have met them, and we know them in a way that the majority of those now living cannot possibly imagine. They have no concern for our realm, or for human-kind, except insofar as we may serve their purposes. When we travelled into the west we learnt something of their intentions. A war is coming and it is a war which we ought properly to have no part of. But it is coming here, and when it comes the elves will come too.

"When that happens, you, the rulers of the realm, will have to make a decision. There can be no ambiguity about this. Those who stand with the elves are against human-kind. You have some years left to decide, but that decision will have to be made.

"In the meantime, we shall be waiting and working, quietly and unobtrusively. If we are revolutionaries, then we are agents of a slow revolution. Slow, but sure. We already have associates everywhere, in every corporation, in every level of government. Most of them do not even know that they are our allies yet. But to any and all of you who have ever wrestled with your conscience over some cruelty or injustice enforced by this regime, I say to you that you are one of us, whether you accept it or not. There are six of us here. Each and every one of you can be the seventh member of our company, and I hope that, when it is least expected, you will make your stand in whatever small way you can.

"And finally, I say this to those of you who are determined to oppose us. To those who think that we represent a threat to their security, to their homeland, and who wish us ill. Remember that we came here and could have taken power today. You saw how rapidly Beau Exelon was willing to change sides. You delude yourselves if you think that his was an isolated voice. Remember that we came here through all of your guards and bars and obstacles. We will leave again with as little difficulty.

"Remember all that and imagine what we might do, if we ever decided that you posed too great a threat to us, or to the realm."

Even as Beau Exelon backed away, looking around him anxiously at the lords and masters that he would have so willingly betrayed, the group drew together in the centre of the room. Elyssa swept the room with her startling blue eyes. When she spoke again, the soft voice carried everywhere and filled every ear.

"Now, sleep…"

Tomas felt himself nodding forward, saw all those around him similarly slumping in their seats. At the last moment he felt as if Elyssa's eyes were staring directly into his, and he heard a voice, quietly, laughingly, inside his head, that said "… and sweet dreams, Investigator!"

Then there was only blackness.

EPILOGUE

Rivertop, 9 months later

Tomas and Idony stood in companionable silence, gazing down at the crib where their daughter lay. The armoury's newest investigator-general felt the stresses melting from his shoulders, the weight of the day's problems lifting from his back. His arm tightened around his wife's waist.

"What shall we three do with our weekend, my love?"

Idony leaned closer in to him. "Victor's promotion dinner is tomorrow night, and I have some correspondence to deal with, but otherwise we are at liberty, I believe."

It was still an unfamiliar experience – the enhanced staffing to which Tomas was now entitled as a consequence of his improved rank meant that there was very little around the house which either of them needed to do. Most weekends they had busied themselves with social commitments, reintegrating Idony into society after their daughter's arrival. Tomas felt the urge to make the most of their unusual freedom.

"Perhaps we might pack a pique-nique? The days are getting warmer and it would do us all good to be out in the fresh air and sunshine."

"Perfect! I will ask cook to make up a basket." Idony laughed to herself, and in the crib their daughter stirred as if in response to the merry tones. "Come husband, we must not waken her. Let us continue our promenade."

Their nightly tour of the property was one task that Tomas and Idony still made a point of doing personally. It afforded them a rare opportunity to share their news – about Tomas's day, or about items of information that Idony had picked up from other mothers as she had strolled in the park, or taken tea at the salon.

"Did you hear that Beau Exelon is missing?" Tomas knew that his wife would remember the significance of the name.

"I did indeed. Lady Exelon will not have it that there was any foul play. I am told she has written to the half dozen of his mistresses that she knows of, including one in Rivertop, demanding his immediate return!"

"My goodness! Victor and I had received a less salacious report. It cannot be any great surprise to those who were there. I am only really shocked that it has taken so long for the blade to fall."

In the candle-light, Idony's eyes sparkled. "I am so very proud of you my darling. To think of the part that you have played."

"I did not do so much."

"You are too modest. Every time we hear one of these snippets of news, some signal that the realm is moving into a brighter future, I feel so grateful for what I know to have been your role in it."

Tomas smiled at her, but it was a smile touched

with a hint of regret. "You are too kind, my wife. I own that I feel pride in these little victories. But I cannot help but wish that I had not lost the opportunity to play a deeper role in events. Merson, Forba, Raour and the others, they have vanished without trace, and I strongly suspect that I will never see them again."

"It is selfish, I know," Idony's arms squeezed tightly around Tomas's waist, "but I cannot regret it. The fear I felt when you were away from me over Fest – I could not bear a life of that. You have played your part, my love, and the new world will need investigators just as much as the old one did!"

Tomas sighed. "You are right, as so often."

"As always, dearest!"

Now it was late. Idony's sleeping breath was the only sound to disturb their bed-chamber. Tomas gazed up at the skylights above, the gleaming moonlight casting its familiar strange shadows across the roof spaces. Tomas knew the impatience that he felt inside him, he recognised it from long familiarity. Every year, as the days lengthened and the sun grew warmer he felt himself yearning to be more active, pulled in the direction of new thoughts and ideas. For the first time, he recognised his instinctive rejection of those emotions as part of the pattern that Merson had sketched out for him during their travels, a pattern which he now saw everywhere.

Frustration darkened his thoughts. Was he really doomed to pass the rest of his life as a spectator to the events which he now knew to be taking place below the surface? He was fortunate, he knew it, and ought to be content with all that he had. It was so much more than he had ever dreamed to achieve. Nevertheless, as his eyes finally closed, his last thought was one of regret, and of longing.

Dreams claimed him. Tomas found himself standing on a large open plain, the Dragon's Back mountains visible as a grey blur on the horizon. He did not recognise the immediate landscape, but the emptiness and solitude comforted him. It was far removed from his old nightmares of fighting through ever thickening crowds.

The warmth of a high summer sun beat on his shoulders. The fresh smell of the drying grasses at his feet filled his head with a sense of exuberant delight. He laughed aloud, and was shocked to hear an echoing musical voice ringing in his ear.

"...and sweet dreams, Investigator!"

Turning, he saw her, and found himself captivated once more by those piercing blue eyes. Elyssa, glowing from within, clothed in shining white, danced closer to him across the grassland.

"You desire a greater role in our future plans?"

He nodded, even though he knew that it was not really a question.

"Then make a wish!" She laughed, even as she pirouetted around him. Even though he knew that he was dreaming, Tomas was slightly ashamed of the ridiculous thought that immediately entered his head. Before he could provide a more considered response, however, the thought was greeted with a delighted smile and a peal of laughter.

"It shall be!"

She leant forward, kissed him on the cheek, and vanished.

Scarcely daring to believe it, laughter bubbling out of him at the sheer surreality of the moment, Tomas hastily started to unbutton his shirt. Soon he stood with the midsummer sun bathing his bare torso and arms. He felt like a child, believing in this one perfect moment that everything was possible.

Then he tensed his legs, spread his wings, and soared into the perfect sunlit sky.

- THE END -

WAKE UP…

A MESSAGE FROM WILL DAVIDSON

Thank you very much for buying and reading this book – I hope you have enjoyed it and, if you have, please do tell your friends and perhaps even post a short review of it online. For a self-published author who is trying to compete with the large publishing houses, word of mouth is incredibly important, so I would be eternally in your debt.

Tomas and the other characters will return in the next book in this series, and if you would like to hear more about that, or just to make contact, I can be reached through Twitter (@WordDruid) and on Facebook. I also have a website at www.the-seventh-colour.com, where you can sign up for my occasional newsletter and read more about the realm of Askuria.

There are several people who have given immeasurable help and encouragement as readers during the drafting process – they know who they are and I have thanked them individually. Without diminishing their contribution I do just want to specifically acknowledge the work of my good friends Martin Lewis-Enright, who created the incredible cover for this book and Dan Hand who made the map inside. By doing so they have brought the realm I created to life before my eyes for the first time. Thank you.

W.D.